THE DOOR THROUGH WASHINGTON SQUARE

Elaine Bergstrom

ACE BOOKS, NEW YORK

This book is an Ace original edition,
and has never been previously published.

THE DOOR THROUGH WASHINGTON SQUARE

An Ace Book / published by arrangement with
the author

PRINTING HISTORY
Ace edition / August 1998

The Penguin Putnam Inc. World Wide Web site address is
http://www.penguinputnam.com

Check out the ACE Science Fiction/Fantasy
newsletter, and much more, at Club PPI!

ISBN: 0-441-00544-6

ACE®
Ace Books are published by The Berkley Publishing Group,
a member of Penguin Putnam Inc.,
200 Madison Avenue, New York, NY 10016.
ACE and the "A" design are trademarks
belonging to Charter Communications, Inc.

PRINTED IN THE UNITED STATES OF AMERICA

10   9   8   7   6   5   4   3   2   1

For Barbara,
who's been with me since the beginning,
with thanks.

"People like me, who believe in physics, know that the distinction between past, present and future is only a stubbornly persistent illusion."

—Albert Einstein

PART ONE

Dierdre,

March 1991

"The most common cause of failure in life is ignorance of one's true will."
—Aleister Crowley
Magick in Theory and Practice

ONE

March 1991

Grandmum's hands were the hardest to look at.

With the face, Dierdre MacCallum could easily remember the energetic older woman her great-grandmother had been. With a bit of imagination, Dierdre could even transpose the sunken, withered features with the young, vibrant woman in the sepia-toned photographs that covered a portion of one wall in her family's ancient house in Aberdeen, then add to it a background scandalous enough to be hinted at in the occasional vague whispers and strange glances at family reunions.

Only the hands with the thin spotted skin stretched like parchment over fleshless bones, the yellowed fingers and the palsied nerves, gave no hint of the woman's past.

One clutched at the sleeve of Dierdre's silk blouse. The woman's eyes focused on Dierdre for a moment, then seemingly exhausted by even that small effort, relaxed into near blindness again. "I never thought you'd really come," the old woman said.

How could Dierdre answer? When she'd received the letter her great-grandmother had dictated to one of the Hudson Manor staff, she'd wanted to ignore it. Now nearly thirty, she'd finally begun to organize a life of her own—a job as an executive assistant for the vice president of operations for a department store in Calgary, a suburban apartment where she lived alone, even the first serious lover of her life, a corporate attorney she'd met through work. After only a few months of casual dating, she and Frank were already talking about living together. By the end of the year, there might have been a wedding to plan.

But Bridget MacCallum Dunglass Stewart, called Grandmum by everyone under sixty in the family, had checked herself into a nursing home soon after her ninety-sixth birthday and announced that she intended to die there in the presence of her favorite great-grandchild. Such a request, issued by the keeper of the family fortune—a matriarch rumored to have the blood of Scotch kings in her veins—could not be ignored. After Dierdre sent a vague reply to the royal summons, Grandmum wrote again, this time to Dierdre's mother and the surviving members of the MacCallum family branch in Scotland. Their disapproval of Dierdre's refusal to drop everything and go at once to New York easily crossed both ocean and continent—first by letter; later, after Dierdre ignored them, by a late-night phone call from Stella, Dierdre's mother.

It was still afternoon in Scotland. The call had cost an exorbitant amount per minute. The family was serious.

"You go. You were closer to her. After all, I barely knew her," Dierdre insisted to her mother.

"You spent a good part of every summer with her when you were a little girl. You used to be close. Besides, she asked for *you*," Stella responded, petulently, as if Dierdre should know that the request itself settled everything.

"But I love my apartment. I just got a promotion at work and the store is starting to plan the summer sales," Dierdre said, knowing immediately that it was the wrong thing to say.

"I'll pay your rent. As for the store, since when does a MacCallum *need* to work?" Stella replied.

Someone created our fortune, Mother, Dierdre wanted to say. *Someone ought to add to it.* But of course, someone already was. The MacCallum bankers were wise at investing, and the family net worth was growing by a good fifteen percent a year. With the MacCallums by nature so thrifty that they were the stuff bad Scotch jokes were made of, her mother's observation was more than right.

"And since you've become such a smart businesswoman, you can visit the two New York industries that Fairchild has invested so much of our money in. It's always nice to have a firsthand report on what sort of companies we're supporting," her mother went on, throwing Dierdre a bone for her obedience.

"I can't leave for at least another three weeks," Dierdre insisted.

"Three weeks! Grandmum is on her deathbed and you're worried about a job you don't even need? What in the world have all those counselors done to you?"

Undone, Mother, Dierdre thought. *Undone, at least as well as anyone could.*

Misinterpreting the silence, her mother asked again, "So go on, tell me again what those counselors gave you for all that money we threw at them?"

"They gave me independence, Mother," Dierdre replied, holding her anger in check. No use exploding now. That's what the old Dierdre would have done, then followed the outburst with tears, apologies and complete capitulation to the family's demands.

Which was exactly what her mother expected. She waited while Dierdre considered the situation, then asked, "If she dies without seeing you, how many more counseling sessions will we have to buy to alleviate your guilt?"

One of Mother's more valid arguments. Of course Dierdre had caved in, then hated herself for it. Another half year of counseling either way, but why should a MacCallum settle for less than perfect mental health?

Dierdre thought of using her boyfriend as an excuse and decided against it. Mother would only say that any relationship worth having can survive a few weeks of separation then ask a hundred tactless questions about the man. Dierdre's fragile calm would shatter under the pressure.

And so, unable to fight the inevitable, Dierdre agreed.

After she hung up the phone, she looked at her little apartment—at the old hobnail-trimmed sofa she'd found at a yard sale, at the antique mirror she'd purchased just last week, at the legal bookcase with its beveled glass front, at the pair of goldfish in their enclosed tank. The fish been a housewarming gift from her landlady. Dierdre, accustomed to loss, had never named them.

Dierdre knew she ought to call about plane reservations,

clean up a bit or sort her clothes. Instead she sat on the sofa and considered her life.

Dierdre's mother had left her husband and two children for what was supposed to be a brief vacation with her husband's family in Scotland. She never returned. Without warning, Dierdre was thrust into the dual role of housekeeper to her father and surrogate mother to her four-year-old brother, Mark, a silent, precocious child. Barely eleven, she was hardly good at either, a failing her father pointed out often, sometimes painfully. Looking back on it now, she found it odd that someone as emotionlly dead as her father could have been roused to anger so easily. At the time, she'd been simply terrified, then grief-stricken when her mother sent for Mark but not for her.

Mercifully, Dierdre could remember little of her early years, save for a few happy respites in those summer weeks with Grandmum and one seemingly insurmountable instinct—a need to cringe and raise a hand to protect her face whenever anyone reached toward her too quickly.

If her mother had endured that sort of treatment, she'd had every reason to leave the house. But for years Dierdre could not comprehend the woman's decision to abandon her children and move in with the branch of her husband's family that lived in Scotland. Now she understood all too well.

The few times Dierdre had visited the family, she had found them listless and oppressively dull. They shared an old mansion just outside of Aberdeen, simultaneously ignoring its upkeep and behaving as if its stone walls were a fortress against a hostile outside world. They barely left the place except to stock the pantry or to consult their bankers about the ebb and rise of the MacCallum fortune. They rarely smiled, never laughed and spoke only when necessary. Her brother, by nature reclusive, soon fell into the habit so perfectly it seemed that he had taken a vow of silence. Stella had tried to change everyone, and when it wasn't possible, ignored them and did exactly as she pleased—playing Lady MacCallum without the annoying appendage of a husband and children or the financial inconvenience of a divorce. She'd been the only one there with any real life in her. Now, nearly sixty, that was fading. In the last few years, Mother had begun to resemble Grandmum; independent, yes, but ordering everyone about as if they were servants or pawns with no choice but to obey her. Dierdre would have never fit in. Not with her parents; certainly not with her father's family. Nor anywhere else, it seemed.

Dierdre had been a terrible student in grade school and the first years of high school. Math came easily to her but she'd been barely able to read until a sharp-eyed freshman English teacher realized she had dyslexia. With tutors and a great deal of effort, Dierdre ended her high school years on the honor roll and became the first MacCallum since Grandmum's brother with the inclination to try college. As soon as she got there, she realized she'd been far too optimistic. Though she absorbed the lectures well enough, no amount of studying could overcome the handicap of a reading speed a fifth of normal. She dropped six credits but still couldn't keep up. She left college after her freshman year and set out to find some place where she felt she belonged.

During her quest, her mother sent disapproving letters and demanded that she join her in Aberdeen—a move Dierdre considered no better than slow suicide. Grandmum, at least, sent money instead of sermons; often more than Dierdre had requested. That in itself was a curse. Dierdre eventually stopped asking for anything. When the checks continued to come, she stopped writing. For months the family didn't know where she was.

In the last five years, Dierdre had lived in six major cities and had little to show for any of it but an associate degree in accounting earned through a correspondence course. She settled finally in Calgary, not out of any real affinity for the city, but because she'd become far too weary to pack up and move again.

Not weary, sensible, her most recent counselor had suggested. The woman had been a wonder, slowly weaning Dierdre off the antidepressants she'd been taking for years, showing her how to contain her emotions inside an orderly, logical facade, slowly establishing what should have been an innate self-esteem.

And with a great deal of help and her own effort, Dierdre managed to land the first real job of her life, the first lover—or at least the first man she'd ever gotten to know well enough to call that—and her first glimpse of the sort of life she wanted to lead.

Though she'd been born in New York and raised in Toronto, Dierdre never considered herself an urban girl. She'd compromised on Calgary, a city large enough for opportunities but located on the edge of an incredible wilderness. Sometimes, when the rush of people and cars and buildings pressed too close, she'd get in her car and drive toward the mountains, park somewhere and wait. Often, she'd be rewarded with the sight of deer foraging in a meadow. Once an injured fox limped up to her car and begged. She rolled the window partway down and tossed out the remains of a fast food hamburger. After the stars came out, bright in the thin, clear air, the coyotes would begin their lonely calls.

An hour would pass, two, and she'd return to her little apartment on the edge of town feeling a real sense of emotional peace. On those nights she would get a feeling—irrational yet certain—that now that she'd stopped her perpetual motion something unexpected and wonderful would occur.

But after a single phone call, everything had changed. Her mother might argue that it was only a visit, but Dierdre knew better. She would be moving again.

Dierdre heard her landlady's stereo playing softly in the apartment below her. Before she changed her mind, she unplugged the fish tank and carried it downstairs.

After listening to Dierdre explain her problem, Molly agreed to take back the fish and tend to Dierdre's plants while she was gone. She took the tank from Dierdre and carried it to the huge freshwater aquarium she kept on the inside wall. She netted the fish with her spread fingers and dropped them in with the rest. Though they'd lived most of their lives in the large tank, the sudden uprooting unsettled them. They dropped into the weeds to size things up. Such a human trait—the instinctive wariness that came with going home.

Home. If Dierdre thought of any place that way, it was Grandmum's apartment building on Washington Square. The only place from her youth with happy memories. And the one place that, for some reason, made her feel real fear.

The next day Dierdre went to work and explained her situation. Her supervisor tried to be supportive. "If it's only for a visit, well, we can get along without you for a week or so," he said.

"It may be longer than that. She's asked me to remain there until she dies."

Dierdre half expected the man to ask how ill Grandmum was, but he politely avoided doing so. Instead, he arranged to hire a temp to replace Dierdre. The girl was just out of business school, smart and ambitious enough that Dierdre knew her job would be over if she was gone more than a few weeks. Even so, her mother insisted on prepaying three months rent on her Calgary apartment.

As for the lover and her hopes for marriage—well Frank always said he had no patience for separations. He told her this over lunch, saying he'd probably start dating someone else while she was gone and suggesting that she do the same in New York. He'd left early for a two o'clock appointment. After he'd gone, Dierdre remained in the restaurant. As she finished her dessert plus the remains of his amaretto cheesecake, she reminded herself of how lucky she'd been to learn how little she meant to him before she wasted too much of her time. Mother, unfortunately, would agree.

The grass will have to be greener somewhere else, Dierdre thought as she and Frank pecked a sterile goodbye outside the airport. Nonetheless, saying goodbye to him brought tears to her eyes. Well, she'd held together for her last day at work, she could continue for a few more minutes. She turned away from Frank and walked to the line at the ticket desk, not looking back, wiping her eyes only when she was sure Frank had left.

"Going home for a funeral?" the woman in line behind her asked.

Dierdre nodded. It would end in a funeral, after all.

"It's always hard to lose someone you love," the woman continued, trying to seem sympathetic but succeeding only in being intrusive.

Dierdre reached the plane with her calm intact and sat in the first-class seat until after takeoff. As soon as they were in the air, she requested a blanket and pillow and the first of a pair of double scotches and cried all the way to her stopover in Toronto, thankful that people were so thrifty nowadays and she had the cabin almost entirely to herself.

Grandmum squeezed her hand again, pulling her back to the present. "I'm glad you came," she said.

"Of course, I had to come," Dierdre said, fighting the urge to pull away. She felt only a hint of the great affection she'd once held for the old woman who'd dressed her up in long, black lace gowns and wide-brimmed hats trimmed in red silk roses, who fed her hot chocolate for breakfast, and who had told the most incredible stories.

In the hall outside Grandmum's sterile, pale-blue room, a nursing home aide wheeled another old woman past, a woman whose bony knees stuck out from beneath the blue hospital gown she wore. What tests had someone run on her? Dierdre wondered. Was there no end to their poking and pricking? No end to the indignities they inflicted on those whose time had come to die?

Squeeze another month of life out of them, then another, another. Squeeze as long as the money held out. And Grandmum had plenty of money. They could squeeze until she was a hundred and twenty or more and not use up a tenth of it. "Are you comfortable here?" Dierdre asked.

Grandmum didn't answer immediately. It wasn't resentment at being forced from her home, Dierdre knew. Grandmum, not the family, had chosen this place as well as the time that she would enter it. "Comfort is hardly the point," Grandmum finally replied. "The building will be yours soon. I've made sure of that. Are you staying in the flat now?"

Of course, Grandmum had to be worried about all the keepsakes she'd collected over a lifetime. And she had entrusted them to Dierdre. Some of the irritation Dierdre'd felt at being summoned here evaporated. She smiled and kissed the old woman's cheek. "I flew in late last night and got a hotel room near the airport. I'll sleep in my old room tonight," she said.

"There's memories inside."

"I'm sure there are," Dierdre agreed.

"They'll be yours, too. Today when you go there, you'll see."

"How will I get in? Do you have a key here?"

"The keys and some signature cards are waiting for you at the bank. The account's been changed to your name and there's a power of attorney for you to sign. The nurses have the papers locked up for you." She lowered her voice. "You just can't trust the help here. At least half are on drugs, you know."

Grandmum had little else to say. Dierdre remained sitting beside the bed for a time, her hand on the institutional green covers, Grandmum's hand resting above it. A few times, Dierdre thought the old woman was asleep but when she tried to move her hand away, Grandmum gripped it, painfully, tightly.

So Dierdre waited, watching the clock, until one of the aides came in carrying a lunch tray. She was a broad-hipped, young woman with a jovial smile pasted on her chubby face and a mop of henna-colored hair. She nodded to Dierdre, then without any warning began cranking up the head of the hospital bed. "Time for lunch, Bridget," she called cheerfully, setting the tray on the bed table and positioning it over Grandmum's lap.

Grandmum jerked herself to full consciousness, looked down at the food, then scowled at the woman.

Dierdre never wanted to get old. Not if it meant living the last months of her life being called by her first name by rude aides a quarter her age, staring at painted walls and gingham-trimmed ducks and white linoleum floors, eating bland food in a room that smelled faintly of urine and disinfectant. Dierdre stood and smoothed her cotton skirt. "I should go and settle in," she said.

Grandmum reached for her hand again, but Dierdre had already moved away. "Go with God," the old woman said. An odd choice of words. Grandmum had never seemed particularly religious before. Maybe approaching death had changed that.

"Thank you," Dierdre mumbled and moved close a moment longer to kiss the old woman's cheek.

TWO

Dierdre took a cab from the nursing home to her hotel, asking the driver to wait while she went inside to retrieve her suitcases. From there, she stopped at the bank then went on to Grandmum's house on the north side of Washington Square. Though she and the driver had spent the better part of an hour together, the man left her and her three suitcases and overnight bag on the sidewalk before she could ask for help getting them inside.

"Be careful of the crime. Don't carry any more than one credit card at a time. Carry a handbag, not something hanging from your shoulder, and never put your keys in it. And don't let those cabbies rip you off. New York is nothing like Calgary. Thank God you took that self-defense course," her mother had warned her the night before she caught the flight. The advice had seemed deliberately incomplete, a way of cautioning her about everything New York from the people to the traffic to the high rises looking down on the city streets like temples to some modern gods.

The late March weather was warm, almost balmy compared to Calgary, and college students sat on the steps around the fountain, most listening to some folk singer playing a protest song reminiscent of Phil Ochs. But there were others milling on the streets around the square—some appeared rich, others not so rich and some looked so tattered that they seemed frightening. Dierdre was trying to decide which bags to carry inside first when a panhandler in his fifties walked toward her, brushing against her arm to get her attention. As soon as she made eye contact, he held out his hand.

Dierdre still held the extra tip she'd intended to give the cab driver for helping her. She sized the man up, decided he was harmless and said, "I'll give you the five dollars if you take my two larger bags to the top of the steps."

He shrugged and picked them up, grumbling to himself as he climbed the white marble stairs and dropped them just outside the locked entrance. Dierdre waited below until he'd finished. He took the money, then spat on the sidewalk in front of her and headed off, continuing his private conversation as he went on his way. Dierdre waited until he'd turned the corner before carrying the smaller bags up the stairs, unlocking the door and quickly pulling everything inside.

The heavy outer door closed behind her, shutting out the city. In the silence, she felt as if she could breathe again.

Everything was as she remembered. The foyer's black and white ceramic floor, the thick rail of the dark oak staircase leading to the apartment and small storage room on the second floor. The tall entrance windows of frosted amber-toned glass shed a golden light through the foyer. The tall carved oak apartment door seemed darker than she remembered, and the brass knocker and the family name engraved on the plaque above it were new. It wasn't an old building as the world measured time; only old by Dierdre's standards, and with a sad history. It had been in the MacCallum family since its construction in the mid-1800s. Around the turn of the century, a sudden fire had taken out the second floor end unit. Two children had died in the blaze, and though Grandmum would have been too young to remember them, the effect on her parents must have been terrible. Nonetheless, Grandmum's father had rebuilt it immediately, taking care to see that the two sides of the apartment matched as closely as possible.

Then, to house his growing family, Grandmum's father had merged their lower apartment with the rebuilt one by breaking through the fire wall at the front and back of the railroad style flats. Two doors off the double wide living room led to two long hallways, mirror images of each other. Off each were two large bedrooms, a smaller den, a large bathroom then a kitchen on one side, a dinette on the other, separated by a wide, curved archway. Across the back was a sunroom the width of the two apartments with two sets of doors leading to a single yard enclosed by a high stone wall.

Life was crueler in Grandmum's childhood. According to the family history, by the time Grandmum was twenty, two of her brothers and her mother had died during one of the great influenza epidemics of the early 1900s. Her father died a few years later, leaving the house and a good part of his fortune to Grandmum. Grandmum had been wise enough to stay clear of the stock market speculation and keep the money in real estate through the 1920s, so the fortune was actually greater after the Crash than before. Since then, the family fortune had increased dramatically, soaring on the coattails of the new industrial leaders—Ford, DuPont, and more recently the major computer firms of Silicon Valley. No one could pick a stock better than Grandmum, the family said, and the MacCallum bankers had followed her advice with their own portfolios. She'd made them all rich.

Dierdre had been in the building only a few times in her life, and not since she was a little girl. But as soon as she stepped out of the sunny front hallway into the dim light of the living room, the memories came back, real as the scent of peppermint and lemon oil that permeated the space. Dierdre remembered playing in Grandmum's kitchen, putting together antique wooden jigsaw puzzles packaged in plain blue boxes. With no picture of the finished piece on the box top, each design was a surprise. She remembered eating ice cream kept hard in freezer trays stored in the bottom of the little metal compartment of Grandmum's ancient Kelvinator, kept in favor of newer models because it still ran. Dierdre had dreamed of becoming a concert pianist while pounding on the keys of the mahogany baby grand, and told her own fortune with decks of strangely patterned Tarot cards.

Little had changed in the old apartment in the years since her last visit. The beautiful Galle mahogany table and sideboard with its inlaid pieces of contrasting wood veneers were still draped in lace cloths, more to decorate than protect them. The back and arms of the tapestry-upholstered furniture were covered with small lace doilies, all of them made years ago by Grandmum's mother. As she walked down the hall, Dierdre saw that the bedrooms were made up, and the kitchen table set with four placemats as if Grandmum had been expecting company when the stroke had felled her.

Dierdre opened the solid wooden doors that connected the dinette and kitchen to the sunroom. In spite of the warm stale air, she shuddered as from a sudden chill. This room had always seemed the strangest to her, first because of the mystery that seemed to surround it, and later because of the dreams its strangeness had undoubtedly created.

The sunroom, with its wall of windows, should have been the brightest room in the house, but Grandmum had always kept the doors leading to it closed. As a result the only light that had leaked into the kitchen had come from the windows at one side of the room. These had been far from adequate to light the space, so the kitchen's dining area had always seemed close and oppressive in spite of the cheery opal-colored wallpaper and white dinette set. Dierdre could never recall having been alone in the sunroom. Grandmum had always been with her, usually carrying a lunch tray to or from the enclosed yard at the back of the house.

Perhaps Grandmum had avoided the room because of the history it so obviously revealed. The two young boys who had died in the fire had made it to the rear doors only to discover them locked. They had been found clutching each other, their faces pressed against the single small pane of glass they had managed to crack. As an additional reminder of the tragedy, this was also the room where the old and new halfs of the apartment were most obvious. The new section of the sunroom had been remodeled in the early 1950s to add a sliding patio door with a narrow oak frame, covered only at the top with a short blue velvet valance.

The older half still held the original French doors, doors Dierdre had never seen except from outside. Heavy blue velvet draperies had always covered them, hiding both the tiny beveled squares of glass and the view beyond them. Even in the warmest summer weather, they had never been pulled back or the door opened.

And Dierdre had never attempted to peek beyound them. Not because she was that obedient a child, but rather because

having been told to stay away from them, her imagination had
begun supplying reasons, none of them exactly pleasant. Then,
one night when she was staying with Grandmum, she dreamed
of a storm, vivid with electricity but nearly silent. She'd stood
in the kitchen doorway and stared at the windows, at the lightning that pulsed around the heavy curtains, at the curtains
themselves moving slowly from the gale breaking outside.

She'd walked to the curtains, and pulled one corner back.
A man's face pressed against the glass. His features were distorted. His dark hair dripped water from the driving rain. He
stared at her as if the weather made no difference, as if he
wanted her soul. With the curtain still in her hand, she backed
away from the window until she put enough distance between
herself and the glass to let the curtain fall. She ran from the
door, the room, the sunroom itself, down the hall to her bed
where she lay trembling, afraid to call out for help because
someone else might hear.

She'd never experienced a more intense nightmare than that
one. Even today, she was half certain that she had actually
been awake that night and the figure real.

In late fall, when Frank had found the time to move their
relationship from casual dating to romance, he had borrowed
a friend's cabin in the mountains. They'd sat in front of a
warm fire, drank wine, made love. Sometime after midnight,
a storm came up, its thunder rolling from peak to peak, its
rain beating against the single-paned windows. The dream returned in all its intensity. She woke screaming. Frank had been
less supportive than irritated by her terror, especially since
he'd planned on starting the next day early so he could turn
on his laptop and finish up some work he'd brought. Perhaps
she should have seen his flaws then.

Now, even though it was daylight, Dierdre still had to force
herself to walk over the grey ceramic floor past the worn
wicker furniture to go to the old doors and push the drapes
apart. The rod was an old-fashioned white enameled one, the
curtains attached with tiny metal clips that moved only with
effort. As they did, a cloud of dust fell on her. The rod itself
seemed ready to fall. Holding the drapes well away from her,
Dierdre studied a section of the old wood molding. Though it
was scratched and missing varnish, a little polish would make

it more than presentable and bring out the beauty in the odd carved pieces across the top. As for the windows themselves, the eighty or so small squares of glass were filthy. Dierdre wondered why Grandmum, who'd used a maid for years, had ignored them for so long.

Perhaps the window glass itself had clouded and yellowed? Dierdre found some vinegar in the cupboard and cleaned one small square. It sparkled. Through it she saw that the sun had broken through the clouds. She looked out happily at the familiar brick patio and marble bench, at the lawn and garden with the contrasting clumps of early blooming yellow, white and scarlet tulips. Later there would be peonies, then lilies and roses, all arranged according to a plan created a century before by Grandmum's mother. Dierdre saw a fluffy white cat sitting in one corner, paws curled peacefully beneath its chest as it basked in the afternoon sun. Could it be Grandmum's? The old woman hadn't mentioned a cat. Perhaps there was a hole in the wall and the cat didn't live here at all.

Dierdre lowered the draperies slowly, and returned to the kitchen. Someone had cleaned out the refrigerator of everything but some ground coffee, a couple of half-full bottles of wine, gin and vermouth and an unopened bottle of orange juice. She put on a pot of coffee to drink in the garden. While it brewed, she decided to settle in. She'd already chosen the same guest room she used when she was a child, a front bedroom in the new section. As she went to get her suitcase from the living room, she heard the sharp sound of the brass door knocker.

Not certain if she had locked the front door, she rushed forward and attached the chain, then cracked it open and peered out.

The man standing outside was around forty, drab-faced, tall and a little thick around the waist. He held a brown paper bag and a stack of books. "Are you Dierdre MacCallum?" he asked, with a bit of nervous hesitation as if he feared he might be disturbing her.

She nodded, then realizing that he couldn't see her clearly through the cracked door, said, "I am."

"I'm Bill Coleman. I rent the flat upstairs. We share the

entranceway." He held out one hand. They brushed palms
through the narrow space.

"You were expecting me?" Dierdre asked.

"In a way. Grandmum said you would be coming."

The use of the family name for her relation convinced Dierdre that she was being too overly-cautious, and far from neigh-
borly. She unchained the door. "Come in," she said.

He did and stepped aside so she could shut the door. He
seemed awkward, almost shy. His khaki suit was a bit baggy
and a little too long at the cuffs and sleeves, as if he had
recently lost both weight and height. His hair was light brown,
but dull and wiry as if much of it had gone to grey and he
dyed it to match the rest.

Not at all like dear Frank, with his custom-tailored suits and
carefully arranged salt and pepper hair. But then look where
she and Frank had ended up. Odd that she should be compar-
ing a stranger to her ex-lover. Did she really feel that hard up
so soon?

Bill stood in the center of the room, frowning slightly, apparently trying to think of something to say, then deciding on
the obvious. "This is such a beautiful room. I'm always bit
awed by the antiques. I've never seen this much art nouveau
outside the Paris museums." Bill ran his finger along the edge
of the carved mahogany Majorelle mirror, lightly as if he were
afraid he might break it.

She was supposed to ask him what he thought of Paris or
what other places he'd visited but she felt a perverse sort of
pleasure in keeping him off balance. "All I can think of when
I look at them is that my mother would never allow me to sit
on the chairs," she eventually replied. "Tha family has always
viewed them as a sort of investment."

The silence was longer this time, and he stood clutching the
bag, looking so mournful, so much like she was certain she'd
looked often enough in her life, that she took pity on him.
"Would you like some coffee?" she asked.

"Love some."

He followed her to the kitchen then thrust the bag into her
hands so unexpectedly that she almost dropped it. "I brought
you some lunch or you can save it for dinner."

She looked at him curiously. "Grandmum may be a little

bit psychic, but I doubt she told you the exact time I'd be arriving.''

"There wasn't anything odd about it," he said. "I heard you come in just as I was going out to grab a sandwich. I knew there wasn't much left in the kitchen, so I thought I'd get you something. Fat Albert's is just around the corner. Now, you have your choice of pastrami and peppers or the infamous Al's Stuffed Turkey—Thanksgiving on a bun and nearly impossible to eat.''

"Pastrami, thank you.'' She reached in the cupboard for cups, wiping out the non-existent dust with a paper towel before filling them.

"It's amazing how a house that hasn't been lived in for weeks can look so clean,'' Bill commented.

"Is the cleaning lady still coming?''

"I don't think so. As far as I know, you and I are the only ones with a key. After Grandmum's first stroke, she gave me one to use if the newspapers started piling up outside her door, that sort of thing. After she left for the home, I cleaned out her refrigerator, not that there was much in it. Even at her best, Bridget's always been an eat-out sort of person. While I was here, I borrowed these from her library. I didn't think she'd mind since I borrow books all the time.'' He set three on the counter.

Dierdre glanced at them. The worn leather covers told her that they were old, and possibly valuable, but the titles meant nothing to her. Bill seemed disappointed when she didn't comment on them, then began paging through one of them as if her lack of interest didn't matter.

"Have you been feeding Grandmum's cat?'' Dierdre asked.

He looked up from the book. "Cat?'' he asked.

"A big white one. It's in the garden.''

"She doesn't own a cat. I don't think anyone in the building does.''

"It must have wandered into the yard. I suppose I should check for a collar.'' She walked to the sliding sunroom door and opened it.

The sun had retreated behind a low-lying cloud. In the dimmer light, the garden looked less inviting, the beds need of care. The wind felt as cold as it had in early morning, and it looked as if it would storm that evening. Taking a hint from the fickle weather, the cat had also vanished. Dierdre called hopefully for it a couple of times, but it was gone. "I just saw it a few minutes ago," Dierdre said, more to herself than to Bill.

"Cats come and go. They're everyone's property in this neighborhood. I've fed half a dozen different ones myself in the last five years. Just when I think one is going to adopt me, it disappears. I like to think they all lose interest in me and go home, though most of them look like they sleep in the sewers and prefer that life. Unfaithful creatures, cats."

"This one looks like it has a home." As Dierdre spoke, a few drops of rain landed on her bare arms. She shivered and followed Bill inside.

While they ate at the kitchen table, Bill acquainted her with the neighborhood. Speaking so fast that he barely paused to breathe, he gave directions to Fat Albert's, to the cheapest grocery store, to the best-stocked five-and-dime. "The rest is a matter of taste," he said. "You'll have plenty of time to scout out your own favorite spots."

"Have you been visiting Grandmum?" Dierdre asked.

Bill finished the bite he had in his mouth and lifted a dollop of spiced mayonnaise and cranberry jelly off his lapel. "I did once, right after she'd gone into the home. I went to tell her that I'd take care of things, and put her mind at ease. She didn't like seeing me. I think it embarrassed her to be so helpless. I went back just once more, but things were no better."

"When did she tell you that I was coming?"

"Some months ago. She was talking about her family and said you were the only one left in this country. She said you'd be coming here soon."

Dierdre frowned.

"That's when she told me, really," Bill said, quickly and a bit defensively.

"I believe you. It's just—" Just what? That no one had ever asked her to come until after the stroke? That Grandmum could be so certain that Dierdre would obey her command even months before she asked? Again, Dierdre felt a surge of anger. How dare the woman ruin her life so . . . so easily, that was it.

"I didn't mean to upset you," he said, putting down his cup and glancing toward the kitchen door, already plotting his retreat.

"You're not. It's just that I hadn't been asked to come until last week," she admitted.

"And then you did exactly what she predicted. Of course it's nearly impossible to refuse a request from a woman as forceful as Grandmum." He smiled, briefly, his face becoming almost handsome for that moment.

Dierdre laughed. Bill was right. No matter how much she resented being here, she could hardly refuse Grandmum's request. Accepting that made her feel a little bit better, enough that she told Bill a few insignificant things—about her job, and Calgary, and her summers with the family in Scotland. Bill responded in kind. He was a salesman for a pharmaceutical manufacturer in New Jersey, working with physicians and clinics in New York and the surrounding states. He didn't like the job all that much, but he was good at it and the money was excellent.

"I'm surprised you rent in New York," Dierdre said. "You could move to some smaller town closer to where you work, buy a house and take the train in every day."

Bill wrinkled his nose and faked a shudder. "My father used to say that houses were like children. I've never had a desire for either. I used to move to a new apartment every year or so. When I think about it, I'm astonished that I've actually been here nearly five."

"The neighborhood's that interesting?"

"No, Grandmum was . . . is, I should say. We usually went to dinner once a week or so just so I could listen to her talk. Did she ever tell you that she knew William Butler Yeats and Aleister Crowley?"

The first name was familiar to her, the second not at all, and she said so.

"Really, you never heard Grandmum mention Crowley's name?"

Dierdre shook her head. "The family has always been well off and a bit eccentric. Grandmum probably met a great many interesting people."

Irritation had crept into her voice as she began to suspect

that a neighbor knew more about her relative than she did. Bill didn't appear to notice. "It was more than just a few casual meetings," he said. "Have you ever taken a good look at the books in Grandmum's library?"

"I haven't been here since I was in my teens. Usually it would be for some family gathering and everything was always so rushed. I never had a chance to talk to her much, let alone get involved in any books."

"And you'll probably be rushed now, but do take some time to look at the photo albums. For the last few months until her recent stroke, Grandmum was cataloging her old photos. Her eyes aren't strong, so I helped her match the damaged prints with the old negatives, and took care of having them developed. We mounted the pictures in a pair of grey albums. They're on a shelf behind the desk. After you look at them, you'll know what sort of questions to ask. Once you get her started, she'll go on for hours. It will give the two of you something to do while you're sitting next to her bed."

He lived to give suggestions, Dierdre decided. She shouldn't see this as superiority, more likely a lack of confidence and a need to appear helpful. She tried to feel some compassion for his anxiety as she showed him to the door.

As soon as Bill had gone, she rinsed the coffee cups then carried the books Bill had returned to the library.

Grandmum's library was in what had once been the larger bedroom in the old side of the house. An interior room, it had no natural light. Instead two large brass chandeliers lit the space. The white mosaic floor was partially covered with a round oriental carpet that through lack of care had long since lost any value it might have possessed. A huge mahogany desk and office chair in the center of the room claimed most of the space. In one corner was an antique maroon mohair settee— the fainting couch Grandmum used to call it—and a fabric-shaded Victorian hanging lamp, the pair arranged for more comfortable reading.

Dierdre scanned the shelves, pleased to see that Bill had been considerate enough to mark the places where the books belonged by pulling out the volumes kept beside them. With his comments in her mind, she stayed awhile, studying Grandmum's collection.

There were Crowley's books, held together on a center shelf by a pair of polished silver and onyx bookends. Beside them was a silver-framed photo of Grandmum at about twenty-five and an older heavyset man. A pair of votive candles beside the photo made the space seem enshrined.

Dierdre turned her attention to the books. They were an odd collection, some by Crowley and others about him. She opened a beautifully illustrated volume on the Tarot and recognized the cards as the same ones she had played with years ago. There were also diaries, some written in an odd sort of shorthand. Others were more easily understood, with sections on Crowley's travels, his philosophy, even his politics. She stared at the photographs contained in these, each of them showing the man in one fantastic costume after another. In one he wore full Masonic dress; in another a sort of Egyptian crown. Even his hands were held in odd manners. The captions described these as ritualistic poses. Dierdre suspected that she knew better.

More appearance than substance, she thought. Just like old Frank.

The albums Bill had mentioned were on a shelf beside the door. She paged through one of them, noting the unfamiliar names, the occasional allusion to some old New York landmark, but she was too exhausted for any of it to hold her interest. She glanced at the book titles. Some were yellowed paperbacks, undoubtedly favorite light reading from Grandmum's recent past. Others were far older, many leather-bound and dating from the turn of the century. These had been arranged alphabetically by some unlabeled categorization. Dierdre determined that one section was on witchcraft and magic, another on mysticism, another on what seemed to be psychic phenomenon. It would have been interesting to someone like Bill, Dierdre thought, but wasted on her. She doubted that she'd read a book for anything but work in the last decade; reading always seemed too much a chore. She glanced at a magazine on the desk, a science journal open to an article titled, "The Psychological Effects of Relativity."

"I bet Grandmum was a great fan of *The Twilight Zone*," Dierdre mumbled as she switched off the light.

• • •

The sun had faded, leaving behind the long gray shadows of evening. Dierdre went to the living room window and stared out at Washington Square. The rain had stopped and a crowd walked the streets in the balmy evening. At this time of the day in Calgary, she'd be just getting home. She'd change into sweats, fix herself something light to eat, and curl up in front of the TV for the evening news. Some things were the same everywhere, she thought, as she closed the heavy draperies, and returned to the bedroom she had claimed to unpack.

She always traveled with twice as much as she needed and usually wore a quarter of it. This trip would probably be no execption. She'd brought six dresses in styles ranging from casual to almost formal, and two good business suits. She pulled these out of the garment bag and smoothed out the wrinkles, then carried them to the closet and opened the door. Half the rod was taken up with old clothes. After hanging her own things beside them, she paused to study what she had found.

There was ankle-length black skirt, a frilly nylon blouse, a knitted wool shawl, a trio of high-necked cotton blouses with cameos carefully attached to the necks. On the shelf above was a black hat, tight fitting with a narrow brim. In a box beside it were gloves, a muff and a number of other hats— broad-brimmed, narrow, fur-trimmed and something Dierdre could only describe as stuffed pheasant. On the floor were six pairs of shoes—heeled pumps, ankle-strapped and two pairs of black leather high-button shoes. Clothes from another era, perhaps things Grandmum had worn when she was young and hadn't been able to part with. In a garment bag, she found more treasures. The first was a rose-colored silk gown, long and flowing, its low-cut bodice delicately embroidered, the skirt painted in a similar floral design. Beside it was a dress so incredibly beautiful that Dierdre was almost afraid to touch it. Slim cut and sleeveless in black and midnight blue brocade, it featured tiny jet beads in intricate patterns over the front and along the scalloped hemline. The cape covering it was in the same blue brocade with a black mink collar so wide it could have easily been mistaken for a stole. Dierdre held the dress up to herself. Apparently she and her great grandmother had once been nearly the same size.

She looked for a label to see where it had been made. The only mark there was a hand-sewn tag with the word 1916 written in black marker. Probably an antique store label, Dierdre thought, and turned over the hem of the gown to see how it had been made.

Machine-stitched, so as far as she could tell it was a reproduction or an altered original. She looked at the rest of the garments. All apparent reproductions, all identified by dates ranging from 1860 to the early 1900s. The hats, while authentic, also had dates penned into their labels.

They'd probably been purchased from a theater costumer, Dierdre thought, though she had no idea why Grandmum would own them. She put her things beside them and continued with her work.

The top drawer of the dresser was empty except for a few pieces of antique jewelry and some scarves. She filled it with rollers and dryers and one of those oversized drying irons that had promised to give body to her limp blonde hair but only succeeded in making it look bouncy enough to seem uncombed. She opened the second drawer and saw that most of it was taken up with a long box. Wondering what new treasure she might find, she opened it.

Clothes for a little girl—frilly petticoats, blouses and long skirts, tiny woolen jackets, buckled pumps and sailor smocks. There were no dates on these, but all of them seemed to be from the same period, probably around the turn of the century. She held up a bright red smock and smiled, certain that Grandmum had once dressed her in it.

Ah, well. Those times were over and from the way Dierdre's life was progressing, she'd have no children of her own. She packed the little clothes away and moved the box to the top shelf of the closet to make room for her own things.

After she was finished, she put on the terry robe and matching slippers her mother had sent for a birthday present, went to the living room, opened the doors of the old console TV and turned it on. Nothing but a fuzzy screen and a buzzing through the speaker. She tried different channels and adjusting the antenna with no success. Apparently she was being forced to read, she thought, as she listened to Bill walking through the apartment above her. He had to be on the phone, pacing as he talked, She heard a dimmer sound of canned laughter. No absence of cable there.

She wondered what he'd do if she showed up at his door and asked to borrow his company for the evening, then decided against trying. He'd probably think she was being too pushy, or worse, that she was coming on to him. Instead, she went into the library. She found a book on superstitions, light enough to require no real effort to understand, and sat down to read. Soon after, taking a clue from the text, she went clockwise round the circlular hallways to her bedroom. As she'd expected, sleep came early and hard. She couldn't recall dreaming, which surprised her.

THREE

The following morning, Dierdre had her breakfast in the
living room. With the draperies open, she could watch the flow
of traffic on the streets near the Square. When it had thinned
to what would be considered a major jam-up in Calgary, she
called for a cab to take her to Hudson Manor. The driver had
nothing to say to her, but plenty of four-letter observations to
yell to fellow motorists. Dierdre decided it was time to acquire
a map of the subway system and a good pair of walking shoes.
It took over an hour to reach Hudson. She suspected that she
could have walked the distance faster and with far less aggra-
vation.

While she was signing the guest book, the nurse on duty
put down her pencil and looked up from the magazine quiz
she was taking. "Bridget's still sleeping," she said.

"I'll wait," Dierdre replied.

She walked softly down the hall and sat in the green vinyl
chair beside the old woman's bed, scanning the headlines of
the *New York Times* that came with the breakfast tray. The
food was untouched, the carton of milk for the cereal half
buried in a bowl of ice. This small courtesy made Dierdre feel
more comfortable about the staff here, enough that she walked
down the hall to speak to the nurse.

"I noticed that Mrs. MacCallum hasn't eaten any breakfast.
Will she eat it later?" she asked.

The nurse was finished with the quiz and ready to be atten-

27

tive. "Sometimes she does. If not, she usually drinks the extra milk along with her lunch at noon. She's far more alert then."

"Is that a good time to see her?"

"Wait until two. By then she's had her bath and a change of clothes and bedding. It's the best time of the day to find her ready to visit."

Dierdre decided to spend the time settling into Grandmum's apartment. She had a taxi drop her off at the corner grocery, picked up a few things and went home. After fixing a salad, she carried it through the sliding doors to the enclosed rear yard.

The space was mostly given up to shrubs and flowers but there was a small patch of lawn and a brick patio midway down from the newer doors. Once it had only a single bench made from the same marble as the front stairs. Grandmum had added a white iron table and chairs. Dierdre sat there, sipped her coffee and considered how little the yard had changed in the last twenty years. There were still the same flowers, the same leafy ferns, the patch of daffodils and jonquils just opening in the mild spring weather, the section of lawn where she and some older girl from the neighborhood whose name she had long since forgotten had played croquet and the perennial garden where they'd buried cheap costume jewelry in cigar-size treasure boxes. Once she'd forgotten where they'd dug their last hole and Fred, the building's caretaker, had helped her look for it. They never found the box. For all Dierdre knew, it was buried there still, the gilded plastic settings peeling and covered with mildew, the box itself rotting in the damp earth.

Dierdre opened the paper and scanned the accounts of muggings, and gang attacks and a grisly double murder. Calgary had its problems with crime, but nothing to match one day's worth here would happen there in half a year. Two children were missing in the Bronx; a prostitute's body had been dumped next to a trashcan in south Central Park. Police thought the woman had been killed in a ritual murder. There'd been a bank robbery gone bad in Manhattan and now an old security guard was dead.

Knives, guns, cults, anger. With no clear concept of the city's true size or layout, every horrible event felt like an immediate, almost personal, threat. She switched her attention to world news but even that seemed more chaotic and immediate here, probably because the United States government was so involved in international affairs. As expected, the tension in Iran dominated, but the chaos was so confusing that she quickly lost interest in the subject.

The feature columns were at least familiar—and after a quick dose of Dear Abby and the comics, she picked up her tray and started toward the house. The French doors with their heavy draperies were an odd contrast to the open expanse of the newer sliding doors. One set seemed open and staring, the other shut, as if the two sets were winking at her, sharing some private joke.

Both doors were clean on the outside, but dirt caked the inside glass of the French doors and cobwebs hung like Spanish moss from the yellowed drapery lining. The draperies had to be replaced, she decided, perhaps with something lighter, airier. The yard had a wall around it. Even if the windows were completely uncovered no one would be able to see in.

Well, at least she had something to occupy the next few hours. Dierdre poured a second cup of coffee and found a bucket and some ammonia under the sink. She stood on a chair and began unhooking the filthy curtains from the rod, slowly lowering the heavy cloth to the floor. She had gotten halfway through when she lost her balance and gripped the rod for support. One end of it broke loose from the wall. The curtains slid off the rod, raising a cloud of dust as they hit the floor. Dierdre sneezed, retreated to the kitchen and waited for the dust to settle before continuing with the work.

After the curtains had been dragged through the sliding doors and spread lining-side-up on the lawn, Dierdre began cleaning the beveled panes, washing each small square of glass three times until it sparkled. She'd finished only the top two rows before the water became too filthy to do much more than move the dirt from one square to another. Washing more quickly, she took the first layer of grime off another dozen panes. She paid little attention to the view through them, but as she was going into the kitchen to change the water, she happened to glance out the sliding door. Something in the yard was wrong. Even when she realized what it was, it still took a moment for surprise to turn to curiosity, then fear.

The dusty velvet draperies she had spread across the small patch of lawn covered nearly all of it. But when she'd looked through the old French doors, the curtains were nowhere in sight.

The angle could not have changed much in a mere dozen feet. She noted exactly where she'd placed the curtains, then returned to the French doors. Peering through the clean panes, she saw only grass where the draperies should have been. Her eyes could not be deceiving her, but to be certain, she looked again, noticing other far-from-subtle differences, though none as obvious as the yards of deep blue velvet that ought to be covering most of the lawn.

She backed away from the windows, one palm held out as if she could push the odd scene away. She thought of her dream, and for a moment the terror threatened to return. Her mind fought it, seeking refuge in the advice of her therapist.

Think logically. Think reasonably. Think calmly.

Didn't Grandmum have books on magic in the library? Perhaps someone had set up some trick with mirrors, the way David Copperfield made the Statue of Liberty disappear on TV. If so, couldn't the mirrors stay in place forever, one long marvelous joke to play on unsuspecting guests?

Except, of course, that the windows were covered and filthy, as if Grandmum had wanted to hide the illusion. If she was tired of it, why hadn't she simply had the mirrors taken down?

Logically. Reasonably. Calmly.

Dierdre managed to diminish her fear to something more like uneasiness, enough that she was able to approach the windows and study the view from a number of different angles. She saw no sign of an illusion. The frame on the old doors also had nothing out of the ordinary, save the beautiful Egyptian style carvings across the top that looked old enough to have been part of the original woodwork. After reminding herself that she'd used the sliding door a dozen times in the last day with no ill effect, she went outside through it and studied the wall and window frames, even made the rounds of the garden wall itself. She saw nothing at all but roses and lawn and bricks and a few airy maidenhair ferns.

Well, there was only one way to solve the riddle.

Though emotion had stolen much of the strength from Dierdre's hands, she managed to undo the rusty bolt on the French doors. The hinges were harder to move, but she was able to crack the door open far enough to stick the mop through.

She could see it in the glass, and when she pulled it back, it was still whole. Though her knees felt weak, she did the same with her hand. She could see that as well. It felt perfectly all right while held outside, and no different after she pulled it back. Heartened, she stuck her head and shoulders through.

Her stomach fluttered from more than nervousness. She felt for a moment as if she had fallen. Gripping the door frame to steady herself, she stayed where she was only long enough to take a quick survey of the yard.

There were the early-blooming tulips in delightful swathes of colors, the lawn just greening out, the sky a hazy shade of blue. She saw no sign of the draperies, or of the wrought iron table and chairs where she had sat and eaten breakfast only hours before. The wall still extended the width of the old flat and the one beside it, but when she looked to the right she saw not the newer sliding door but an exact match to the doors at which she now stood. Before she could understand the revelation, the white cat appeared on the top of the stone wall, jumped onto the the lawn and lazily started walking toward the house as if it belonged there.

Could mirrors have changed the texture of the sky? The style of the doors? Could mirrors have conjured up a cat? Dierdre shut the door as quickly as the rusty hinges would allow and ran to the newer doorway. Yes, it was still sunny, but now there were clouds in a far bluer sky. As she already expected, there was no sign of the cat and the draperies lay where she had left them.

Her forced calm abandoned her, replaced by fear all the more potent because it was directed at something so utterly strange.

Dierdre backed away from the windows. When she reached the kitchen door, she turned and ran to the front of the apartment as if whatever had altered the view through those doors would break through them and charge down the narrow hallway after her. She stopped just before she reached the front door, then sat in Grandmum's old rocker facing the hallway,

her feet bobbing the chair anxiously back and forth, her mind
trying to grasp, to accept, to understand her discovery.

It was as if the garden and the cat existed in the past or
future or even some other similar world and that all of it was
waiting for her just beyond those doors. If she thought that
Grandmum would be coherent enough to answer questions,
she would have phoned the nursing home and asked her about
it. She could ask later, but if she did and got no logical answer
to her questions, would she ever be able to set foot in the
house again?

And in these circumstances, what could possibly be logical?

This couldn't wait, she decided. This was a mystery she had
to solve on her own, and quickly, before her imagination got
the better of her and she was forced to abandon the house.
Though later she wondered where she discovered the courage,
she returned to the sunroom, and cracked open the door. The
cat responded immediately, running to it, then pausing just
outside. Dierdre crouched down and picked it up, drawing it
through the doors and letting it go in the sunroom. It curled
around her legs, its soft fur warm from the sun, its purrs comforting. Having said hello, it made straight for the kitchen.

The animal's calm vanished as soon as its feet touched the
floor's new ceramic tile, as if like Dierdre, it suddenly realized
that it had wandered into a world where things were not quite
right. It sniffed the air, the tile, the walls, then began rubbing
against the corners of the cupboards, leaving its scent on the
unfamiliar surfaces. Dierdre found a can of tuna fish on the
shelf and opened it. At the sound of the electric can opener,
the cat jumped, though it ran to the bowl eagerly enough when
Dierdre put it down.

It ate only a little before a car sounded a horn. The cat
stiffened for a moment then went back to eating. When Dierdre held out one hand and approached the frightened creature,
a paw shot out, its claws retreating as soon as they touched
her skin.

"Poor scared thing," Dierdre said in a soothing voice.
"You're as confused by all of this as I am." She continued
to talk to the cat until it had finished. It approached her again
and sniffed, purring, relaxed enough that she could pick it up
again.

"Maybe you'd like some milk, huh?" Dierdre crooned. She opened the refrigerator. As soon as the cat saw the light, and heard the hum of the motor, it pushed out of her arms and through the French doors. By the time she reached them, the cat was gone. If it hadn't left a dusting of white hair on her blue cotton shirt and three deep scratches on her arm, Dierdre might have doubted that it had ever been there at all.

Yet the cat had readily come into the house, as if it had perceived this place as home.

If Dierdre stood in the center of the sunroom, she could look out both sets of doorways. Staring through both made the small differences far too clear, and far too unsettling. If she lived in this house, she would have to do as Grandmum did and keep the old set covered. But now that she'd discovered the room's secret, no hasty covering of sheets or blankets or rotting draperies could make her any less aware of her discovery.

Someone knocked on the door, the meeting of brass to brass harsh, insistent. Dierdre jumped, and ran to answer it, pulling it open without fastening the chain. The thought of companionship, even if it was only as brief as a delivery by the mailman, calmed her.

It was Bill, a rumpled topcoat over a different ill-fitting suit. "I thought I'd take a chance on finding you in," he said. "I keep a company car in a garage near here. I'm going up to Boston on business for a couple of days. Since the nursing home is between here and the turnpike, I thought I'd offer you a ride over. I'll be leaving in half an hour."

Bill was leaving? She hardly knew him, but once he was gone she would be alone in this section of the building, an idea that bothered her far more now than it would have an hour before. "When are you coming back?" she asked.

"Day after tomorrow. If you need anything in the meantime, Angelina Petra lives in the lower apartment in the next entrance from you. She and Grandmum were good friends. I know she'd like to meet you."

"Has she lived here a long time?"

"She never mentions a time when she didn't. You might ask her about that."

Bill certainly spent a lot of time suggesting conversations,

Dierdre thought. Did she look so incapable of handling social amenities on her own?

"As soon as I get back, I'd like to show you around," Bill went on, speaking quickly, as if he were afraid she would turn even that vague invitation down. "Now, I'd just like to offer the ride."

"Oh . . . yes, I suppose it's a good time to go back," Dierdre replied, thinking it high time she discovered what Grandmum knew about the old doors.

"I've got to load my suitcase in the car then fix a sandwich and a cup of instant coffee for the road," he said.

"I just made a fresh pot. Would you like that instead?"

"Absolutely." He started to follow her to the kitchen—far too close to the oddly-matched views. "Wait here," she said. "Everything's such a mess since I started cleaning the cupboards."

She stopped at the end of the hall and turned. "I forget how you take it. Just . . ." He had an odd expression on his face. Triumph, perhaps, blended with a bit of concern. "What is it?" she asked.

"Grandmum. I think it just hit me that she'll probably never be coming back. I'll like having you for a neighbor, Dierdre, but I'd rather it be some other way." He looked toward the grate in the old gas fireplace, obviously embarrassed by his sudden rush of emotion. "Cream. One sugar," he said, answering her first question.

She rushed to pour them each a cup. While he sat in the living room, she changed her shirt, smoothed her hair and joined him.

"You said that you often borrowed books from Grandmum's library. Do you have any suggestions on what I might find of particular interest?" she asked.

"Well, as I said, there are the photo albums. I would start with them. Once you've gone through them, you may want to read about some of the characters in them. Crowley's works are in the section on the occult. Yeats is in literature. Noah Hathaway isn't described by any biographer, but there are a couple of books of his poetry and a stack of letters Grandmum received from him in a carved wooden box on the shelf behind the chaise. I always wanted to ask permission to read the letters, but it seemed like too great an imposition. But since you're a relation . . ." He left the thought unfinished.

"Since I'm a relation, I can ask what she wants done with them," Dierdre replied stiffly.

"I hadn't implied anything else," Bill said, looking confused by her sudden shift in tone.

"I'm sorry. Your suggestions are probably natural to Americans. Canadians are friendly, but not nearly so direct, especially to casual acquaintances. I guess I've started to think like them."

"I've been told that I am way too direct by more than one woman, and they were all Americans," Bill replied. "It's the salesman in me. Tell me when I come on too strong."

He smiled to show that he wasn't entirely serious. She did the same.

The rear of Bill's late model Taurus wagon was filled with boxes, piled so deep they nearly obscured the view out the rear window. In contrast, the passenger compartment had only an atlas and pile of maps on the seat, a half-full litter bag hanging from the cigarette lighter.

They took a circuitous route away from the Square. Bill pointed out some of the nearby restaurants, a pizzaria where Woody Allen could occasionally be spotted on Friday nights, the places he believed had the best Chinese, Thai and Ethiopian foods. Later they passed a house where Mark Twain had once lived, and a secluded row of apartments that once housed Eugene O'Neill, e.e. cummings, Louise Bryant and her husband John Reed. "Close together, but then I suppose Louise liked it that way," Bill commented.

"She and Cummings were lovers?" Dierdre asked.

"She and O'Neill." He pointed to a three-story building, so narrow it seemed to have been compressed by the wider structures on either side of it. "That's where Edna St. Vincent Millay lived. It's rumored that she used the third floor to hold an orgy of such vast proportions that it stunned even the scandal-proof bohemians. Grandmum said she'd been invited but had gotten wind of the sort of event the hostess planned and had politely declined. Of course the building is so narrow that the participants all had to lie sideways like sardines in a can.''

He stared at her, his faded blue eyes intent, his hands shaking. Years ago, she'd had a blind date with a college boy who'd looked at her that way, the look his only warning before he thrust his hand between her thighs. ''Did you want to stop for some lunch on the way?'' she asked. ''I'd like to buy you something. You've been so helpful.''

The comment diffused some of the tension. The moment passed.

''The quick sort since I'm running so late,'' Bill said and pulled over, double parking beside a street vendor's cart.

Dierdre bought them hot dogs and lemonade. They ate standing up, close to the cart to keep out of the press of pedestrians around them. ''Does it ever get quiet in New York?'' she asked.

''Between the hours of three and five in the morning. Of course, then you don't go out for fear of being mugged,'' Bill replied. ''Visitors always complain about the crowds, but we New Yorkers are used to them. With so many people, you can lose yourself among them.'' He laughed, the first time she had seen him let down his guard around her. ''I love being just a faceless cog in this giant wheel. Anonymity is such a beautiful thing.''

''Most people would hold the opposite view.''

''Most people haven't been subjected to scrutiny as I have all my life.''

''Were you an only child?''

''Worse. I was the youngest of five, conceived so late that for the first four months of her pregnancy, my mother blamed me on the change. She only wised up when I started kicking. She was fifty-one when I was born and determined not to make the same mistakes with me that she did with the older kids. I spent most of my early years hiding out. It's a habit that's hard to break.''

A half dozen cars had queued up behind Bill's. One of the drivers gave a loud blast on a horn. ''I guess we ought to go,'' Bill suggested, waving affably to the waiting drivers while holding the door for her.

Once they were underway, Dierdre wondered aloud how

anyone could own a car in this city and not go insane.

"We use them as restaurants." Bill held up the remaining bit of his lemonade. "As social clubs." He pointed to his cellular phone. "I even know someone who powers his laptop off his cigarette lighter and does his correspondence during morning rush hour. He's never had an accident. That's how slow things move. Eventually, we may never get to work at all. We'll just use our cars as portable offices, driving for four hours in one direction, then four in the other."

She laughed, encouraging him to continue. She paid close attention to his descriptions of New York's longest traffic jam, worst accident and the crazy drivers he'd seen on the road. The banter felt comforting, and kept her mind off the mystery, and the questions she had to ask her dying relation.

"I even heard of someone who died in his car. It happened right in the middle of rush hour. By the time the driver pushing him along realized what had happened, the corpse was nearly to his office. Marvelous funeral. Friends sent donations in his name to AAA."

"That one isn't true, is it?"

"Urban legend. Slightly embellished à la Bill. And speaking of destinations . . ." He pointed to the iron fence and beautifully kept gardens in front of Hudson Manor.

The nurse on duty had been right. Grandmum did seem more like her old self in the early afternoon. She sat in a wheelchair in the visitor's room, her short thin hair washed and blowdried, even a hint of powder and lipstick on her face. She was dressed in a deep blue cotton robe decorated at the front and sleeves with an embroidered grape-and-vine pattern. Dierdre had seen the robe many times before and it always reminded her of Greece and Rome and all the other far-off places Grandmum had visited over the years. She sat up in bed in front of a low dining table, her glasses low on her thin nose, reading a book. To one side was a lunch tray containing some sort of overdressed mayonnaise pasta salad, a few lonely peas its only splash of color. The sliced banana covered with dollops of vanilla pudding looked equally bland.

When Dierdre was a child and stayed with Grandmum, they had eaten bright curries surrounded by sliced mangos and tan-

gerines, mixed-green salads with ripe tomatoes, desserts lush
with chocolate and cream. No wonder Grandmum had no interest in the home's food. Dierdre took the woman's hand, and
saw how alert Grandmum appeared once she realized she had
a visitor. "Hello," Dierdre said. "You look so much better
today."

Grandmum stared at her. Recognition took only a moment.
When it came, her expression brightened. "It's having you
near, Dierdre," she said in a hoarse whisper. She cleared her
throat and went on, sounding more like the woman Dierdre
remembered. "How did you find my house?"

"By cab," she replied. Grandmum smiled, thinking as Dierdre was of the word games they'd played years ago. "Much
as I remembered it," Dierdre continued more seriously. "Interesting how much of the past has come back to me, even
after decades away."

"Did you find something good to read in the library?"

"You know how I am with reading. I did see a few pos-
sibilities but I was too tired to start any of them. I settled in.
Today I've been cleaning a little. I even washed the windows
in the sunroom."

Grandmum must have heard what she'd said, but if the old
woman knew about the strangeness of the old doors, she gave
no indication of it. Instead she picked at the meal as if she
had already eaten. Considering the appetizing appearance—
and most likely taste—Dierdre hardly blamed her.

"Would you like me to take you out for an early dinner?"
Dierdre asked.

"Would you really like to take me?"

A blunt question, but a natural one given Grandmum's apparent condition. Dierdre would have to call a nurse for help
getting her dressed, then phone for a cab. She had no idea
what Grandmum could eat, or what she would do if the old
woman needed help in the bathroom. Dierdre didn't even
know if Grandmum was capable of getting out of bed. And
all that effort for perhaps an hour away from this place hardly
seemed worth it. Dierdre looked at the food again, and the
expression on Grandmum's face. In all her life, she had never
lied to the woman except for the little things children are too

embarrassed to admit to. "It's probably not such a good idea," she said.

"Smart girl. I'm not too steady on my feet anymore, even when they're not drowning me with drugs to help me rest."

"Are they really?"

"They were. Not anymore. After I saw you last night, I refused to take any of them. By tomorrow my mind, at least, will be as sharp as ever. We have a lot to discuss."

"Is there anything you'd like me to bring you?" Dierdre asked, thinking of the books.

"Just one. Tomorrow, bring me a reuben sandwich from Fat Albert's the way Bill did last time he came."

"You like sauerkraut?"

"Love it, especially the way it makes that broad-beamed aide gag when it comes sliding out the other side."

Dierdre grinned. Grandmum always had spark, and the cagiest ways of getting even with anyone in the family. That probably explained the obedience she still got even now when she didn't control the bulk of the MacCallum fortune any longer. "I could check the phone book and see if someplace around here delivers," Dierdre suggested.

"You'll do nothing of the sort, child. I can bribe the help for that. Now sit here and tell me how your life is going while I try to stomach this marvelous feast."

Dierdre did, telling her what she thought of the Canadian Rockies, and all the beautiful places she'd discovered in them on her frequent trips there with Frank.

"I knew a mountain climber once," Grandmum said. "He told me that Lake Louise was the closest place to paradise he had ever seen. Paradise is always somewhere on a mountaintop for people like him."

"Did you ever visit the Rockies?"

"The American ones. I was about twenty. I went by train. It took nearly three days to reach Yellowstone. It did seem like Paradise, especially after that."

"People value most what they have to strive for," Dierdre said, reciting from memory the advice at the end of the letter Grandmum had written her after Dierdre had graduated from high school. It was one of the many she had kept and read from time to time until her last move from Toronto to Calgary when the movers had lost them.

"I took pictures of the trip. You'll find them in my scrapbook, tucked away in the library."

"I haven't been in there much. I've been far more interested in the sunroom doors."

At this second mention of them, Grandmum seemed to understand. She stared at Dierdre as if waiting for her to go on.

"The view isn't the same through each set of glass. And there was a cat, a white one. . . ." Dierdre blurted.

"Buddha," Grandmum said.

"What?"

"The cat's name is Buddha. It belongs to Angelina. It's fond of chopped liver."

"It scratched me." Dierdre showed the old woman her arm.

"Long-haired cats are often timid. Take a plate into the garden and sit with it."

Dierdre was beginning to understand this odd conversation. "You want me to go through the doors, you mean?"

"Want? You're the one who's so concerned about the damned cat." Grandmum managed to spear a piece of tuna from the salad. Though her hand shook, she managed to get the fork to her mouth, eating the one choice morsel triumphantly.

"I'll be all right there?" Dierdre asked.

Grandmum threw down the fork in disgust, lay back and stared at the ceiling as if petitioning God for patience. "It's our own damn garden, for pity's sake. What could possibly harm you?"

She doesn't know about the doors, Dierdre thought. Or perhaps she's forgotten. Or the past and present are all jumbled together as often happens when people get old and confused.

"The cat is just fine. It's the people that you can't trust. Read the books I left out for you; then you'll understand." Advice given, Grandmum shut her eyes.

Dierdre tried to get more information out of the woman, but if Grandmum heard her questions, she gave no indication. She might have drifted off to sleep that quickly, she might be half-deaf, but Dierdre didn't believe either. No, the woman was ignoring her. Grandmum knew well enough how strange those old doors were. She wanted Dierdre full of curiosity, ready to throw all caution aside and step through them.

"I suppose I should be going," she whispered, in case Grandmum was already asleep.

"Going?" the woman blurted. "You just got here."

"You look sleepy."

"Not sleepy; remembering. I was thinking of Angelina and the cat. She and I have known each other so long. She was born in the building. I was seven years older and used to watch her when her mother went out. She's my last friend there, only because she was the youngest. There was her and Leah and Alma; what a group we were."

"Tell me about them," Dierdre prompted, thinking that Bill might be right and she might learn something important if she just let the old woman pick the topic, and ramble on as she wished.

FOUR

A year ago, when Bridget had still been alert and active and feeling half her actual age, she'd read an article describing how the brain of an old person gradually ceases to absorb new information while retaining the old. She'd found this a curious fact and had waited for some sign of that in herself. It never came, not even after infirmity assaulted her, leaving her feeling every one of her years.

She'd received the first of its blows one quiet summer afternoon. She'd been sitting in the garden when she'd sensed a dull throbbing deep in her brain. She had time to put down her coffee mug and take a deep breath before a searing blast of pain exploded in her temples. She pressed her hands against her forehead, surprised for a moment to find skin and skull still intact. Though her conscience felt surprisingly pure given the details of her life, she mumbled a prayer for forgiveness of her sins while she waited for a second, probably lethal, jolt.

It never came. Instead, she felt a tingling then a heaviness in her left hand. She'd picked up her cane and struggled to the house. There, she sat at the kitchen table, breathing deeply while she waited, not certain if the climax was coming or had already passed.

Certainly, what had happened had been climax enough.

By the following morning, she felt nearly normal except that her left hand seemed swollen and hard to move, the left arm heavy and difficult to raise. It was all in her mind, of course,

42

the lack of feeling caused by a sudden bursting of some small blood vessel, the resulting death of nerves. Ah, what tricks an old brain could play, and she was powerless to prevent any of them.

Some weeks later, with her arm still stiff, she had a second attack that left the same limb weaker and her balance somewhat skewed. The cane she had used for extra support became a necessity.

She'd seen these mini-strokes in her friends. Since she was well over ninety and aware that she would die soon, she didn't bother to waste time and money on a doctor. Instead, once she felt up to it, she phoned for a cab. The driver had been Russian, his English precise though heavily accented. Together, they'd made the rounds of a half dozen nursing homes. Some smelled as bad as neglected diaper pails. Others had aides who were so cheerful they made her nausous. The rest seemed to be painted in various shades of lime green, as if some pop psychologist had said this was the color of incipient death.

Not for her, thank you. She wanted her death site to have some semblance of taste. So she picked Husdon Manor with its blue-and-cream-flocked paper in the waiting room and halls, the little ducks and country quilt photos on the bare spaces of every wall, placed there in a futile effort to create a serene, country feel in the heart of the city. Not her taste, of course, but tasteful enough for an old lady.

She could have died in the home she had always lived in, of course, but she thought that being among her own things would make her struggle to breathe, to live, to prolong the inevitable one more time. She was ready for death, and she thought it would come easier in a place like Hudson Manor.

With her choice made and the papers signed for an admittance at some unnamed date, she went home and reviewed her will, organized her books and documents, and arranged to have the cleaning service do some extra work in her apartment. Then she packed her suitcase. When the next painful stroke hit, all she had to do was crawl to the phone and dial Hudson Manor. The staff took care of the rest.

And then, after the necessary doctor had come to examine her and tell her what she already knew, she lay in one of their infinitely uncomfortable adjustable beds and contemplated the truth about old age.

No matter how she lay, she felt pain. It radiated from the point where her body weighed heaviest against the mattress out to the farthest tips of fingers and toes. The nursing home food looked tasteless, but she could hardly judge it. Even if it had been perfectly flavored, she doubted she would notice the subtleties of herbs and wines and spices. Reading gave her headaches. She envied other residents who actually liked TV, but had nothing in common with any of them. From the way they all looked at her and each other, it seemed the feeling was mutual. Perhaps they were all like her, she thought, rebellious adolescents trapped in aged dying bodies.

The only time she felt any sense of comfort was when the aides bathed her in one of the huge step-in tubs used mainly for the younger, temporarily disabled clients. They would have preferred to give her showers, but a daily bath had been the one luxury she had demanded before signing the papers that would commit her to this place, and she made it clear from time to time that she still had wits enough to notice if they broke the agreement. As one of the few residents not on Medicare, she had some clout.

But even the baths had their own misery. The aides would not let her sit in the swirling water with any kind of peace. Instead their hands were constantly on her body, reminding her of its frailty and their own omnipotence.

She could focus on the pain and all the rest, but doing so seemed to stretch each hour into the length of a day. Better, to ignore the present and live in the past—in the time when she had been young, alone and daring. In the time when death had not seemed possible. There, the hours whirled by so quickly that she would often wake from her journey into her memories to find her food trays stacked on her bedside table, and a visitor waiting patiently for her attention.

Sometimes, the caller was one of her distant relations, asked by the family to check on her and make certain Hudson was treating her right. More often, it was Angelina, but the poor old dear seemed far too uncomfortable in the sort of surroundings she would probably be entering in the next year or so. During her last visit, Angelina had begun to breathe too fast, to look a bit paler than usual. Bridget had suggested that she either go home or order up a bed and replace the "cellmate" who snored too loud. Since then, Bridget made a practice of phoning Angelina every other afternoon to tell her how she was getting along, and assure her that there was no need for her to make such a long, tiring journey when the phone was so close and convenient. Bill had also come by, though only a few times. His attempts to cheer her up had been so obvious and disgusting that she had made it more than clear she did not want to see him there again.

But now there was Dierdre. Dear sweet young Dierdre. Emotional, cautious, almost fragile. She reminded Bridget most of her own mother, a delicate woman, thin not from genetics or choice, but because the constant conflict of emotions within her had pulled too much energy from her body; and of her own son, Dierdre's grandfather, an excitable man, always full of great ideas, who nonetheless refused to make a decision without first consulting her.

The family's fragility surprised her, for the MacCallum's had always been of stern, strong stock. Had her decision so altered them? No, she could not think that way, for to do so now would be to condemn herself, to offer God one more mark on her conscience. If she did, she feared she would be damned.

In any event, Dierdre was stronger than her father or grandfather, or even her mother, a second cousin of Dierdre's father, one quarter MacCallum but still of a disposition that could only be called flawed. They flocked together in Aberdeen, called to their ancestral home as salmon were to the place that spawned them. If so, Bridget understood. She alone knew how their history had changed in a single afternoon, so she did not fear the dreams or the times that reality seemed to shift and reform like fog in a faint morning breeze.

At least Dierdre seemed to understand the need for a life independent of her clannish relations. Bridget admired her for that, enough that she'd decided to name Dierdre as her heir—the keeper of the family's most treasured secret. The one who would make the decision on whether the door should be left open or closed forever. And here she was asking questions about things she certainly needed to know. Better to tread carefully, to make her understand slowly lest she fall into the hysteria that seemed far too common in this family. And perhaps that time with her and Angelina and Leah was the perfect place to start.

She smiled at Dierdre. "Take me back to my room," she said. "Even this story is one best told without interruption."

Dierdre did as she asked. Once they were settled in, close to the window with the bed table between then, Grandmum asked Dierdre to pour her a glass of water. She took a long drink and shut her eyes. "If I stop talking, give me a poke, dear. In the meantime, this is the easiest way for me to recall the past, the real past, and you have a right to know of it.

"And besides, this is the part that isn't written down; things no one should ever know but me and now you."

"I don't understand—"

Grandmum cut her off. "In time, child, you will." She took a long drink through the plastic straw and began.

"I think the time to start is when I was fifteen. Mother and the boys had been dead for nearly two years. During that time Douglas MacCallum, my father, had been fighting a growing depression. Sometimes it got the better of him, and he stayed home and drank. Then he would rally, and head back to work. But in time, the rallies began to space farther apart. The grief was claiming him.

"I hardly blamed him because I missed mother and the boys, too. I'd even gotten drunk myself and found the two hours of giggling far preferable to the constant mourning for the dead.

"Albert had been nine and always prone to catching every illness the huge and dirty city had to offer. Edward had been only two. At least they'd both gone quickly. Mother had hung on for weeks, fighting off one bout of fever after another. Perhaps, she didn't die of the same thing as my brothers, perhaps it had been of a broken heart. No matter, she was gone. Now the silence of the house was broken solely by the clink of ice in my father's glass, my own stifled sobs.

"I didn't want him to know that I was crying. Mother always told me that seeing me unhappy over my brothers' deaths always made her sorrow worse."

She opened her eyes and glanced at Dierdre. The girl was

looking out the window, her eyes bright. "My mother left me as well," she whispered.

"They all do. Perhaps those old buildings in Aberdeen are the one solid thing in their lives."

Dierdre looked at her, frowning. "What an odd way to put it."

"But appropriate, believe me. Now put away the tissue," she said, patting Dierdre's hand. "Things were bad but not that bad, though they soon got worse. You see the deaths in our family weren't the first losses in Father's life, nor were they the cause of his drunkeness. He had always been fond of good bourbon and when drunk would often sadly say that the MacCallum fortune had been built on the lives of others.

"But if lives had built our fortune, we MacCallums had built a good part of every city we'd lived in. It was rumored that a MacCallum had built the first municipal buildings in Aberdeen, the Trade's Hall in Glasgow. Perhaps some MacCallum ancestor had overseen the construction of the ancient St. Macher's Cathedral. But unlike our ancestors, Douglas MacCallum thought not of buildings but of dams and dikes and tunnels.

"And the greatest of these, the precursor of all the miles to follow, was the first subway tunnel in New York. Father was in charge of the crew. His foreman might have determined when conditions were safe or unsafe for digging, but Father was the one who gave the final order to proceed. Mistakes happened. Men died—not Scotchmen or Americans, but Italians and Irishmen, Poles and Hungarians. For years he saw the isolated deaths as accidents; tragic, but unavoidable. Then there was the single huge accident, one that claimed nearly a dozen lives in a single blast. Even that he managed to shrug off.

"But years later, when the influenza claimed my mother and brothers, the guilt he had ignored for so long returned, haunting him more potently than any ghost of a dead worker might have done. He began to view the deaths in his family as retribution. Revenge by men was one thing; by God something entirely different.

"And so he drank, and in those hours between sobriety and misery, his guilt somehow lost its hold on him.

"But around the time I turned sixteen, his misery seemed even more intense. He'd sit at home, staring at nothing in particular, paying no attention to his fortune or his work. 'We've plenty enough to live on for at least another century,' he would tell me, but I didn't believe him. Bills were piled high on his desk, and one morning I'd heard him on the phone arguing with a creditor for more time.

"I was always smart with figures and budgets. I used to sit with Mother in the kitchen, watching her pay the bills, asking her to explain about checks and rents, ledgers and interest. It had hardly been a business education but it was enough that when I stole into Father's study that evening and went through the mail, I could see that our situation had become desperate.

"Father hadn't worked in months so our income was limited to the rents he collected from the ten apartments in the building he owned. I looked in the book of rental receipts, hardly surprised to find that only half the tenants had paid for the previous month, none this month and it was already the eighth.

"A brief look into the savings account book showed the effect of my father's grief. A year earlier, there'd been nearly five thousand in the bank. The account was now down to less than four hundred and there would be another mortgage payment due on the building the beginning of the month.

"If my brother Andrew had been home, he could have handled things. But he was away at West Point learning to be an officer. That left me to deal with the situation. I lay awake that night, debating what to do. When I finally reached a decision, I slept easily, never doubting for a moment that I was up to the task I'd chosen."

She paused to bend forward. Dierdre held up the water glass so she could reach the straw a little easier. "I didn't know you were so poor," Dierdre said.

"No one knows. The story I am telling you took place long ago in a world that never really existed, at least not anymore."

Dierdre looked at her, trying to find a diplomatic way of telling Grandmum that she had no interest in fiction, when the need for facts was so pressing.

"In a few years I would change everything," she said.

"You turned things around, you mean?" Dierdre asked.

"In a manner of speaking, I sure as hell did," Grandmum admitted, laughing before going on.

"While Father slept in on Saturday morning, I put on my best blue dress. With the rental receipt book and the real estate ledger clutched tightly in my hand, I knocked on the second floor center flat, a tiny one-bedroom apartment owned by two brothers, both immigrants from southern Italy. Michael conducted a streetcar. John seemed to have no obvious job but was always well-dressed.

" 'And we all know what that means,' my friend Alma said soon after the pair had moved in. She said they had more money hidden away in their mattress than my father had in the bank. At that moment, I prayed that she was right.

"I hadn't seen any sign of the brothers' wealth, but if they were wealthy, they would probably not mind paying their rent, which was why I went there first. I listened outside the door for a moment, and when I heard their voices and knew they were awake, I knocked with what I hoped was the proper amount of force to show I was serious. John opened the door a moment later. He wore a sleeveless undershirt, black pants and suspenders. A cigar hung from one corner of his mouth. Michael lay on the couch in the living room with a bottle of beer beside him in one hand, the morning paper in the other. Smoke rose from a second, thinner cigar, in his ashtray. The smell of them combined with my own nervousness made me queasy. 'I've come to collect this month's rent,' I said.

" 'Hey, isn't that your papa's job?' Michael called from inside.

"I told them that he was letting me do it for a change.

" 'Why don't I believe you?' Michael continued, but in a good-natured way. I think he was trying to find out how bad things were, which was none of his affair.

"Even so. I began to have doubts about what I was doing. Whatever had made me think I was capable of doing this, and what would Father say when he learned what I had done? I wanted to apologize and go home but thought of the desperate situation I was in. They had to pay. They had to. I concentrated on this, only on this, and stood my ground.

"Nearly a minute passed before John called from inside the house. 'Go on, Michael. We've got the money. Give it to the poor kid. Who knows. It looks like she'll grow up to be a real beauty. Maybe one of us can marry her and take it all back.' John took the cigar out of his mouth and laughed. I stared at the end of it, black from his saliva. I couldn't imagine what something that smelled and looked so horrible might taste like.

" 'What's the matter? You don't like my smoke?' John asked me.

"I shook my head. John got up and stuck thirty dollars in my pocket, then blew smoke in my face and laughed again. 'Save the receipts, little girl,' he said. 'And if anybody in the building gives you a hard time about paying, you come see me and I'll break their legs if they don't pay. OK?'

"Thinking Alma was probably right about the pair's shady connections, I fled, stopping at the opposite side of the hall. The brothers may have been rude, but I was old enough to know they were probably the same way to everyone. And I had gotten the rent. With that success firmly in my mind, I knocked on another door. Ardeth Hirsig, my friend Alma's mother, answered. She balanced her youngest, two-year-old Joanie, on one wide hip and held a bottle in her hand. 'Have you come to see Alma?' she asked. 'If so, you'll have to wait. Leah has off work today and took her shopping.'

"I told her what I wanted and that she owed two months. I said the last reluctantly. The Hirsig's were my friends, after all.

"If Mrs. Hirsig was offended, she gave no sign of it. 'Your papa has been negligent,' she admitted. 'So was Mr. Hirsig and in the same way, I think, though with far less reason. Come in. Sit down. Have some lemonade.' Before I could say anything, Ardeth Hirsig gave Joanie to me, filled a glass and handed it to me with a glance of pity. She asked about Father.

"I said that he was a little better but nothing more. Mrs. Hirsig moved through the cluttered kitchen, pulling ten dollars from a covered bowl in the cupboard, another five from beneath the loose corner of the shelf lining, five more from a can in the back of the freezer. All the while, the baby was staring at me, sucking on her finger, waiting patiently for her mother to return with the bottle. Joanie was the youngest of eight children, and had already been well-trained in that virtue.

"Finally, the woman dug into her purse, pulling out two

more dollars. In total, she gave me twenty-two. 'I'll have another three after I go to the bank and Leah pays me her rent on Friday.'

"I wanted to remind her that she would still owe us for this month but this was the family of my best friend, and I just couldn't do it. Instead, I wrote out a receipt for the rent already paid.

"She asked if I wanted to stay for breakfast. But I had just taken their money. It hardly seemed right to take their food, too, so I declined.

" 'Ah, well, you go and make your Papa some breakfast,' she said. 'Put a lot of pepper in the eggs. That's how I used to wake up Mr. Hirsig.'

"She talked about her husband a great deal, but no one in the building had ever met him. Alma told me that she didn't even know if her father was still alive, though Mrs. Hirsig spoke as if he were and received a check from Switzerland every month. It was sizeable enough that the family of nine could live, not comfortably but with some comfort. There were so many of them that I could never keep track of them all. I recall that Edward and Wilhelm Jr., the oldest, had gotten good educations before taking jobs with the city. Recently, they'd moved into their own flat in a nearby building. I often saw them entering or leaving our building, usually carrying groceries. There was something wonderful about the way they stuck together but I didn't think about it often because it reminded me too much of my mother and brothers.

"In the next hour, I visited all but two tenants in the building. They all paid at least their back rent. Angelina's mother, Mrs. Laughran, even paid a month in advance then asked me if I would watch Angelina on Saturday when she had to work. 'Now that she's almost ten, she could stay alone, but she gets so bored all by herself,' she explained.

"Alma and I had plans. I asked if we could take her along.

" 'With Alma. Of course! She's such a sensible girl. Not like her older sister. That one, even with the good job and school and all, whew!' Mrs. Laughran waved her hand in front of her face, a gesture that seemed to imply that Leah was some sort of smelly cheese. I doubted that was exactly what she meant by it. Flighty, more likely, and on that I had to agree.

"I arranged to come over at eight on Saturday, then left the Laughran flat smiling. I had two hundred and six dollars in my pocket, more than many people earned in a month.

"On the way to my flat at the end of the building, I met Alma and her sister, Leah. Alma carried three library books on accounting and law, Leah a half dozen on a variety of topics pertaining to spiritualism. She also carried a bag from Chumley's Books on Fourth Street.

" 'Look what I found at Gotham, and on sale besides,' she said as she pulled out a copy of *Isis Unveiled* by Helena Blavatsky. I was hardly surprised. Leah had a deep interest in spiritualism and Eastern religions. I thought her dabbling at this hilarious but rarely said so, especially since Leah had impressed some of her beliefs on her little sister.

" 'Come over Saturday morning,' Leah said. 'Mama's going out and we're holding a séance. Alma said she'll sit in if you will.'

" 'A séance? In the middle of the afternoon?' I forced myself to keep a straight face.

" 'Spirits don't flee from daylight, Bridget! At least the good ones don't,' Leah said, speaking as if she were her mother's age, and not twenty-something. 'We're going to try to contact our dead grandmother but who knows who else might show up.'

"I thought of my mother and younger brothers, and was surprised at my sudden surge of excitement. I believed in God and souls, so the existence of ghosts and spirits could hardly be dismissed. But would a spirit be able to contact the living? Would it want to?

"I decided that Mother would. Mother would want me to know that she was all right, and in a happier place. I agreed to attend, trying to make it sound as if I only did so because I had nothing better to do. 'I have to bring Angelina Laughran, though. I told her mother that I'd stay with her on Saturday,' I explained.

"Leah whined. She thought Angelina was too young. She said that Angelina would spoil things, that if any spirit really did show up, the girl would leave the circle screaming. 'She's nothing but a baby,' she concluded.

" 'She's nearly ten,' Alma said. 'You were doing all this

stuff when you were that age. You told me so.'

"I promised her we'd leave if Angelina didn't behave. I said it so earnestly, and as I did, I wondered why I felt the need to reassure Leah about anything."

An attendant came in with juice and cookies. She gave some to Dierdre as well, then left, her cart's wheels squeeking on the waxed linoleum in the hall. Grandmum's voice had grown hoarse and she rested it awhile, letting Dierdre tell her a bit about Frank and her job in Calgary. When she'd exhausted the topic, they returned to Grandmum's story, "You were telling me about Angelina?" she prompted when Grandmum asked where she'd left off.

"Angie?" Grandmum pulled herself back into the present and smiled at Dierdre. "Angie . . . Angelina, though at that time she despised her whole name. It took nearly an hour to convince her that even good Catholic girls dabbled a little in spiritualism. I finally succeeded by suggesting that she was too young to understand a séance, let alone be able to contact anyone. Once I'd stated that, there was no way she would have stayed away.

"Leah and Alma had used those same hours to rearrange their kitchen to accommodate us. As soon as their mother left for work, they had tacked an old scrap of red chintz over the tiny kitchen window so that the yellow linoleum took on a bloody hue. The walls, normally a faded shade of blue, had a purplish cast, eerie and well-suited to the event. They moved the bleached oak table to the center of the kitchen, covered it with a white bedsheet and placed a pair of squat yellow candles in the center.

"Leah had dressed for the occasion as well. Her dark hair, normally pinned up in a severe bun not at all in keeping with either side of her personality, lay heavy on her shoulders. She wore a red blouse and a half dozen dimestore necklaces. Hoop earrings dangled almost to her neck. It was the same costume she'd worn the previous Halloween. I wondered if the spirits would be insulted or impressed.

"We took our seats at the table. There were the four of us and Brian Howard, a myopic boy about my age who lived on the next block. His twin brother had been run over by a streetcar the year before and I suspected that was why Leah had invited him.

"'Join hands and stare into the candle flame,' Leah ordered.

"When we were settled and quiet, she went on. 'Think of the person you wish to contact. Picture the face in your mind, the way that person spoke, the room he died in.' I thought of Mother."

The account was so detailed that Dierdre found herself knowing these people, feeling sympathy for their tragedies as if they were her immediate family. "Were you there when your mother died?" she asked.

Grandmum nodded. "She didn't die in bed. She had seemed better that morning, more alert than she'd been in days, so Father moved her to the living room before he left for work. She sat in the chaise that's now in the library. I propped up her head with pillows so she could take in the afternoon sun streaming through the windows and watch the people rushing past, all of them oblivious to the tragedy taking place inside.

"I had been reading *David Copperfield* to her, and had become so engrossed in the story that I never realized the moment when she took her last soft breath.

"During the séance, I thought of that room, and how bright it had seemed for an instant. I began to cry, to beg her to come. Then I heard a commotion and opened my eyes for a moment. Brian was thrashing in his chair. Angelina was crying as well, tears leaking from beneath her shut eyes. I wanted to hold her, to comfort her, but I dared not break the circle. Not yet. Something was close, close enough that I could feel it standing behind me, so close we almost touched. I waited for the sound of Mother's voice, a kiss on the cheek."

"And did she speak to you?" Dierdre asked.

"No, but I knew someone else had been in that room with us, someone I knew. Someone who loved me.

"Brian jerked his hand out of mine. Startled, I turned to him in time to glimpse his pale face, his damp forehead, before he stuck his head between his knees. 'I'm gonna be sick,' he groaned.

"'Then get to the toilet before you make a mess on my mom's floor, you moron!' Alma ordered, pointing the way, then following him, pushing him when he moved too slowly, making certain he got there in time.

"Angelina began to cry, softly, as if everyone were still trying to concentrate and she was afraid to distract them. I looked at her and then at Leah. We three stayed in the kitchen while Alma went to check on Brian. 'Did you feel something?' Leah whispered.

"Angie nodded and moved close to me, taking my hand. I didn't say anything to her. I could still sense the presence and I didn't trust myself to speak.

"We knew what had happened. We all became believers in that moment, changed by a single event. How quickly that bond was formed between the three of us in spite of the differences in our ages, and what strange journeys it's led us down. Different journeys, of course, but from the same source.

"Leah had always been interested in spiritualism. Now she'd pulled us in as well. She and I went to every spiritualist meeting, dragging little Angelina along whenever she could sneak away. We bought books by every purported master. We discussed it all, attended the lectures and practiced when we could. Sometimes we obtained no results, at others something would happen, usually vague but nonetheless real enough to keep up our interest. In the end Leah had her magic and Angelina a gift with spirits that became her livelihood. As for me, I was always the practical one who had the least time for all that foolishness; but in the end I got the best gift of all, the door."

"The door?" Dierdre asked. "The rear door you mean, the old one that goes somewhere else?"

"Some time. Some time else," Grandmum corrected. "It's in the journals. They explain it all."

"The journals? Are they in the library?"

"Some of them," Grandmum replied, looking past her to a cleaning lady coming in with a mop and pail. She seemed ready to make another comment, then thought better of it, waiting until the woman had gone to finish. "This is a secret, my dear. Tell no one here or there. And accept one small thing—what you've discovered is strange, incredibly so, but it's still only our own backyard."

FIVE

Damn it all, Dierdre thought on the way back to the apartment. She'd spent most of the afternoon with Grandmum and all she had learned about was some childish attempt to contact the dead, and some little-known facts about the family history. What did that have to do with anything? Why hadn't she pushed a little harder, made Grandmum say something to clarify what was going on, and how she should deal with it?

Instead, Dierdre returned to the apartment more worked up than when she'd left it, wondering if she had the courage to walk through the apartment's front door let alone the rear ones. Though she managed the first, she could hardly bear to look at the doors leading to the sunroom. Even the kitchen's proximity to them bothered her, and after she fixed some coffee and toast, she carried her plate to the living room. The paper she'd only glanced at that morning held little interest for her, except for the weather forecast. When she realized why, she threw it into the center of the room.

Damn it! Grandmum had a thousand books on the occult in her library. She'd lived with this secret, probably longer than Dierdre had been on this earth and it had never brought her any harm. What logical reason did Dierdre have to fear anything?

Logic could not erase her fear entirely, but it could diminish the feeling enough that Dierdre was able to once more stand in the center of the sunroom, and look through both sets of doors. This time, she was not seeking differences that would verify what she already knew, but similarities.

Though the shape of the rosebushes was different and the wysteria vine covered different sections of the courtyard wall, the shadows thrown by the setting sun were falling at the same angle through both doors. And the cat had returned, sitting with its paws curled under its chest in a far corner of the yard where the sun still warmed the dark brick wall.

Dierdre retreated to the library in search of the books Grandmum had mentioned. Grandmum had told her she'd left them out but there were none set aside. As for the ones on the shelves, she could be there forever and never find the ones she needed. Bill had mentioned the photo albums. If Grandmum had been working on those recently, those might be the books she meant. She found them exactly where Bill had told her. Along with them were a pack of letters tied with red ribbon, and three journals whose entries were dated from 1910 to the early 1970s. The writing was small and more precise than Dierdre remembered, but undoubtedly Grandmum's. Unfortunately, it was also so faded that she could make out only a few words from each sentence. She decided to decipher the journals in the morning. Now, it was better to concentrate on the albums.

Some of the people were familiar to her. There were Douglas and Kendra MacCallum, Grandmum's parents, looking stiff and formal in the reproduction of an old daguerreotype. And Grandmum herself, holding her little brother in her arms, the two older boys standing behind her. She recognized the oldest, Andrew, from other pictures. He had gone on to distinguish himself during the First World War. Dierdre knew nothing about the other two boys, not even their names.

The pictures seemed to be arranged chronologically and as Dierdre turned the pages she saw Grandmum grow from girl to young woman. She saw her with friends, all the names carefully printed on the back of each photo. And the last photo, a sepia-toned picture of a pretty, oval-faced young woman holding a fluffy white cat.

Dierdre dropped the album on the desk and stared at the photo. This could be anyone's cat, she told herself. White persians all look alike. This was probably even the cat Grandmum had mentioned when she confused past and present. Nonetheless, Dierdre's hands shook as she pulled back the protective plastic cover so she could turn the photo over.

Angelina and Buddha, June 1918, she read.

Over seventy years apart. Could it be?

The past? Dierdre had only one way of knowing. Nothing had happened to the cat when it entered through the doors. Nothing would happen to her when she left through them. And until she did, until she actually stepped through those doors into what Grandmum said was nothing more than her own backyard, Dierdre would have no peace in this house.

Before her emotions could drain her resolve, she headed for the sunroom. She stopped in the kitchen only long enough to pour a large glass of brandy from the bottle in the cupboard. Drinking half of it before she reached the old doors, she pulled them open.

The cat had come through the ordeal all right. Dierdre hadn't lost an arm or a head when she stuck those through, she reminded herself. It would be all right. All right. All right.

Taking a deep breath, she stepped through.

A wave of dizziness rolled over her, similar to the one she'd felt when she put her head through, but so strong that she had to grip the doorframe before her knees gave out on her. The feeling lasted only a moment, but it made her heart pound. She stayed where she was until she felt calmer, then stepped forward onto the lawn.

The air was the first thing she noticed. It seemed denser, purer, but thicker somehow, as if one set of pollutants had been replaced by another less chemical mix. Was that manure she smelled? It would be likely. If she were in the early 1900s there might be horses on the streets, perhaps a few early autos belching diesel or whatever they had used for fuel.

She walked through the yard. It seemed better maintained than in her time, the lawn free of weeds, closely cut and edged. The stone patio was newer. At the rear of the yard, half hidden by a lilac bush, was the gate that had been bricked up when she was still a little girl, after a burglar had broken its lock and gained access to the yard and house.

Now it had only a simple latch to keep it shut.

Not certain where the gate would lead, she pulled it open.

She had never been in the alley behind Grandmum's house, but she doubted that it still contained stables in her time. As she saw them now, most were ill kept, their paint peeling, their doors padlocked. A few had been converted into apartments, others were still apparently in use. Horses were tethered in front of them and she heard workers shouting to one another from inside.

After determining that the gate would not lock behind her, Dierdre started for the main street, stepping back as she neared it to allow a pair of riders to pass. One of them tipped his hat to her, then reined in his horse and stared at her curiously.

"Can I help you, Miss?" he asked, polite but confused, He spoke slowly and distinctly and she realized he must think she was foreign.

Damn it, if she'd been thinking rationally she would never have come into the past wearing a sleeveless red silk shell and her favorite pair of Calvin Klein stonewash jeans, ripped at one knee. But then, she'd never expected to find the courage to travel beyond the yard. "No, I'm quite fine," she replied.

"One of the new artists, are you?" he asked, pointing to a larger cottage near the center of the alley.

Artists. Of course, they could dress any way they liked. Next time she came here, all she'd have to do was put on a paint-smeared smock and she'd fit right in. Or she could use one of Grandmum's special dresses, kept no doubt for just that purpose. She smiled and nodded to the man and continued on her way, her hands locked over her forearms to keep them from trembling. She turned right at the street, walked to the corner and found herself on Washington Square, easily recognizable in spite of the changes on the streets around it where apartment buildings stood in place of the Loeb Center and Trinity Chapel. When she'd been in school, Dierdre had despised history. Now she wished she'd paid more attention to it. Her myopic history professor would undoubtedly feel right at home here.

Washington Square was, if anything, more crowded than in 1991, pedestrians vying with horses as well as automobiles. The drivers of the last were ruder than any she had ever seen, honking at horse and man alike as if they lacked brakes as well as manners. Still, the activity seemed less guarded, less hurried. People called out greetings to each other, many stopped to talk, often in a language she thought might be Italian. There was something comforting in this intimacy. It made Dierdre feel as if she had stumbled into a some small town's central square on a busy afternoon.

A newsboy on the corner was selling *The Times*. "Paper, Miss?" he called to her.

Dierdre crossed the road, reaching into her pocket for some coins before realizing they would look foreign to him, or worse, counterfeit. "I'll have to go back for some change," she confessed, scanning a headline that meant nothing to her, and more importantly noting the date.

March 19, 1919.

"Do you have a watch?" she asked the boy.

He shook his head and called out to a fellow newsboy on the diagonal corner. "Willie, what time is it?"

"3:15," Willie answered.

The same time! Dierdre's confidence was growing so quickly that she felt almost euphoric. No gangs here. No guns. Nothing to fear, except being discovered, apprehended, judged as mad.

A mounted policeman noticed her and began edging through the foot traffic. Enough for now, she thought, and retreated to the alley, the door in the wall, the almost-familiar yard.

Buddha met her at the gate, curling around her legs as if they were old friends. She picked him up and rubbed him under the chin, listening to him purr. "You remember the tuna fish, I suppose," she said. "I'll have to tell Grandmum that you like that, too. What do you suppose she'll say?"

Carrying the cat, she started toward the house. As she did, she glanced at the far door, then stared at it, recalling a moment later what made it seem so strange. According to family history it had burned at the turn of the century, but in 1919 it was still intact.

"Everyone lies to me. They probably lied about the little boys as well," she mumbled to herself. As she neared the building, two men and a woman came out the far door. The woman wore a long blue dress, tightly fitted at the bodice. In spite of the warm weather, the smaller of the two men had on a suitcoat.

They stopped just outside the door, the three of them partially blocking her way. Not certain if they would consider her an intruder or a guest, Dierdre dropped the cat and continued toward the house. When she got close enough that it would be suspicious not to introduce herself, she looked directly at them.

The larger man was perhaps forty, tall, muscular and a bit stout. He wore an odd garment—a pale green loose-fitting tunic with an embroidered cowl. The second man looked somewhere between twenty-five and thirty, tall and thin, with reddish blond hair and freckles and a mustache, probably intended to make him look more mature, though the thin pale line of fuzz he'd managed to acquire had the opposite effect.

She noted nothing else about him, because her attention was fixed on the woman. Dierdre knew her well! This was the young Grandmum of the photo album, far prettier than the black and white pictures had revealed but certainly the same woman who now lay dying at Hudson Manor.

Dierdre's heart began to pound. As she ran for the house, the younger man reached for her. She pushed her way past him and through the door. Pausing just inside, she made certain she was back in the sunroom she had left. Then she turned and saw the group still in the yard. She could even hear them speaking, their voices muffled as if they were a long way off.

"Did you see what she was wearing?" the younger man asked.

"Some new lunatic in the neighborhood. One more's of no consequence," the young Grandmum replied. She stared at the glass, as if she knew exactly where Dierdre had gone. From the way the woman's eyes were focused, Dierdre knew she could not see her. Nonetheless, the woman winked.

"Well, I don't think it was of no consequence. Sane or otherwise, the creature went running into your house, after all." The man started toward the open door. As he neared it, his features distorted, flattened, vanished.

Dierdre suddenly realized that she knew him as well! He was the man from her nightmare, the one from the storm whose face had been pressed against the clear window glass.

This was one shock too many in a day filled with them. Dierdre's vision clouded and darkened at the edges. Her knees lost their strength and she backed onto the divan, sitting with her hands over her eyes, her eyes shut. When she opened them some moments later, she felt vaguely disoriented as if she had dozed off and had some swift, vivid, forgotten dream. But she was not one to fall asleep anywhere but in bed and never so early in the evening. She glanced at the door, still slightly ajar, at the the hair on her blouse. She struggled to remember.

Part of what she'd done came back—the yard, the alley, the Square so altered by time. But the rest? She looked at the doors, shaking with fear and not certain why, and saw the young man sitting in the garden with the cat on his knee. She watched his long-fingered hands stroke the cat's back, his focus on the door all the while. And she remembered all of it.

He was waiting for her. But he hardly looked frightening now, only a bit shy and almost as confused as she'd been when she'd first noticed the odd view through the little panes of glass.

Without thinking, she went to the door, standing just inside. She wanted to go to him, to speak to him, but caution held her back. She shut the door slowly, ready to slam and lock it if he came toward it. But he only sat awhile longer, then got up and walked toward her, disappearing, as he had before, into another time.

She pressed her palms and the side of her face against the tiny panes. She smelled dust and old varnish, and a hint of incense from long ago.

SIX

The toast had hardly been sufficient for an evening meal, but Dierdre had no interest in grocery shopping. However, she did want to get some air, the modern polluted variety, so she picked up the second photo album and walked the few blocks to Fat Albert's. She'd hoped to find some secluded table where she could eat and study the photos but the little deli was more crowded than she'd expected in early evening on a weekday.

The kitchen was dominated by a three-by-fifteen butcher block and two burly stackers—she could hardly think of them as cooks, the old stoneware plates and tall, thick blue glasses for the chocolate and vanilla phosphates and the three German beers kept on tap. The white iron bistro chairs seemed far too delicate for constant use, and the tables too small for the huge sandwiches the deli served, easily enough for lunch and dinner combined.

Which explained the crowd, she decided. No lunch here. Instead they'd left work early and gone directly to lunner.

The invented word stuck in Dierdre's mind, the repetition of it making her giddy. She sat in the corner, fighting a smile. She'd come here to get out of the house and to try to stop thinking for a time about the mystery of those doors, but the more she tried the more her emotions seemed to shift and grow into a sort of silliness bordering on hysteria. Now she watched the patrons of what could only be a local establishment, trying to gauge their eccentricities, as if they had also been affected by the mystery in Grandmum's apartment.

Was the thin man in the straw hat an alien? A visitor from another time? What about the obese woman with the snake tattoo and ankle bracelet? The man in the three-piece suit daintily eating, with pinkies extended, a concoction oozing thick globs of thousand island dressing? A more likely visitor would be the barrel-shaped old woman in the tie-dyed full-length caftan and love beads, her faded copper and gray braids tied at the ends with flag-colored ribbons. Dierdre watched the silver rings on her fingers flash as she paid her bill and walked out the deli doors.

Yes, definitely a refugee, probably a hippie from the mid-60s, prematurely aged by drugs and wild living in some place like San Francisco or Boulder.

"Yo, Angelina! You forgot your change again," the deli cashier called after her.

"Put it on my tab!" the woman yelled back, her voice surprisingly strong.

"That's over thirty-five in credit. When are you gonna use it?"

"When business sucks," the woman replied and laughed.

The name! Could this be the woman Bill mentioned, the one who lived upstairs? She hardly looked old enough, but Dierdre doubted there were two old women named Angelina in the same neighborhood. She grabbed the rest of her sandwich and the album, laid ten dollars on the register and started after her.

"Dinner change, Miss?" A panhandler with a dirty bedroll blocked the exit, his hand held out, waiting. Dierdre thrust the remains of her sandwich into it and followed the old woman down the street, hardly surprised when she saw her head up the stairs to the second entrance of Grandmum's building.

That mystery solved, Dierdre pulled out the key to Grandmum's flat and started up her own stairs, stopping just outside the entrance to take one final look at the woman. Dierdre wanted to call out, but the moment when it would have seemed natural to do so had already passed. She had no idea what to say.

The woman sensed her staring and looked her way.

"There's no one home over there right now," she called, then paused, frowning. "Are you Dierdre?" she asked.

"I am. Have we met before?"

"A long time ago. I'm Angelina Petra. I doubt that you remember me. I certainly wouldn't have recognized you, but Bridget said you were coming. Come over, have a cup of tea and tell me how she's doing."

Another reprieve from the doors, the mystery. Nodding, Dierdre joined the old woman, following her through another strange door, this one painted black with an ankh-shaped iron knocker.

The furnishings in the apartment seemed as ancient as those in Grandmum's, but mismatched and worn, and arranged with little thought to proportion. In the living room, a threadbare, maroon, mohair couch dominated the space between two green velvet wing chairs. A long, low table held a pair of pewter candelabra, a Bible and a crystal ball mounted on a black iron base. A pair of Russian-looking icons took up most of the wall space above it, creating an ecumenical sort of mix.

The small dining room had no table but instead a huge oak desk piled high with magazines and catalogs. A chrome and Formica kitchen set was covered with little bottles of herbs and spices, dried sage bound tightly with twine and a clear glass salad bowl half filled with colored marbles. There was no electric light. Instead, a handful of hanging iron candle-holders must have supplied the nighttime light, since their bases were all well-coated with wax drippings and wax stalagmites rose from the floor beneath them. Angelina carefully skirted the wax mounds and walked into the narrow kitchen. Dierdre followed.

Angelina unhooked a ceramic teapot from the rack above the stove. "Lemongrass, raspberry and sage, or chamomile?" she asked.

Tetley would be all right, Dierdre thought. "Whatever you like," she replied.

The woman started the water, then threw open the doors leading to the sunroom. "Go in and take a seat," she said.

Light streamed into the kitchen from the single set of sunroom doors, near perfect matches to the old ones in Grandmum's apartment. The room had no furniture save four iron chairs surrounding a square iron table. The rest of the space was filled with potted plants. Some were probably the source of the dried packets in the kitchen. Dierdre recognized sage and basil, violets and dumbcane, ivy and geranium. Some were blooming and healthy; others half dry or nearly dead.

"Anywhere is fine," her hostess called from the kitchen.

Dierdre moved two potted plants off the end of one of the benches and sat down, taking a deep breath of the scented air. There was something calming and familiar about this cluttered place, something that made her feel at peace within the building's walls for the first time since she'd come here. When Angelina entered the room, carrying a serving tray, Dierdre looked at her and smiled.

"So you've remembered," Angelina said.

"Remembered?" Dierdre asked. Angelina did not elaborate, but instead seemed to wait for Dierdre to consider her comment.

And as she did, Dierdre did have a memory, not of this space but of the garden beyond it. She walked to the doors, not surprised to see the trellises mounted on the walls and over one corner of the small yard, the hanging wysteria vines, their blooms unopened but still beautiful in the late afternoon sun. "You used to let me play in the yard," she said.

"Of course I did. You liked it there. You said it made you feel safe."

"Safe?"

"You had nightmares, dear. Terrible ones. When they got too bad, Grandmum would send you over to me. We would drink tea and play checkers all afternoon until Mr. Petra came home from work." She handed Dierdre a cup. The scent of the tea made the memories more vivid. Though Angelina was older, she had not changed much in the years since Dierdre had known her.

Angelina took the seat across from hers and poured the tea, a scented blend of green pekoe and lemongrass. "It was Mr. Petra's favorite. I like to drink it and think of him. Sixteen years and I still miss him."

"It's delicious," Dierdre admitted.

"So how is that old witch doing?" Angelina asked.

"That what?" Dierdre asked.

"Old witch. Your great-grandmother. For pity's sake, Bridget and I have known each other long enough that I should be allowed some familiarities. Now how is she?"

"Weak. Her hands shake. She seems confused, too, but not always."

"Confusion is normal in this house," Angelina commented, holding out her hands as if inviting Dierdre to look around her.

"I suppose you'd need a good memory to find anything," Dierdre said.

"In this house, memories shift like sand in a tide." Angelina sipped her tea, leaving Dierdre to wonder if the woman had been exaggerating the clutter or merely making a comment about her own mental ability.

"Did Bridget talk about why she sent for you?" Angelina finally asked.

"She wants me to stay until she dies," Dierdre said.

"She didn't mention the building?"

Dierdre thought she understood. Of course the woman would be concerned about her future. "She said that I would inherit it, but don't worry. Though I probably won't live here, I don't intend to sell it either. If you've been here so long, I wouldn't think of changing any terms of your lease."

Angelina laughed. "You are more like Bridget than I thought. No, I wasn't speaking of that. I was curious about what you think of her apartment and the strange things that happen there."

The woman didn't know the truth, Dierdre decided. And if Grandmum had kept the doors a secret, so should she until she had a chance to learn more about her discovery. "I haven't noticed anything strange," Dierdre replied, looking down at her teacup, the few leaves moving slowly in the bottom, forming patterns, an old memory. "You used to read these for me," she said.

"As I do for everyone, only I never charged you. Your company was payment enough." She looked into Dierdre's cup. "Drink a bit more," she said.

Dierdre did, leaving a few tablespoons of liquid in the bottom. Angelina turned the cup over on its saucer and rotated it. Setting cup aside, she pressed her stubby fingers together beneath her chin and looked intently at the pattern in the leaves as if she were praying for guidance.

"I made nearly the same reading before," she finally said. "I told the gentleman that he would embark on a long and difficult journey, chasing an impossible goal. I told him the goal was worth it."

"Did he make that journey?" Dierdre asked.

"I don't know. We never spoke of it again. Ah, well. I hardly have Bridget's precognitive powers."

Dierdre wanted to ask what the old woman meant, but Angelina had gone back to studying the leaves, and when Dierdre tried to speak, Angelina gestured for her to keep silent. "During this journey a time will come when you must go against all advice and make an important decision. Don't back away from this task though at the end . . ." Her voice trailed off, she kept looking down but something in the woman's posture convinced Dierdre that she was troubled.

"And then?" Dierdre prompted.

"Nothing. I made a mistake. I don't see any more."

Dierdre frowned. "I have no idea what you mean," she said.

"The leaves have no concept of time. But I don't think they speak of some event in the distant future. This reading should be clear soon." She stared at the leaves a bit longer then picked up the saucer and rinsed it off at the sink before refilling Dierdre's cup, mumbling to herself all the while.

Dierdre walked to the window and stared out at the yard, thinking of tragedies, and what she'd glimpsed of the past. "You said you lived here all your life. Tell me what you know of the building."

"Goodness, Bridget hasn't?"

"Bits and pieces over the years. I don't remember much of it, and certainly not with any order. I've been studying her photo albums, which brings some of it back." She pointed to the second album that she'd placed on an empty chair.

Angelina looked at it, then at Dierdre, and frowned. Dierdre stared back, wondering what she'd said to make the woman so suddenly concerned. Before she could ask what was wrong, the old woman dismissed her worry with another quick wave of her hand. "Well, you were pretty young last time you visited. You can hardly be expected to remember much. But telling what I know will take some time. I'd best boil more water.''

Angelina moved from stove to table to pantry and round again, a colorful bumblebee in her hive. The tea she served this time was black and smoky, probably with as much or more caffeine than coffee. She maneuvered her bulk into the chair beside Dierdre. ''Should I start at the beginning?'' she asked.

''Please.''

Angelina picked up the photo album and paged through it quickly, picking one of the first photos, an old daguerreotype of the building taken soon after it was finished.

''The building was constructed in 1831 by a wealthy man whose name escapes me. It isn't important except for you to understand that he spared no expense. As you know, the outer stairs are white marble as are the floors in the foyer and parlors of almost every apartment. Bridget's grandfather purchased the building in 1844 from the original owner's estate. He did so just in time for the Village rennaisance, or so I understand.

''Those were the days the greatest artists and writers called the Village their home. Annie Lynch lived just a few blocks east of here. In its greatest moments, her parlor hosted Herman Melville, Washington Irving and a number of starving poets, including Edgar Allan Poe. When she was a little girl, Bridget's mother met Ms. Lynch, who had been one of Poe's more ardent supporters. Ah, the stories she told! Bridget and I were in envy of her.

''Henry James's grandmother lived in the building next door. More to my interest, Madame Blatavasky, the spiritualist, lived just around the corner in the 1880s. She's the one I would have wanted to meet, if only to touch her hand in the hope that some shred of her power would transfer to me.'' Angelina laughed, and sipped her tea. ''Forgive an old woman a bit of exaggeration,'' she said.

''But what about this building? What was it like when you were growing up here with Grandmum?'' Dierdre said, trying to steer the woman back to the actual question.

''This one, well, this one had its ups and downs, but nowhere near as serious as other places in the neighborhood, if only because it sits on the north side of the square which was always a bit more fashionable, and because the MacCallum fortune kept it from ever getting the slightest bit seedy.'' She pointed to a few older pictures of the area, showing row houses in disrepair, a huge gothic structure partially torn down, its tall central window bare except for the frame, one turreted wing still standing. ''Looks like a castle that lost the attack, doesn't it?'' Angelina asked. ''So it did, damn that university and their stupid plans.

''As for this building, things got really strange for awhile. There were some real eccentrics in here.'' She laughed. ''Now, I'm the only one left. ''

''And the others?''

''Crowley's people, mostly. A strange bunch, and coming from someone like me, that's saying a lot. They took over the place after he moved in. Every time there was a vacancy, one of them would fill it. Close to the temple, they were. Pretty soon four of the seven apartments were filled with them. I could understand how Bridget let it happen, since she was a bit taken with him. That was natural enough under the circumstances, but I never understood her father's allowing it.''

''Circumstances?''

''Her power. I'm telling you, what I trained myself to have is nothing compared to the powers she simply ignored. I can see a future in the tea leaves or the lines of a person's palm, and I'm right more often than I'm wrong. But Bridget, ah, even before she met Aleister, she was always right.''

''Lucky guesses,'' Dierdre countered.

''Uncanny guesses. And there was more. Bridget always knew how to handle her father's depressions or how to settle fights between the neighbors. She had no training but it still seemed that she could use her will to control others. If you need an example, look how certain she was that you would come here.''

Dierdre tried to hide her scowl. The woman was right about that, but did she have to be so wounding in her honesty?

Angelina shrugged. ''No matter, dear. She has the same power over me. I think if her head had been less filled with ledgers and business law, she would have been a great magician, perhaps greater than Crowley himself. Crowley even used to tell her so, but by the time she was thirty she lost what little interest she'd ever had in arcane matters." Angelina paused, then added, "Pity."

"When she had interest, what did she do?"

"Read mostly. Half the library she has is filled with the books she bought. We practiced together, but her best work came when we were apart, though she never spoke of it."

"Then how did you know?"

"If you have any sensitivity to magical forces at all, you know. Stay here long enough and you'll begin to understand."

Angelina began pointing to pictures, identifying the photos of men and women in odd Egyptian-looking costumes. People holding candles, congregated in Grandmum's yard, of Grandmum herself similarly garbed, and pictures of Crowley in yet another wild headdress, flowing robes, and once stark naked sitting in lotus position in the middle of the rose garden, his spare tire making him look like a partially-deflated Buddha.

"Not the most comfortable place for so much skin, eh? And I'll tell you, people didn't often get photographed in the buff in those days. Not like now when everyone seems ready to bare it all. Of course, now we have airbrushes to ease the flaws before publication." Angelina laughed.

She turned the page to a photo of a young, thin-faced woman, her long dark hair parted in the center, falling over her bare breasts. She held a staff in one hand, a candle in the other. On her chest was a strange circular tattoo. "Aleister's scarlet woman, Bridget's best friend, Leah. Aleister called her the Ape of Thoth—now isn't that the most romantic pet name you ever heard?" She laughed and turned the page. "Ah, here's Noah with Aleister! A marvelous picture of Noah, I think."

Dierdre hid her reaction, forced her voice to remain calm. "Was he a follower as well?" she asked.

"Follower? No. But a believer. As he did with Bridget, Crowley seemed to have some hold on the man. But Noah was even more level-headed than Bridget. He and I used to tell her over and over, 'You've got to get rid of those people, even Leah though she is your friend. Something bad's going to come of it.' We were right. I only wish my premonition wasn't so damned accurate."

"Was it the fire?"

Angelina nodded. She seemed ready to speak, but caught herself and went on, "And there were other things, particularly . . ."

Dierdre refused to let the matter drop. "How did the fire start?" she asked.

"During a ritual, but I don't know anything else, I really don't because I was only eighteen and away at the time. But Bridget knew, and Noah. Bridget never speaks of the fire because she thinks it was her fault."

"When did it happen?" Dierdre asked.

"Nineteen . . . nineteen, sometime in early summer, I think. I used to always go away with my family in summer but that year I graduated from secretarial school and took a couple of weeks before starting my first job to visit a cousin in Boston. That's the only reason I can remember the date so exactly. As for the rest, I know nothing."

"I heard that two little boys died in it."

The old woman shrugged. "Maybe they did. Maybe it was Noah or one of the children. Maybe no one died. Details aren't important, the fire did damage and it's been repaired."

"You can recall the year, the season, but you can't remember who died?" Dierdre asked incredulously.

"You're not the only one troubled by that oddity, dear. I just get one set of memories straight and then they seem to change. Then I get my mind used to a second, then there comes another different set, then another. I can't explain it. It makes no sense, but every once in awhile I wake at night convinced that . . . dear, this will sound like the ravings of a senile old woman . . . that it was me who died."

Dierdre thought the woman far from senile and said so.

"Thank you, Dierdre. You're not the only one who's re-assured me over the years. Bridget and Noah used to say the oddest thing about my memory lapses—that I had a gift for seeing alternate consequences. I never could get them to explain what they meant."

Dierdre paused. This was probably one of Grandmum's oldest friends, but Grandmum had never told her about the door. Perhaps she couldn't. Perhaps if it was magic or even some miracle it would all go away if she spoke of it. Bizarre thoughts, but no more bizarre than the door itself. "If someone did die in the fire. it would have been in the news," she replied carefully. "You could go to the library, get an old newspaper and read the facts."

Angelina gave a short laugh, went to a kitchen drawer and pulled out a brittle, yellowed square of newspaper. A piece of it broke off as she handed it to Dierdre.

The photo, or at least the reproduction of it, had probably never been good and time had only made conditions worse. The two children seemed to be blond, and somewhere between eight and twelve, but the features were blurred. Half the caption was missing as well as most of the second column of the story. She deciphered the family name, Draper, and noted that the boys had been visiting the building when the fire occurred. "So now you know," Dierdre said.

Angelina shook her head. "Facts of the moment, nothing more. I know you must think I'm just a crazy old woman, but trust me I'm not. Articles change just like memories. Sometimes I can almost see the print on the page flicker, as if the past isn't finished with itself yet. No, I don't believe the papers."

The old woman's voice had become louder, quicker; approaching a hysteria Dierdre knew all too well. "You said there were other odd things," Dierdre prompted, relieved when Angelina let her change the subject.

"Little things, really. One was how Bridget would hole up in her apartment, sometimes for days at a time. I never understood knew why she sometimes turned into such a hermit. But each time I'd start getting really worried, she'd show up and act like nothing unusual had happened. Strange, don't you think?"

Not so strange. Dierdre was beginning to get a fairly good idea of where her great-grandmother had gone. "Can you remember when she started acting so secretive?" she asked.

"Let me see. It was just after Aleister and Leah moved into the building. And that was sometime around Christmas the year before the fire."

Dierdre calculated the date. "Christmas, nineteen eighteen," she said.

"And there's something else that's odd," Angelina continued. "People connected to this building keep returning to it. Mrs. Lockeer, in the apartment above me is one of Mrs. Arnold's granddaughters. Mrs. Arnold moved in here just after her husband died; that was nineteen seventeen I believe. Ronald and Eugene Ryan, in the other flat on the second floor of this entrance, are descendents of Carlotta Whyte, one of Crowley's supporters who lived in the apartment Bill now has. Mrs. Minelli across the hall was born here, as I was."

"And Bill?"

"Bill . . . ah, that one who's always snooping in Bridget's library. He's the exception, I think, though I'm not certain. But we all know full well why he's here. Like me, he has a gift for sniffing out magic. Now that he's found it, it's the spells he's after; as if Bridget would share such things with him, even if she could remember what she's tried so hard to forget."

"Could he be related to one of Crowley's followers. You said they used to live in the building?"

"He says no, but maybe he doesn't know the connection. In any case, I'll never understand why Bridget lets the little worm have a key to her apartment."

"He borrows books from her library," Dierdre said, not knowing Bill well enough to defend him yet.

"And keeps them, I'd wager."

"He brought two back the day we first met. I suppose that Grandmum must have had her reasons for being so trusting. But you're right about it not being a good idea, especially since I don't know him as well as she did. As soon as he returns, I'm going to ask for the key back."

There was more, but Dierdre kept the thoughts to herself. In the morning she was going to have the locks changed. Then, if Bill made a copy of the key, he wouldn't be able to use it. If he did, he wouldn't be able to admit it. One less unpleasant scene to face.

"And there's something else," Angelina continued. "Sometimes I wake late at night and hear the most wretched sounds—whimpers, moans and stifled screams—as if whatever happened in these walls years ago somehow lives on."

"Does anyone else hear them?"

Angelina shook her head. "Contacting the dead is my gift, but one I would gladly trade for some other."

Dierdre wanted to ask another question but Angelina seemed to have said enough. She sat, rocking slowly back and forth, looking down at the leaves swirling in her own cup, a vague, contented smile on her face, as if she knew what Dierdre was thinking and agreed with it all. When Dierdre left, Angelina didn't even say goodbye.

It was nearly dark by the time Dierdre returned to her apartment. She locked and chained the door then showered, put on her terry robe and dried her hair. After, she padded down the hall to her bedroom, opened the closet door and looked at the clothes inside.

Hers were so plain, so drab next to the ones Grandmum had left. She pulled the cherry cheval mirror from Grandmum's bedroom into her own then began trying on one antique design after another. They fit so beautifully they seemed to have been made for her. She paused before putting on the black gown, fingering the exquisite beadwork.

This wasn't a dress, it was a costume. One worthy of all the finishing touches. She found underclothes in the drawer, put on a black garter belt, black seamed hose and black high heels that were only a bit too large.

She looked like a Victorian whore, she thought, as she stood in front of the mirror, applying powder and mascara and bright red lipstick. Only then, when she felt she was ready, did she lift the dress above her head and let it fall over her raised arms.

The loose knit underskirt stretched as it covered her chest then clung to her hips and thighs as if it had been designed especially for her. In spite of the many jet beads, it felt surprisingly supple against her skin. Dierdre finished the costume with the coat, and pulled the mink collar close around her face. Her hair was too short, too plain, but the rest seemed perfect.

She went to the kitchen and looked at the wine in the refrigerator, then fixed a martini instead, pouring it into a Waterford wineglass, adding the obligatory olive.

Walking carefully in the unfamiliar shoes, she carried the glass to the sunroom. After moving one of the wicker chairs

close to the French door, she pulled it open and sat in the
darkness, looking out and sipping her drink.

The fur tickled her face, the alcohol made her giddy, but
not nearly as giddy as the shadows she saw moving on the
lawn outside thrown through the little panes of glass in the
door by a light burning in another time. She heard music,
the ripple of laughter, the murmur of voices.

She wanted to go there, to join them. She wondered if she
dared.

Then *he* stepped into the yard. Noah. The man from her
nightmares. His black suit made him look so formal, so young.
He carried a drink which he stirred with an index finger as he
moved to the far end of the yard. Once there, he faced the
house then leaned against the wall as if he were waiting for
her.

She stood and walked toward the door, standing, frozen by
doubt and fear, blotting tears from her eyes with a tissue, trying not to run her mascara, not certain why she cried.

SEVEN

March 1919

Months before he first saw Dierdre MacCallum, Noah Hathaway had been taking a leisurely autumn walk across Washington Square. A small crowd had congregated at the north end. Curious, he headed toward it, not surprised to spy Aleister Crowley at its center, sitting cross-legged on the cement steps surrounding the fountain. Crowley's odd posture might have escaped notice, but his odder clothing—a black wool tunic embroidered with an assortment of red and yellow Egyptian hieroglyphics and a pair of knee-high, lace-up sandals, made it impossible for even the most polite New Yorker to overlook the man. And of course, once he started speaking, people could not help but listen and react.

Noah knew this was exactly how Crowley liked it. Discussions led to disciples, and disciples to donations, without which Crowley would likely starve. Noah himself had fallen for the man's pitch, more than once since Crowley had returned to New York. In all, Noah had donated well over a hundred dollars to further the man's work. Noah wasn't a believer, but he'd seen close up the damage that rigid religions caused, and Crowley's devilish remarks on them, in both lectures and inflamatory letters to the local papers, made him worthy of support.

But that didn't mean that Noah had to like the man, or ever socialize with him. He started to cut a wide circle around

Crowley and his audience when Crowley looked up and noticed him.

"Mr. Hathaway!" he called. "Come and join us. This group can use another level head."

Meaning Crowley expected Noah to take his side. "I have an appointment to get to," Noah responded.

"Then come by tonight, I've just moved into a French flat there." Crowley pointed to a brick building with white stone stairs. "My landlady has arranged a small reception for me in her apartment tonight. I think you'll find it interesting."

Interesting? Noah was suddenly intrigued, and a bit irritated by the emotion. What was it about Crowley that made Noah feel like an imbecile for buying printed copies of the man's nasty little essays and attending the overpriced lectures, yet made him unwilling to break with Crowley completely?

"Come at nine. First floor, end apartment. Incidently, I think you might know my landlady, Bridget MacCallum," Crowley added.

Noah looked toward the building again. It did seem familiar somehow, though he could not recall having been in it.

But that evening, when he walked up the concrete steps and stepped through the tall, carved entry, he realized that somehow he did know the place. And when Crowley introduced him to Bridget MacCallum, the young lady Crowley and his mistress rented rooms from, Noah was certain they had met more than once, but he could not recall where. When he mentioned this to Bridget, she looked at him and admitted that she felt the same way. They spent an hour trying to decide where they had met, but without success. Then she asked him to fill the ice bucket.

He went into the kitchen and pulled a block from the icebox. As he was chipping away at it, he tipped over a drink someone had left on the counter. The glass bounced off his foot and broke on the hardwood floor. He sponged up the mess then went to the closet for a broom and dustpan and rummaged under the sink for soap to clean the newly refinished hardwood floor.

He'd known exactly where to go to find what he needed, just as he'd known the floor had been recently refinished. He looked at the closed cupboards around him. The one closest to the stove would have blue canisters of sugar and flour on the bottom shelf, canned goods above. Though Bridget didn't drink coffee, she kept a can of it in the icebox so it would stay fresh for guests. Over the years people had given Bridget little tins of chocolates and hard candy. She'd filled these with loose tea and bulk spices and kept them in the drawer to the right of the stove.

Noah was a believer in the paranormal, but that didn't make him any more comfortable when the paranormal unveiled itself so abruptly to him. Though he really didn't want to know if his new-found powers were real, curiosity was too irresistible a force. He pulled open the drawer and looked down at the colorfully painted lids. None of the boxes were labeled. But of course Bridget always knew what they were.

Bridget came into the kitchen. "I was wondering where you . . ." She stopped, midsentence. Since she caught him gaping down at the open drawer as if he had just discovered some scandalous family secret, Noah could hardly blame her for sounding angry. "What in the hell do you think you're doing?" she asked.

He couldn't look at her. She would only distract him. Instead, he continued staring at the bright red and blue and yellow flowers on the little tins, letting their patterns lull him into a sort of waking dream.

"You make a marvelous sponge cake. We ate it with fresh strawberries I picked from my mother's garden. It was just last summer, right after I came home from England. I'd been wounded in the foot and caught influenza in an army hospital and so had been sent home early. I lived here. You rented me a room because you needed the money." He hesitated then walked down the hallway to the front bedroom and stood at the closed door. "This one," he said.

"That's my father's room. That's why the door is locked. He's in Virginia on business," she whispered.

"You father is dead," Noah replied.

She slapped him. "How dare you go along with his sick joke."

"Joke? What are you talking about?"

His confusion enraged her further. She dragged him into the front room and pulled Crowley from the group surrounding him. "I want you both to apologize," she demanded.

"Apologize? For him?" Crowley looked beyond her to Noah, standing by the end of the hall. "I would never have invited the man if I thought he would act so contrary to his nature as to offend you."

"I only told her that I believed her father was dead," Noah said softly. "I may be mistaken, but I meant no offense."

"What did you mean?" Crowley asked.

"I don't know exactly. I believe that I once lived in this house and that I had used the bedroom belonging to Mr. MacCallum because he was dead. I just can't recall exactly when I lived here."

Crowley smiled. He seemed genuinely merry. "Bridget, my dear, if you don't forgive Mr. Hathaway it will be most awkward. Because, you see, I never said a word to him. He has a gift, one so strong that I suspect he will be as useful to you as a friend as he will be to me as a pupil."

"What gift do you mean?" Bridget asked.

"The rock beneath the shifting sand," Crowley replied, looking at Noah as he spoke.

Noah thought the man was joking, or else trying to sound far wiser than he actually was. But Bridget turned and stared at him so intensely that Noah realized the comment had been meant for her alone, and that she understood it.

Bridget moved close to him, taking his arm. "Aleister is half right," she said. "I am angry, but I'm also curious. Do you really think we knew each other in a different life?"

"This life. I rented your father's bedroom. I was there because . . ." He knew why but he could hardly describe his beliefs about the man's death to the man's daughter. ". . . because he died. You rarely spoke of it. You said that the details were too painful," he concluded, wincing, waiting for her temper to flare again.

Instead Crowley said something to her. She looked at him curiously. Her expression softened. "This really isn't the time for this conversation. Come tomorrow as Aleister suggests, Mr. Hathaway. When the place is quieter, I would like to hear everything you can recall."

• • •

Noah did as she asked. Crowley was at their afternoon meeting but only for a little while. Noah told his story to both of them, then arranged to rent an apartment in the building. Sight unseen, but then he'd been in it before. Later, he and Bridget went into the garden to sit on the lawn. He told her what he could of happy times, a bit about the tragic ones, softening only those tainted by her father's bloody end. He thought the visions some sort of fantasy, brought on by some hypnotic suggestion or a drug Crowley had slipped him. But Bridget was a sensible sort of woman, he could see it in her expression as she listened to what he believed was true, nodding as if she had shared the scenes with him.

"And we knew one another?" she asked when he had finished.

"More than knew," he replied, taking her hand, pressing it between both his own, looking into her eyes. He wanted her to believe him, to accept him, damn it, to kiss him without his having to ask, or worse beg.

She leaned forward. Her lips brushed his cheek. Not exactly what he'd hoped for, but more generosity than he'd expected from an almost complete stranger.

She wore, he thought, the most incredible perfume.

After that evening, he began visiting often. Soon, he moved into the place on the second floor. It was an expensive apartment and far larger than he needed, but it gave him an excuse to see Bridget every day. It wasn't that he'd become obsessed with her, but rather that he feared that if he stayed away for too long he might go back to the building and find her gone, and all traces that she had lived there gone with her.

Soon they had an informal agreement that when the time came that their friendship had grown into love they would announce an engagement. He'd been ready from the first day he'd met her, but he sometimes doubted that she would ever feel that way.

Friendship was enough, though at night, alone, he admitted that he wanted so much more.

He had nothing to judge the feeling on. He'd never thought himself in love before, and he was still a virgin. Not that there hadn't been opportunities, or that he was a prude. He had a number of women friends, some who made it obvious they wanted to be more than friends, but none of them appealed to his spirit, only to his body, and he wanted both in a lover.

He thought he'd found perfection in Bridget MacCallum.

Her fierce independence, and the careful way she tended her little garden reminded him of the Amish women he had so admired while he was in college in Lancaster. Bridget was well-read and sensitive, and when he shyly showed her the little book of poetry with the Amish theme that had been published while he was still in school, she had read the first few poems, the three glowing literary reviews, and looked at him in astonishment. "Why in God's name are you working for the government?" she asked.

"What's wrong with that? Every writer from Poe on tried to land just that sort of plum."

"Poe was starving," Bridget replied.

"So he knew that steady income has its advantages." He didn't admit that one of the conditions his father had given before agreeing to pay for his education, was that he would go to work for the government. Noah couldn't blame him for wanting that security for the family. After all, Noah was the only son, his family comfortable but hardly wealthy.

"Then write when you can," Bridget said.

She was right, he knew, and so he tried. But even Central Park with its vast stretches of lawn and woods did not give him the inspiration of the simple community he'd almost been a part of during those few years in Pennsylvania.

If he was to write, it would be in that kind of place, and about that sort of life. And he wondered if Bridget—intelligent, free-thinking Bridget—would ever want to live in such a pastoral environment.

That decision would come later. Now he was merely content to be with her, to share what he had written, to hint about the plans he hoped to pursue.

As the Christmas season approached, his visits to Bridget were marked with odd, strained silences and moments when she would stop in midsentence, frown and look away. Whatever troubled her troubled him too, and not just because he cared for her. Something important was about to happen, and he dreaded it.

The Customs Department was holding its annual Christmas

party on December 17th. Noah arrived at Bridget's door at seven to pick her up. He knocked and got no answer. Then, thinking she might have the water running, he pounded.

"I don't think she's going to answer, Noah," someone said from the front door.

Noah turned and saw Angelina Laughran standing there. Her long strawberry blond hair was braided and curled on top of her head like a crown. The red dress she wore gave a soft color to a face that usually seemed too pale. The elegant attire made her look older than eighteen, and the gold ankh necklace more like a fashionable accent than the sign of a practicing medium. "You look beautiful," he said.

"And you look as if you've been stood up," she replied.

Too direct a statement, and almost cruel. "This isn't like Bridget. Something must have come up," Noah said.

"I think you're right. She went out rather suddenly."

"I should wait for her then."

"You'll do nothing of the kind," Angelina replied. "At the very least you should come round the corner with me to Nora Baxter's party. You can check back here later."

He shook his head. "I have other plans, even if I have to go alone. I'll just leave her a note." He pulled a pen from his suit pocket, a business card from his wallet and began to write.

"Too bad," Angelina said. "Nora would have been delighted to see you."

"Later, perhaps," he said, writing until he heard the foyer door close, then turning and looking at the door.

Blast it! The girl barely said two words to him every time they met, and here she was, suddenly as friendly as her cat. It seemed as if someone had asked her to intercept him and get him away from the house.

He stuck the note in the door and left, circling the block, coming down the dark alley behind the building. Even here he kept to the darkest shadows, wondering at his sudden suspicion. There was no reason for it, and yet . . .

Yet he felt as if he had every right to sneak into Bridget's garden. Once there, he stood in the shadows and stared through the French doors at the darkness within, praying that darkness was all he would see.

He waited nearly half an hour. The air grew colder and

damper. Light snow began to fall, sticking to his coat and hair. He waited until he was so chilled that he risked his health if he stayed any longer, then decided to meet Angelina at Baxter's and stay long enough to warm up. "Five more minutes," he mumbled to himself.

A match flared inside, lighting a candle, another, another. Soon there was a circle of light on the sunroom floor. It revealed Aleister Crowley, in a long white robe, standing outside the circle. A woman sat within it, her back to the door. When Crowley raised his hands, undoubtedly to chant some unholy verse, the woman stood and turned toward the door. Naked, expectant, she held out her arms.

Bridget!

Noah wanted to run but no amount of running, no distance would make him forget that he loved her. He wanted to rush to the door, breaking through the glass if need be to stop them both, but he was in the wrong to be spying on her. And more wrong now as he stayed where he was and watched, despairing yet too fascinated to look away.

What spell had Crowley used on her to make her lie with him so willingly? To let him kiss her with such passion in places only a whore was used to? To mount him when he asked, riding him as if he were one of her many conquests? Or was it magic at all? Bridget was hardly one of the man's feeble-minded slaves. Perhaps she was actually attracted to him.

No, she would have told him if she was, would have broken their relationship off.

Something else was going on here. Noah felt it more strongly now than he had on the first night he stepped into the building, but this time he sensed that he was only an insignificant part of it. He looked down at the snow-covered ground, and stepped through the broken gate.

A few buttered rums at a tavern near the Square took the chill from his body, but nothing could lift the sorrow from his soul. As soon as he was warm enough, he walked over to the Square, setting up his surveillance of the building from the leeward side of the arch, holding his coat tightly around him to keep out the damp.

Midnight came and went. He saw a light switch on in

Bridget's parlor, then in the hall. Moments later, the light in Crowley's second floor apartment came on.

Crowley had gone, but still Noah waited, giving Bridget a chance to dress. He started for the door when he saw a cab pull up in front of the building, and Douglas MacCallum step out of it.

Though he had no reason to dislike Bridget's father, he could not shake the irrational belief that the man was supposed to be dead. Nor could he dismiss the strange, haunted look in the man's eyes, as if he shared some part of Noah's vision, or had seen the fate that waited for him after his soul was judged, and found it lacking. On the rare occasions when Douglas MacCallum visited New York, they rarely spoke to each other beyond polite greetings. Noah always tried to arrange his visits to times when the man would be out for the evening.

Well, now he'd have to wait until the father went to bed.

He studied the pattern of the lights in the house, waiting until the one in Douglas's bedroom switched off. A few minutes later, Noah went into the building, knocking softly on the front door.

It opened immediately. Bridget wore a white robe. Her hair was loose and tangled, and smelled of some sort of odd musky perfume. Though it was late, she hardly seemed surprised to see him standing at her door. "Noah," she whispered. "Father's sleeping. Let's go upstairs to Aleister's. I know that he's up, and probably Leah as well. We can talk there without disturbing anyone."

Without an apology for how she had treated him, without even a glance at his shocked expression, she grabbed his hand and began to pull him up the stairs to Crowley's room.

Just outside the door, Noah broke away and ran, down the stairs and outside. Bridget followed, but stopped at the entrance door. He turned and glanced back at her—a motionless, silent shadow, watching him leave.

He had a few more drinks, then joined Angelina at Nora's party which as usual went on until nearly breakfast time. He didn't want to go home that night, didn't want to hear a knock at the door, or a ringing phone or, far worse, find himself walking up to her door to listen to her explanation of what in the hell had gone on that night.

• • •

In the weeks that followed, Bridget never mentioned that night. He tried to bring the matter up once, but she evaded his questions with the single comment, "Just trust me to do the right thing."

Trust was impossible, though, when she spent so much time with Crowley. She helped edit his books and essays. She attended every lecture. She moved like some queen in the circle of weaklings and libertines that followed him so slavishly.

Then her pregnancy became far too obvious. When she supplied only the briefest explanation for that, Noah abandoned all thought of marrying her. Now, when he talked with her of his future, he did not include her in it. If she noticed, she didn't seem to care.

But one thing had not changed; he still spent some part of nearly every day in Bridget's apartment. He was waiting for something to happen, for the magic she hinted that she and Crowley had worked to touch him as well.

Noah had thought himself in love with Bridget, but he had wooed her too gently, and far too slowly. If he had moved more quickly with her, he might have claimed her before Crowley pulled her into his circle to use and probably impregnate. Perhaps she and Noah would have married, and now she would be carrying his child, not one more bastard out of the many Crowley had undoubtedly sired in his years of disguised whoring. Noah vowed that the next time he felt a strong attraction for a woman, he would fight his nature, throw all caution to the wind and the consequences be damned.

Then he saw Dierdre standing in the yard, looking pale and confused and completely out of her element. The clothing she wore—the plain demin trousers of some Kentucky farmer and the beautiful silk blouse, both cut in an unfamiliar style—added to the effect. There was also an exquise sense of wonder and confusion in her expression, as if she had been lifted from another, far different place and plunked here, into Bridget's elegant enclosed garden off Washington Square.

And this was more than mere attraction. The woman made him feel like a schoolboy. He was actually afraid to speak to her lest he stutter.

Noah realized that he was not the only one looking at her

intently. Beside him, his barrel-shaped body filling the open half of the French doors, stood Crowley. If Crowley were attracted to the woman, he had the means to make her his, just as he had done with Bridget. Noah would not allow it.

Noah rushed toward the woman, one arm outstretched. She looked at him, seeing him for the first time, though he had been in the garden since she entered it. Startled, she pushed her way past him and fled through the open door. Noah followed. Though he entered the room only seconds after her, he saw no one there but an old man, some friend of Bridget's whose name Noah had never bothered to remember, sitting at the limed oak table, drinking coffee laced with brandy.

"Did you see a woman rush by?" Noah asked.

The man shook his head. He was more than a little drunk already though it was only late afternoon.

Aleister lowered himself into an empty kitchen chair. "I saw her," he said to Noah. "But she's gone away from us. She isn't accustomed to being here yet, you can see that on her face."

Noah didn't ask what Aleister meant. He was used to the man's mysterious references. In time, if Noah were lucky, all would be made clear or at least less obscure.

Even so, when the door or whatever Crowley referred to, opened again to let her through, Noah would be the one waiting on the other side, arms outstretched to catch that innocent prize. He poured himself a drink from the bottle of scotch that Bridget kept in the icebox and returned to the garden. He sat on the bench near the far wall, staring at the doors through which the woman had vanished, waiting expectantly for her to step through them again. Buddha joined him, stretching out on Noah's knee, purring loudly whenever Noah gave him some small bit of attention.

It grew late, making it far too awkward for him to remain in the yard. He left reluctantly, knowing he had no excuse for returning until the following evening when Crowley was hosting a more intimate gathering.

That evening, Noah arrived a bit late. All the better to say a quick word to Aleister and to Bridget then make his way through the house first to the kitchen to pour a bourbon then to the yard. He sat in the shadows where hopefully no one from the group inside would notice him. He waited.

The cat came first, walking softly from some hiding place in the yard. Buddha didn't like Crowley, and from what Noah knew about the man, the cat was right to be wary. Buddha curled around his legs, leaving traces of its affection on the dark wool trousers. Noah crouched, scratching the cat under the chin while he sipped his drink.

Everyone but Angelina would think he was crazy, but he could sense the woman watching him from somewhere just beyond his reach.

EIGHT

As Dierdre walked slowly toward the door, she kept her attention on Noah and the cat. She paused at the threshold, almost too long, then in a sudden burst of resolve stepped through. As she did, the glass she held seemed to hit against something solid and fall to the kitchen floor, splattering the drink on her legs. As she bent down to wipe them off, the vertigo she'd forgotten gripped her and she stumbled.

Noah hadn't seen Dierdre enter the crowded sunroom, or move to the doors. Instead she seemed to have materialized from the shadows just outside them. She stumbled as she walked toward him. He dropped the cat and rushed forward to help her. "Are you all right?" he asked.

She leaned against him a moment then pushed away and looked at him. No menace here; just an earnest young man trying to help. "So much for a grand entrance. I spilled my drink," she replied.

He pulled a handkerchief from his pocket. "Use this," he said.

As she wiped her legs, he spied the olive from her drink, visible in the dim light by the white plastic toothpick spearing it. He reached for it, but before he could grab it, she did. Pulling off the olive, she tossed it into the grass and quickly put the plastic pick in her coat pocket.

"Shall I get you another?" he asked.

"Please. Martini. I might as well stick with gin since I'm going to reek of it all night long."

He walked inside. She hesitated then took a chance on a theory she'd formed and walked through the other door.

As she expected, she stayed in the past, joining him in the kitchen where he was mixing her drink in a shaker of ice. He took a glass from the china cupboard. As he filled it, she saw that the glass was the same design of cut crystal as the one she'd been carrying earlier.

"Second revelation, basic physics," she mumbled.

"Did you say something?" Noah asked as he handed her the drink.

She smiled. "Just to myself."

"Ah, well we haven't been introduced. I'm Noah Hathaway."

"And I'm Dierdre ..." she hesitated, wondering if she shouldn't use some other name, deciding against it. "Dierdre MacCallum."

"Dierdre. A beautiful name. You're related to Bridget, I presume?"

"I'm a cousin. Distant cousin." She wanted to giggle, but managed to hide the mirth behind what she hoped was a mischievous smile. Turning, she took stock of the room, noticing that in seven decades the main changes had been in modernizing the appliances, changing the color of the walls and putting new tiles on the floor. She sipped the drink, letting Noah lead her down the hall to the parlor where Grandmum ... Bridget ... was sitting close to the fireplace. Her dress was deep green, high-cut and loose fitting. She wore a bright tapestry-print shawl over her arms and shoulders, its yellow fringe falling into her lap. Her honey-colored hair was loose, the soft curls glowing in the firelight. So young, yet she seemed regal, confident, composed.

Behind her was the other man Dierdre had seen in the garden and in the photo album, the magician Aleister Crowley. She recalled all the pictures of Crowley in turbans and robes and the way he'd looked when she'd seen him before. He was not so fantastically dressed now. The suit was probably conservative, or at least as conservative as the one Noah was wearing. He'd attached a gold Masonic pin to the lapel and he wore a Masonic ring as well. Minor adornments, no where near as eccentric as the woman in the flowing black pajamas standing beside him, her long dark hair braided with gold and silver chains, the old man with the turban on his head leaning heavily on a tall carved staff, the pair of adolescent boys in matching liederhose smoking a substance that smelled nothing like tobacco from a long-stemmed brass pipe. In spite of them, and the others almost as oddly dressed, there was no mistaking Crowley if only for the way the crowd seemed to form a circle around him, vying for a chance to speak to him or to at least remain within listening distance.

As soon as he saw Dierdre, Crowley pointed her out to Bridget then motioned for her to come forward. Dierdre could feel Noah's hand, warm where his fingers pressed too hard against her arm, as he followed her through the crowded room.

Dierdre concentrated on the wink her relation had given her. She held out her hand, astonished that it wasn't shaking. "Hello Cousin Bridget," she said.

"Cousin indeed," Bridget said softly, stood and embraced her. "You grew to be as beautiful as I expected. But then you always were the prettier one," she whispered, her mouth close to Dierdre's ear. She moved back and continued. "And here. I don't believe you've been introduced to my houseguest. This is Master Therion, Aleister Crowley."

Noah's grip on her arm tightened as Crowley took her free hand. "I see the MacCallum in you well enough, but there's a bit of Nordic blood there too. Remarkably striking, particularly with the black."

"Miss MacCallum and I have just popped in for a moment. I'm taking her to dinner," Noah said from behind her.

"Dinner?" Bridget frowned as she looked at Dierdre. "Is that what you want, Dierdre? We could speak in private."

What could Dierdre tell the woman? That seventy-two years in the future she would be lying in a nursing home waiting to die? Not the most upbeat conversation for a gathering such as this. "I just came for a visit," she said. "I'd like to get to know my family a bit better, that's all."

"I'm glad you're leaving. I think it would be much too distracting to be near you tonight, darling Miss MacCallum," Crowley said, kissing the back of her hand, holding his lips against her skin a moment too long to be polite. "Besides, Noah has been lonely of late, and he's far too civilized to speak of why. Perhaps you can educate him."

The dark-haired woman laughed, a bit too loudly and with more malice than mirth. Bridget flushed and adjusted her shawl over her chest. As she did, Dierdre detected a swelling in the woman's stomach. Had she been married yet? Dierdre didn't think so, yet Bridget was unmistakably pregnant. No wonder that even decades later, the family whispered about her.

"And, Dierdre, the lady in black is Leah Hirsig, Master Therion's scarlet woman," Bridget said. Dierdre started to extend her hand but Leah only joined her long-fingered hands beneath her chin and bowed, slowly and solemnly.

Dierdre gulped the last of her drink and set the glass on the mantle. "Shall we be going, Noah?" she asked.

As he escorted her to the door, Crowley called after them, his voice booming even in the crowded room. "Do what thou wilt," he said.

"Shall be all of the law," Noah finished as automatically as an "amen" at the end of a prayer.

Before they left, Noah asked her to go upstairs with him. "I've got to look in on my nephews before we go," he explained. "I'll be just a minute."

She stood in the front room of his apartment. One wall featured mismatched bookcases filled with volumes of poetry, novels and biographies. On the space above them, she saw photos of barns and pastures, of children playing in the river, of old men sitting in front of buldings in some country town. There was a desk in front of the window with a typewriter and stack of paper on it, and a Victorian-design sofa with a brown brocade cover. Everything was compulsively neat, from the carefully stacked papers to the spotless marble floor.

She turned toward Noah, who had stopped at the first bedroom door. "Now if anything goes wrong, you go downstairs to Miss Bridget's for help, all right?" she heard him say, followed by a mumbled reply.

Noah joined her. "They'll be fine. I just wanted to let them know I was leaving," he said. "Excuse me, I think I need to dress a bit warmer."

As soon as he'd disappeared into what was probably the second bedroom, one of his nephews called for him then padded into the hall.

He wore blue flannel pajamas that made his pale blond hair seem nearly white by contrast. His face was round and Dierdre could see the resemblance to Noah around the boy's eyes and the shape of his mouth. "Hullo," he said, immediately holding out his hand.

She took it. "I'm Dierdre MacCallum," she said. "And who might you be?"

"Louie," he replied.

Dierdre felt a surge of relief. She couldn't recall much of what she'd read on the yellowed scrap of paper but didn't believe that either of the fire's victims had been named Louie.

"Are you one of Miss Bridget's family?" the boy asked.

"I'm her cousin."

"Is she coming up later."

"She'll be checking to make sure you're in bed," Noah replied as he came down the hall. He'd put on a long wool topcoat and scarf. He carried a second scarf which he wrapped around Dierdre's neck, then scooped up the boy and carried him back to bed.

When they left, Dierdre noticed that he didn't bother to lock his door. "There's no need for locks here. Besides, Bridget will be coming up later. She's fond of them," he explained.

Dierdre thought of the fire, and wished that Angelina's photo had been less faded. She should be able to remember, but crossing the portal had somehow dulled the details. Only the fire and the mention of the deaths remained. "Are there other children in the building?" she asked.

"Three. My nephews haven't gotten to meet any of them though. The boys have only been here the last two days, dropped off while my sister and her husband are in Baltimore on business."

"How long are they staying?"

"They go home tomorrow."

"Do they stay with you often?" she asked.

"Just a few times a year."

Just what she'd hoped to hear. Dierdre relaxed and followed Noah down the stairs. "Is Crowley always such a beast," she asked Noah once they were outside, as if speaking of the man in the building would invite some sort of demonic reprisal.

Noah gave a dry laugh as he took her arm. "So he's called and so he calls himself," he answered as they walked to his car. "He says that his mother gave him the nickname when he was still in short pants. Some people might spend their entire lives trying to prove a nickname wrong, Aleister's spent his reveling in it."

"What do you think of him?"

"Think? Aleister would say that the important thing is that I think of him at all. Ah . . . here!"

They'd reached his car, a deep mahogany-colored convertible with a long engine compartment and wide running boards. It looked far more modern than the Model T's she'd seen terrorizing pedestrians the day before, and the dramatic way Noah pulled back the top convinced her that this had been a new purchase. He helped her inside and she leaned against the dark leather seat, pulling her coat collar close against her neck, turning to look at him. "So what do you do to afford such luxury?" she asked.

"I manage a department in the New York Custom's Bureau. The money's excellent but it's a boring job; not at all worth talking about, believe me."

"All right then, I won't. Where are we going?"

"You said we were going to dinner, so dinner it is."

They headed down a Broadway softened by gaslights, moving at a speed that was probably remarkable for its time, or for her own given the heavy 90's traffic. Dierdre wished she was a native New Yorker, for it would be delightful to note which buildings had changed and which had remained much the same in the space of so many years. They pulled up in front of a cafe with an intricately carved wood exterior. The windows were deep gold-and-olive stained glass, the floor wood parquet polished to a deep russet patina. A dozen or so diners were scattered through the room, eating at tables set with white linen and floral-patterned china, each lit by a pair of candles that flickered when Noah closed the door.

"A table near the back, please," Noah requested.

The man nodded and led them through the room to a quiet spot in the corner. He lit the candles and asked about drinks.

Returning with the bottle of burgundy Noah had requested, he poured out two glasses and began reciting the menu.

A limited selection, but no less than some rural supper clubs Dierdre had gone to with Frank. The restaurant specialized in German food and they decided on pork with red cabbage and dumplings. Rye bread and cheese, soup and relishes preceeded the main course, a dessert followed. All of it was served in such a leisurely fashion that Dierdre never got a chance to become completely full. She did feel a bit drunk though, and more anxious each time she glanced at the cuckoo clock on the wall beside their table.

Were their rules to this odd travel? Some time limit she ought to know about? Certainly, she ought to keep it all a secret, and she did the best she could, answering Noah's questions about her life as evasively as possible. She lived in Montreal, she said, choosing that city because it was so old and she familiar enough with it to answer any general questions he might ask. She worked as a secretary for her father's firm, she said, and had taken some time off to travel. "More of a trip than I expected," she explained with a sincere smile.

Soon after they'd started the main course, a string quartet began playing, giving her a chance to stay silent for a time. When the group took a break, she turned the conversation around, slowly drawing out details of Noah's life.

"So you write poetry? I've never met a poet before. Have you been published?" she asked.

"Two years ago a collection of the poems I wrote while in college in Lancaster was published here. I've recently had three published in the *Little Review*. They're not as good as I would like, though. I have difficulty composing in the city."

"You don't find all the activity inspiring?" she asked.

"You're smiling. You must be joking. Just look at all the rushing about, and for what end? No one has time to think anymore. Poets especially need quiet and ordinary lives."

"Do you ever give readings?" Dierdre asked.

"I do. As a matter of fact, I chose this place because it's close to Healey's Cafe. There's a group of poets meeting there tonight. Would you like to go?"

"If you'll promise to read something," she replied with real enthusiasm. Poetry was the one form of literature she truly

loved. Every word was important and the total pieces usually
short enough that her reading speed was not a handicap. Besides, people were expected to read poetry slowly, to roll the
words around in their mouths, savoring their sounds as well
as their meanings.

"You'll inspire me," he replied and for the first time that
night, took her hand.

It must have been the atmosphere that made the simple gesture so arousing. She smiled at him and for a long time, they
said nothing at all.

They had dined in elegance, and Healey's was the antithesis
of it. But though the pub was dark and smelled of cigars and
liquor, Dierdre noted a few women nearly as well dressed as
she was, drinking and laughing with a group of wild-eyed men
with loose ties and rumpled shirts. The main crowd had congregated near a bookcase full of slim volumes and loose pages,
a bar chair and a single light hanging overhead. Dierdre looked
at the people sitting around them, then at Noah, so fastidious
in his dark suit and ascot, and wondered how he managed to
fit in.

A man called for them to join him. Noah introduced her to
a half dozen or so people, but the names were given so quickly
that she never committed them to memory. Instead of waiting
for an order, the bartender brought them mugs and a pitcher
of beer which got passed around the table. The evening's main
attraction was the man sitting beside Dierdre, Edgar Masters.
She didn't recall his name until he got up and began to recite
poetry she had learned in high school, speaking in a soft, cul-
tured voice. Two other poets followed, but their work seemed
overly dramatic and far too flowery after she heard Masters's
simple lines. She wondered why anyone ever let him read first.

Then it was Noah's turn.

He took the seat to a scattering of applause, found his book
and a copy of the *Little Review* on the shelf behind him.
Though he held the magazine open, he glanced at it rarely,
reciting from memory a short poem about an old couple he'd
observed walking in Central Park, the woman arthritic, the
man nearly blind. Sweet, too sweet for this city, Dierdre
thought. As the crowd clapped politely, he opened his book
and began to read a piece on an old farmer in Lancaster. It

described his birth, his youth, his family, and finally the emptiness of his old age.

> "... *Now they are gone, one with the earth we*
> *loved too well,*
> *Dark silence fills the house with memories*
> *That fade each morning with the waxing light.*
> *I hold what little I remember*
> *Close and wait for another night to fall."*

Two other poems followed; simple and sad of the sort that Edgar Masters would have written. A real poet might be able to find all sorts of flaws in them, but to Dierdre they seemed so pure, so perfect, so full of emotions that reflected her own heart. When Noah returned to the table, Dierdre wiped away a tear and on impulse kissed him with far more passion than she had intended to display. The crowd that had clapped when he'd finished, clapped louder now. Someone ordered them both a shot of bourbon. Noah tossed his back. She followed, then deliberately loosened the scarf he wore around his neck then ran her fingers through his hair.

"That's it, girl!" one of the women exclaimed. "Make the poet behave like one."

Letting the woman's approval egg her on, Dierdre kissed him again. Pulling back she saw his shocked expression and laughed. Good Lord! When was the last time she'd had more than three glasses of anything alcoholic on a date? When had she ever touched anyone, even Frank, with such abandon? But now, when she should have been on guard, she found herself feeling more daring than she'd ever been in her life.

Ah, well, she would consider that strange matter tomorrow. Now she was content to drink the beer, down another shot and listen to Masters give an encore, new works from a book of poetry that would be published forty-five years before Dierdre was born.

It was well after midnight when they left Healey's. Dierdre hadn't turned into a scullery maid and the motorcar, not a pumpkin, was waiting outside.

"Where should I take you?" Noah asked.

"Back to the Square. I'm staying in the neighborhood."

She leaned her head against his shoulder and looked at the lights shining in the windows of the houses and apartment buildings they passed. The people that lived in them would likely be dead before she was born. They'd never know who she was or where she'd come from.

Such freedom!

She had stepped back into a time when casual sex wasn't lethel and her mother did not exist, and there was no one to condemn everything she did with quiet disapproval. A time when Dierdre was free to make as big a fool out of herself as she wished, and escape the consequences forever if she chose to simply by walking through a door.

She hadn't even needed the alcohol. No drug could intoxicate as well as that sort of liberty. She rested her hand on Noah's knee and shut her eyes.

When he'd first seen her, Noah had been infatuated with the mystery of this woman. He'd expected that if he ever got to meet her, the infatuation would fade at least a bit. Instead, by the time they left Healeys he was more smitten with her than before—with the shy nervous smile and unruly hair, the vague comments about her past and her family, the refreshingly liberated attitude he would have found delightful in any woman. And she seemed romantic enough to understand his desire to chuck it all and get away from the city to write. And when she took his hand and leaned over the table just before they left Healeys to confess in a sincere whisper, "Someone who loves you would do everything she could to support you in whatever you wanted," he moved from being merely smitten to completely in love.

He had to see her again. She had to let him. He wanted to tell her this, and more, but instead parked near his apartment. "We've arrived," he said and he helped her out of the car. "Which building are you in?" he asked.

"It's not important. I can walk from here."

He longed to tell her that it was important. That no woman should be walking the streets unescorted. That he had to know where she was staying, if only to know that she trusted him. But she had her hands on his shoulders and her body close to his and it was not the moment to make a stand for manners she seemed to care so little about.

She kissed him for the third time that night; lightly, nervously, as if fearful that one of them might break if she pressed too hard.

"Will I see you again?" he asked. "I'm free all day tomorrow."

"Then wait for me in Bridget's garden. I'll be there around three if I'm able," she said.

"Able?"

"I'll be there. I promise," she said.

Noah watched her walk down Fifth and turn into the alley. She could be one of the artists, perhaps, though the dress spoke of wealth not Bohemia. And that last, cryptic remark. Why wouldn't she "be able?" Concerned, he followed her. If caught he would say that he wanted to see her home safely, though it was more than that. She was a mystery he had to solve.

And it might take longer than he expected. By the time he reached the entrance to the alley, she was gone. He ran a few yards down it, stopped and listened. A rusty hinge creaked. A small animal rustled through a windblown pile of last autumn's leaves. He heard drums beating slowly in Bridget's yard, the sound muffled by the stone wall around it. Nothing odd about the drums at this hour; Crowley's ritual had begun. Someone stifled a cry.

"Dierdre?" Noah whispered, then concerned called louder. "Dierdre?"

Dierdre heard Noah's voice, but it seemed to be coming from a long way off. Perhaps she was in shock, or perhaps she'd become caught in some spell woven by the ritual into which she unwittingly walked.

A huge stone bowl had been placed in the center of the garden, a fire started in it. She could feel the heat of it even from her place by the gate some twenty feet away and she wondered how the men and women who stood closer could keep from being blistered, especially since every one of them was naked.

Men alternated with women, all holding hands and arranged in a large triangle around the fire. At the two points farthest from the house, men in black robes stood outside the group, pounding softly and slowly on huge floor drums. The air vibrated with the sound. Dierdre felt it pounding in her ears, her mind, her chest.

"Noah!" she whispered and tried to leave, but a black robed man stepped from the shadows and grabbed her arm, pulling her back from the door, closing and locking it then standing between her and freedom. She turned toward the man and gestured for him to move. "I don't belong . . ." she began in a frantic whisper.

He put his palm against her lips, a gesture for silence, then pointed to the corner of the triangle nearest the door.

Crowley stood there, robed all in white and wearing a huge Egyptian sort of headdress decorated with a golden triangle. He held a short knife in both hands, the hilt decorated with a single polished stone that glowed blood red in the firelight. Leah Hirsig, the woman Dierdre had seen with him earlier that evening, was still beside him. She wore the same loose black pajama pants but she had shed the top, though her long hair hanging over her small breasts provided some modesty.

The door opened behind them. The drumbeat increased and Bridget MacCallum stepped into the firelight. Like the others she wore nothing, but her presence here seemed all the more obscene because of the swell of her stomach, the innocence of the life growing within her.

She moved between Crowley and Leah, letting the woman tie back her hair with a thin silver clip. Bridget knelt in front of Crowley. Leah knelt behind her, taking Bridget's arms, lifting them straight over her head then back so that her spine was arched, her breasts and stomach stretched, her knees slightly apart.

Crowley began to chant, the language Eastern-sounding, unfamiliar, his booming voice rising and falling. As he did, he held the flat edge of the knife against the tips of Bridget's breasts, the sides and center of her stomach, between her thighs.

Dierdre didn't need to understand the words Crowley spoke. This was obviously a rite insure the health of Bridget's child. As Dierdre watched, she began to see a certain primitive beauty to it. She tried to relax, to accept that she was an audience to this ceremony whether she wished it or not. Then

Crowley lifted the knife above Bridget's belly, lowering it swiftly, stopping just as the blade broke the skin above the navel. Blood welled from the nick as he raised the knife to his palm, wounding it as well. He held his palm toward the fire, waiting until the blood flowed then covering the cut he had made on Bridget with his own.

A blood mingling, perhaps a declaration of fatherhood or something more. The drums grew louder. The chanting increased then abruptly stopped. Crowley held up his free hand. "Now!" he shouted.

Leah moved to the fire. Picking up a cup, she scattered its contents on the flames. The flames decreased, their color changed from gold and yellow to bright red. The drums' tempo quickened. The couples, silent until now, began to chant some refrain from Crowley's ritual in a quick sibelant whisper that seemed to brush against Dierdre's bare face and hands like a soft kiss.

Crowley lifted Bridget to her feet and led her closer to the fire while Leah joined hands with the man and woman on either side of her, closing the gap.

The chanting grew faster. Bridget picked up a second cup and threw its contents onto the flames. They died completely to throbbing red embers. Leah broke hands with the others and kissed the man to her right then the woman on her left. They in turn embraced the persons next to them. Leah sat down, dragging down those on either side of her. The others followed her lead, hands exploring, arms embracing, lips seeking lips. A woman cried out and broke from the group, heading for the doors. Someone caught her before she reached them, clapped a hand over her mouth and dragged her back to the circle.

Dierdre stood motionless. The man holding her loosened his grip. She moved away from him and toward the orgy beginning in front of her. As she expected, he let her go, thinking no doubt that she intended to join it. When she was some feet from him, she bolted for the doors and the freedom of the future.

She almost made it. Two black-robed men moved out of the shadows and blocked her way through either door. "Please," she whispered. "Please." They looked quizzically at each other, then at Crowley who had noticed her and paused long enough to watch the exchange. He motioned to them to step aside. But as she walked to the doors, she saw Louis and his brother crouched behind them spying on the group, hiding in the place where the two children must have died.

So it had been Noah's nephews after all. She had to warn them, to warn him. She veered to the right toward the center doors. As she did, Crowley cut her off, holding her wrists tightly. "What in the hell do you think you're doing?" he demanded.

"The boys. They're going to die in a fire. I have to tell them to get away from here. I have to talk to Noah."

Crowley gripped her arms so hard that she cried out. "You bothersome little bitch!" he growled. "This is no child's game you're playing, no fascinating fairy tale little excursion you're on. There are rules to magick. Go back and learn them before you meddle in my affairs again!"

He punctuated that harsh advice by pushing her away from him with such force that she lost her balance and fell toward the boys. They froze, too shocked and startled to move. The last thing she heard as she stumbled through the door was their cry of horror, cut off as quickly as it began by the years between them.

NINE

Dierdre woke on the floor, bruised and disoriented, called back from wherever her dreams had taken her by the insistent ringing of the phone. Light was streaming through the uncovered sunroom windows. As she groped for the phone, her stomach lurched. She let the answering machine pick up for her while she rushed for the bathroom. There she sat on the cool white slate tile, waiting for the nausea to subside, trying all the while to remember why she had been sleeping on the floor.

The phone rang again. This time she answered it.

"Miss MacCallum?"

Had that been her name, or had she chosen something else? "MacCallum . . . oh, yes."

"Sorry to wake you so early. This is Liz Brauden at Hudson. I'm calling to tell you that your great-grandmother has been asking for you. I think you should come at once."

The woman's tone was crisp, businesslike, with just the slightest hint of sympathy. In a place like Hudson, she undoubtedly made the same sort of call a few times every month, certainly often enough to perfect her delivery of the message.

"Has she had another stoke?" Dierdre asked.

"No, but she seems quite certain that you should come this morning."

"I'll be there as soon as I can," Dierdre responded. She hung up and got to her feet, nearly falling. She was missing

one of her shoes. She slipped off the other. Looking down at
the dress she wore, she remembered the wine and the beer and
bourbon and martinis, if only because of a sharp headache and
sour taste of gin and olives on her lips. From that reminder
came the memory of Noah and some tavern and his poetry.
But the rest, the terrible rest, was still elusive as a midnight's
dream.

If she only had time to remember. But of course, she didn't.
For all she knew Grandmum was dying. She had to go.

In the bathroom, Dierdre stripped off the dress. As she did
she saw the bloodstains on the back of her wrists, the bruise
on her arm caused by her fall, the ripped seam under her arm.
She splashed cold water on her face and looked at herself in
the mirror. Her eyes were puffy, her cheeks flushed. "Good
lord, what did I do?" she said aloud, trying to remember.
Some memory of the evening's gathering returned, but the
ritual itself remained cloudy, seen only in brief, terrible
flashes.

She remembered something about a bonfire in the yard, so
she returned to the sunroom and looked at it through the old
doors. There was nothing to indicate any sort of gathering had
been there except for a small burned circle in the center of the
lawn. Dierdre's shoe was just outside the doors, a sign that
part of what she recalled had actually happened. She could
step through the doors to retrieve it, and take a closer look at
the burned patch in the lawn but decided to wait until later.
For now it was enough to realize that she had lost it. She
frowned, trying to recall why.

Then it came to her! The boys crouched behind the glass,
and Crowley pushing her through the door.

Showering and dressing as quickly as she could, she caught
a taxi and headed for the nursing home. Halfway there, she
leaned forward and tapped on the bulletproof glass. "I've
changed my mind," she called. "Take me to the library first."

"Which branch?"

"Central, I think. I'll be looking up an old newspaper article."

"Central it is." He cut through two lanes of heavy traffic

without a blinker and made a hard right so quickly that Dierdre thumped her head against the grimy window.

Bulletproof glass. Probably a good idea the way this man drove. He screeched around three more corners, and about the time she began to suspect that they were going in circles, he pulled up in front of an immense building, its white marble making it look simultaneously elegant and cold.

Libraries always made Dierdre uneasy. The stacks of books in even the smallest ones seemed to wall her in, setting off the claustrophobia she'd first experienced in grade school. While her travels had given her a unique ability to memorize the most complicated street maps, she'd never managed to master the Dewey decimal system. Librarians, helpful in the beginning, soon lost patience with her. At least now she wasn't an inept student looking up sources for a school report. With periodicals everyone needed help.

The aide at the periodicals desk set her up with a microfilm viewer and takes for the May and June 1919 issues of the *New York Times*. She scanned them quickly, and found the story in the issue for May 25th. The story made page one, hardly unexpected given the prominence of the site and the human interest seen all too clearly in the accompanying photograph of the two boys. One was undoubtedly Louis. The other boy, a bit older, looked a lot like Noah. Dierdre ran off a copy then scanned the paper for follow-up articles. There was an obituary the following day and a short article noting that the fire had apparently been caused by someone knocking over an oil lantern. There was no mention of Crowley living in the building or of any gathering. Someone had apparently hushed up the more lurid details of the building, most likely the MacCallum lawyers.

Work done, Dierdre stepped outside. It was less than a dozen blocks to Hudson Manor, easier to walk than to take a taxi. She moved quickly, instinctively holding her purse tightly and sticking to the the more crowded streets. She arrived at the nursing home less than an hour after she'd been called. "She's still in her room, isn't she?" Dierdre asked the nurse on duty.

The woman looked at her sympathetically, got up and walked down the hall with her. "I'm Liz, the one who called you this morning. Since then, we've been trying to give her something to help her rest," she explained. "It's hardly an extreme measure but she refused it just as she's been doing since you first came to visit. She turned down the painkillers as well. I think she wants to say a few words to you before the end."

The end. A strange euphemism, one that held no comfort for those who lived on. Though Dierdre would miss the old woman, she felt little sorrow. That was scarcely surprising. After all, Grandmum had led a long and obviously more interesting life than Dierdre had ever suspected. But Dierdre wondered what she would do if Grandmum died before they could talk, and before she could get answers to the countless questions that would have seemed insane in any other circumstances. "How does she seem this morning?" Dierdre asked.

"I haven't noticed any change, but in cases such as hers, I like to trust the patient's instinct. With Bridget, that seems more than justified. She has a great deal of insight into her condition for one so old. Many times I've noticed that she even seems to predict every turn in her health, an odd gift but . . ."

Dierdre let the woman prattle on, knowing Liz was only trying to prepare Dierdre for the sight of imminent death.

But Dierdre had seen death before, just once when she had been barely nine. Her paternal grandfather had come to Calgary for one of his rare visits. In the year since Dierdre had seen him, his salt and pepper hair had gone completely grey. He'd lost a great deal of weight, enough that his clothes hung on him, making him look even thinner than he'd become.

Dierdre asked if he'd been sick.

"Not sleeping well, not for a long time," he'd replied.

"A normal complaint in this family," Dierdre's mother had commented, then suggested he try one of her prescription sleeping pills.

That first night, he took one. The next night he took the entire bottle. Dierdre found him in the morning when she went to tell him that breakfast was ready.

It was hardly a terrible sight. Other nine-year-olds might have been told that he had gone to sleep forever, or some religious superstition to cushion the reality. But Dierdre's mother had made certain she knew the truth, then sat at the kitchen table, holding Dierdre tightly. "I gave him the pills. I should have known. It was all my fault he did it," Mother whispered between her sobs.

The memory stayed with Dierdre on the slow walk down the long hall, and the brief consultation between kin and nurse and aide. It seemed to grow even stronger as she walked toward Grandmum's bed. The old woman's head was propped up, her hair combed. Someone had even applied a bit of powder to her face. She looked rather good for someone about to die and her expression was almost mischievous.

Dierdre took the seat beside the bed. "Are you in any pain? Can I get you anything?" Dierdre asked.

"You could have brought the sandwich," Grandmum complained.

"It's not even ten. Besides, I thought you were dying," Diedre countered.

"Good Lord! Not just yet though I somehow lost track of the date. Well, you can bring me food tomorrow when you come. Now tell me what you were thinking when you walked in. You're expression was so odd."

"I was thinking of Grandpa Bruce," Dierdre admitted, feeling a bit guilty that Grandmum wasn't the only person on her mind.

"Ah, the one I didn't save."

"Save? But you were miles away when he died. What could you have done?" Dierdre asked, then felt a rush of shame and confusion. How could she expect Grandmum to be rational, to remember everything exactly? How could she possibly ask for an explanation of the fantastic from a woman on her deathbed?

"I knew what I knew. I could have warned your mother. I didn't. I understood how much life troubled him and so I let him go."

"How could you know what he planned?"

"You told me. Do you remember coming to visit me soon after Grandpa Bruce's death?"

Dierdre had been there many times, but none of the visits seemed clear in her memory except for an occasional quick flash of memory, gone almost as quickly as it came. "I remember that we played Monopoly in the garden," Dierdre said.

"And later, just at five, I opened the old doors. Do you remember that?"

Dierdre shook her head. She truly could not remember, but the words caused a sudden surge of fear in her, and not just because of her two journeys into the past. She suspected that had she known nothing about the doors, she would have felt the same way.

"You spoke to me there. You said that Grandpa Bruce was dead. I remember how hard you cried, so hard that I became worried. I know it must have felt like a dream to you, but try to remember."

Dierdre shook her head, not wanting to remember, not seeing the point of any of it. "Why are you telling me this now?" she asked.

"Because in two days, at exactly eleven on Thursday night, the stroke I have been expecting for decades is going to hit and I am going to die, swiftly and I hope painlessly. I know that, child, because you're going to walk through the old sunroom doors as soon as it's over and tell me of it. And if you are as intelligent as I think you are, once you deliver the message you'll cover the old doors again, and forget they exist unless there is some terrible need to use them. Perhaps in time, you may even find the courage to do what I could never do. Close them forever and let the magic end."

"I've already been through the doors twice. The second time, I met Noah Hathaway. Later I saw you in part of some strange ritual but I don't remember the details clearly."

"Ritual? Ah, there were many in that year. But none of it is happening in your natural time, so when you leave that place it feels like a dream. Grab onto any memory of those trips that you can. Fix it in your mind and the rest can all be recalled. Now what is clear from last night?"

Dierdre frowned. "Buddha. He was in the garden when I walked through the doors. Later I remember being with Noah. He took me inside the house. I spoke to you at some social. There was a whole crowd of people. You were . . . pregnant and later Crowley took a knife and cut you. It was . . ." Dierdre's voice trailed off. She didn't want to try to explain any of the vague memories just starting to surface.

"Yes, the night of Aleister's ritual. We did it to make certain that Bruce would be strong and wise. Given his parentage, he should have been heroic, or at least a blatant libertine. But he was never either of those things. A more timid and conservative son, I could not have imagined. And scientists speak so confidently of genetics."

"How many times did you force the poor child through those doors?" Dierdre tried to speak without malice but couldn't hide her feelings entirely. Grandmum looked away from her as if ashamed.

"Only twice," she confessed. "The first time was when he was seven. I went with him. I had no real reason for doing that, except to see if he could go back as Aleister said he could. He was only in the garden with me for a few minutes. Then he must have realized that something was wrong. He rushed for the house and went in the other set of doors. So much of the house looked different that it terrified him, and he came running back to me. I took him home immediately, but he was hysterical for hours, and unwilling to go into the sunroom for days after."

"And you put him through again?"

"A year later. I thought that it would make him less frightened if I explained everything to him and he took the journey again. It was a terrible mistake. After that, he was never comfortable in his own house. I sent him away to school. When that was finished, he took a job with my brother's firm in Scotland. He never set foot in the house again."

"Did he remember?"

"No more than you did, but I was more careful with your father. I never sent him through the doors. I couldn't go with him and by then I knew there was really was no point to it since it was so long ago I could offer no advice to anyone. Besides, I'd seen the effect on poor little Bruce.

"You were the real marvel, though. When you were a child, you loved it there. I think you loved the young me, too. What a pair we were, only two years apart and both of us so young and adventurous. Then later, you came back, all grown up and so beautiful."

"That was just last night. Noah took me to a place called Healey's. I heard him read his poems, and I heard Edgar Lee Masters as well."

"That must have been a treat. Shall I tell you who I met?" Grandmum's voice fell to a whisper, as if someone might overhear and actually understand. "My mother knew Annie Lynch. She used to talk about her all the time. I did one better. I read everything I could about where to go then I stole into Annie Lynch's parlor one night to listen to Edgar Allan Poe read *The Raven*. Aleister would have thrown a fit if he'd known what I did after, but I warned Poe to stay well away from Richmond. Apparently, he didn't listen." She laughed, then coughed, and gripped Dierdre's arm. "I did give Poe one odd thing to occupy his mind. I bought two of his collected poetry anthologies and paid for them with a silver piece that wouldn't be minted until a year later. Poe would have noticed the date, I think."

"I have questions," Dierdre blurted.

Grandmum nodded, waiting.

"Where did the door come from? Why is it there? And if I want to close it, how can it be done?"

"I've written down everything I know for you, child, exactly as Aleister told me to. When you go home, look in my journals. I've recorded the dreams when they came. But unless someone knows their purpose, I doubt the message would be understood."

"I found some early journals but the words were all faded. I couldn't read much of them," Dierdre explained, guilty that she hadn't tried a bit harder.

"So I noticed on the occasions when I've consulted them. I know my own writing but I could hardly expect anyone else to make a decent guess. So last year, I had Bill buy me a used computer and a simple word program. I was always a good typist and I've entered a lot of the early stuff for you. If you look in this drawer, you'll find a print out of the first few entries. I didn't want to leave them in the house for someone to find. Sit with me awhile and read it."

"I could read it later," Dierdre suggested. "We can talk instead."

"Talk? I'd rather have you understand what we are talking

about first. Besides, foresight is a marvelous luxury. I think I should spend my last days on earth praying for my soul. When you're finished with the reading, give me your opinion on whether God will understand what I did, and forgive me.''

"I could call the doctor. There might be something he could give you to put it off," Dierdre suggested.

Grandmum smiled. "Thank you, Dierdre, for thinking there might be something of me left to save. But I should have died, you know. Eighteen years ago when I had breast cancer."

"They caught it early."

"Of course they did. As soon as I was told I had only months to live, I made certain it would be diagnosed right at the beginning. A two inch scar is all I have to show for it. I have to thank you for that, too. It was your last trip through the door, until recently that is."

Dierdre shook her head. She couldn't doubt what her own experience had revealed, but the effects of this time travel were more difficult to accept. Actually, Angelina's odd explanation of what was happening in Grandmum's building was beginning to make a great deal of sense.

Grandmum pointed to the bedtable drawer. "The journal is in there," she said.

Dierdre pulled out a light blue ring binder filled with a few dozen pages. The first few pages were all unreadable handwritten scrawls. "To put off the prying help," Grandmum explained. "Go on."

Some pages in, the typed account began.

"Sit beside me, where I can touch you, child. If you have any questions, ask. I'll understand. And some of the words . . . well, they are necessary to explain things clearly. As to my state of mind, well, I think you'll understand."

With Grandmum's hand on her arm, Dierdre began to read.

PART TWO

Bridget

"Wealth—the most dangerous of narcotic drugs. It creates a morbid craving—which it never satisfies after the first flush of intoxication."
                                                    —Aleister Crowley

TEN

October 13, 1918

Aleister has told me that there will be one precise moment in time, a moment that cannot change. He calls it a pivot because it is there that both past and future change. It is coming tonight, and before it does, I must set down my thoughts and my position at this moment exactly. If I do not, he tells me that I will lose my way when past and future shift. So I sit in the center of the circle he drew on the floor of my sunroom, scribbling furiously in shorthand.

If all goes as I plan, a descendent will read this someday. I want whoever it is to know what I have done and why. I want them to know what led up to the moment to come—the history of the family that they, hopefully, will never know—so I will begin earlier. With Leah and Alma and myself and what we meant to one another.

First of all, you should know what my life was like before tonight, and I must remember it as well. So now I set it down as best I can describe it. To summarize my early years, I was one of four children, and the only girl. When I was thirteen years old, my mother and two little brothers died of influenza. My father never got over the shock, and slowly began to sink into a deep, terrible depression.

By the time I was eighteen, I not only collected the rents for the buildings, but also handled most of the business of my father's construction firm. I kept the ledgers, hired and fired its foremen, even bid on the jobs. I only stayed away from the job sites themselves, aware that a woman, no matter how independent, would not be welcome there.

Through it all, Douglas MacCallum, my father, remained at home and drank. He had long since stopped taking any interest in his friends or his religion. On the rare occasions when my brother Andrew visited, Father would say nothing, staring at both of us with quiet annoyance for trying to put a brake on his slow suicide.

In early 1916, Andrew left his teaching position at Beal College in Maine to join the Navy. In short order, he was transferred to England. Soon after, he sent his first letter to us, announcing that he had married a Scotch girl and intended to settle in Aberdeen after the war. "I know you would approve," he wrote. "In a sense, I have decided to come home. We still have relations here, your mother's cousins, Mary and Duncan, and a number of MacCallums as well. They all say hello."

It was Andrew's last letter. Four months later, he was killed while on patrol in the North Sea. His wife sent a terse note stating that Andrew would be buried in her family's plot in Aberdeen and announcing that she was expecting Andrew's child. It was the last contact we ever had with any of my brother's new family.

Dierdre had been reading the account slowly, pausing from time to time to puzzle out an unfamiliar phrase. But though she was certain that she understood what she read, there was still something wrong with the meaning. "Your brother didn't die in the war," she said, looking to Grandmum for some explanation.

"Not in the world after I was through with it, no," Grandmum replied, waving her arm toward the book. "Go on. Read!" she ordered. "And speed things up a bit, we only have a couple of days."

"If you want things speedy, you'll have to read it to me," Dierdre retorted.

"It's still so bad?"

"It's not something you grow out of." Dierdre tried to hand the notebook to the old woman.

Grandmum pushed it away and whispered, "These aren't words to read aloud, especially here where the aides have nothing better to do than hang on every sound."

"Patience then," Dierdre said, and returned to her task.

Father took the news stoically, too much so for my comfort. But he seemed more alert after Andrew's death, more curious about how the business was going in my hands. When he was certain that I no longer needed even his advice, he took his revolver into the sunroom. From everything I could determine later, he had been facing the garden my mother had labored to create when he blew the top of his head off and went to seek solace in whatever the afterlife had to offer him. I cleaned the room myself. It was months before I could enter it again without bursting into tears.

But Father underestimated his human purpose, without him there was no sham of a figurehead for MacCallum Construction. Clients found excuses to cancel their contracts with a girl not even twenty-one. Debtors put off paying, blaming the war and making me feel unpatriotic for demanding anything at all. The two construction foremen who had once expressed an interest in buying the business were fighting somewhere in Europe. I had no other takers. With no choice left me, I collected what debts I could, then gave my last few employees a week's severance, sold off the equipment and closed Mac-Callum Construction forever.

In the years before Father's death, I had managed to pay down the mortgage on our building. I used half the money from the equipment sale to pay off all our remaining debt. If I lived carefully, I wouldn't have to touch what was left of the family fortune. I thought I could invest it, and live on the income the other apartments provided.

A grand scheme, but not in keeping with the changes in the neighborhood. The Laughrans moved away, leaving only Angelina and her two older sisters to pay the rent. They often came up short, and I had no idea how I could evict some of my oldest friends. One of the Italian brothers disappeared. The other married and moved to New Jersey. I rented their flat to a bookkeeper and his wife, then learned that they both worked for an art gallery that only showed enough of a profit to pay them every other week. Even the Hirsig family left, moving to a larger, cheaper house a few blocks away. In spite of it all, I held on to the savings by taking an office job with an architect and living as cheaply as I could.

The building became my lover, my child, my shrine to our family's magnificent past. I spent my salary on tuckpointing for the chimneys, plastering in the front halls and arranging new windows on the second floor. Much of the work was done by some of the firm's old employees for as low a price as they could afford. Still, the building was huge, and my resources too slim. I slowly lost ground.

Within two years, the money had run out and I started selling our heirlooms. The Galle etagère went first, sacrificed for a third its value. The Hummel figurines my mother had collected went next. The silver service followed, then the antique Chinese pitchers and bowls. I kept only the old portraits of the family and the Waterford goblets. These were valuable but I was unable to part with the glasses in which I and my father drank a toast for Andrew's marriage. Instead, I took in boarders, single men just back from the war. They stayed a few months, then moved on to be replaced by others. I remember only a few of the names, and in the end counted only one as a friend. Dear, sweet Noah. The most sensitive man I will ever know. I suppose that now I will never see him again.

One January evening, the Friday after my twenty-third birthday, Alma and Leah came over for a potluck dinner. They brought a cake and a bottle of wine. We ate in the sunroom, spreading an old red blanket on the worn carpet as if we were at a nighttime picnic outside.

As usual, Leah drank far too much. Though she was usually the center of the conversation, always ready with a witty retort, tonight she was quiet, withdrawn. "Is something wrong?" I finally asked.

"I've been evicted," Leah admitted, biting the inside of her mouth nervously. "No warning, just 'clear out your things by the weekend, Leah, and may I never see you again.' The bastard! Alma, can I move in with you for awhile?"

Judging from Alma's shocked expression, Leah had apparently kept this news to herself, something I found astonishing given her inability to keep any sort of secret for more than an hour. *"This has happened to all of us at one time or another. It may take some time, but you'll find another place,"* I said.

"But I loved him," Leah wailed and covered her face with her hands.

"Here's an idiot for you," Alma said. *"She thought the bastard might actually leave the huge brood he's sired just because she spread her legs."*

Love was one thing, adultery another, and I could not imagine Leah, no matter how drunk, doing such a thing. *"How can you say that?"* I demanded, one arm over Leah's shoulders to comfort her.

"Isn't that why you damn near fainted while we were walking across the Square and why you're picking at your favorite casserole?" Alma asked her sister.

Leah sat, face still covered, saying nothing, her silence admitting everything.

"There was only one thing stodgy old Edward could do well, Leah. You found out exactly what that was, didn't you?"

Alma was baiting her sister. Knowing Leah's temper all too well, I half expected Leah to throw the wineglass at her, more likely the bottle. Alma deserved it. But instead, Leah wiped away her tears with her fingertips and smoothed back the few strands of dark hair that had fallen from her carefully arranged chignon. *"I'm going to get him back,"* she said.

"How? Light a red candle and recite the Song of Solomon? How about a bit of Eastern meditation? Maybe you could send your astral self to his bed at night to torment him," Alma poured herself and me more wine and held the bottle out to Leah, who took it and filled her glass again.

"Perhaps you can send one of Angelina's spirits to haunt him until he gives up the ghost," I joked, trying to lighten the argument, though it was probably impossible.

"You shouldn't speak so casually of the dead," Leah countered. *"And I do know someone who can help me. The Beast himself."*

"Aleister Crowley?" I asked. The name had been in all the papers. He was a writer, a mountain climber, a mystic and a magician. In spite of these many accomplishments, not one reporter had showed the slightest bit of kindness in his account of the man. Instead they all spoke of him as if New York had

just been visited by the Devil's chief disciple, or worse.

"Angelina and I went with Alma to hear him speak. We met with him afterward. Even Angelina was impressed," Leah retorted, staring at Alma as she said this.

"That was months ago," Alma said. "He might not even remember us."

"But we met him. We can see him again."

"I suppose we could, but to what purpose? During his lecture, he made certain that we all understood that he is not a medium or a fortune teller. He does not work any sort of magic for money. And I think that any man who revels in being called The Beast would consider love charms far beneath him."

Leah seemed ready to cry again, when Alma added even more coldly, "But I will take you round to see him tomorrow you, you fool. Perhaps he can think of some sort of herb or tonic to solve your little problem. It would be for the best given your situation."

"I'm going to get him back," Leah repeated.

"You don't know how little you really want that," Alma countered, somewhat prophetically it later seemed.

So the following afternoon the two sisters went to Aleister's dingy apartment on University Place. They promised to stop by my house when they left him, but only Alma arrived some two hours later.

She paced my living room, wringing her hands like a damsel in distress in a bad movie. Finally, she stopped in front of the two remaining pictures on the wall, portraits of my parents. "What would my own mother say if she saw Leah this afternoon?" she complained. "She'd call Leah a whore. But she's wrong. Leah is a crazy whore, there's a tremendous difference."

Her voice grew louder as she spoke. I thought of the old woman who had taken the flat above mine, and how prehensile her hearing seemed to be. Any moment now the woman would be pounding her shoe on the floor, unless she had heard enough to press her ear to it. Without asking if Alma wanted any, I poured a shot of brandy and handed it to her.

Alma wasn't much of a drinker but she flung it back anyway then poured herself a second and sat in one of the old straight-backed chairs. "Maybe she's possessed," Alma continued. "Nothing else can explain it."

"What in the world happened?" I asked, taking a chair beside her. I hoped that as Alma related the facts she would calm down a little.

"We went to see Crowley. I phoned him up, so he was expecting us. He lives in an ugly studio apartment in a run-down building on University Place. The stairs leading up to them sag and the railing is wobbly and I thought we would both break our necks before we got there. All the way up Leah kept muttering something. More than once I heard her say her damned boss's name."

"Your magician must have been impressed."

Alma snorted. "He impressed her is more like it. No sooner did he answer my knock than Leah looked at him and fell completely silent. I said a few polite words, but neither of them seemed to hear me. I think that if I had told Leah that her precious Edward was standing behind her she would not have bothered to turn around. It would have meant not looking at him, and that would have been impossible."

"You never told me that he was good looking," I said, trying to find some obvious explanation for Leah's sudden enthrallment.

"He isn't. Many would find him quite horrid. For one thing, he shaves his head like a monk and his nose is far too big for his face. It's his eyes and mouth that are irresistible to her I think. That and his reputation. But you can judge for yourself when we go over there to bring Leah back."

I let her idea slide. Though I was intrigued by the situation, I hadn't made up my mind if I wanted to be a part of it. So I offered her another drink. She refused. "She stayed?" I asked.

"Stayed! No sooner had I seen the futility of breaking the spell both seemed to have fallen under then he took her in his arms, bent her backwards like a green twig and began to kiss her. If he'd tried something like that with me, I would have slapped his face or stuck a knee in his crotch and deflated his ego, but Leah just kissed him back. I didn't know what to do, so I waited for someone to notice me. When he picked her up and carried her to a threadbare seetee by the window, I wanted to say something, but I was struck dumb by the sight of their display. When he began undoing the buttons on her blouse, I yelled some insult and left. On the way down, I missed the last step and nearly broke my arm in the fall, not that they would have paid any attention if I had called for help.

"I went home before I came here and tried to phone them. No one answered. You know what that means."

"That he won't think a love charm beneath him?" I asked, stifling a giggle. I should have shown more sympathy, but some perverse part of me relished this situation. Leah's actions were shocking but Alma had always been such a prig.

"She went from infatuated to possessed in a matter of moments," Alma continued. "No, I don't like this at all."

"Maybe we should wait an hour or two then go over there and see what's happening?" I suggested, far too curious not to see firsthand the end of this odd drama.

"Would you really go with me? It would be such a relief. I don't want to be alone with them."

I turned to the cabinet where I kept the liquor and poured myself a shot of gin. I was about to meet the Beast up close and like Alma, I needed a little easy courage to steady me.

Alma had not exaggerated the state of Crowley's building. When I had been a child, the place had possessed a certain faded elegance. That had long since departed. The concrete steps outside were streaked with mildew. The wooden entrance door was cracked, its once beautiful carvings worn, its finish dull. The stairs were as Alma had described but she had somehow forgotten to mention the musty reek of the entire space, as if the basement sewer regularly backed up and the floors were never cleaned after.

This is what real poverty is like, I thought, and prayed I would never sink so low.

We climbed the stairs carefully, pausing in unspoken agreement outside Crowley's door to listen before knocking. I heard a man's deep voice singing some stupid popular song, the name of which I've forgotten, then Leah's familiar nervous giggle.

With one hand on Alma's arm to steady me, I knocked.

Crowley answered. He was wearing a Chinese-style silk

dressing gown with a blue dragon embroidered down the length of one lapel. He had a huge body, somewhat gone over to fat, but still obviously powerful. Curious about Leah's sudden infatuation, I stared at him trying to determine what Leah had found so attractive. As Alma had noted, he shaved his head. His face was puffy as if he indulged too often in drugs or drink, the skin weathered but pale as if he were usually an outdoorsman and had been confined or convalescing the last few months.

But those eyes! They must have been Leah's downfall. Their color, a diluted shade of brown, seemed less like that of a man than of some sort of wolf or large cat. But they were large, bright, intelligent, unblinking as they stared at me, as if he were afraid that were he to look away I might snatch up Leah and bolt from the room.

I don't know how long we stood staring at each other before Alma swept past me and over to the rumpled fourposter on which Leah lay, her bare legs splayed, her naked body sheened with sweat, her hair unbraided, falling in thick damp strands over her shoulders. "Have you lost your mind?" Alma said, her voice low and stern, the superior tone of a parent. She often used it with Leah, but never for so obvious a reason.

Leah only smiled and stared at the ceiling. I thought I'd never seen the girl so drunk before and never in such a state. Out of respect for what little Leah might remember of this afternoon, I focused my attention to Crowley.

"What have you done to her?" I demanded.

"Done? Nothing she didn't want me to do, I'll guarantee you that." The ripple of humor in Crowley's voice made me furious. "Trust me, I did not take advantage of her, but never have I experienced such a powerful mutual lust. Ah, the way I used it."

He pointed to a screen that must have been used to hide the bed. I walked to it and saw that he had painted one side. And what a picture! It was Leah, but a Leah I had never known. Naked, emaciated, the pallor of her body all the more evident in contrast to the colorful parrot on her shoulder, the grotesque demons at her feet. "She said I should paint her as a dead soul, and so I did," he said. "She inspired my greatest masterpiece."

I didn't doubt it. It was grotesque, but with a strange sort of beauty. Even if I had never seen the painting again, I would not have forgotten it. "She came here because she was troubled," I continued, *trying to make him understand her mental state, trying to appeal to a conscience I later discovered did not exist.*

"Ah, yes. A child and a suddenly disinterested lover. A bland sort of drama, don't you think. Now at least her mind is settled on that matter."

Alma looked up at him, her arms still around her sister, her expression hopeful. "You'll help her end the pregnancy?" Alma asked.

"End? Dear woman, no! She has life in her. A marvelous thing, and a completely natural state for a young woman. It's the morality of the so-called Christian masses she has to learn to ignore. I told her that she should stay with me and I'll teach her to hold her head up no matter what calumnies rain down on it."

I suspected that he was an expert at that. I looked at Leah, staring at him as a nun might a crucifix. But I had to admit that I hadn't seen her so calm in weeks. I also began to see that I was wrong about her being drunk. She'd merely ceased to care what her sister or I thought of her actions. Based entirely on first impressions, I felt almost a grudging respect for the man, though I doubted I would ever really like him.

"If you stay here, don't come to me later for help," Alma said to her sister.

"I won't. Not ever again," Leah whispered.

I believed her. I don't know why but I did. Perhaps I have a bit of the "sight" in me.

After we left, I told Alma that her sister was better off with Crowley. She looked at me as if I had suddenly joined league with the devil. It was months before I saw her again.

Meanwhile, Leah visited me a great deal. This was hardly unexpected. We had always complemented each other. I was her rock; she my adventure. I couldn't think of another person I preferred to be with, and yet there was always something too frantic, too unfocused about her. If often seemed as if the woman had no idea what sort of a creature she was, and was waiting for the right person to tell her.

And too many had tried which explained her swelling belly and her sudden departure from the New York City school system. At any other time in her life, she would have been distraught, but now she had a radiance about her that I thought might be due to her pregnancy as much as Crowley's influence. When I asked straight out if she was doing anything to harm her child, she denied taking any drugs except for an occasional puff of hashish to quell the nausea of pregnancy, and to drinking not at all.

"Aleister won't allow it. He said he lost his own child that way. I listen to him, because he's right," she explained. "But he is worried about the influenza reports and other things too. You noticed how unhealthy the air in the building is. Sometimes it's actually hard to breathe in it, and we have only that one room between us. We have to get out and with the shortage of apartments now that all the soldiers are coming home . . . well, I was wondering if you had any space to spare."

"Everything's taken," I replied.

"You could split your own until something opens up. He would pay. He's sold a lot of books in the last few weeks, and supporters have been sending money. We have more than enough."

What could I say. I needed the money. And she was my closest friend. With great misgivings, I agreed.

I gave Aleister and Leah what would have been the end unit if the apartments were still split. They moved in the following day. Before they did, Noah and I carried what little furniture I had into my half of the apartment or into storage in the basement. The couple might have next to nothing, but I would not share my few family treasures with them. I needn't have worried for them, though. Within a few days Aleister had the place furnished with the most incredible array of hand-me-downs I've ever seen, all of them donated by his followers.

There was a chair, more a throne really, so large it could easily seat two with two more perched on its flat arms. His threadbare setee had been replaced by a courting seat, the sort where the couple sit facing one another, and a pair of oxblood leather chesterfield chairs worn a bit at the feet because a terrier had gnawed them. The old metal bed I'd seen in his dismal room had also been discarded, replaced by a mahogany one with tall head- and footboards featuring painted nymphs cavorting among flowers and vines. The last was given to Aleister by a newlywed whose wife, most appropriately, disapproved of it.

As soon as they arrived, Aleister set up his folding screen in the center of the large living room we shared, dividing the space in half. We would still have to share the single front entrance and the kitchen, but the rooms between would be separate. Since the sunroom was the largest space and, since I'd long since sold the wicker furniture now the emptiest room in the flat, he asked to use the entire space for his rituals.

This arrangement might have worked well except for his guests. They were a motley bunch, mismatched in education, temperament, and manners. They usually thought that the entire space belonged to Aleister so that I was constantly having to throw them out of my living room, kitchen and even bedroom. Many of them felt that, like Leah, they should view clothing as optional and took advantage of the open-mindedness of their hosts to shed most of what they wore. They also seemed to believe that I belonged to Aleister, something I found as ludicrous as it was insulting.

In fairness to Aleister, he did not often intrude on my privacy, at least not directly. But there was no ignoring the presence of the man within our shared space. I smelled his incense. I heard his chanting at odd hours. Leah would sometimes come to sit with me in the sunroom while Aleister made good use of the castoff bed with one or another or his devotees. Leah showed no sign of jealousy. She said that he used sex as a form of magick act—the word "magick" always spoken to draw attention to the hard "k", no doubt to separate what he does from some cheap sideshow act. I suppose she thought he was working. I thought of it as lusting, but I kept silent, trying to judge him as she did, by a different set of standards.

Most disquieting were the times when I swore that some ghostly presence or another was in the apartment with us, conjured up by the mage from the afterlife or the spirit world, or someplace far from pleasant. This made me anxious. Often I did not sleep well. I might have done as others have and consulted him about *my* problem, but I would not be beholding to the man.

Then, in short order, a number of events changed my life forever.

ELEVEN

It began two months after Leah gave birth to her son, Hansi. The delivery, assisted by Aleister, who seemed to have acquired some medical training God knows where, was quick and relatively painless. Hansi was a large and healthy child, but given to sniffles and the damp New York weather didn't seem to agree with him. Influenza was taking a terrible toll on the city, so much so that, at Alsister's urging, Leah took him south to Florida to visit Aleister's brother who had a grapefruit farm there. I thought that Aleister would use the time to practice whatever rituals might require women purchased or seduced for that purpose, but I was wrong. Instead, he shut himself up in his half of the house, studying and meditating, both thankfully in silence. I hadn't felt the place so still since the pair had moved in with me. When I did see him and inquired about his work, he told me he was on the edge of the most marvelous revelations, some sort of great leap forward in his abilities. This was one of the few times I've sensed real excitement in his tone. I asked for details but he refused to reveal them.

Some nights later, as I was reading in my half of the living room, I heard a scream from Angelina Laughran's apartment, followed by the sound of running water. A moment later my bedroom wall caved in and the room started flooding. I screamed myself, then, and Aleister rushed in. He immediately saw that a pipe had broken and rushed to the basement to turn off the water.

He'd moved quickly but the damage had already been done. Angelina's bedroom wall was ruined, as was mine. Worse, the break was buried somewhere in the damp plaster, and until we located and repaired it, we would have no water for cooking or sanitation except for what we pulled from the basement.

I'd had some old pipes replaced before, and knew that I couldn't repair this myself. The cost of having someone else do the work was well beyond anything I could afford. The building would be condemned and sold, probably to the university. It would be ripped down as they had done to so many fine places near the Square, replaced by some ugly ediface with no charm or character.

I didn't fear poverty, for I was already poor. But I would not have the last and oldest possession of my family, this house I grew up in, and all its memories, destroyed. I sat on the edge of my bed and began to cry.

"That will do no good whatsoever," Aleister said to me sternly.

"Unless you can conjure up a few hundred dollars, I fail to see any way out of this situation. I might as well give in to how I feel," I retorted.

"I have never met any woman with such a disgusting need for wealth," he replied. He must have known he was baiting me, but he spoke as if he had just made an offhanded comment about the weather.

"You don't understand. It's not the house, it's what it means to me. I grew up here. My mother died in this room when I was twelve."

"Twelve! How fortunate for you," Crowley replied. It seemed a terribly distasteful joke, made even worse by the absence of any mirth in his expression.

"I miss her very much," I added.

"Perhaps she would have been kinder had she waited a year or two to leave. Nothing like departing when a relationship is at its ugliest."

He spoke from his own experience. Leah had told me that his parents had been tyrants and worse, his own mother telling him he bore the mark of the Beast when he was scarcely old enough to understand the term. So I could hardly blame him for his feelings. What I could hold against him was his damnable lack of respect for my own. "Illness gave her little choice," I replied. "My father followed her eight years later. He killed himself, again in this room. I'm surprised you have no empathy for how I must feel."

"I save my empathy for my work."

Horrible. Yet people came to him for advice. I could scarcely understand it, though even now when all I wanted to do was to throw him out of my house, I felt myself drawn to his power like a moth to the lethal flame or a mouse to the cheese in a trap. There was something fascinating about him, and oddly our constant proximity had only deepened it.

He was staring at me, the flecks of gold in his milky brown eyes catching the light from the lamp. His expression had become almost merry, and I began to sense that he received far too much satisfaction from wounding me. "Dearest Bridget, there is too much empathy in the world. What a smart person truly starves for is a good dose of truth."

A relative term—truth. It hardly seemed worthwhile to argue that with him especially when I was so miserable.

"Besides, there is always a way out of any difficulty. We just have to find it." Having reached a fine level of crypticism even for him, he started for the door. "I, for one, have no intention of leaving no matter what the state of the plumbing. This space has been far too good for my work."

After he left me, I went back to my handkerchief, feeling somewhat better for my all too feminine outburst.

Hours later, after my crying jag had run its course, I washed from one of the buckets of water Aleister had carried up from the basement, changed into a nightgown and robe and sat on the sofa reading.

Aleister joined me, sitting beside me and taking my hand. The gesture, one of comfort, seemed so unlike him that I had to fight back a new batch of tears. "There are people coming by soon," he said gently. "Some of them are wealthy. Perhaps we can find some mundane way out of your prickley little problem. Join us."

It was my house. Perhaps he did mean to help, if only to impress me or himself with his influence. I went to my bedroom to change, deliberately picking a loose-fitting silk kimono with an embroidered peacock feather design at the cuffs, front and hem. In my own house, at least, I would compete with The Beast for center stage.

By the time I entered the parlor, a half dozen people had already arrived for the evening ritual. Someone had crossed to my side of the apartment. One had discovered my liquor cabinet and was pouring the best of my father's remaining scotch into my Waterford goblets and passing the drinks around.

"Excuse me. There's been a mistake," I said. I took the glasses back and poured the contents into less costly containers then carried the Waterford to the kitchen to hide away until the evening had ended. I heard scratching in the sunroom, cracked open the door and glanced inside. Aleister had rolled back the old carpet and was on his hands and knees, drawing a pentagram on the wood floor. He motioned for me to be silent and continued with his work.

On my way to the front of the house, I passed the room Aleister was using as a library. Some of his followers were paging through his books, paying particular attention to the rarer volumes. I wondered if Aleister seached his guests as they left.

Aleister kept himself hidden until after the ritual began, all the better to make the grand entrance. And so he did, wearing an Egyptian sort of headdress, the long robe embroidered with hieroglyphics, and covered with a cheetah skin ("The Beast had slain the beast," he'd informed me when I first asked about it.). Pharoah. Priest. Warrior. He was all these things and more. His deep voice boomed, howled, growled over the chants of the worshippers. For a time, he was no longer Aleister the man—intelligent, grating, and far too addicted to earthy pleasures. For a time he was Master Therion, invoker of the gods. No one, even myself who was hardly a believer at the time, could doubt his power.

The ritual itself, a sort of early Solstice ceremony, was as marvelous as anyone would expect from The Beast. The incense, so thick that it coated the ceiling of the room, curled around his face and body, swirling as he moved from one corner to another to another, chanting the words, in English now. *"I dedicate this room and those around it to the great Ptah, father of the gods, that he may allow those who seek his favors and the favors of his children to find them in this space."*

And so he consecrated the room, making it his. On this, he swears he acted on instinct. I believe him, for in the time I knew him I often saw the evidence of an incredible second sight.

After the ritual ended, I stayed close to Aleister, letting him insinuate what he would about who I was, more interested in the help he had promised me. He tried, in truth he did. He explained my problem every time someone complained about the lack of water. He described me as an ardent supporter, the closest friend of his mistress. He even went so far as to say that I had offered the sunroom and courtyard for use as a temple, and that he would accept the offer if the place were in better repair.

But though he obtained a great many offers for new lodgings for himself and Leah, he found no one willing to help me. I felt worse than before, because for just a little while, I had dared to believe someone might actually decide to rescue me.

Though it was nearly dawn when the last of the guests had left, sleep was hard to find. I gave up and went looking for Aleister. I found him in the sunroom, reading by the light of an oil lamp. Books were spread around him on the floor. He still wore his ceremonial robes and there was a heavier scent of incense in the air than usual. He must have heard me come into the room, for he asked without looking up, *"How old is this building?"*

"It was built around 1800 I think," I replied.

"Old enough for a magickal number," he commented.

"You propose to fix a busted pipe with magick?" I asked, trying not to laugh.

He looked at me with a curious expression. *"Have you never done something for the pure and marvelous pleasure of determining that you can?"*

"That hardly seems a reason," I replied. *"There is enough to do with purpose."*

"Purpose? Ah, my sweet child, you know nothing of your limits unless you test them. And without that knowledge, how

can you possibly determine any purpose? For example, I swam the width of Loch Ness in the middle of winter just to see if I could. I climbed the highest mountain in Nepal.''

"Three people died on one of your climbing expeditions, as I recall. As for the outcome, what did it serve?" I was arguing for the sake of doing so, for by then I knew very well what Aleister was trying to explain. Nonetheless, the clash of wits excited me. I admit that if he had not become so attached to Leah, and if I had any inkling that he might possess some usual virtue, I might have been attracted to him. I have always liked men I see as my equals.

"Three men died because they were fools! Hopefully, in their next lives they'll be more prudent. As to what it served— simply this, when the time came to sample the best whores India had to offer, I knew that I would be more than up to the task. I made them scream with passion.''

It was like him to pick the most inappropriate example just to see my reaction. I stared at him without commenting, not even with a frown. He moved close to me. His hands gripped my shoulders, pressing lightly, moving me backwards. I cried out when my back reached the wall, then tried to slide sideways and out of his grip. He held me there, his face moving close to mine. "In normal circumstances, it's the other way around," he whispered as if we were lovers sharing some private joke.

I put my hands on his chest and felt the heat of his body. For a moment, I hesitated, wondering if kissing a man with such experience would feel different than kissing Noah. Perhaps it would, but there was danger in it. I could see this in the way his licked his lips, anticipating. In the way his hands held me, challenging me to try to refuse him. And most, in the way his attention was fixed on my dressing gown, loosely tied, exposing most of my chest.

Had he already worked some magick, that I would go looking for him so seductively dressed?

"The right wand combined with the perfect cup can accomplish anything," he said, as if I cared about that lewd logic or joining him in his work.

I pushed him away. Not hard, but enough to convince him that I was serious. He lowered his arms, but did not move. I *had to brush against him to leave. He laughed. "What is self-respect worth at the end of a life, my dearest Bridget? Missed opportunities, every one no more than a regret."*

"I will miss only those I chose to miss. There should be no regret in doing as thou wilt. If that isn't a part of your law, it should be," I replied, throwing his own beliefs back at him as I walked down the hall toward the bedroom, never looking back. His laughter continued, following me, but it was empty of all mirth, a hollow sound.

"I'm going to help you whether you like it or not. Actually, if you don't things should go all the better," he called after me.

In response, I slammed by bedroom door, though I could not shut out his laughter.

By the following morning, Aleister shed his ceremonial robes, replacing them with a sort of loincloth that made him look like an overgrown and somewhat pudgy baby. The shaved head only added to the effect and when I came upon him sitting in a full lotus position in the sunroom, I wanted to laugh. However, since he sat with his eyes closed and his hands palm up and resting on his knees, I knew he was meditating. I stifled even a giggle and left for work without saying a word.

As I look back on those words, it seems that I make the man too trivial, too much a sort of pompous clown. Sometimes he is. At other times, he seems to be the most powerful man I have ever met; certainly the most disturbing.

When I came home from work that afternoon, he was sitting in the same place and position. I wondered if he had moved at all. By dinner time he was more than ready to eat, and after consuming nearly all my meal as well as his own, he retreated once more to the sunroom to continue with his research. He was still hard at it the following morning. Books were piled around him and notes scattered across the floor. At the moment, however, he was ignoring them, concentrating instead on an intricate arrangement of Tarot cards spread across the carpet. "Ring up your boss and tell him you won't be in today," he said without looking up.

"I need the income now more than ever," I replied.

"Then money you shall have, and more."

"Do the cards speak so well?" I asked.

"No, they're a disaster. Far worse than I thought. Now call your boss."

I did as he asked, then went and sat beside him. *"Start with the worst,"* I said.

"This is not your reading, or mine, but Leah's. It isn't good."

Exactly, given that she'd thrown in her lot with his, I thought, but at a time when he seemed so concerned about her, I didn't say this aloud. Instead, I listened as he pointed out the various cards, patiently explaining their position and meaning. I confess that only a few weeks have passed, but I remember nothing except his sad predictions.

"She will not see the child she now carries raised to adulthood. And the one she and I will conceive together will be sickly, and perhaps die young. I would send her away from me, but the cards show an even worse future for her apart from mine, though that is how she will end her days."

He paused and took both my hands, squeezing them as he continued, *"You have to understand the first rule of magick. Magick requires purity. No, don't smile, I am speaking of purpose, not ritual. An adept learns magick for its own sake and to bring him a certain amount of luck and success for his own life, but he does not sell his skills. Many times I have added to an individual's luck or monetary fortune, but always only to see if I could do so. And if the recipient rewards me, well, that is his choice not my demand. Now, though, I am going to stretch that rule just a little and request a payment from you. Before we solve your problem, you must make me a promise. When your fortune increases, as it undoubtedly will if you do exactly as I tell you, you will make me two promises. First, you must always provide for Leah and our children when we are no longer together."*

"You're planning that! How can you do that to . . ."

"I do not plan. I see. And it may surprise you to learn that I do indeed care about her, more than she knows. Certainly more than I ever want her to suspect. I will not have her end her life alone and friendless, undoubtedly penniless. I want her to have you to count on, Bridget—for herself, her children, even for those who will come after."

*Was he telling me the truth? I think he believed this, though
I have seen him milk a wealthy matron for every cent she'll
part with. As for his affection, I doubted I would get a straight
answer by asking him, so I kept silent and nodded while saying
nothing.*

*I loved Leah as I would a sister. But there was always a
terrible, nagging thought. What would be left of the woman
when Crowley was through with her? And what scars would
be left on her children? But at least Leah would have my
support. "I promise," I said. "And the second?"*

*"That you never tell her about this conversation. I will not
give her that sort of power over me."*

Now that was honest. Again, I agreed.

*"Good, you've put my mind at rest. For that I will give you
what you wish."*

*What I wished for was enough funds to fix the building
properly, though I sensed he spoke of more than bricks and
pipes and concrete. After all, he knew what this place meant
to me.*

*He gathered up the cards and put them away before con-
tinuing. I confess that I recall too little of what he told me,
only that he showed me a book on Egyptian symbols and made
me pay particular attention to three.*

*The first was the god he had invoked in the ritual some
nights before. Ptah was symbolized by a standing man clutching a walking stick with a ram's head for a handle. "This is
the Opener, the god who can bridge one realm and another.
Or one time and another," Aleister explained.*

*The second was Thoth, the measurer of time, symbolized by
an ibis.*

*The third was Ap-uat, the opener of the ways, symbolized
by a human figure with the head of a jackel.*

*Aleister began drawing these three in his sketchbook, add-
ing symbols to the cloaks and staffs of each small figure. I
admit that he has talent and that in spite of how quickly he
sketched the reproductions were beautiful. He later carved relief figures from small pieces of oak and affixed these to the
frame above the sunroom doors, but I am jumping ahead of
the story.*

While he sketched, I listened to him explain the gift he in-

tended to give me, one he hopes will be complete power to end all my misfortunes.

"If what we attempt works, you will have the gift of ultimate hindsight. With it you will be able to alter not only the present but also the past. Now how long have you known Leah?"

"We've been friends as long as I can remember. We were both born in this building."

"Good! And so she has seen your family at its most prosperous. You would still be friends with her had your fortune not changed?"

"I know so."

"And what would you change, if you could?"

"I would warn my father of the accident that killed those eight subway workers. I would make certain my mother and brothers were visiting the family in Canada when the influenza hit. I would watch my father closely for any signs of despair. Should I see any, I would not leave him alone even for a minute, until I was certain he would not harm himself."

"A dozen people saved. Would that be enough or would you feel the need to warn passengers of the sinkings of the Lusitania and Titanic?" He smiled as he asked this.

"I would have that much power?"

"I cannot give you a shred of hindsight. You will have it all or none. Think about this first—how you will limit what you receive, for if you do not limit it, this gift will become a curse far worse than any you might face from poverty. Once you make your decision, I will tell you the other things you must do to make the magick work. And now, I must rest." With that, he stood, stretched and headed down the hall to his bedroom. Minutes later, I heard him snoring as large men often do.

He could have gone on working for another day or two. I've seem him do it often enough. Instead, he'd left me to consider his words.

I did. I even consulted my own Tarot deck. Every card was a call to action save one, the queen of swords, a card Aleister believed signaled prudence and careful planning, laid in the place that signified myself.

So I set out to do what the cards said I must.

I made a list of what I would change, and many of the things

I would not. My family came first, I decided. I would limit my actions to them and them alone. With the rest of the world's misfortunes, I would try to adopt Aleistair's own attitude, complete willed indifference.

When Aleister rose some hours later, I told him what I'd decided and repeated my promise to take care of Leah.

He clapped his hands, then rested them above mine. "Then here is the rest of what you must know," he said. "I plan to create a doorway into the past. It will give you the means to change the most important events that you have listed. These will be limits to the power I intend to give you. First, I do not believe that you can go back to a time in which you lived, for I believe that each of us has an eternal soul and it cannot occupy two bodies at the same time."

"Then how . . ."

"Silence! Let me finish. "Second. The door will be locked to all but your own family. You may send a close relative or your own descendent, with only one limiting factor—the person you send must not have been a result of the changes you make. In short, it must be your own child, conceived before you dare to change the past, or better yet conceived during the ritual of change itself.

"Why my own? My brother Andrew left a son."

"You intend to save your brother's life. If you warn him that he will die in the war, he may never go to England. He may never meet the woman he married, indeed he is likely not to."

"Then I will save one life and insure that another is never born," I replied bitterly.

"Never born? Don't believe it. Souls always find their way to earth eventually. Now, as to the third, you can only go back in time. The future is closed to your present self."

"Can someone from the past come here?"

"I don't think so," he said.

"Think so. You don't know?"

He laughed. "I've never tried something like this before. And I must tell you that the price for doing it will be high. I'll want to scream this triumph from the mountaintops, but if I do all the magick will end. So for Leah's sake, I will have to practice modesty—a virtue I know too little about.

*"Now as to the fourth and last limitation, the years sepa-
rating the present and the past must be exactly sixty-six plus
six years; that is, seventy-two."*

*"I have to wait seventy-two years to know whether the spell
has worked?"* I asked incredulously.

"No." He thought a moment, then told me what he believed, pausing often as he tried to find the proper words to
explain. *"I'm not certain exactly what will happen, but I think
that as long as you do what you intend and send someone
back, things will change from the moment the door opens. The
. . . world as it now exists will be remembered like a dream.
The world as you have . . . altered it will become the reality."*

"Then how will I remember what I have to do?" I asked.

"Because, this moment will have its own reminder." He
pointed to the drawing he had made, the strange carved heiroglyphics he would place above the doorframe. *"If you can
recall the part of any dream, you can recall all of it, every
precise perfect piece. Here . . ."* He thrust a pad of paper into
my hand. *"On the day of the ritual, you will write down what
you want to tell yourself and what we are planning. Write
down every detail except the exact content of the ritual. Wait
until the evening we open the door. In the middle of the ritual,
put the account and instructions in a ledger, a bible, or some
other book you consult often. Then you will find it later, and
can save it for the generation to come."*

"Why don't you do this for yourself?" I asked. In truth I
could not believe he would be so charitable.

He laughed. *"My child. If I thought that there was any way
I could live with this sort of power, I would do it in a moment.
I couldn't. My best work comes when I am in the worst of
circumstances. This would ruin me. It might even destroy
everything I am."*

"How soon will we know if we have succeeded?"

*"We'll know, and immediately, I think. The signs will de-
pend on the changes we make. We're going to make powerful
magick, you and I. Yes, I think we should conceive your child
then."*

He moved close to me and gripped the back of my neck. I
was too shocked to resist, and half convinced that I should
not anger him. So I submitted, letting him kiss me, letting his

hand slide beneath the neckline of my dress, his palm cup my breast, his fingers rub the nipple, squeezing. I thought myself made of ice or steel, unyielding.

He released me and laughed. "What a night that's going to be," he said. "Have no doubt that what we do will work. I suspect that it may work too well.

"What do you suppose happens? When time folds in on itself, what part of memory becomes illusion? What part of the future suddenly ceases to exist? I tell you Bridget dear, only one scene will be completely real, and provide the link between what should have been and what is. Ah, what a night we are going to have! Tell me, are you a virgin?"

I only looked at him. Dazed, angry and too confused not to nod and admit it.

"The knowing wand. The chaste cup. What power!" He laughed. I remember how hard he laughed as he walked down the hallway to his room.

TWELVE

Dierdre laid down the little ledger and looked toward the hospital bed. Grandmum lay awake, watching her, waiting. "You're not finished," Grandmum complained.

"Why did you let him touch you like that? How could you even think of him being the father of your child?" Dierdre asked with disgust.

"Because I had seen enough of his magick to believe he could accomplish everything he said. And because if he didn't succeed, I would at least have someone to hold on to, an American MacCallum to love."

"You were that lonely?" Dierdre's words were whispered now, compassionate.

"Not lonely. Alone with my memories and the dreams they brought. All too often, I dreamed of Mother's death and of that charming sunroom, its walls streaked with my father's blood. Don't be so quick to judge, child. You've lived a remarkably peaceful life by comparison."

"But him. Why did you pick him?"

"I would have to mate with him anyway. It's part of the ritual."

"But to have the tie a child would bring."

"Times have changed. Leah's having a child out of wedlock was scandalous. Anyone I might have chosen would have refused the request, especially when I told the man the reason I wanted to have sex with him. So if I would have to mate with

141

the lowest sort of man, I decided that it might as well be someone I knew. At least with Aleister I was picking someone my equal in intelligence. If he'd been half a gentleman and not living with my best friend, I would have been his lover from the start."

She paused and smiled, lost in the past for a moment, then went on. "And since I was a virgin, I thought that losing my virginity to a man who had undoubtedly deflowered hundreds would be far more pleasurable than some inept fumbling with a half-drunk beau. Besides the beau might actually want some part in raising the bastard afterward."

Dierdre stared at the old woman, struck dumb by her candor.

"Well, you asked me to answer. Did you expect I would lie on my deathbed?"

Dierdre replied with the first words that popped into her head, "Actually, I thought you more likely to lie than to dance on it."

Grandmum grinned. "That's my girl! Now go on with your reading. And try not to blush."

Dierdre picked up the binder, turned the page and began. She was only a few sentences into the account when she turned her chair so that she was facing away from the woman who had written it. No use having Grandmum snort at the color rising on her cheeks.

And so Aleister and I reached our agreement. While I waited until my body was at its most fertile, Aleister exhausted himself with private rituals to make certain that I would conceive. If I didn't, he assured me that he would know immediately, and we could always try the ritual again later, and again, and so on. Libertine that he was, he could not help but leer when he noted this. I found his lust repulsive and prayed that we would be successful at once.

We decided on tonight, September 17. I spent the better part of today preparing for the event. I had to bathe in a certain blend of herbs, to sit and let the moisture dry on my skin afterwards. I annointed my breasts and vulva with oils. Since then I have sat naked on the cheetah skin in the center of the sunroom, scribbling this account as quickly as I am able while

Aleister, robed in royal purple, black and gold, prepares the room.

He has set incense burners in every corner, affixed the small, carved figures above the doorway, covered the floor around the rug with sweet grass and rosemary, covering that with some oddly scented powder whose source he will not reveal.

When he had finished, he moved beside me, asking me to put down the pad for a moment, but to keep it always within the circle of greenery and powder. He picked up a palette and brush and joined me where I sat.

"Lie on your back and shut your eyes," he whispered.

I did as he asked, expecting that now he would touch me. But instead, he arranged my arms slightly out from my side, my legs slightly apart. I felt the paintbrush moving over my face—the lips and cheeks and eyes—then over breasts and belly. He was painting me, slowly and meticulously, and each brief touch had all the effect of a kiss.

I don't know if this part of the ritual was required or if he was doing it to relax and arouse me. No matter, I was thankful because by the time he had finished, I did not dread what was to come. Just to be certain, he had me open my lips and drink some bittersweet liquor that burned in my throat, spreading its fire to my stomach and outward to my limbs.

"Finish the journal. We begin a sunset," he told me. He stood at the window, staring in the direction of the setting sun, raised his arms and began to chant. I glanced at the long shadows in the yard, gauging my time as less than an hour.

My instructions to myself and my descendents are as follows:

In the years from 1970 to 1975 one of my descendents must go through the door and make the family feel confidence in his advice. The person who goes through the door must warn my father of the accident in the tunnels that will occur in October 1903, and warn my parents of the illness that will claim the life of my mother and brothers should they stay in New York during the summer of 1909. Someone should also warn my brother, Andrew, about his death in the war. And say a prayer that they will listen to the advice.

Aleister said I can hold on to the dream if I remember any part of it. I will set the notepad aside. Later I will finish the account. But not now. No, not now.

September 18 (ledger continued at dawn)

Let me finish. Let me set everything down as I remember it, so clearly that it astonishes me. Yet my world is fading fast and no wonder. It now has all the substance of dream.

The drug's langour wore off almost immediately, replaced by a heightening of my senses. I could feel the paint drying on my skin, feel the symbols he had written there—strange hieroglyphics from an ancient age. The cheetah fur pressed softly against my back as I stared at the whisps of incense curling like vines through the room.

The space seemed to grow dark suddenly, as if clouds had flown in to blanket the sky. Aleister set candles around the circle he had prepared for us and stepped into the center of the flickering light.

He had set a stage as much for me as for the gods.

"Be wanton," he whispered. "Magick flows from desire. Be the woman of your own fantasies. Give your passion to your need and to your child."

And in that moment the man I knew ceased to be, replaced by someone I trusted, someone I desired. I arched my back. I spread my arms and inhaled, I felt as if my soul was growing, expanding to fill all of me.

His next words were foreign, a repetition of some phrase of the chant he'd begun earlier. He whispered them, breathing them out on my legs, my thighs, my belly, my breasts, and last as he pressed against me, onto my mouth, my eyes, my ears. I don't know what they meant but I know what they meant to me.

"Be wanton. The magick flows from desire."

The words opened me to him. I took him in with hardly a moment's pain.

I matched him thrust for thrust until, lifting my body off the fur, he rolled over, putting me above him.

His words grew louder, still with the same meaning, stronger now.

Be wanton.

And so I did, taking from him as he had from me, not caring

that he had moved beyond me into the realm of the gods he invoked.

His hands and fingers wove complex patterns in the air separating us as he pulled the energy from our approching climaxes, holding us back, offering our passion to the gods.

I know when I conceived.

For in that moment, the candles flickered, dimmed, then burned more brightly. The fur beneath my legs seemed softer as if the skin no longer rested on a bare floor. Something rustled in the darkness beyond our flickering pool of light. I smelled earth, flowers. I saw shadows of leaves against the windows as if the earth herself was putting forth new life.

"Aleister," I whispered, frightened.

"Shhh," he replied, voice soothing for a moment.

The chanting continued. Be wanton.

And so I was until passion reached its natural end. I screamed. I thrashed. I tried to break from him but he anticipated the move and held me tightly, shifting again so he was above me before pulling back. While still in the circle, he pushed my thighs apart and placed his hands against my crotch, digging into me, wetting them with what he called the elixir. I watched him step out of the circle. I saw him reach for the figures he had fastened above the door.

Arms high, fingers spread, he carressed the carvings, annointing them with ourselves, chanting one final string of words.

Joining me once more, he kissed me for the first time, a kiss of celebration, of triumph. "It is done," he said.

With difficulty, I managed to stand, to step over the candles, to fall onto the wicker chaise in the corner. For a moment, it seemed strange to find the chaise there, though an instant later I was certain it had always been in that spot. I was naked, and not quite certain why. I pulled Mother's quilt over me and tried to remember what I'd done that evening.

I believed that I had been ill. Leah and Aleister had been living in a flat on the south end of the Square. They'd stopped by to visit, then Leah left Aleister to cheer me up while she went off to some meeting with a friend. One thing had led to another. He suggested that brandy would make me feel less queasy. I'd had too much of it, and for reasons I couldn't quite recall because the present was a lie, I'd let him take advantage of me. Oddly, I felt no anger toward him. Far from it, though that was somehow correct as well. Father had never approved of the man, but he was out for the evening so he need not have known any of what we'd done.

Aleister made some excuse for leaving, winking as he left the room.

I picked up the book of poems by Shelley that I'd been reading before his arrival. A stack of papers fell out of it. I recognized my own handwriting. Intrigued, I began to read.

And remembered. And wrote this down. And cried, out of thankfulness, and hope, and a certain anxiety for how could I ever explain any of this to anyone?

Now, bathed and dressed, I walk through the apartment, running my hands over the little Hummel figurines and the beautiful furniture that I did not sell in the more prosperous past I had created, and marveling at the pictures of Andrew and his family arranged on the mantle.

I hear the front door opening. Father coming home.

Aleister has given me a miracle. For that I will always love him.

There were a few more typewritten pages, but Dierdre could read them later. She glanced at her watch. It was after eleven. Grandmum lay silent, looking at her. Dierdre went to the bed, and looked down at the frail form in its center. "Are you sure I shouldn't call a doctor?" she asked.

Grandmum pushed herself higher in bed and winced at the pain the movement caused. She took a deep breath. "There are things you should never change," she said. "Aleister told me some of them; others I learned the hard way. Now you won't have to. Whatever you do in the past, if you want to keep the door open don't tell anyone about it. It isn't your time, don't stay there too long. And never try to bring someone back from the dead. Life and death belong to God, and no one else."

Dierdre nodded, not certain she would be able to speak. There were tears in her eyes.

"Catholics believe that no matter how terrible a person's sin, she can confess and be absolved at the end of her life? I haven't been to church in years but this evening a priest will be coming to hear my confession. I wonder what he'll make of it. Ah well, nothing like a bit of insurance, my father always said. And nothing like knowing what hour to plan for."

Dierdre smoothed back a thin strand of Grandmum's hair. "Is it really better to know?" she asked.

Grandmum nodded. "Knowing meant that you would be here, my child. And there is no greater comfort than your presence. It was always so."

THIRTEEN

On the way home from Hudson Manor, Dierdre finished
reading the pages in Grandmum's binder. The typewritten account had ended soon after she'd stopped reading; much of
what remained was nothing more than scrawled suggestions
for future MacCallum investments and instructions for dispos-
ing of the family treasures. Most of them were going to Dierdre. A cash settlement to help her end her days in comfort,
the little Hummel figurines and all the books on astrology and
spiritualism were to be given to Angelina. Any of the other
books that Dierdre didn't want to keep were to go to Bill. No
one else was listed. Grandmum, it seemed, had outlived nearly
all her friends.

The final words were directed at her.

*It isn't the journey that is the problem. It's the people you
will meet there. When in doubt, trust Noah.*

Noah. Dierdre sat in the living room, on the beautiful
tapestry-covered sofa, her feet curled under her and Grandmum's photo albums piled beside her. She started with the
earliest pictures. There were Grandmum and her brothers,
taken in 1902 when they were small children. They were in
formal dress, looking seriously in the direction of the photog-
rapher. There was Grandmum and Angelina and a dark-haired
women whom Dierdre recognized as Leah. Angelina was the
shortest, slim in spite of her round face, and thoughtful. Leah

was painfully thin, with features like a painting by Modigliani, a vague smile on her thin lips. Grandmum, or Bridget as Dierdre thought of her in these early pictures, was the prettiest of the three, her eyes bright beneath the evenly bobbed bangs. All them wore their hair loose, and it seemed some mussed by the wind. THE THREE FATES, LONG ISLAND, JULY 1916, PHOTO BY ALMA, Grandmum had lettered beneath their names.

Next was Leah and a bald-headed man, though only Aleister's name was printed beneath the picture as if Grandmum didn't want to bother to name those already identified. The album followed with additional pictures of Dierdre's family, the building, the places Bridget had gone on vacations, a scene of a crowd in what looked like Central Park. And on the next to last page was a formal colorized photo of a younger Noah with an intense expression in his artificially blue eyes giving hints of his talents. The pipe in his mouth had possibly been intended to give his youthful face more maturity. If so, it failed. He seemed most like an adolescent who had stolen his father's prized meerschaum. There was writing on the corner of the photograph as well but it had faded with the years.

Dierdre turned the page, and looked at the last photographs, all candid snapshots in black and white. And all of her when she was a child. She remembered the dresses she wore, the garden as it was then, but the girl about her own age standing beside her was the most familiar.

BRIDGET AND DIERDRE, 1902.

The past roared back. How they'd played croquet on the lawn. How they'd eaten homemade ice cream in the front parlor. How they'd buried treasure in the yard. Then she'd gone to Grandmum's gardener seventy-two years later and asked the poor man to help her find it.

Had Grandmum kept the picture in the open all these years, or had it been tossed in some box of old photos for Dierdre's mother and grandmother to see? Had the entire family always known the secret she had just learned?

Had they thought her so unstable that they wouldn't share it?

Or had it been something more insidious, more deceitful? A photo planted, perhaps, as a sort of insurance to send her on her journey should Grandmum meet with some accident before she had time to explain the door.

When Dierdre had been at the nursing home reading Grandmum's journal, a part of her had already begun calculating parallel dates, giving her clues to her purpose in Grandmum's plans for the family.

Seventy-two years difference between past and present meant that Crowley had worked his magic only months before the time that Dierdre could now visit, though Grandmum had already possessed decades to use the gift he had given her. But logically, how much of the distant past could Grandmum have changed? The further back she went, the less she would know and the less any messages given would be believed.

Dierdre had visited every summer from the time she was seven until she turned twelve, corresponding to the years 1898 to 1904, ideal times to warn Douglas MacCallum and his wife of the fate of their family.

Had she succeeded? Grandmum's account made it clear that for her father and brother she had, but what about the others? Dierdre wished she knew more of the family history. Well, Grandmum had undoubtedly taken care of that as well. She returned the photo albums to the shelf and began looking for the journals. There were a half dozen, covering the years from 1925 to the end of the Second World War, but nothing from the times before or after, the ones that would have really mattered.

And there was no sign of the computer, either. She checked the room's little closet and found it in an unmarked box on one of the storage shelfs. Well, if she couldn't find the printouts, she could read off the screen.

It didn't take her long to get the machine running. But she was used to a Mac system and the IBM clone was running DOS. Frank was the expert on these machines. She glanced at the clock. He'd still be at work. No possibility of talking to her replacement there.

Frank sounded so happy to hear her voice that she felt a brief stab of self-pity. Had she really thought he would find someone else so quickly? She explained her problem and he helped her open the program and get into the text files.

Problem solved, she wanted to get on with her reading, but

Frank wanted to talk. He told her how he'd run into some of her co-workers at a downtown bar, and how much he missed her. "I'll be coming to New York in the next couple of weeks to settle out some matters with a new vendor. Would you like to show me the sights?" he asked.

"I . . ." Dierdre didn't know what to say. "I think Grandmum's fading fast. I don't know if I'll be here."

"You're coming back here, then?"

He actually sounded hopeful, but oddly she felt nothing toward him, not even triumph. "I don't know. She's leaving the building to me. It may take some time to sort out this inheritance. Or I may stay awhile just to see how I like it here."

"Oh. Well, if there's anything I can do here, just call."

"I will, and you call when you know your New York schedule."

She wondered if she would see him when he came to town, or if she'd feel like inventing some excuse to avoid it. Odd how her feelings toward him had changed after just a few days of separation.

It was the dress, she thought. And the martini. And the soft yellow glow of the gaslights. More, it was the notion that she shouldn't look for just a "good fit" as her mother would call it. She should look for someone to cherish her. The word came to her again—Noah.

The computer screen was glowing. Waiting. She forced her attention to the files.

The program was a crude prototype of Windows, with folders for every year and files arranged in three-month sections within them. None of them seemed to be more than a dozen or so pages long.

Dierdre hit the ENTER key to bring up the earliest files. While she waited for the old program to open them, she got up to bolt the front door. She'd just reached it when she thought she heard a soft creak from the floor above her. Could Bill have come home? She phoned him, listening to the ringing in the apartment above her. No one answered. After ten rings the machine picked up. She hung up without saying anything.

The building was playing tricks on her just like it did on

poor old Angelina. Nonetheless, she felt far more secure now that the bolt was in place.

Before going on with her work, she called a locksmith. She told him that her keys had been stolen. He promised to be out within the hour.

Retreating to the library to wait for the man, she pulled the throw off the fainting couch and wrapped it over her shoulders, sat in the plush desk chair and began to read the account, scrolling forward until she came to entries immediately following the ones she'd finished at the nursing home.

October 20, 1918

I read the letter I found a dozen times, trying to make sense of it, trying to do as the letter I wrote had suggested and remember. It's so hard. The memories fade so quicky even when I stand in front of the matching doors and look out at the rear yards, the one on the left so changed since yesterday. There is no garden in my view of the little yard, nor even any wall, only an ill-maintained patch of lawn and a low fence leading to the alley and stables. That should have been proof enough, but I had to be certain of the rest. I woke early this morning and could not get back to sleep until I was certain about what Aleister and I had done. Without thinking of the time, I stepped through those doors into a New York much changed, but still recognizable. I made my way to the square where a glance at a copy of the New York Tribune *showed the date to be exactly seventy-two years earlier, that is 1846.*

I had no way to pay for the paper so I snatched it up and ran past the stables, through the gate and the doors. For the last two hours, I have been sitting at the kitchen table reading history, trying to grasp the reality of Aleister's magic.

In that place I visited, there has been no world war; slaves still work the estates in the South. Horace Greeley is publisher of the New York Tribune *and there is some letter inside my edition from a friend of Edgar Allan Poe saying that things in Fordham aren't nearly as pathetic as the paper has made them out to be.*

The letter I had written myself seemed to describe a dream. But this? For all the moments of disorientation I felt immediately after I returned through those doors, the newspaper in front of me provides a concrete reminder of where I have been. As I read, this certainty grew stronger until I had no choice but to get up from the table, run the few blocks to the dingy apartment Aleister shared with Leah and pound on his door.

Aleister answered, a book in his hand. He smiled when he saw my bare feet, my exultant expression, the newspaper I clutched in my hand. "What a miracle!" I exclaimed. "What an incredible miracle." I threw my arms around him. Then I kissed him as if we had just survived a battle together.

To his credit, I think he could have done anything he liked with me at that moment, but did not try. Instead he laid his hands on my shoulders and look directly into my eyes. "It was as much your doing as my own," he told me, solomnly as if I must believe him. I cannot understand how a man like him can suddenly turn so modest.

October 24. This evening I had a small surprise party for Father's birthday. During it I found myself wiping tears of joy from my eyes. I cannot believe how a single night could affect so many so wonderfully. Yet now as I reflect on what I have done I understand that the future is filled with uncertainty and strife. How can I possibly explain to Father what has happened when I can scarcely understand it myself? Yes, I have a letter written in my own hand, apparently when I was awake. Yes, the letter coincides perfectly with my vivid dream. But the dream and the letter are both so fantastic that I know that no one will believe them.

We are the MacCallums—wealthy, always wealthy. My brother, Andrew, lives in Aberdeen, working with a distant relation in a manufacturing firm. My father runs a successful construction business just as he has for most of his life. As for myself, I am going to school just across the Square, taking business courses, preparing to add my talents to the family trade.

No, for all our Scotch ancestry, we MacCallums are not the stuff of great tragedy.

Except . . . except. Ah, words fail me but instinct does not, and in truth reason doesn't either.

Aleister, dear Aleister. After all that you have given me, how do I protect you from my father's wrath when he learns the

truth? Better to wait and name someone else, or some nameless someone else—some predator on the street who attacked
me while Father was away on business. I can make a good
case, or at least a reasonable one, for trying to put the whole
terrible matter behind me until my body made that impossible.

But if I tell Father a lie such as that, will guilt make him
belatedly do what the letter says he did? Will he force me to
give up the child? Will he always despise it? Before I make a
decision about this, I must confer with Aleister. He is the only
one who can help me, as he is the only one who understands
what has happened.

October 28. Aleister was furious when I explained about the
lie I wanted to tell my family. He says I must tell Father the
truth if only because he believes that Father has already
guessed it. I demanded that he explain.

"How many people died in the subway construction?" he
asked.

"Four," I replied.

"And your mother and brothers, when did they die?"

"Three years later than in the letter, but of the same illness."

"Where were they when that first round of influenza
struck."

"Visiting cousins in Scotland."

"A difficult trip for a woman and two small children don't
you think? Do you recall telling your father to send them
away?"

I shook my head. He must have known, but I had no idea
how.

"Why not ask him what happened. If the answer leads you
to believe that he knows part of the truth, tell it all to him."

Last evening, I did as Aleister asked, approaching the subject obliquely, surprised that he even understood my question.

"It was your friend, the little girl who would come and play
with you in the garden. She used to tell me so many things,
and all of them came true. When she warned me of your
mother's death, of course I listened."

"Dierdre?" I asked, incredulously. It had been years since

she'd visited me and until that moment, I had almost forgotten she'd ever existed.

"Yes, Dierdre." He spoke her name emphatically, and with just a hint of sorrow.

I told him, then, where she had come from, and why. I left out only the details of how he had died and the lewd aspects of the magick ceremony which had opened the door. I then explained my promise to Aleister and that I was going to have his child.

He knew about the door already! From the way he looked at me as I told him, he knew! He kissed my cheek. "You've sacrificed so much," he said, his voice soft and resigned, as if a part of his soul had died in that alternate reality, and could not be revived.

"Not so much, when through it I gave you back your life," I confessed. I'd begun to cry, so filled with relief and emotion that I did not see the sad surprise in his expression until I pulled away to look at him.

There was a pain in his eyes that had nothing to do with my plight, nor with the explanation I had just given him. No, it had been there for over a year. At night, I would wake and hear his footsteps in the hall. Sometimes, I would go into the sunroom and find him sitting there in the dark staring out the window into the yard, silent tears rolling down his cheeks as if he remembered his despair and could not quite shake it off.

This was how he looked at me while I told him what I'd done. For a long time after I finished he said nothing at all. When he finally spoke, his voice was wooden, drained of all but the shadow of life. "I'm leaving for Scotland on Monday," he said. "The business can survive without me for awhile now that Bob Dunglass is working with us. I think it's time I pay a long visit to Andrew. I'll be staying until the holidays, or perhaps until late spring if work can stand me gone so long."

I was expecting a child, and whatever scandal that would cause would be easier faced alone. Some men might have thought Father's act cowardly, but when I thanked him for his decision, he understood. "How are you going to explain the child?" he asked.

I hadn't considered anything beyond what I would tell him, but the first idea that came to me seemed the right one. "Al-

eister says he doesn't care how I explain except that I be truthful with you. So I think the child should be the result of some quick, doomed courtship with a soldier just back from the war who died before we could be married. I can refuse to name him out of respect for his family."

"Noble. Tragic. People will still talk but not so disparagingly, I think." He paused to turn away. He wiped away a tear, then spoke with more emphasis than I had heard in his voice for months. "Bridget, listen to me. If anything happens to me again, let me die as I let your mother and brothers die so many years ago."

"You knew it would happen?" I asked incredulously.

"I knew. Dierdre told me everything but I let it happen. I did it without asking your mother's permission, and felt as if I were their executioner. But I had to let them be at peace."

"Peace? I don't understand."

He seemed to be looking through me as he spoke, at the room around me and the rooms around that. "You were ten when the nightmares started, but you could hardly know about them since the boys and your mother were in Scotland when they began. Lucas started first. Three nights later Phil started dreaming as well. They would wake screaming that their throats were closing up and they couldn't breathe. Mother would go to them and hold their hands and try to calm them. She even resorted to giving them shots of brandy at night, but though it should have knocked them out quickly, the alcohol did no good. Neither did laudanum. If anything it made the nightmares worse, because now they couldn't wake from them. By day they were exhausted, at night terrified to sleep.

"Then, just before they returned from Scotland, Mother started having the dreams as well.

"Do you remember how she would walk the house at night, visiting your brothers' room? Can you remember how you would sometimes find her sleeping with one or the other of them? They all had these dreams, terrible ones. I was no fool. I saw that these had begun around the time they should have died.

"In time, I couldn't stand to be near them, and be reminded of what I had done. And so, when I learned what would happen that last time, I let it happen. It's only recently that I

*understand how right I was to let them go because now I've
began to dream as well. I know how I died, Bridget. I see
myself walk into the sunroom and take a seat by the window.
I feel all the despair that caused my decision. I wake with the
taste of gunoil and powder on my lips. And in some horrible
part of my mind, I remember feeling the impact of the bullet,
then my death.''*

I shook my head. I'd started to cry, from pity as well as
guilt.

*"Now I'm going to Andrew. I'll explain what's happened
to him and help him understand his nightmares."* He squeezed
my shoulders hard as he went on. *"If anything happens to me
or Andrew again, don't try to save us. The choice to claim a
soul belongs to God and no one else."*

"Will you remember that?" I asked.

*"I will. And, Bridget, thank you. You didn't really save a
life with what you did, you saved my soul from certain damnation.''*

"Is God that unjust?" I whispered. If he heard me, he gave
no indication.

*November 20. Two days after Father left and with his per-
mission to give this gift, Aleister moved into a small second-
floor apartment. I charge him a quarter of the usual rent and
give him full run of the sunroom in my apartment and rear
grounds. He didn't ask for it, but the letter I wrote myself
made it clear that he will have use for them and I wish to give
him something more in return for all he has given me. Now
that he has proven his power to me, like doubting Thomas, I
feel that I ought to support the work he does.*

*As for Aleister, I know that he recalls every sordid detail
of our night together. He's hinted often enough that he does,
and told me more than once that he would use me in another
ritual if I were willing. Though something in his presence still
repulses me, his occasional touch, his brief stolen kiss makes
me weak from desire.*

*That part of me remembers most and seeks that pleasure
again. He tells me it is my destiny to become the woman that
Leah cannot be. I ask him to explain and he hands me books
instead and tells me to study.*

I might if the books were more like the ones I'd read when I was younger. Instead they're filled with dry information on the proper poses for meditation, on the scientific basis of Eastern religion, on little tricks I can use to perfect my innate ability to practice magick as he does.

It's all so ridiculous! Angelina has a gift. I suppose Leah does as well. But from the night of our youthful excursion into spiritualism, I've had an interest in it, nothing more.

But even Angelina sides with Aleister on this, though she despises the man. She tells me that it is my duty to develop my talent. Fools both of them. Don't they understand that I have property to manage? And even with Mr. Dunglass picking up a good part of Father's work, I still feel I must help out there at least now when we're preparing the tunnel bids. So I hardly have time for such nonsense, though half the building seems to feel otherwise about themselves. Aleister's rituals seem to be dragging most of them in.

Two, however, are positively terrified about having him in the building, and have given notice. I'm sorry the family on the far end is leaving but I won't miss the old biddy from upstairs a bit. I do give her credit for facing the two of us directly to tell us why she was leaving. "I won't live in the same house with a man who worships the devil through ravishing women," she told us.

"My dear woman, whatever gave you the exaulted opinion that I would want to ravish you?" Aleister retorted before I could answer her.

"How dare you—" she began.

"Because daring is the only way to be certain one is still alive."

Her face reddened, more with anger than embarrassment. "I'm leaving this weekend," she said and slammed the door behind her as she left.

Thankfully, there's a shortage of apartments in the city these days. I'll have no problem finding someone to take her place. One of Aleister's supporters inquired about it the very next day.

There were other mundane entries concerning the firm, primarily a glowing account of Mr. Dunglass's business sense.

Dierdre could already see how someone like Grandmum would choose a business partner over a soul mate when picking a husband. Then Dierdre saw another name she recognized and began reading more carefully.

November 20. Tonight I took a stand against all the gossip in the Village and hosted a party for Aleister. Few of my friends came, of course, since they think I've lost my mind for having "The Beast" occupy the building. Angelina was one of the exceptions, arriving early and looking radiant in a deep green skirt and cream-colored blouse. Aleister's friends, however, showed up in abundance and they were undoubtedly as obnoxious in this present as in the one I altered—drunks and libertines of the lowest sort. But there were the surprises, too. A thin woman arrived carrying a violin which she played magnificently for most of the evening. A number of artists came by to admire the "Lost Souls" painting. Some reporter from the Evening World *showed up carrying a notebook. After a few drinks, he began asking guests what they thought of Aleister. I doubt he got more than two or three honest answers as everyone was so horribly drunk. I was thankful that I had followed my instincts and placed locks on my bedroom and library doors. At least nothing valuable will turn up missing unless the guests start walking off with the furniture.*

I found the crowd amusing at first, but soon overwhelming. I was about to retreat behind the locked library door when I saw a man about my own age standing just inside the doorway, his hat in his hand, looking not at Aleister or the German woman sitting on his lap in a near state of complete undress, but at me. I frowned and walked across the room to him. "Have we met?" I asked.

"I believe we have, but for the life of me I can't recall where," he replied. "My name is Noah Hathaway."

I knew his name, of course, from his brief mention in my letter to myself. But I couldn't understand how he could remember me. Later, I discovered him going through the drawers in my kitchen. When he began to describe my habits with uncomfortable accuracy, I pleaded confusion, but he held his ground, speaking reluctantly of my past as if he were afraid he would distress me. He did, but not at all for the reasons he suspected. I was irrational by the time he had finished, almost certain that Aleister was testing me. I pushed my way through the crowd and accused him of playing some horrible joke.

With one hand, he motioned for me to be silent. The other had long since slipped beneath the thin wisp of a slip the German woman still wore. He was rubbing the tip of her breast with the same sort of motion someone else might use to rub the carvings on a chair arm, paying little attention to the effect he was having on her or on my temper. Instead, he continued a discourse on eastern mysticism. It took a few minutes for him to finish, then he pushed the woman off his lap and turned his attention to me.

By then, of course, I was livid. It took him some time to calm me down. When he discovered what was going on, he laughed. "Stay close to that one," he told me. "Invite him to lunch tomorrow."

"You'll be there?" I asked Aleister, unwilling to be alone with the young man though he seemed harmless enough.

"I will. It's not often I meet a true adept," he replied, rubbing a finger down the side of my neck. I shivered. I couldn't help myself. He has that affect on me.

And "that effect" was similar, I think, to the one I was having on poor Mr. Hathaway. He sat alone in the corner, obviously uncomfortable in this odd company but unwilling to leave.

Late arrivals pushed into the apartment until half the crowd was forced to spill out the sunroom doors into the yard. I turned on the outside lights so that the guests could see where the lawn ended and the rose garden began. Someone squealed. I heard a lewd giggle. Moving closer to the window, I saw a small group in the shadows near the house. They were kissing each other, pulling at their clothes. I had an uncomfortable feeling that an orgy was about to begin. Someone else might have found it erotic or at least entertaining but my only inclination was to throw the lot of them—naked or otherwise—into the street. Aleister moved beside me. I was about to ask him if he planned to join his guests when I saw the tight set of his lips, the disapproval in his eyes. I'd expected him to be at least amused. "What's wrong?" I asked.

He stared out the window. The German woman had removed the few garments she'd been wearing. Many of the others had already shed their tops. "Fools!" he said. "Licentiousness without purpose. Why waste such a potent force as sex on such perfect pointlessness?"

"I suppose they would argue that they are paying tribute to Dionysus," I said, trying to sound droll and sophisticated in spite of my displeasure.

"Dionysus would demand that they display a bit more enthusiasm, don't you think?" he replied.

Astonishing! What was going on outside was actually making him uneasy. I watched the couples and trios go at it and sensed their forced ardor. I could not help but contrast it with what Aleister and I had done, the incredible passion in that working, the incredible result.

I've begun to understand that the man is lonely, hungry for someone with an intellect at least approaching his.

I left him standing at the window, poured myself another glass of wine and walked down the long hallway to the front room.

The lights had been turned off hours ago. The votive candles that had been lit to replace them were burned nearly to their bases and flickered in their colored glass bowls. Noah sat alone in the corner, his hat in one hand, a bottle of scotch in the other. I crouched beside him. "How did you get here?" I asked.

"Live here," he replied, then shook his head to clear it. "Drove," he corrected.

I took the bottle away from him and set it on a table on the other side of the room. "Well you're not driving now. You can stay here until you're up to going home." I locked myself in my room and went to bed. Just before dawn I decided to check on the house. The guests in the yard had gathered up their clothes and vanished, taking Noah with them.

November 21. Noah arrived precisely at noon, and sat stiffly in my parlor. He looked a bit ill from last night's excess. He again insisted that we had shared this apartment and may have had a private agreement to one day marry, but he could not recall ever meeting me before the previous night. I began to feel real pity for him, mixed with admiration at how un-

shakable his convictions were. "I understand that you have an apartment for rent," he said.

"Actually, there are two," I replied and described them.

"I'll take the two-bedroom one that's just above us," he said, referring to the end unit upstairs, the one just across the hall from where Aleister and Leah are living. *"I'd like to move in immediately."*

"You haven't even seen it yet," Aleister reminded him.

"No matter. I belong in this building," Noah replied and reached for my hand, just touching it before I jerked it away as if I had been burned.

"Give it to him. He's meant to be here," Aleister said, more by way of a suggestion than an order. I complied, though I had a strange misgiving about it.

After Noah had signed the lease and left, I asked Aleister if I could ever be truthful with the man.

"Not if you want to keep the door open," he replied. He walked back to the sunroom, pulling open the draperies I instinctively kept shut. *"What do you see?"* he asked.

I told him that the sky was a muted shade of pink through the outside window. The sky through the door closer to the center of the building, the opening we had created, was cloudy. It looked like it was about to rain seventy-two years ago.

"I see the rosy color of tonight's sky, nothing more. I helped you create this and I can't even glory in what I've done. This is for your family, no one else. If you try to speak of it to others, you'll likely end the magick. Besides, no one will believe you."

"Mr. Hathaway would," I retorted.

"So he would, all the more reason to keep it to yourself. You could become some man's errand girl."

"Never that," I said. My smile faded as I saw how he was watching me, the intensity in his golden eyes devoid of any friendliness or affection. Cats mate like this in the heat of a moment, I thought. I believe it was my last coherent thought, for my brain felt suddenly muddled.

He was kissing me, as he had undoubtedly kissed Leah. I responded. It was all the invitation he needed now that we were utterly alone. He pressed me close to him, his hands

*hurrying down the buttons on the back of my dress. When it
and the rest of my clothing lay in a heap on the floor, he knelt
in front of me and kissed my belly then lay the side of his face
against it. We remained that way for some time, both of us
meditating on the life growing within me. He said something,
softly, in a language of ritual and pulled me down to where
he crouched waiting at my feet.*

*Intense. Magnificent. Perhaps more than the last time, my
first time. And yet, there was something missing. In spite of
his words, spoken no doubt as a hasty afterthought to provide
some use for his lust, I felt there was no real purpose to our
coupling, and of course no anticipation of the act. I miss both.
Does this mean that I'm condemned to become what he is, an
adept obsessed with the acquisition of power, unable to feel
passion or love for its own sake?*

*Then I think of his strange confession concerning Leah.
Oddly, the thought of his love comforts me.*

*November 29. I haven't seen Aleister for the last two days,
nor have I heard him moving in the apartment upstairs. Once,
I went up and knocked softly to see if he was all right, but got
no answer. Later, when I went up again, I found a note on
the door—a rude one—saying I must not disturb him. I don't
know what it means but I sense that I am a part of it somehow.
This evening, though, I found him in my kitchen raiding the
refrigerator. He'd laid a banquet of cheese and bread and
cold meats across the table and was sampling a bit of everything, washing it all down with a bottle of brandy. He grinned
when he saw me, like a little child caught with the cookie jar.
"You'd let it all go stale anyway," he grumbled as if that
justified his rude intrusion.*

*"Noah rang you up. He'll be moving in on Saturday," he
added.*

*So he answers my calls as well. "Is anything here really
mine any longer?" I grumbled.*

*"Only what's in yours," he said, pointing to his head.
"Ideas are the only thing anyone really owns. You ought to
start working on acquiring a few of your own."*

*I scowled, but I understood what he meant. That night, for
the first time in so many years, I opened a book not related*

to school or to business. I fell into it like a man dying of thirst might an oasis pool. I was up half the night, astonished more by my interest than by what I was reading.

December 10. I wonder if Aleister and the others are right about me. I admit that I have been trying a few of the exercises. They seem silly, and impossible, but I have been able to focus on a candle flame and make it flicker through my will. Three nights ago as I lay on the edge of sleep, I felt my soul leave my body and move through the building stopping finally in Angelina's kitchen. I would have thought it one of those vivid dreams that seem to have come with my pregnancy but this morning Angelina commented on how strangely Buddha had been behaving and how she felt some presence in the room. She claims it's the work of spirits sent to encourage her that her studies are going well. I didn't contradict her. Let her believe whatever she will.

Noah moved in two days ago. He is with me as often as I allow it. The feelings I had for him in some other present are still real, and tinged with sadness. I've no interest with him in this life save for friendship, though he apparently is hoping for much more. I don't lead him on, but I don't dismiss him either. I've been hiding my condition well, but I can feel the pressure growing in my womb, the occasional nausea in the morning. In a few weeks my pregnancy will be apparent and I may lose even his companionship. I try not to think of the future when we're together; the moments with him are too precious to be ruined by regret.

And, ah, what he remembers! I hold on to some shred of a dream, he gives me the details. Then it all comes back. Today we both began to study the books Aleister has suggested I read. Noah is astonished by my belief in the man's magick— even though I dare not tell him the root of it!

Aleister is obviously pleased that I'm studying and tells me that hard work is the key to mastering magick. I don't think that's the entire truth. You have to be sensitive to the forces you are trying to control, and confident enough to handle the unexpected. I have no false modesty. I am aware that I possess both traits in abundance.

And one other thing is going as I hoped. Mr. Dunglass has

*been handling things at the office so splendidly that I finally
have the time to relax a bit and to travel through a New York
so different from today.*

*I find the excursions strange, and somewhat frightening as
I do not think the 1840s were as tolerant an era as that of
today. I do my best to fit in, but every slip makes me anxious.
I speak little when I'm there, but listen a great deal trying to
get a feel for the more common expressions and wondering
how best to fit in.*

*I finally decided to do a bit of shopping. The exchange has
been awkward. The choice seems to be between buying old
coins now to spend in the past (far too expensive) or some
awkward sort of exchange of goods. I did find a pawn shop
in the past, located a few blocks south of the Square. I took
two plain gold rings back with me and sold them to the owner
for a fraction of what I paid for them today. I used the money
to purchase a pair of hats, a coat and some shoes. It didn't
go very far. I'm certain the pawnbroker gyped me. I'll have
to think of some other, less costly way, perhaps a store that
sells stage costumes or a seamstress with an eye for historical
detail. I'm certain Noah would know of one since he's so
interested in the theater.*

*November 15. Leah came north for a visit and brought her
son, Hansi, with her. He's a nervous child, up half the night
with cholic. Their nursery is right above my bedroom. Last
night I heard him scream for two hours and finally went into
Father's bedroom so I could get some sleep. I wondered how
I will behave when I have my own child, and pray that I will
be patient.*

*When I woke late this morning, I discovered Aleister sitting
in a puddle of sunlight in the center of my garden. He was
naked and crosslegged on the cheetah skin, deep in meditation. Pens and papers and books were scattered across the
sunroom floor. I have no idea how he got in without a key,
but it looks as if he means to stay for a time. So it is happening
that some of the most important aspects of the events I altered
are starting to realize themselves in spite of what I've done. I
think of Father and Andrew and shiver as if someone were
walking on the graves they should have occupied.*

FOURTEEN

Though she'd been reading far less than two hours, Dierdre put the book aside. The information was incredible, and best doled out in small batches if she was going to make any sense of it at all. Her head hurt. When she stood she felt a bit shaky, then realized that it was after three and she hadn't eaten anything all day. She went into the kitchen to fix a sandwich. She'd just sat down to eat it when the locksmith arrived.

He'd been in business nearly thirty years, he told her. "And business was never so good as this year. Too many people look for an easy way to get rich. Now, how'd you part company with your keys?"

"In a restaurant. I went to get a second cup of coffee and someone lifted them off the table. I don't think they have any idea where I live but I can't be sure."

"How'd you get back in here?"

"The neighbor has a set. Fortunately, he was home."

"Don't give them out to anyone. Not ever. You can never tell who's a crook in this town. Psychopaths and saints look alike. Crazy, every one of 'em. That's why they live here."

"And you?"

"I'm from Queens." He paused. She suspected that she was supposed to laugh, but wasn't certain. "Any more entry points?" he asked.

She showed him the front and side windows. He sold her a set of security bars that would keep the windows from being raised more than a few inches. "Anything in the back?" he asked, pointing toward the closed sunroom doors.

"They're fine," Dierdre said. "You've done more than enough."

"You sure? You can never be too certain."

"I'm sure."

While she wrote him a check from Grandmum's checkbook, the locksmith dug through his toolcase, pulling out a handful of pamphlets on crime prevention. "Now you read these, hon," he said as he handed them to her. "Losing keys is bad enough. There's a lot worse that could've happened to you. I see it every day."

She showed him to the door, thinking that con artists ought to be on this list as well. He'd been in her apartment twenty minutes. He'd charged her $250.

Before putting away the checkbook, she paused to look at what had been paid out. There were the usual checks for taxes and repairs, a small one to Angelina, and one for $500 for Bill. Grandmum must have had her reasons, probably something connected to the computer work. Dierdre decided to ask her about it next time they visited.

Now that the mystery of the door was at least partially explained, she felt less apprehensive about it. She took her now-soggy sandwich into the sunroom and sat on the wicker chaise. As she ate, she considered what had been done on the floor and how the carvings had been made and annointed. And the yard, its tulips and crocus colorful in spite of the drizzly day; what might she see if she simply sat and watched the yard?

Crowley and his minions caught up in pagan rituals. Grandmum herself in the center of them. Much better than home movies, far more flattering to the subject. No wonder Grandmum didn't bother with cable. What she had was much more interesting, but sad. Grandmum could view the events, but she could no longer be a part of them.

Some time later, Dierdre saw her much younger relation walk into the garden through the rear gate. She circled the lawn, no doubt inspecting the damage from the night before, then disappeared inside.

If the weather cleared, she'd be back. She'd sit on the bench and read. Now, decades later Dierdre could sit and watch her, just as Grandmum must have done. Dierdre had been no more than four when she'd first visited here and played in that yard. If she moved into this apartment and lived to her late seventies, Dierdre could watch herself.

The thought fascinated. Terrified. She wished she'd never come here, then thought of Noah. No, though she'd just met him, it was right that she'd come here, so right that Bridget might say the Fates had a hand in it.

And in less than two hours, she'd be with him again.

Laying aside the journal she went to shower and dress, this time in the long black skirt and blue chiffon blouse. Thinking of the dampness and the drafty car, she found a long wool coat trimmed in persian lamb and a black hat. They were going to explore the city and her only choice of shoes were the heels she'd worn the night before. Hardly appropriate, she thought, and decided to take a chance and wear the lace-up granny boots she already owned. She took one final look at herself in the bathroom mirror then walked purposefully to the doors. Holding her breath, she stepped through them.

The vertigo was less intense than the last two times, though still far from pleasant. No wonder she'd been so terrified when she was younger. She would have had no idea of what was happening to her. But then, there would have been Bridget, the company of a friend to reward her for stepping through.

The events of the night before had been hazy. But as soon as she moved into the past, they became clear, so clear that Dierdre actually blushed when she saw Grandmum . . . no, that was far too old a name for this woman . . . saw Bridget step outside. Bridget's hair was loose, hanging over her shoulders and the peach color shawl over the loose fitting dress hid her pregnancy to anyone who didn't know about it.

"Hello," she said to Dierdre and held out her arms. Dierdre took her hands but Bridget pulled her close, holding on tightly as if Dierdre would flee if she let go. "I wanted to say so much to you last night but it was hardly the time for a family reunion. It's been so long! I'm so glad you came when we'd have a chance to talk."

"For a bit. I'm meeting Noah soon."

They sat on the bench, knees touching. Bridget looked at

her intently then said, "So I have seventy-two years, is that what you've come back to tell me?"

"And two days, I think. At least that's what you told me."

"Ah, two days." Bridget shook her head and smiled sadly.

"I believe so. You said I am to come back and tell you the exact time. I don't think it's right but you insist. You said it was better for your soul."

"My soul? Ah, my soul may require a bit of deep cleaning by then. I suppose I should be thankful, in time I suspect I will be." She hesitated, then went on, "Since you told me this much, add a bit more. Will I die of some terrible disease?"

"A stroke. It will be quick, I think. You seemed all right when I saw you this morning, just tired and willing to let life pass." Dierdre went on, telling what little she knew, cut off only when the account became too detailed for Bridget's taste.

"Leave some things to chance, please," Bridget whispered.

"For myself, I'd prefer to leave all of it that way," Dierdre replied.

"You haven't had the opportunities I've had to experience things differently."

"So now can you take up stunt flying, mountain climbing, whatever you want and not worry about an accident?"

Bridget shook her head. "The future is never certain, and you don't want to take risks. I've seen what saving my father's life has done to him. I'm not sorry I did it, nor is he, but I'm certain that I don't ever want to be brought back from the dead, so to speak." She shivered and rubbed her arms. "It's getting colder. Let's go inside and have a quick cup of tea."

Dierdre followed her to the house, through the sunroom and into the kitchen. She sat, saying nothing, content to study the room she'd been in before. There were few changes, primarily in how cluttered everything seemed here. Papers were strewn across the table; some handwritten, others apparently ripped out of books. The handwriting wasn't in Grandmum's elegant script but a hasty scrawl intended for the writer's eyes only.

"Aleister," Grandmum said. "He said this is the most important work he's ever done and I'm a part of it. He rarely leaves the apartment anymore, and only allows guests so that he can keep his following."

"Is he here now?"

"We just passed him, child. He's meditating in the sun-room."

Dierdre glanced in. It took a moment then, yes, she did see the man, sitting motionless on the floor to the right of the window. There was nothing odd about his clothing, or the absence of it, except that she couldn't imagine how she'd gone by without noticing him.

"He's so remote when he's working," Bridget said. "He'll probably join us later. I can't wait for you to meet him when he's not with his crowd and showing off; he's almost human then. In the meantime, tell me the future, the better parts, that is."

"Well, I've met an old friend of yours, Angelina Petra . . . ah, Laughran."

"Angelina! Is she still alive?"

"And still working."

"Really? Séances?"

"Readings. She said seances are too draining, but she's very busy. And she still lives in her same apartment."

"Well, how could she move out with all that clutter? It is still cluttered, isn't it?"

"A complete mess," Dierdre admitted.

"Well, I'm glad some things don't change and that she's well. And the others? Leah and Hansi and the rest?"

"I don't know anything about them."

Bridget frowned. "I suppose they would be awfully old. We can't all live damn near a century."

What did Dierdre sense in her tone? Triumph. Self-satisfaction. It seemed terribly cold, disinterested. "Angelina says you have a marvelous gift for second sight," she said.

Bridget frowned. "I suppose she would call it that, since she had no idea what it really is. But I don't think it's a gift, really; there are too many obligations which come attached to it."

"I've already seen some of them," Dierdre said. "I'm meeting Noah soon but I want to talk to Aleister before then. I'm worried about a fire that I believe will . . ."

"Kill Noah's nephews," Bridget said, finishing for her.

Dierdre nodded. "Who told you?" she asked.

"You did. Such a long time ago that you probably don't

remember. I've tried to prevent it, but there's nothing I can do.''

''You're speaking of something that hasn't happened yet,'' Dierdre reminded her.

''I do what I can,'' Bridget said. ''Did you see how careful I was to extinguish the fire in the yard? Did you see the men at the doors, placed there to keep anyone from going inside while the ritual was in force? Before that, I told Noah I didn't like the boys upstairs so that he would send them away. The second time they came, I all but sat in the lap of Noah's brother-in-law so his sister would demand they cut their visit short. I'll tell you what the moral is, dear. Some things are better left to the Fates, or to God if you prefer to call them that.''

''But we may be the ones responsible,'' Dierdre said. ''Angelina believes a ritual caused the fire.''

Bridget shook her head. ''I've done my best to assure that won't happen. I'll continue to do so. That's all I can do. Do you understand?''

''No, no I don't. Why not just tell Noah the truth. He'd keep the secret.''

''Things aren't that simple, dear. Besides, we all have a time to die just as we have a time to be reborn.''

This hardly sounded like the reborn Catholic woman Dierdre knew. She wanted to say as much, then ask a hundred questions, but it was too late. She heard Noah's voice calling to her then saw him walking through the doorway—the same doorway she'd just used to come here.

''Noah is taking me sightseeing,'' Dierdre said.

''And to dinner and to the theater afterward if she'll let me,'' Noah added.

If Bridget had any bit of romantic affection left for Noah, she gave no indication. Instead, she held out her arms again. As Dierdre hugged her, Bridget whispered, ''Not too long.''

''Or else what?'' Dierdre responded in the same low voice.

But Noah had moved close to kiss Bridget on the cheek and the woman never replied.

Well, whatever it was couldn't be too terrible, Dierdre decided. After all, she'd been with Noah for hours last night and all that had happened was that she'd gotten far too drunk and made a complete fool out of herself. A charming fool, though, if Noah's happiness at seeing her was any indication.

The afternoon was still, cool and overcast with a soft drizzle adding to the dreariness. After they got into his car, Noah took a wool blanket from the back seat, unfolded it and laid it over her legs. The gesture touched her more than his poetry or his earnest presence. She murmured a thank you and stared out the window, seeing little. Her mind was on Noah, and the attraction she felt for him.

Did it stem from his chivalry? She doubted it. More likely it came from the feeling that, unlike Frank, love for him would have to possess more meaning than a physical attraction and swift mutual agreement to a nocturnal meeting in some expensive hotel room.

God, she'd been so hungry for someone like this. Someone to cherish her. Then she'd found him, living right above her in what would soon be her building. Only decades separated them and now it seemed that even time could be ignored.

"Is something wrong? You seem so quiet today," Noah said.

She wiped the back of one hand over her eyes, slowly so he would not know she was wiping away tears. "It's the rain. I was hoping for sunnier weather," she said then turned toward him and laid her hand over his.

"So was I," he admitted. "I'd hoped we could drive out to White Plains or up Long Island and I could show you some of the countryside. With this weather, it will hardly be a pretty trip, so it's the city instead."

"You don't think much of New York, do you?"

"I'd probably find more excitement in it if I weren't constantly in the thick of things. That's why I spent most of a year's income on this motorcar. Now, at least, I can escape on weekends." He ran his fingers through his hair. When he spoke again, he tried to sound more cheerful. "I don't mean to say that I'm disgusted with it all. I'm not. I'm just not an urbanite at the core."

In her day, he'd have more options. He could live in the country and work in the city if he chose. Of course the country was not like his country and the city was filthier and far more crowded, and the world had little use for poets.

"What would you like to see?" he asked.

What could she request? She had no knowledge of what was here except, of course, for the huge stately edifices she could easily visit in her own time. "I don't know much about New York at all. But I would most like to see what you find interesting and beautiful." And it was more than a pragmatic answer; it was the truth. She wanted to know everything about him.

"Interesting? Well that's for later. Let's start with the beautiful, or at least the most beautiful places I can think of on such a dreary afternoon."

He headed west then north, down a road paralleling the Hudson River. Piers reached into the water like grasping hands, the tips of them lost in fog and mist. With the windows half open, Dierdre could hear the muted blasts of ships' whistles as they moved unseen through the water, the lonely response of fog horns.

"Could we stop?" she asked.

"In a little bit, not here. It's too dangerous," he replied.

They headed north, nearly another mile. The docks became wider and less frequent. Noah turned onto one of them, parking near a group of trucks and horse-drawn carts some distance down. He pulled an umbrella from behind his seat and walked around the car to help her out. "Bring the blanket," he suggested, then handed her the umbrella so he could wrap the blanket tightly around her shoulders.

"Come under it with me," she said and they walked close together down the dock.

On the south side, workers were unloading cargo from a Portuguese ship—crates of olives, oranges and lemons, figs and dates; casks of wine and brandy; cases of rum; wooden boxes filled with spices, the names stamped on their sides. The combined scents were marvelous; the voices of the workers, calling to each other in a dozen different languages, even more exotic.

"*The Conte de Savoia* comes into port four times a year. I like to stop by here then," Noah explained.

"All these marvelous things," Dierdre said.

"Venice and Morocco. Greece and southern Spain," he

said, rolling the names around in his mouth as if he could taste them.

"A lot of it seems to be alcohol," Dierdre noted, then wondered if she sounded like a prude.

"A high demand item since Congress passed the Eighteenth Amendment. Odd, most of my friends gave little thought to liquor before," Noah replied with obvious disgust.

"Prohibition?"

"Next January sixteenth most of this cargo will be illegal, not that the law will stop anyone's vices. Laws never do. I've got a half dozen cases of bourbon in storage. Even Bridget's laid in a few cases of port and sherry to take her through the next couple of years until the country comes to its senses."

"It's going to take a lot longer than that," Dierdre said.

"You may be right. Governments are notoriously pigheaded where morality is involved."

They continued on, past the workers to the end of the pier where an old man had set up a makeshift restaurant under a metal-roofed shelter. The stove was nothing more than a coal fire in a trash barrel and a huge cast iron pot on top of it. His offerings were mussels freshly steamed in wine and lathered with garlic butter, bottles of wine and shots of brandy.

"Red or white wine?" Noah asked.

"Red, please."

He bought them a bottle, and two dozen steamed mussels. The shellfish came wrapped in newspaper, accompanied by a pair of long wooden picks to pull them loose from their shells. It looked like it would a real trick trying to eat them standing up even if they weren't carrying a blanket and umbrella.

"Bring the wine," Noah said and headed down the pier.

A half dollar tip soon got them a sheltered spot on a quieter part of the ship's deck. They sat on a bench with the paper spread over their laps, pulling the sweet meat from the open shells and sharing swigs on the bottle.

A fitful wind blew out of the northwest, a sudden gust beating the mist against Dierdre's face. She caught her breath at the coldness of it, then laughed. "Don't apologize for the day, Noah. It's marvelous." She kissed him on the cheek, then rubbed off the spot of butter her lips had left with the back of her hand.

He glanced toward the nearest workers to see if anyone had noticed her gesture. "Noah," she whispered. "If they saw, they would think it charming." She moved her face closer to his and waited. But instead of kissing her, as he must have known she wanted, he brushed back a damp strand of her hair then wrapped his arms around her, holding her close.

"We should go; you're so cold," he said.

"I'll be fine."

"To the fire then. I'm freezing."

He wrapped the empty shells in the paper and they headed down the plank and toward the end of the pier. The air had grown colder, and the fog increased, rising off the warmer water. For a time it grew so thick that they could see nothing but the wooden pier beneath them, the boat looming like a dark spectre on one side. For a time the rest of the world ceased to exist.

"Noah," she whispered, loving the sound of his name on her lips.

"Yes?" He looked down at her, his blue eyes drained of all color, almost as gray as the fog itself.

"Noah, I don't think we're ever going to be more alone."

This time, he did kiss her, softly as if still not certain that was what she wanted. She linked her arm with his and they walked on to where the little fire was waiting, a tiny gold beacon in the pressing isolation.

They stayed at the fire for a time, finishing their wine while their jackets dried. Noah held the blanket close to the fire until the dense wool steamed. When it seemed more warm than damp, he wrapped it around her shoulders. "We should go. The fog may be lighter inland," he said.

As they approached Noah's car, they passed an old man loading fruits and vegetables onto a horse-drawn cart. "Por la señora," he said, handing her a tangerine.

"Have you ever thought of how marvelous it would be to just chuck it all and hop on one of those ships?" Dierdre asked as they drove.

"I've thought. It isn't possible. Just before I went off to school, I made an agreement with my father to always take care of my mother and sisters. His health was already failing. He died just after I got my degree."

"How long ago was that?"

"Eight years." He smiled at her astonishment. "Yes, I am a bit older than I look."

"Where are they now?"

"My sisters? Doing well enough, each in their own way. Sylvia married a banker. They have the boys who were staying at my apartment. Barbara is living in White Plains and taking care of my mother. My father left a decent pension and some savings. I send them money every month to supplement it."

"Are they well?"

"If my mother's lungs don't fail her, she'll probably live well into her eighties. I think my father was frightened that the money would run out long before she did. My younger sister, Barbara, is well physically. Emotionally, however . . . let's be polite and say that she's fragile and easily influenced. She took our father's death very hard. Some months after it, she converted to a particularly strict sect of Calvinism. Thankfully, she spends most of her time with a Bible study group then uses what few hours she las left in her day making dire moral pronouncements about our family and friends. Her minister holds her up as the epitome of virtue. Mother merely tolerates her. I try to do the same but I don't have Mother's patience. I suppose that's why I find Aleister's frank opinions about puritanism so refreshing."

"But you don't believe them, do you?"

"Not his morals, but the rest . . ." His voice trailed off. She could tell he had something important he wanted to say, but wasn't certain he should.

"Bridget has told me some of what he's capable of. What have you witnessed?"

"Not witnessed. Experienced. I'll tell you what I can just a bit later," he said. They drove away from the river in silence, past all the huge museums, turning finally into Central Park. As Noah had hoped, the fog was thinner here, thin enough that when he parked near a lake Dierdre could make out a pair of swans circling slowly in the dark water, and an outline of the sun behind the low-lying clouds.

The drizzle had stopped, and they decided to walk awhile through what Noah said was the wildest part of the Park. He led her down a set of wide steps and along a path that wound through a section of gorges and rocky outcroppings. Rhododendron grew everywhere, their leaves curled and wilted in the chill, the buds fully formed, waiting for warmer weather before they opened. The path curved down to the lake they'd seen earlier. There it widened so they could walk side by side. Noah took her hand. "You asked what makes me believe in Aleister's powers and I told you it was my own experience. This is what happened."

And in a logical tone of voice he told of encountering Aleister in the park, of going to Bridget's that evening and of realizing, with complete certainty, that he'd lived in that apartment not in some other life, but in this one.

"I have no idea how it can be but I actually saw myself sitting in her father's room, composing poems at the little desk in the corner. I even know how her father killed himself, though I didn't tell her so in any detail. Bridget was furious. She thought Aleister was playing some sort of nasty joke. He wasn't. I swear he never told me anything about her.

"But the oddest thing of all is that after he told her as much, her reaction to my story changed completely. I am convinced that she believes it as much as I do. All of this makes me certain that the man performed some sort of magick that changed things from the way they should have been."

"And what do you think you were to one another?" Dierdre asked, afraid to look at him and see some love in his expression when he answered.

"I think we were lovers or perhaps engaged. That isn't clear, but today it makes no difference. Bridget belongs to Aleister. No, not like Leah, the stupid fool; Bridget is much too practical to become his next scarlet woman, but she does believe and support him, and let him use her however he wishes." He shook his head and kissed the back of her hand then held it as he went on. "Whatever Bridget and I should have been to each other isn't important. It's as if we knew each other in a previous life, and in this one moved in different directions. I'm sorry for the loss, but resigned to it. I don't blame her. I blame him."

"And yet you believe in him."

"Believing is not the same as supporting, as any man of the cloth will be happy to tell you. Of course, they'd be speaking of the devil. I am too, I sometimes think. I know this must all sound crazy to you, but it's all the truth. I know it."

Dierdre stared out at the water, the pair of swans skimming the water, side by side. She considered what she'd read in Grandmum's journal. The hints of how deeply the woman had cared for Noah. Perhaps it was wrong for her to step between them. Perhaps she should be doing whatever she could to make the relationship whole again.

Dierdre thought of the child that would be born in a few months, and of the ritual she had witnessed last night, then of the people who had witnessed it. Noah had scarcely been able to kiss her when she asked him to. Even if he knew the truth about what Bridget had done, he'd never be able to forgive her.

Thank God his nature made her decision so easy.

She leaned against him, resting her head on his shoulder. "I believe you, Noah, because I feel that way toward you," she said slowly. "We've only known each other two days, yet now that I've found you, I haven't the strength to ignore the attraction and leave as I should."

He kissed the top of her head. "I'm glad you're so weak." He held her close, so close she could feel his heartbeat. "You'll be staying in New York, then?"

If she said no, whatever relationship they might have would be over. If she agreed, how could she ever explain those strange absences? "Yes," she replied thinking this wasn't really a lie and that everything could somehow be settled later.

They continued on the path, following the shoreline for a time then cutting overland in a long circle leading back to the stairs. Through it all, they saw only a few other hikers, most of them alone. She thought of the news account she'd read about the body found in the park. Would anyone dare to hike alone in this park in her time?

Noah checked his pocketwatch. "It's nearly six. We should think about a proper meal, served slowly somewhere warm so we can dry off."

"Someplace where there's a fire, if possible."

He thought a moment. "Do you like Hungarian food? We have some of the best in the world right in the Village. It's early enough that we should have our choice of tables and when it's this cold there's sure to be a fire."

FIFTEEN

He was right about the hour. Though this would be the beginning of dinnertime rush in Calgary, there were only a handful of patrons scattered through the little restaurant. The walls were paneled in dark wood, warmed by gaslights along the walls and candles on every table. The floor was thickly carpeted. A stone fireplace dominated one wall; its blaze flickering on the crimson tablecloths. The maitre d', a bald man of about sixty who looked as if he'd made a hundred too many trips to the pastry cart, eyed them with disdain. "Sir, you need to wear a tie to dine here," he said. His accent was Hungarian and from the protective way he spoke Dierdre guessed he was the owner.

"I'm sorry. I hope you can make an exception."

"No. No exceptions." The man crossed his arms and moved to the center of dining room doorway.

"Then perhaps you have one I could borrow?"

"Gentlemen, sir, know to bring their own."

"It's all right, Noah," she whispered to him. "We can go somewhere else."

"I promised a fire, and a fire we shall have. Give me a moment," he said, and drew the man aside, speaking low and earnestly. Dierdre couldn't hear the conversation but from the way the man's expression slowly changed, Noah must have been persuasive.

"Of course," the man said with a wide grin. "I understand

completely. We'll make an exception.'' He led them to the table closest to its blaze. "If it gets too warm, we move you," he told them.

They'd just settled in when the sole waiter on duty at that hour brought them two snifters of brandy and a tray of cheese spread and rye rolls. "I didn't order . . ." Noah began.

"Julius says it is on the house. To help the lady warm up." The young man winked and moved to another table to take an order.

Dierdre pushed her damp hair back from her forehead and covered her smile with her hand. "Noah, what on earth did you tell him?" she whispered.

"I told him that we met in this restaurant. I said that I had decided to ask you to marry me while we were out walking this afternoon and that here was the only right place to do it. I added that I hoped you wouldn't die of exposure before the wedding."

"You must be a great actor."

"Actor! Why wouldn't they believe me after the day we've had?" He leaned back in his chair and stared at her with a vague contented smile. "Just look at us."

Dierdre knew that if she were looking in a mirror, she would see that she was blushing. Usually it took an unexpected insult joke or crude remark to redden her cheeks. Not tonight. Her emotions were too obvious, too strong.

They started with clear chicken broth and fluffy liver dumplings, followed with a plate of spicy goulash and spaetzle. Dessert was spectacular, apricot jam folded into a sort of crepe and flamed with spiced brandy. Through it all they said little more than an occasional comment on the meal. Noah seemed content to just be with her, and Dierdre, thankful she had no awkward questions to answer, managed to relax.

The waiter brought the final course, brandy-spiked coffee heavily laden with sweet whipped cream and shaved chocolate. "When does the play begin?" she asked.

"Eight-thirty. We'll have time for another cup. We can even walk from here, if you like. After this meal it might be a good idea."

"After so much brandy, I'm not sure I could."

"I'll hold you up. I promise, and we're only going a couple of blocks."

"What are we seeing?"

"Two plays actually. The first, *The Peace that Passeth Understanding* is a Reed-sized slice of anarchism, I believe. One of the other members called it too experimental for his taste so he gave me his ticket with the comment that he'd outgrown Punch and Judy years ago. When I asked him what he meant, he refused to answer except to say I have to see for myself."

"Was it reviewed?"

"Yes. As I recall one of the critics said, 'there's always been a touch of socialism in the Provincetown presentations. Now they've gone completely Bolshevik. Not surprising given that the author of this month's trash is John Reed, who will likely live his last days in exile in Moscow.' Punch and Judy were never mentioned."

"What's it about?" Dierdre asked, wondering if she'd understand much of it.

"Versailles. Mr. Reed is apparently upset about the peace treaty." He explained something of Reed's checkered background as a journalist, Bolshevik and, some believed, Russian spy. "It's only the first offering though," he added, and said a few words about Susan Glaspell, the author of *Bernice*, the second play.

"You said you were a member of the players. Do you act?"

"I buy tickets which in a roundabout way makes me a member. I haven't missed one of these shows in the last two years. I don't find the regular theater nearly as interesting but if you prefer . . ."

"No, I specifically asked for interesting. I can see something on Broadway some other time."

"Good. This is the last night."

He signaled for the waiter. "Another cup of this please." The young man, who'd been hovering nearby, went off to get it. After he'd gone, Noah glanced in the direction of the maitre d' hovering just outside the dining room door, then at the other diners who all seemed to be trying not to stare at them. "Our waiter seems to have a talent for gossip," he said, then reached across the table and took both Dierdre's hands.

"Now, try to look happy or at least impressed, because my

dear it's time to make dour old Julius happy and propose. And so, my darling, I cannot survive another day without you. Would you do me the honor or becoming my lifemate, my beloved, my wife?''

He said it with such near sincerity that Dierdre suspected he would use nearly the same words were he ever to propose for real. As for herself, she responded in kind. "Yes! Oh, yes!" she said, loud enough for the diners nearby to hear. The restaurant broke into applause.

"I take that as a hopeful sign for the future," he whispered.

Someone started beating a fork against a waterglass. Others followed. Noah moved to her side of the table to kiss her. "If we want any peace, we'd better get out of here," Noah said.

He had to kiss her again at the doorway.

"A smart young man. He doesn't buy the ring until he gets answer," Julius confided to her while she waited for Noah to get her coat.

"A smarter young man than any I've ever met," Dierdre agreed. She felt dry and warm from the fire, the meal and the excellent brandy, and joyous enough that it seemed as if Noah had proposed and she could accept. When he came back with her coat and the maitre d' shook his hand, Dierdre actually expected Noah to invite him to the wedding.

Noah told her a little more about the theater company as they walked the few blocks east to MacDougal Street and the unimposing little storefront with the folding wood doors that had housed the players for the last year. The ticket box was nothing more than a weathered wooden table separated by a curtain from the playhouse proper. It was a narrow room, some fifty feet long with dark wooden pews for seats, a simple wooden stage and worn curtain with a faded tapestry design. The place reminded Dierdre less of a theater than a church.

Most the close seats were taken so she and Noah sat near the back. "All the better to make a hasty retreat over to Polly's if the play is too obscure," Noah whispered.

And it was, but interesting too, with its cardboard cutouts of political figures, and biting caricatures of Lloyd George and Woodrow Wilson. She understood perhaps one joke out of three, but most of the audience seemed to love it, applauding wildly when the farce was over.

Some of the group she'd met the night before were in the audience. She and Noah joined them in the lobby between the plays. The subject was political, and though Dierdre was cloudy on the details of the treaty, she knew the outcome of it. "We've stolen Germany's dignity," she said when asked her opinion. "Eventually, they'll want it back. In twenty years, we'll be back in Europe, fighting a war that will make this one seem nothing more than a skirmish."

The woman beside her frowned. "Do you really think so?" she asked.

"I think this would be an unwise time to have a child," Dierdre replied.

"And what about Russia?" someone else asked.

"Russia?" She considered how much to say before answering. "Russia will side with Germany at first. Later, they'll be betrayed and become our ally. They'll finish the war as a great power, almost equal to America itself."

She'd said the right thing. A man congratulated her on her sense of destiny, then introduced himself as John Reed. He asked her for the source of her information.

"Just my opinion," she replied.

"Well, a damn good one it is!" He shook her hand and was about to ask her another question when one of the women drew her aside.

"I hear Noah is living in that house on the Square," she whispered. "I'm worried about him."

Dierdre forced a smile. "Don't be."

"But with that man right across the hall from him. I hear they even hold séances or something in the yard. And Noah is so sensitive."

The woman was fishing for information, and Dierdre had no idea what to reply. "Things aren't nearly as scandalous as you've heard," she said. "I understand that Mr. Crowley spends most of his time writing."

"And fucking his landlady right under his own mistress's nose, or so I understand." She saw Dierdre's shocked expression, and hesitated a moment before going on. "I'm sorry. I shouldn't repeat such gossip."

"My *cousin* rents the man a room, that's all," Dierdre said then moved closer to Noah, taking his arm. "Could we go back inside and sit down?'' she asked. ''The open doors are giving me a chill.''

The playhouse proper was nearly empty and those still seated faced the stage. They paused in the shadow of the rear curtain long enough for a quick passionate kiss before taking their seats. Though the second play, a convoluted sort of ghost story, was probably excellent she had trouble following it. Her mind was fixed on Noah, his hand warm against hers, the fantasies she had of how the night would end. And yes, she had to admit it, on Bridget and Crowley and the gossip circulating about them.

When the play was over, most of the audience talked of going to the club upstairs for a drink. ''Should we?'' Noah asked her.

She shook her head. ''Take me home,'' she whispered.

They parked the car just off the Square and walked to the corner of Grandmum's building, close to where she had left Noah the night before. ''Just tell me the way,'' Noah said.

She faced him, pulling him close. ''I meant *your* home, Noah,'' she said.

He pulled away from her, reacting with the reserve she'd expected to see surface. ''So quickly,'' he mumbled.

''Doesn't that seem right, too?'' she asked and kissed him, putting all the passion she felt into that moment. He started to pull away then changed his mind and took her arm, holding her close as they walked down the street to the familiar white marble stairs, the tall entrance door.

The scent of incense was strong in the lower hallway, stronger still on the second floor landing. A drumming, so soft and deep that it was felt rather than heard, made it seem as if the building was alive, its huge heart beating slowly.

Dierdre stood at the top of the stairs, marveling at how little the space had changed. Only the foyer windows were different—clear and beveled now, amber in her present. Grandmum must have loved this place so much to have agreed to what she did. Dierdre, always the traveler, could nonetheless understand.

She heard Noah's door open, turned and saw him waiting for her, his expression almost grim, his eyes so brilliantly blue even in the dim light. She followed him inside. As soon as the door was shut, she kissed him again. She could feel his hands shaking a bit as they slid under her coat and moved over the soft fabric of her blouse. She could feel her own do the same as she held him, though for a different reason. She was afraid, perhaps irrationally so, that if she let him out of her sight even for a moment one or the other of them would vanish into some unknown past or uncharted future.

"A brandy?" he asked, more for himself than for her, she guessed.

She followed him to the kitchen. No sign of the boys, thank God, except for their photographs hanging in the hallway and a few chalk drawings taped to the refrigerator. The chalks were still on the table along with a stack of paper. "They left this morning. I haven't had a chance to clean up." He pulled a pair of glasses from the cupboard and dusted them out.

As he rummaged for the bottle in the cupboard, she asked, "Do they visit often?"

"A few times every year, why?"

She didn't want to frighten him, so she chose her words carefully. "A feeling I have, one no less strong than yours when you stepped into Bridget's apartment. Don't let them stay here again, Noah. It isn't right considering what goes on downstairs. This is more than just a prudish opinion, believe me and promise me, please."

There, she'd said it. And to hell with Grandmum's warnings, and Crowley's dire predictions. She had her own instincts and she'd followed them.

His back was to her as he poured the drinks, but she could hear the concern in his voice. "Odd that you should feel so strongly about this. Angelina has said much the same thing. And though she likes them both, Bridget agrees."

"Then listen to all of us, Noah. Please?"

"All right. No boys here again. Is that enough?"

"Enough."

He handed her a glass, but the intimacy she'd felt had vanished, pushed away by her concern. She stepped away from him, walking to the back door. He opened it so she could walk onto his narrow back porch, scarcely wide enough for a single chair. But the view was marvelous. She could look over the alley to University Place and Broadway and the city beyond.

The golden gaslights on the road below were soft, diffused, no match for the brighter electric lights of the skyscrapers to the north. The sky was hazy, glowing. The silence so deep she held her breath. All the better to listen. It seemed that here, in a less hectic time, she was able to see the beauty of the buildings, the roads, even the people.

He moved behind her, standing just inside the door. Without thinking, she whispered, "Oz. Xanadu."

"Did you say something?" Noah asked.

"Say? No, just thinking aloud." Her heart was pounding. She would have to be more careful than this or someday she'd slip and give everything away.

"Can you point out where you live?"

"Not from here. Besides, that's not important."

"It is to me. Especially since I'm going to want to come round and see you tomorrow."

Even if she weren't such a mystery, he'd naturally want to know these details. And Dierdre didn't dare say a word. She felt a bit like Cinderella at the ball. She might even use the allusion if she were completely sure that the story wasn't some piece Disney had dusted out of obscurity before animating. "Give me a little time, please," she replied. "It's all so complicated."

"You're not married, are you?"

She turned and faced him. "Not married. Not engaged. Not even seeing anyone except for you. I'll tell you everything soon, though. I promise." She took a sip of the brandy and stepped inside, close to him. "This isn't a time for questions, Noah. Please, no more."

The breeze had mussed her hair. He pushed back a strand that had fallen into her face then fumbled with her scarf, his hands brushing her neck as he did, each touch sending a shiver to the tips of her breasts. Was it the man that aroused her, or the place? Or, admit it, the time?

She looked at the studs on his shirt, wondering if they unfastened through buttonholes or hooks or something less familiar. "Forgive me," she said. "I've never undressed a man before."

He looked at her with incredible relief, and she understood what he had been hinting about all evening. This would be his first time, and no matter what happened between them in the future, they would always share this bond.

She wished she'd never met Frank or had the two swift affairs before his, had never chosen to lose her virginity to someone whose face she could barely remember. She wanted this night to be as special for herself as it would be for Noah. Instead, she would have to settle for the being the more experienced—a role hardly suited to her in her own time. Here, though, things seemed so different that she almost felt the part.

"Are there any precautions I need to take?" he asked. "If so, I'm not prepared. That is, I never expected that tonight . . ."

Frank had been so careful about using protection. Even so, she knew that protection sometimes failed. Since she'd been more concerned about pregnancy than disease, she never let him near her during those times when failure might lead to conception. At least her affair with Frank allowed her some certainty now. She rested her fingertips on Noah's lips and answered, "It's all right, dearest."

For a long time they stood, pressed together, not moving, each waiting for the other to decide.

Finally, he stepped away and took both her hands, leading her down the hallway to the quiet warmth of his bedroom, to the narrow bed covered with a blue quilt with a handstitched wedding ring design.

He pulled this back, then turned his attention to her, moving slowly even while undressing her, as if the feel of every fabric-covered button sliding through its hole was a unique experience, the dainty lace trim of her bra almost as arousing as the flesh beneath. She'd worn her own, but doubted he was much of an expert on ladies' brassieres. If anything about it struck him as odd, he didn't comment on it. Instead, he laid it on top of the rest of her clothing in an orderly pile on the chair beside the bed.

She lay back on his pillow, smelling spice cologne and sweet pipe tobacco. She murmured something, indistinct even to herself as he pressed against her, then kissed her.

His hair was soft, and curled slightly when mussed. She couldn't see his expression in the dim light leaking in from the hall, but his eyes caught the light. They were moist, as if passion moved him to tears.

And at the end, when he moved inside her, slowly exploring, stopping often to hold himself back, she realized that this was the person she was seeking, and that the place was irrelevant as long as she had him.

Then with a cry of joy, his body released. He looked down at her, smiling at the wonder of her, and at the pleasure he had felt. She kissed the center of his chest, ran her nails lightly down the side of his hips. He shivered and burrowed deeper in her, trying to steal the last shred of passion, trying to find some source that would allow him to continue.

"Not yet," she whispered. "Later. We have time."

He rolled off her. She rested her head on his arm, her hand on his thigh. "It's too soon to say it, and I know I'll sound ingenuine, but I do love you," he said.

"I know," she replied. She wanted to say, I love you too, and no matter what happens I always will, but voicing her emotions came hard to her and any promise she made might prove impossible to keep.

She moved closer to him, pulling the blankets up to cover them both.

He was too near to vanish if she slept, she decided. But as she shut her eyes, she recalled the warning.

Not too long.

Or else what? Maybe she'd be trapped here, unable to return. Able finally to tell him the truth and more. That she loved him, and that she knew she had finally found her home.

How marvelous, she thought.

"I have to be at work early tomorrow. Mondays are always hectic," Noah said. "So I won't be here when you wake. But I want you to stay the night if you can. You can let yourself out, though, and lock the door behind you."

She wanted to say yes, to sleep beside him, but Bridget's vague warning kept coming back to her, each passing hour making it seem more urgent.

Not too long.

"I won't stay, then." She kissed him again and rolled out of bed. He started to do the same.

"It's all right," she said. "I can get home from here."

"You shouldn't be walking out there alone."

Alone! She wanted to laugh at the absurdity of his protectiveness. He had no idea about the era she came from, the sort of dangers women faced even by day. "It's all right," she repeated. "It's practically the same building, anyway."

He looked ready to argue, then must have seen the resolve in her expression and decided against it. "When will we see each other again?" he asked instead.

"Whenever you like." She slipped on her panties and bra, back to him, modest now that the urgency had ended.

"Friday night?" he asked.

"All right." She turned and kissed him, then began putting on her blouse.

"I can be home by five."

"I'll see you in the garden," she said.

"Which way are you going?" he asked.

"Not far. Just around the corner."

"Then I'll watch until you're out of sight."

She finished dressing quickly before he could change his mind, then waited while he put on a robe and followed her to the front door. Once there she stopped to kiss him good-bye, pressing her body against his, running her hands down his back, wishing she could tell him the truth, too frightened of the consequences to try.

He switched on the outside light for her. The stairs were dimly lit and she heard the radio playing softly from behind Bridget's door. It would be so easy to knock, but Noah was standing at the top of the stairs watching her. She turned and smiled up at him, and left.

It was after midnight. Monday morning. The street was silent, the air still hazy with fog. She walked to the end of the block and around it, down University Place and into the narrow Mews. All the while, she was aware of Noah watching her from the upstairs window. She waited in the darkness behind the fence, listening to the silence marred only by the occasional creak of a stable door and a distant harmonica played no doubt by some bored stable hand.

When she was certain that Noah must have returned to bed, she stole through the gate into Bridget's yard and up to the door.

The door was shut and the sunroom and kitchen dark as she approached it, but when she was less than a foot from it, she noticed that it was cracked open, the neon light above the modern stove still burning as she had left it. Taking a deep breath and preparing herself for the dizziness to come, she stepped through.

The vertigo was worse this time, so intense that she had to grip the door frame to keep from falling. Not certain she could walk, she leaned against the inside wall, breathing deeply and slowly. It didn't pass completely, just released her enough that she could make her way to the bedroom. As she undressed, she considered taking a shower, then decided against it. She would not wake with Noah beside her, but at least she'd have his scent on her, and the memory of what they'd done still wet between her thighs.

What better way to remember where she'd been, what she'd done, and how she felt about him.

I love him, she wrote on the notepad beside her bed, as if she would need one more reminder of him to jog her memory in the morning.

Letting her go off unescorted had run completely against everything Noah had been raised to do. He'd agreed only because he sensed that Dierdre was a lot like her cousin, and did not want to feel vulnerable. But he cherished her far too much not to worry. So he had gone to the front window as soon as she left and watched her walk to the corner. He had stood just inside balcony doors on the side and watched her make her way to the alley. When she moved out of sight, he went into the bedroom and cracked open the window. Listening closely, he could just make out the click of her hard-soled shoes on the brick lane. They stopped abruptly. There was no sound of a door opening, or as would be more likely, being shut and latched. It was as if the night had devoured her, leaving no trace.

He waited, holding his breath to make it easier to listen. Nothing.

He had just decided to slip on some clothes and go after her, when he heard the familiar click of metal against metal, someone opening the garden gate.

No light flowed from Bridget's doors and there was no moon. The only illumination came from the gaslights on the other side of the high brick wall and what little it shed on the garden was so dim he could make out only the hint of a shadow. Whoever it was moved along the walls, rather than walking straight across the lawn. He heard a step on the stone patio just outside Bridget's doors, nothing more. By the time he'd pushed open the screen whoever had had been there had gone inside.

Could Dierdre be staying with Bridget? If so, why wouldn't she just tell him that?

He could think of only one reason—Aleister Crowley.

He rushed to his front door, and cracked it open. He stood there a long time, listening to the dim murmur of the man's voice, Leah's occasional answer. Below, he heard Bridget's radio, playing softly, nothing more.

He waited nearly an hour, before giving up and going back to bed.

Perhaps his imagination had been playing tricks on him and there had been no one in the yard at all. Perhaps one of the stablehands had spilled straw in the alley and it had cushioned Dierdre's footsteps as she'd headed down the Mews. He'd have to trust her, he thought. Just as he'd trusted her with his body, and more, his love.

Still, the doubt remained. They had met under such strange circumstances and fallen in love so quickly. Was it odd to think that magick might be the cause of it all?

He didn't sleep well that night. On the way to work in the morning, he stopped at a florist to order roses. He sent these to Dierdre via Bridget's, with a note asking Bridget to see that Dierdre got them.

SIXTEEN

Every room at Hudson Manor had a clock on the wall, the LED variety with a light to show if it was before noon or after. All the better for the patients to note the passing of their final days, their long slow slide into oblivion.

Other residents could not be certain of the time they had left to live. Bridget knew. In the last day she'd moved past prayers for her soul to a more philosophical contemplation of what was to come. Possibly there would be an answer to those final, nagging questions. Does God exist? What happens when one dies? Is there any sort of afterlife at all?

Bridget believed in God; she had too much proof of His existence, or at least of the existence of something like Him. As for the rest, she suspected the worst—that there would be no answer; only another forced amnesia, another spin through another life with a new face, a new status and the same eternal questions.

She wondered if she would even have the capacity to ask them next time around. Hopefully she'd be reborn human, though some philosophies were less clear about this. She pictured Angelina coming back as a honeybee or common earthworm tending her plants from a different perspective. Had Noah already been reborn as a mourning dove, lost without a mate? She hoped she would be reborn human, though there might even be something to be said for being a hawk or a cat or better yet, some exotic sort of butterfly. Since souls that interacted together in one life were supposed to return together in the next, would Crowley return as a fat Venus flytrap with some sort of flytrap scent designed to lure unsuspecting virgin butterflies into his stretched and hungry maw?

Could butterflies be virgins or did they mate as caterpillars? If Bridget had the time she'd look up the fact. One more stupid question for the next life. Perhaps it would stay with her on a subconscious level and in the next spin of the wheel she would become a entomologist specializing in their study.

Ridiculous flights of fancy, hardly worthy of a woman who ought to be concerned with the state of her human soul. She'd taken care of a good part of that last night, doing the best she could with the help of a bewildered young priest who kept asking her to be more specific in relating her sins.

As if she could and still expect him to give her absolution.

Though it wasn't even lunchtime, she rang for an aide and requested one of the tranquilizers they were so fond of distributing. Hopefully it would calm her enough to let her have a bit of rest before Dierdre returned. The pill was just starting to take effect when Bill walked through the door. His expression looked serene with the willed calm he must adopt when on a frustrating sales call. She guessed that he was furious. "How's your work going?" she asked him.

"Terrible. I thought I was on to something important late last night and went downstairs to check a fact in one of your books. I discovered that Dierdre had changed the locks on me."

He looked so betrayed that she kept a straight face only with difficulty and commented, "She's not like me, Bill. She's not used to having near strangers walking in and out of her space at odd hours. I'm sure that once you talk to her you can reach . . ."

"Talk! She's never there to talk to. It was after midnight when I pounded on her door and she didn't answer. I expected that she might have spent the night here with you."

"She hasn't been here since yesterday afternoon." Bridget stared at him with a benign smile. She knew exactly where Dierdre had gone and why. "I expect that she'll stop by here late this afternoon."

"I'm surprised she's not here now considering how long

you—'' He stopped midsentence, but he'd already revealed too much.

"You read my journals, didn't you?" she asked.

He didn't answer directly. "Tell me how Crowley did it," he ordered.

"I don't remember. He didn't allow me to set any of the ritual down."

"Tell me the truth. I have a right to know."

"A right?" Bridget wanted to laugh at the absurdity of it. "You never had a right to half of what I gave you."

"Crumbs," he muttered.

"Given out of respect for his memory."

He frowned. "This isn't the time to lie. At least admit there was a certain thrill in having an avid student of the craft under your roof again."

"All right. I'll admit that it was good to see the books get some use. As for the rest, I swear that I don't remember. Given the circumstances, I was hardly concentrating on the words."

"Dierdre can ask him to write down the words for me."

"Why would he want to do that?"

"She can tell him who I am. I have a right."

"He'll argue that you have a right to figure things out for yourself the way he did, especially since you most likely have the talent to do it."

"I've tried! Don't you think I've tried?

"You've dabbled. Not much more than I did when I studied."

"You can hardly know what I've done." He sounded crushed, furious. She was too relaxed to care.

"I can. I watched the master at work, remember?" she reminded him.

"He wasn't like you or me," Bill countered.

The drug was moving through her, muting her anger and concern. "Actually, William, the oddest thing about him was how much he was like you and me." She shut her eyes. In a moment she was certain she wouldn't hear anything more he said. A blessing, she thought, wondering why she had put up with his antics for so long.

He took her hand and shook it, hard enough that she felt a wave of pain roll up her arm to her shoulder, her chest. "He must have given you some hint," Bill prompted.

"Hint?" She laughed. "Just one. He said he was the right wand and I the right cup. What magick we made together."

Crowley's face was forming in her mind, the eyes in sharper focus than the rest. Dreams were coming, marvelous ones in which she was young again and beautiful. Her dream self held out her hand.

From somewhere else she detected a soft growl of rage. She paid it no mind. It didn't concern her any more than the dull aches in her joints, the sharper pain in her shoulder or the slow, faltering rhythm of her weakening heart. With only hours of future remaining, it was better to concentrate on the past. Later, when Dierdre called her name, she'd force herself back. She had a sin to confess to the girl. The only one she had held back from the priest, the only one that might deny her heaven.

If heaven existed.

There was no nurse on duty when Dierdre arrived at Hudson. She scribbled her name on the guest log and headed down the hall to Grandmum's room. She'd gotten halfway there when she heard voices inside, speaking low and earnestly. By the time she reached the door to the room, she'd guessed that Grandmum had died.

Too early. Almost a whole day too early.

Dierdre had not said goodbye, not asked those final important questions. Nonetheless, Grandmum's unexpected death gave Dierdre a certain feeling of peace. Unlike Grandmum and her need for certitude, Dierdre preferred to think that some things were better left unexpected, to the whims of chance, of God.

Three aides were hovering over Grandmum like hungry buzzards. One of them saw her standing in the doorway, and pointed her out to Liz who came and took her arm and led her away from the room.

Liz glanced up and down the hall, then spoke in a whisper, most likely so the other residents wouldn't hear. "We tried to call you as soon as we discovered her, but you must have already left."

"I took my time getting over," Dierdre admitted.

"It probably would have made no difference. Bridget had been dead some time before we discovered her. If you like, we can go down the hall and go over the directions she left for her funeral."

"I'd like to see her first."

"You should wait. Let us clean her up and comb her hair, that sort of thing."

"Just for a moment," Dierdre responded, walking around the woman and into the room.

She stood at the end of the bed, staring down at the body. It looked so much smaller now, so much frailer without that spark of life in it. The eyes were shut, the head fallen to one side as if she had died in her sleep.

Died. Dierdre thought she would have some sense of finality now, some feeling of sorrow. There was none. She didn't mourn the woman. Somehow, she couldn't. But Dierdre did feel a terrible loss: that of the the one person who shared the secret of Crowley's magick.

"Have you done anything to her yet?" Dierdre asked.

"Nothing," Liz said, speaking from just behind her.

"Another stroke?"

"I assume so. Without an autopsy, we can hardly know. You can order one if you want it."

Dierdre considered the matter, then said, "No. It's not what she would have wanted."

Liz nodded. "Bridget would probably have agreed. And she was well into her nineties."

Dierdre stood there a moment longer. What words would she have said if she'd gotten here earlier? Would she have asked so many questions of a woman about to die? Was there anything more, really, to say but goodbye. She stood there a moment longer, then turned and followed Liz out of the room and down the hall.

The rest of the afternoon was spent at Waverly Funeral home. Its director, Sukie Hayes, was a brightly-dressed woman in her forties. She met Dierdre at the door and led her upstairs to a soothing office of plush green pile carpeting, leather chairs, incense and classical music. She had a brass ankh on the wall behind her desk and wore a gold crucifix on a chain around her neck. She poured Dierdre a chardonnay and herself a cup of coffee, then opened Grandmum's file.

As Dierdre expected, Grandmum had been thorough—choosing the funeral home and paying for the mortician's services in advance, picking out the clothes she would wear, the music that would be played, the psalm the priest should read. She had also selected a coffin, the sort that was rented rather than kept. After her cremation, her ashes were to be scattered through the garden. A fitting end, considering what had gone on there, Dierdre thought.

"She did make two rather unusual requests," the funeral director said. "The first was that the rest of her family be asked to remain in Scotland. She saw no reason for them to make a long trip just to stare at a body."

Dierdre nodded, thankful for Grandmum's courtesy.

"The second is more interesting. She wants her body kept intact for one week after her death before it is cremated."

"Did she give a reason?"

"She did, but I'd already guessed it. Certain religions believe that the soul remains with the body for some days after death. The soul cannot feel pain or pleasure but it watches over its abandoned shell and senses what is going on. Watching its former body reduced to ashes would be, as you can well imagine, unsettling even for a spirit. Many religions place the time of the soul's passing at two or three days. Bridget more than doubled that number, but then cautiousness is like her."

"You knew her?"

"My father worked for MacCallum Construction back when Bob Dunglass was running the firm. I didn't know her then, but later we met at a university class on Egyptian religions, one of those non-credit things. I saw her at a few other classes after that, then lost touch with her. Last month she showed up here, barely able to walk but with a mind as sharp as I remembered. We worked out the plans together. All you and I need do is choose the day. Will the day after tomorrow work for the service? I know it's only two days away but it's the easiest to fit in."

"Whatever works best for you is fine," Dierdre said.

Sukie Hayes handed Dierdre a copy of the file. "Now that

the business part is out of the way, let me show you the room.''

They returned to the main level and a huge center room across from the front entrance. ''We may need more space, so I'm keeping the room on the right vacant as well,'' the woman said.

''Should it be so big?'' Dierdre asked. ''Grandmum was so old, and with no immediate family here something smaller and more intimate might be better.''

''She knew a lot of people and she was worth a lot of money. Services like hers always draw a crowd.'' She took Dierdre downstairs to the smoking room, and showed her the corner where the coffee pot would be set up.

Dierdre went back to the woman's office and had another glass of wine. She was reluctant to leave this soft and comforting place and Sukie's understanding conversation, reluctant to face the phone calls she'd have to make to family and friends, to the visits that ought to be done in person to the tenants in the building.

It was nearly dark by the time Dierdre reached the house. She decided not to go into what was now her apartment just yet, not to face the responsibilities that would be impossible to ignore once she went inside. She needed a friend now, someone who would understand without explanations exactly what she was going through. With that in mind, she went in the next entrance and knocked on Angelina's door.

Angelina answered quickly, drew her inside and gave her a quick hug. ''You stay in here, child, until I get rid of the nuisance.''

Dierdre moved aside a stack of magazines and took a seat. Though she wasn't intending to eavesdrop, she heard Angelina speaking, low and earnestly, a man's occasional answer. They concluded a few minutes later and Angelina escorted the man to the door. He was young, wearing a well-pressed suit and designer tie and carrying a soft-sided briefcase so full of papers that he could only zip it half shut. He held himself so straight that he seemed puffed out, like some exotic male bird in a spring mating ritual. As he passed Dierdre, he winked. Dierdre was convinced that he would head to the nearest tavern and order drinks for the house.

As soon as he'd gone, Angelina suggested they go into the kitchen. On the way, she stopped to put away her deck of Tarot cards in a silk-lined box.

"A good reading?" Dierdre asked.

"Who needed a reading?" she replied and went in the kitchen, where she pulled a pair of jelly glasses from the cupboard and a bottle of rhine wine from the refrigerator. "The man was so simple. He couldn't come until 6:30. He shows up carrying half the office files with him. And he's so damn fastidious he doesn't even have a wrinkle in the crotch of his pants. Of course he's going to get the raise. I told him that if his firm is stupid enough to pass him by, he should quit outright and wait for a better offer. If they don't make it, someone else will." She laughed. "Stockbrokers. Lawyers. Accountants. They're all I see these days. And they pay so much for such easy advice, all of it about money. Now, years ago things were different. Then everyone wanted to know about romance. Romance was harder but a lot more interesting. Ten-thirty or so, isn't that when Bridget died?"

The question was so abrupt that Dierdre had to pause a moment to shift gears. "I just know it was sometime this morning," she said.

Angelina poured them each a drink. "A day earlier than she expected. I'm surprised she made a mistake."

"Maybe her abilities slipped a little."

"Possibly. But she passed on peacefully enough. I'm glad."

"You felt her?"

"Don't sound so surprised! The dead are my specialty, after all."

"It's just that I thought you had to be . . . well, looking for the soul, seeking it out?"

"Bridget was my oldest and closest friend. She sought me out. That ought to prove something to her."

"Prove?"

"That I'm not the damn fraud she thinks I am." She poured them each a drink and held up her glass. "Here's to you, Bridget. The most sensible friend I ever had."

"And my most interesting relation," Dierdre added.

They finished their drinks in silence. Dierdre stared out the rear doors into the garden, deep in twilight. Tears welled in her eyes, not for Grandmum who hardly seemed dead since Dierdre could go and talk to her any time, nor out of worry about the tasks facing her over the next few days. Rather, the tears came from the silence itself, and the secret she longed to reveal to this woman, or to anyone who would listen and understand.

Angelina held out her arms. Dierdre fell into them as she had so many times when she was young. And she cried.

Later, when her tears had run their course and left her exhausted, Angelina lit a pair of votive candles on the coffeetable and put a blanket over her. "You'll sleep better here tonight," she said.

Dierdre didn't argue. The flickering candles were comforting, the smell of incense calming. She shut her eyes and waited for sleep.

When it finally came, it wasn't surprising that she dreamed she'd been sitting with Grandmum at the end, conversing about some important matter. She'd expected to dream of Grandmum in this place. She'd also expected to recall the dream when she woke, but it faded soon after she'd opened her eyes, leaving her with an odd feeling, as if she had misplaced something important but could not recall precisely what it was.

SEVENTEEN

The following morning, the *New York Times* ran Grandmum's obituary, not the small-type sort Dierdre had expected but a three-column piece complete with a picture. It appeared to have been taken when Grandmum was in her early thirties and showed her standing beside her first husband, Bob Dunglass, at the ceremony opening the Holland Tunnel. Not to be outdone, the *New York Daily News* moved the story to the second page of their local section, and actually went so far as to describe Grandmum's death as the passing of a piece of New York history. Grandmum would have found this hilarious, though in the MacCallum family the notion of history was oddly skewed.

Dierdre had promised to send copies of the obituaries to Aberdeen. As she clipped them out, she wondered if she should make a copy of them for the deceased as well, then decided against it. Grandmum seemed to have far less interest in her death when she was younger.

That disinterest made Dierdre's predicament even the more difficult to resolve. It seemed to her that her own life had fallen into place when she met Noah. But her meeting him had depended on the time that Grandmum sent for her.

And the day of Grandmum's death had been wrong.

She considered this and what it might mean. It was only a day's difference, but a day might mean so much in the strange altered universe of her family. She might arrive in New York a day or two earlier than she did, might never brush past Noah on that first trip back in time, might never have spoken to him, or become his lover.

Then would she be condemned to dream of loving him as Grandmum had, with some vague, wistful feeling of regret? Would Noah have one more nebulous memory to add to all the others that so clearly troubled him?

But if she lied—or, rather, let the mistake stand—what would the consequences be? Grandmum had lived an incredibly active life, had seen the priest and Dierdre, had made it clear that she had said all she intended to say. She died in her sleep, and from her appearance and Angelina's belief, it had been peacefully. Few wouldn't envy her that death.

And yet, Dierdre sensed something wrong in that shift of time. As if the loss of that day meant that someone had been playing with the pattern of their lives.

Perhaps Dierdre was being too logical, but the feeling kept her awake most of the night, and nagged at her through the hectic day which followed, making her so forgetful that she finally resorted to sitting down and writing out a list for herself.

By the morning of the funeral, she still hadn't reached any decision about what to do. She had lots of time, over forty years to decide, she told herself, but it made no difference. She managed to put the matter out of her mind only after she reached the funeral home where Sukie Hayes was waiting for her.

The viewing room was filled with flowers. The huge spray of peach-colored roses over the casket had come from the family in Aberdeen. There were also ostentatious arrangements sent by the family business associates; and smaller, more artistic offerings from friends and tenants in the building, even one from Hudson Manor though Grandmum had hardly been there long enough to merit one.

"Would you like to see the body?" Sukie asked.

Better now than later, Dierdre thought, walking forward and looking down. She had been to six funerals in her life. Four were for women over seventy when they died. As a result, Dierdre was most surprised that she was surprised at all by what she saw.

Why was it that when old women died they always managed to acquire a diginity to their bodies that had never been there during the last years of life? Here was Grandmum, her hands delicately manicured and folded over her chest, her face carefully made up with a touch of blush on her cheeks, a bit of color on the sewn-shut lips and parchment eyelids, a little length to the lashes, and the last best effect, the pale pink spotlight that gave the illusion of life to dead flesh. She looked as elegant as Olympia Dukakis, as wise as Dierdre suspected that Katherine Hepburn must be. Perhaps she had looked like this just weeks before Dierdre had arrived her, making Dierdre wish that she had visited more often instead of putting so many miles between all but their voices on the telephone.

"She looks remarkably like herself," Sukie said, as if reading her mind. Dierdre smiled. Shut her eyes. Said a quick prayer.

Guests began arriving even before the viewing was scheduled to begin. Bankers in their Italian shoes and tailored suits offered carefully worded condolences. The building's tenants came next, most staying only a few minutes before going back to work. A few retired employees of the MacCallum firm clumped together in the corner, exchanging stories about their families and the past. An oddly matched group of friends— half of whom wore black or long Indian print dresses and had ankhs and pentagrams hanging from silver chains around their necks. The others were a divided group of society matrons in afternoon dresses and middle-aged women in power suits with purses big enough to accommodate both daytimers and cell phones. Local shopkeepers came as well, even Fat Albert himself, looking ready to burst the seams of his black three piece suit. He walked directly to the casket, crossed himself and knelt down so quickly he almost upset the kneeler, then stayed on his knees so long that Dierdre wondered if he needed assistance getting up. When he did finally push himself to his feet, he came over to Dierdre. Pressing her hand in both of his fleshy paws, he said a sincere condolence and, citing the need to get back for the late afternoon rush, left.

Angelina arrived later in the company of Mrs. Minelli, a woman in her late sixties whom Dierdre had met briefly when she'd visited the tenants the afternoon before. She was dressed

all in black and looked nervously at the crowd. She lived behind two key locks and a deadbolt, rarely setting foot out of
her apartment except to go to church, admitting only close
friends and young white delivery boys who had picture ID's
to hold up to her peephole.

The woman's latest phobia had been dubbed the South Central Killer by the news media. His third female victim had just
been found discarded in a dumpster behind the Ritz Carlton
Hotel. She went on at length about the method of strangling
and mutilation details, ignoring Angelina's reminders that the
killings had probably taken place miles away. Some of the
woman's paranoia rubbed off, until Dierdre began feeling a
bit nervous herself. Today, she was astonished the woman had
ventured out for something as formal and pointless as a wake.
The woman's oversized purse looked heavy. Dierdre suspected
a handgun or worse.

Angelina was dressed as colorfully as ever, with her only
sign of mourning the black ribbons in her long braids. Like
Albert, the two women stayed some time in front of the casket.
Mrs. Minelli said a decade of the rosary. Angelina's lips were
moving. Dierdre wondered if she was praying and if so, what
prayer. More likely, she was carrying on a conversation with
the deceased. Later she'd have to ask Angelina what Grandmum thought of it all.

Visitation had started at three. By five the crowd seemed to
hit its peak. Then the leeches arrived.

They didn't look like leeches, not the women with their
sensible flat shoes and tailored coordinates, nor the men in
their Dockers and sport jackets. They all had real sympathy in
their eyes as they expressed their condolences before inquiring
if Dierdre was part of the family. They all spoke in voices so
soft they seemed almost furtive, explaining how they had met
Ms. MacCallum at an opening at the Modern Art Museum, or
at a fundraiser for the Ellis Island restoration project. They
asked about Dierdre's relationship to the deceased, storing the
information in their internal data banks then responding with
the words they'd been programmed to say. "She was such an
enthusiastic supporter of our project to rescue stray dogs. She
was such a patron of our little theater group. You should come
to our fundraiser on Friday . . . Sunday . . . Tuesday. You'll

meet some people from the neighborhood . . . from our board
. . . from the national society.''

To the best of Dierdre's knowledge, Grandmum despised
dogs. If she had supported their project it was only to get rid
of the beasts soiling the sidewalk in front of the building. And
the closest thing Grandmum had to modern art in her apartment was a gilt-framed print of Lord Leighton's ''Flaming
June.'' She doubted that Grandmum had much to do with the
rest, either, but the proof would surely be in the records for
her checking account. She dutifully collected business cards
and pamphlets, until the press of mendacity became too overwhelming. When it did, she backed away from the group, leaving them proselytizing each other while she retreated to the
quiet sideroom that Sukie had not seen fit to open to the public.

The door was slightly ajar, and when she pushed it open,
she saw Bill standing behind it, facing the casket. She hadn't
seen him come in, and from his expression, she could well
understand why. Viewed from this quiet corner, the crowd
seemed far too intimidating for someone like him.

He glanced down at the pair of pamphlets in her hand and
shook his head. ''Isn't it astonishing how people who would
never dare approach the deceased for a handout think nothing
of approaching the heirs,'' he said.

''That's because they know I don't have Grandmum's
guts,'' Dierdre responded.

''You knew how to put me off pretty well. Maybe I should
have made more of a pest of myself just to keep you in practice.''

One of the women—the one representing the art museum—
saw her standing in the doorway, and started toward her. Bill
moved into the doorway, blocking the entrance. ''Sorry, this
room isn't open to the public,'' he said and shut the doors in
her face, just slowly enough to avoid seeming impolite.

''Thank you,'' Dierdre said. ''I needed a break from it all.''

''You don't have to go back in there, not yet at least. Once
the predators realize that you're out of reach, they'll leave in
search of easier prey and things will get civilized again. If you
like, I could find Sukie and ask her if we could hide out in
her office for an hour or so.''

"You know her?"

"We met when I brought Grandmum here to make the arrangements. Interesting woman. Quite a believer in reincarnation, which is odd in her profession. The only thing she doesn't do is cater the buffet after. Which reminds me, did the trays arrive on time?"

"An hour before I left. And they're beautiful. Thanks for suggesting the caterer."

"I get enough free meals through work that I know who's good and who's likely to poison the guests, that's all."

"Are you coming by after this is over?"

"I took the afternoon off. If I hadn't, I wouldn't be able to be here now."

Since he'd read the obituary, Bill had been more than helpful to her. He'd been the one to take her around to the tenants so she could inform them personally about Grandmum's death. He'd answered questions from the pesky reporter at some local Wiccan newspaper who'd wanted to do a feature on Grandmum's relationship with Crowley. He'd arranged for the family spray of flowers, as well as drinks and food for after the wake. He'd helped her and Angelina put together a list of people to invite to the house. Dierdre wondered if she'd been judging him harshly. After all, Grandmum had trusted him, and she'd known him for years. Angelina didn't approve of him, but the feeling was hardly a strong one and could stem from nothing more than a personality clash.

Bill cracked open the door and scanned the room. "The man in the jeans is leaving. The woman in the floral dress is still hovering around the casket. It's a smaller crowd all around. Want to make a break for it?"

"No, but I should go back out there. I'm the only close family here."

"Then here." He picked up the tissue box and held it out to her. "Take a couple of these. Is anyone gets too pushy, sniff loudly, cover your eyes and make a run for this door. I'll tackle anyone who tries to follow; I promise."

"No need to go that far. Just give me some support while I try to be as obnoxious as possible to anyone who deserves it."

For the next two hours, Dierdre stood in the back of the

room, beside Bill, as well as Angelina after Bill alerted the old psychic to her problem. Their presence attracted a number of other people from the neighborhood, all of whom created a buffer that kept the remaining leeches at bay.

There was no special end to the wake. No rosaries or sermons by some minister who barely knew the deceased or the family. Instead, Sukie made a quick announcement that viewing hours were over and began ushering the mourners outside.

Just before she left, Dierdre went the casket for one final moment alone with what had been her closest and favorite relation. "You're only dead now," she whispered. "Not in the past. Maybe not even in the future, if what you believe is true. I'll probably see you far more often now than I did when you were alive." If anyone had overheard her, they would have thought her mad. But the one odd thing about the moment was not her feelings, but the nagging certainty that this funeral was taking place exactly as planned at the wrong time. When she turned back to the crowd, the notion stayed with her, enough that she could almost see the forms of the people that hadn't been able to attend but might have on the following day, and a vague sort of translucence to a few who did.

She pulled a rose from the spray resting on top of the coffin. Should it have been pink instead of peach? She tried to put the matter from her mind as she laid it over Grandmum's clasped hands then walked outside into the late afternoon sun, and up the cab that Bill had hailed for them.

On the way back to the apartment, he rested his hand above hers. She didn't discourage him from what seemed more a gesture of sympathy than one of romance.

And if he misunderstood, she had plenty of time to set things right.

Angelina had left with Mrs. Minelli an hour before Dierdre. The two women had taken the keys to Grandmum's apartment, and settled in to meet any early guests. By the time Dierdre arrived, a handful of people had already stopped by, all of them tenants from the building until James Suskind, the family attorney, put in an appearance.

When he'd been younger, the man must have been irresistibly handsome, and age had only added interest to his features. He looked like someone Dierdre would trust in an office, a courtroom, or with the most incredible of secrets. "I would have come earlier but I'd scheduled clients for most of the afternoon and some matters were urgent," he explained.

Dierdre nodded then thanked him for coming, using a phrase she'd perfected throughout the afternoon, a sort of funereal mantra, far easier than trying to think of the right words for individuals she'd just met.

"Have you read the papers I sent over to you?"

"I glanced at them," Dierdre lied. In truth, she'd spent most of last evening trying to determine the meaning behind the intricate legal wording.

"They're mere formality, anyway; as is the reading of the will. But we should get it out of the way, along with any questions you might have."

"I have one now, if you don't mind."

"Mind? My dear, I'm the one who should be apologizing for even discussing such matters at a time like this. Now what is it?"

"This may sound silly, but Grandmum made it clear to me that she wished certain gifts to be given."

Her voice had fallen to a whisper. He responded in the same low tones. "You're speaking of the rents and the books in the library, those things?"

"Exactly. And my request is that you draw up a paper as soon as possible making certain that any heir of mine will be bound by her wishes until you're able to draw up a will for me."

"You have much in common with your great-grandmother. I'll have it ready when you stop by. And, Dierdre, New York may seem large and a bit frightening to someone used to smaller cities, but I wouldn't worry too much about your survival here."

"Unexpected things do happen, though. There's the lunatic drivers, the mumblers around the Square, even a serial killer on the loose, or so Mrs. Minelli tells me. I just want to be certain that Grandmum's wishes are followed."

"That I can promise you."

"Is tomorrow morning too soon for me to come by?"

"If you can wait until ten, after which I'll be free for an

early lunch. Maybe we can follow that with a little tour and I can put your mind at ease.''

Bill had joined them a moment before and heard the attorney's last comment. "God knows I've tried to do the same. I hope I've persuaded her to stay here, at least for awhile." He apologized for interrupting then said, "Mrs. Minelli wants an escort to her door. Is there anything you need while I'm out? A pound of coffee? A cup of cope?''

She laughed and took a quick walk to the dining room to the buffet spread along the massive cherry sideboard. "I can't think of anything," she told him when he returned.

Nonetheless, Bill was gone nearly an hour and returned with a dozen peach and yellow roses already arranged in a crystal vase. "It's not just the dead who should get flowers," he whispered to her. "So should heiresses, and people settling into new homes, and good friends. Besides the sideboard looks in need of some color.''

He headed down the hallway. She watched him go then turned her attention back to the couple sitting across from her. Later, when Bill still hadn't returned, she went looking for him. She found him, sitting on the wicker chaise in the sunroom, with a book open on his lap, his eyes fixed on the sunroom doors. She stood silently in the doorway a moment, then went back to her guests.

He couldn't see what she saw in those windows, and so she wondered what it was about his presence there that troubled her so much.

EIGHTEEN

James Suskind's office seemed typically New York. Located on the second floor of a converted brownstone a few blocks to the east of the Square, its entrance foyer offered such amenities as black and white ceramic floor tiles, cherry wainscotting and a resident mascot—a roach of such grand proportions that it might have been around as long as the building itself. It exited the building between Dierdre's feet, as if it had been waiting for someone to open the door to let it out. Probably just visiting its hopefully smaller progeny, Dierdre thought, as she watched it amble down the side of the structure and disappear into the cracked window of the tiny Italian restaurant in the basement. Though Dierdre knew that most restaurants in the older parts of any town had problems with roaches, she vowed to never eat there.

The attorney's office held none of the unpleasant surprises of the foyer. Instead it boasted hardwood floors and an ornate metal ceiling from which hung an antique-reproduction ceiling fan. Dierdre took off her coat and settled into the leather armchair beside the desk and began to study the legal papers Suskind handed her.

They seemed even more imposing than the ones she'd studied for hours the night before. Though she suspected that they'd be nearly indecipherable to someone whose brain worked correctly, she paged through them looking for sections she might understand. Those were probably the most important sections anyway. "Aren't you supposed to read the will to me?" she finally asked, somewhat hopefully.

He laughed. "My dear, we'd be here all day if I did that. Now if you turn to the middle of page three we can go over the most important parts."

Perhaps Grandmum had made him aware of her condition, or perhaps everyone had problems with such documents, but as soon as she was ready, Suskind began to summarize their content.

"First of all, Bridget transferred half her personal estate to your family some twelve years ago, but I suppose you're already aware of that. Before she did, she placed a small percent of it into a separate account which had grown through rental income from the building you've inherited. Two thirds of that account goes to you for your needs and the rest for expenses connected with the building."

"Taxes and upkeep. That sort of thing?"

"Exactly. And this arrangement will continue for as long as you live in the building."

"In her apartment, I suppose."

"That isn't specified, and you might want to pick something smaller."

"No," Dierdre thought of Noah and smiled. "That apartment will be just fine."

"Now if you decide you don't want the responsibility, you're free to keep the money alloted to you, and the bulk of the estate—"

"The building?"

"I'm sorry, the building. Should you leave it, all future rents will go to your brother, Mark, provided he resides on the property."

Mark would be able to see what she saw through the doors, but Dierdre doubted that her younger brother, reclusive to the point of eccentricity, would be up to the task of dealing with the responsibility of tenants let alone his ancestors. She looked at the list. Should Mark decline, there was cousin Moira—a far better choice, then Uncle Bertie, and so on. But all of these would be holding the building in trust for Dierdre's child, or Mark's should Dierdre remain childless.

She considered this odd, until she realized that it was likely that only she and Mark and their children would be able to move through that door.

"Bridget apparently believed in the importance of someone from your branch of the family residing in the building at all times. I hardly see the point of it. So many buildings in New York are managed by professional services."

"That wasn't Grandmum's way. And in that I agree with her," Dierdre countered. "Now as to her specific bequests?"

"We'll get to that in a moment. Before we do, I want you to have a look at the summary the Fairchild firm prepared on the building."

The sheet he handed her next was far easier for her to read, but she wasn't certain she understood it. "Is there a mistake? The monthly income is so . . . immense."

Suskind smiled and pointed out his window. "I don't care what anyone says about London or Hong Kong or San Francisco. The most expensive real estate in the world is here in Manhattan and you have just inherited one of the finest chunks of it."

"Nearly sixty thousand a month income? For nine flats."

"For six, actually, and all of them have offstreet parking though two are rented out separately. Parking alone is worth nearly a thousand a space in that area. The other three apartments are treated differently. Now as you'll note the city taxes reflect a property value of eight million which is hardly close to what it's worth. And the money in escrow for maintenance is summarized on the next page."

Dierdre turned to it. Again it took a moment for the amount to set in. She had been raised with the comfort of wealth when she needed to call on it, but this inheritance took her well beyond that, and since it was all hers, she would answer to no one on how she spent it.

The greatest gift in this inheritance was not the wealth itself, but the sudden and certain knowledge that it was not the curse it had been when she was younger. Her mother's veiled insult, *since when does a MacCallum NEED to work*, lost its sting. Of course, Dierdre would work, at whatever she chose. She could run a business or start up and manage some charitable foundation, and no one could criticize her mistakes. No one would even have to know until after she was dead, not even then if she wished it that way.

"I have a personal question to ask you. Are you in a serious relationship with anyone?"

She shook her head. "I was. Not anymore."

"Good. Now my advice to you may sound cold but it will save you a lot of difficulty later. Never get romantically involved with anyone without making it clear early on that you will require a prenuptual agreement," Suskind said.

Dierdre thought of trying to explain such a document to Noah. She almost smiled.

"Now that you understand the value of our local real estate, the bequests might have more impact. Turn to page five."

Listed there were the names she'd expected to see. Angelina Petra, rent frozen for life at $100 per month. Rhonda Minelli, rent frozen for life at $550 per month. And last, Bill Coleman, rent frozen for the next five years at $800 per month.

"I've never been able to get her to explain any of this."

"Angelina always lived in that building. I think she was born there," Dierdre said.

"And the other two?"

"Mrs. Minelli lived there when she was just a girl, I think. As for Bill, I really don't know but I'm sure Grandmum had her reasons."

"I used to tell her that she would be better off providing for them somewhere else."

"Better off?" Dierdre wanted to laugh. Grandmum had been worth eight figures. "She hardly needed to worry about a sinking standard of living. Besides that's their home," she said.

The other bequests were for specific sums to charity, and not nearly as much as Dierdre would have suspected. She asked Suskind about this.

"Until recently, she used to give more, much of it startup money for economic development projects. I think she backed off so you could pick your own groups to support."

He went on, summarizing other points in the document, handing her papers to sign. "I'll have my secretary make copies of these and send the originals over to you tomorrow," he said when they'd finished. "Any final questions before I take you to lunch?"

"Just two. First of all, I'm going to pick up the tab."

"My dear lady, under the circumstances I wouldn't have it otherwise. If I didn't have to be back at the office by two, I'd even suggest Lespinasse."

"Second, is there a store near here that specializes in old coins?"

"Three I know of, but the best is just a few blocks north of here on Tenth Street. There's a marvelous Kosher deli on the way, we could visit both places together if you wish."

"No, that won't be necessary. I'm sure I can manage that part on my own and I have a lot of other errands to run." A far better excuse than trying to explain that she wasn't after rare gold coins, but instead wanted a bit of dated folding money. Dierdre was more inclined to celebrate, not her inheritance but her decision to remain in the city, and she wanted to do so with Noah. No matter how uneasy it made him, tonight she would take care of the tab.

Though it was well before noon when she and Suskind left his office, the streets were already crowded. Unlike the exotic but decidedly American element in the Village, the pedestrians here seemed more ethnic. Their pace was also faster, and as they passed her by she heard bits of conversation in Greek and Italian and Yiddish. Was this the sort of life Grandmum had wanted her to have, she wondered—one of exotic, bustling aimlessness?

"I feel as if we're a part of a giant hive of disorganized bees," she confessed.

"Don't worry, it will pass," Suskind replied, then took her arm and steered her into a slower-moving lane near the center of the crowd.

The restaurant he'd chosen had well-padded booths separated from each other by high wooden backs. The layout allowed them a certain amount of privacy and cut down on the noise of the diners around them.

The lawyer was as entertaining a lunch companion as she'd expected, filling her in on a number of important New York survival skills. "Actually, you've already acquired the most important ones, you carry a handbag and keep it close to your body instead of relying on one of those shoulder danglers that invite petty crooks to cut and run.''

"My mother warned me about the bag. Bill Coleman showed me how to carry it.''

"He's been helpful to you?''

"Not as much as to Grandmum, but he was the first person to make me feel welcome here. There haven't been many.''

"Give that time. Most people you've met probably don't think you're staying so their psychic blinders are well in place. Once you're established here, you'll find it far from lonely.''

She stared out the window. The crowd had gotten thicker. An older woman stumbled, her palm white against the glass for a moment until she caught her balance and hurried on. "Where do you go for silence?'' she asked.

"Some people swear by the Hamptons or the country club estates up in White Plains, but those are mostly wealthy businessmen who are stuck in the city during the week. Since you can afford to be gone a few weeks at a time, I'd suggest getting a place in upstate New York or maybe Maine. You could even fly back to Calgary for a good part of the summer, visit your friends and avoid all the city heat. I can recommend a good management service to keep things in order while you're gone.''

Dierdre shook her head. "I'll handle things personally the way Grandmum did, at least for now.'' The waiter brought their meals and they fell silent for a time. "What sort of law do you practice?'' Dierdre eventually asked.

"I do estate planning and some business law.''

"Nothing criminal?''

"Well, there's my rates or so some of my clients tell me. But if you mean defense trials, not anymore. My ulcers don't allow it. However, civil and criminal law do occasionally overlap, particularly since most of my clients are so wealthy. For example, I have someone in the office who does nothing but background checks.''

"On those prospective spouses you mentioned?''

"And for landlords and occasionally for tenants. With Manhattan rents so high, a little extra security makes everyone feel more comfortable. Bridget used the service on occasion; you may find the need as well.'' He grinned. "Here I go, giving a pitch for my office when you're picking up the tab."

"Humor me, I'm an heiress."

The retort seemed wrong somehow, not to Suskind apparently, but to herself. It was too light, too callous. She should feel some sorrow, some regret, and far less euphoria. After all, she'd expected the inheritance to be huge.

Suskind must have seen her expression many times before. He leaned forward and took one of her hands in both of his. "It's right to feel the way you do. Your great-grandmother lived a long and enviably active life practically to the end. The only thing that puzzles me about her death is how she knew."

"That she was about to die?"

"It seemed that way. When you get the papers in the mail you'll see that she signed them in November, just weeks before her first stroke. No one else with her business sense would have waited so long."

"She had the gift of second sight, at least that's how Angelina Petra describes it."

Not a real answer, but one that seemed to satisfy him, and probably more believable than the truth. He changed the subject to theater, and they talked another hour before she left him standing on the sidewalk in front of the deli. He took her hands again, saying softly, "I want you to know, my dear, that you've made one friend here. Call me if you ever need help with anything, if only for a willing ear or a quick piece of advice." As she said what she hoped were appropriate thanks, she had the feeling, the oddly euphoric hope, that she would never see him again.

She headed down the street, trying to move as quickly as the foot traffic around her. She had a great deal to accomplish today, and half the day was already over.

The owner of the coin store could provide her with only a hundred dollars in paper money, forcing her to pay an exorbinant amount for twenty silver dollars. She might have added a pair of turn-of-the-century gold pieces but she suspected that the hundred or so dollars she'd collected would be more than enough for a night on the town in Old New York.

Main task accomplished, she asked the shopkeeper to recommend a place that specialized in antique clothing. For that she needed to take a cab. On the way there, she recalled how the crystal wineglass had been wrenched from her hand when she'd walked through the door. Not wanting to make too noticeable an entrance into Bridget's garden, she changed her request. "Not an antique clothing store, but one specializing in reproductions."

"You want a costume shop," the man said without looking at her.

"A theatrical resale store."

"Yes, costume shop." He seemed to double his speed as he pulled sharply into traffic, heading west on Fourteenth at an incredible clip, especially given the way he had to weave through traffic. Dierdre sat back and shut her eyes, consoling herself with the thought that Grandmum would never have named her heir if she was expected to die so soon after the reading of the will.

"Costume shop," the man repeated, as he pulled into an alley off Greenwich Avenue. The flavor of the street traffic reminded her of the Square but she wasn't certain how far they'd gone. "Could you wait?" she asked the driver.

"Fifteen minutes, meter on," he said.

She handed him ten dollars. "Twenty," she said, and went inside.

The dresses were a disappointment but she did managed to find a large-brimmed midnight-blue hat and matching fringed cape along with a close-fitting, cream-colored felt hat, both suited for accessorizing the rose silk gown already in her closet.

She left the store owner her size, the period she was interested in and her phone number, then caught the cabbie just as he was starting to pull away.

"I wait twenty-six minutes," he said.

"No doubt," she mumbled, her hand inside the shopping bag, her fingers carressing the soft blue wool.

NINETEEN

Home. Her home. "Now and then. Now and before," Dierdre whispered as she shut and locked the front door behind her. She paused then and listened, as if with so many people on the streets around her one of them must have found a way into the empty rooms.

Satisfied by the silence, she carried her purchases into the bedroom, unwrapped them and held them up to the rose silk gown. Yes, they'd do nicely, even for an evening at Sardi's or someplace equally fitting.

Perhaps she should make a quick crossing—yes, that was the right word—borrow Bridget's phone and make reservations for tomorrow night. She considered it, and decided not to. By all rights the funeral should be today or tomorrow, not yesterday. Not a time for celebrating, and especially not for sharing a planned celebration with the deceased herself.

Grandmum's kitchen had the unfamiliar scents of peppered beef and smoked turkey, sliced vegetables and salads, wine and spiced tea; leftover scents from yesterday's buffet mingled with the faint sweet smell of the flowers Bill had brought her, now brightening the center of the kitchen table. She looked at them as she waited for the answering machine to bring up the messages, thinking of how helpful he'd been yesterday, and how understanding.

The first call was from her mother in Aberdeen, the second from Bill who suggested that if she didn't want to be alone tonight, she should join him upstairs for dinner and a rented movie.

She phoned Bill and left a message on his machine telling him that she had other plans for the evening. That done, she started up the computer system. While Grandmum's files were being printed, she changed into comfortable leggings and an oversized sweater, then phoned her mother.

The conversation went exactly as Dierdre expected. Mother first wanted to know who, if any, of the family relations in the area had come to the funeral. As Dierdre expected, that conversation exhausted itself quickly, since only two distant cousins had bothered to attend and only briefly. That brought them to the real reason for Mother's call—to find out how much Dierdre had inherited.

"Six million and the building," Dierdre replied.

"You don't have to pay for its upkeep do you?" Mother actually sounded alarmed, as if Grandmum had planned to swindle Dierdre out of part of her inheritance.

Dierdre explained about the escrow account then the requirement that she remain in the building if she wished to keep possession of it.

"Good. I never liked you living out in that wilderness anyway. Now you can start doing something useful with your life. And when I come to visit, you can take me to Elaine's or wherever New Yorkers go to be seen these days."

"Give me a few months at least. By then I might have figured that out."

Mother lowered her voice, nearly to a whisper. "Don't hole up in the old place. I like to think you take after me and not the lunatics on your father's side."

By the time Dierdre got off the phone, she was convinced her mother planned to marry her off to Donald Trump. Would that make her wife number three or four? No matter. Struggling poets were more her type and now she could even afford one.

Duties out of the way, she took the printout of Grandmum's journal into the sunroom, lay down on the wicker lounger and opened it.

She hadn't gotten more than a few sentences into it when the phone rang again. It was Frank.

"You said I should call you when I got my schedule. Things were moved up suddenly. I'm at the Warwick now. Can we have dinner tonight?" he asked.

She tried to make an excuse but he was insistent. "It's not like you and the old woman were all that close," he said. "And I'll have to leave tomorrow morning. If time is so important, I can even meet you in the Village. Actually, I'd like to see the sort of place you inherited. I could swing by there, stop for a drink and we could eat somewhere close."

He stopped just short of begging. Did she really have such a dramatic effect on men? If so, this was a new trait, and a disturbing one. "All right, I'll meet you," she said wearily. "Any place you like."

He gave her a name and midtown address and a tentative time of 7:30. He told her he'd call back if he couldn't make reservations, something she suspected that he'd already done.

She wondered what sort of company she'd be and what she could possibly say to him when he asked how life in New York was treating her. Well, there wasn't any time to worry about it now; she had reading to do, and if she put it off, she wouldn't be decent company for him. After, well away from her apartment or his hotel, she would say not goodnight, but goodbye.

She grabbed the journal again and started over.

It began not with another old entry, but with a more recent one set off by parentheses, and probably added while Grandmum was typing the entries into her computer.

(Dierdre. Since the history is so important, I left unchanged the entries made immediately after Aleister and I opened the door. But it occurs to me that much of the truth of our family history is not set down in my journals let alone told to anyone. Some of it, like what I will describe below, is too troubling to relate to the family without a complete explanation. Other events only gained significance in time. But I want you to know all of it, if only to impress on you the responsibility you have inherited. These little asides will serve that purpose. I should also add, that I have skipped some of the original written entries. They aren't important to you or anyone, not even to me any longer.)

• • •

December 17. I received my first letter from Father today. He said the voyage was an easy one and he and Andrew have had a long talk about what transpired here. As I expected, Andrew would not accept the reality of any of it until Father accurately described the dreams my brother had been having (something Andrew had never described in his letters home) and explained the source of them. Andrew has always struck me as overly logical, but Father must have been persuasive, because Andrew professes to being a believer now. Father also sounds much wittier in his letter than I expected. I think being away from this house and the daytime reminder of his night terrors is good for him. I pray that he finds peace.

(I was such a fool, Dierdre. I believed him. If you read some years beyond the entries I have deciphered for you and put on this machine, you will see that Father's visit soon turned into a permanent move. The change was good for him. Perhaps it was in part the slow life in the country and the good Scotch air but he always sounded so upbeat in his letters.

(Then in the year 1925, at Andrew's insistence his wife later wrote me, Father and Andrew journeyed to Dover. They walked to a place where the cliffs rise high above the ocean. I suspect that Andrew must have believed he had been shot down near that place and it was those cliffs he'd seen just before his life ended. He thought that if he saw the place where it happened, he could somehow be at peace—or at least this is what I believe he said to Father.

(I don't know what happened, at least not all of it, though a local guide with them wrote me that soon after Andrew walked to the edge, he became dizzy and fell forward into the pounding sea below.

(The fall should have killed him but Father swore that he saw movement, some sign of Andrew struggling. Father had always been a physically fit man, as at home beside his work crew as he was in his office. And so he did what anyone who knew him would have expected. He pulled off his shoes and shirt, then climbed partway down the cliffs until he found a spot where he thought it safe to jump.

(The doctor who later examined their bodies said that Andrew's back had been broken in the fall and he died from being pounded against the rocks. Father's head had been split

*open. I did not ask if the blow had been to his forehead first.
I'm sure of it.*

*(So it came to be that Andrew died where he should have
died, just as Mother and my brothers died as they should have
died, tormented for years by dreams until their fate came to
pass. And father? Well, not the same way, but the rocks had
the same effect. It almost seems as if these deaths are fated to
happen, no matter how we try to change them.*

*(I like to think that those few extra years of life I gave to
both of them were useful, sometimes happy ones. I like to think
that Andrew's death was caused by a sudden fainting spell at
the place where he died. I think that I delude myself, then find
comfort only in Father's strength and his words to me—that
I had saved his soul.)*

*December 27. Last night Aleister had what he tells me will
be the last public ritual for some months. He also told a number of his supporters this as well, and because of it my apartment has never been more crowded. At the last minute, Leah,
Noah and I were transferring what valuables we could from
the library to my bedroom so that I would only have to lock
off one room. The event, as usual, cost Aleister nothing and
me only the price of a few boxes of crackers and some cheese.
Someone brought a half dozen bottles of scotch, someone else
three magnums of champagne, and so on. The party was fes-
tive and after guests began making phone calls to friends,
growing larger by the hour. Soon there were far too many for
even an outside gathering.*

*With his usual ruthless efficiency, Aleister moved through
the crowd, rudely dismissing the merely curious. I wasn't sorry
to see them go, for he tells me that they are always the most
trouble at these gatherings. Once they had gone, he more tact-
fully disposed of those of little financial or ritual value to him.
I watched him kiss his supporters on the cheeks, the lips, and
pat one young girl on the rump as he sent her out the door.
Good God, he revels in it!*

*Those left numbered nearly fifty, including Angelina and
Noah who were there less for the ritual than to give me some
assistance were things to get out of hand. It was still too large*

a gathering for the house. In spite of the weather, we moved the group outside.

Aleister had thought this might happen and planned for it well. We'd dug a fire ring in the center of the lawn, laid in bricks and filled it with part of the cord I'd bought to see the house through the winter. Though the night is still, I am mindful of the warnings concerning a fire and have placed buckets of water close to the house to protect it.

The drummers began the deep slow pounding. In any other location, the neighbors would be annoyed or worse but here the only neighbors are my tenants and the horses in the stables behind the building. Neither are likely to complain.

So the ritual began.

Leah, her dark hair loose on her shoulders, carried a brass urn of smoking incense to the stone rise near the back of the yard. The smoke seemed to have an affinity for her body, curling around her feet and legs as she began to shed one article of clothing after another until there was nothing left to anyone's imagination. As she held the urn above her head, she seemed too tall, too emaciated, as if life were trying to imitate Aleister's masterpiece—the "Dead Souls" painting for which she had posed.

As Aleister changed, Leah walked through the crowd, smoke falling from the urn. Someone coughed. Someone else tittered nervously. She seemed to take no notice of that or of anyone until the chanting abruptly stopped and Leah halted mid-stride.

She was standing in front of one of Aleister's wealthiest and most ardent supporters, a portly middle-aged woman who should best remain nameless since she obviously regretted her part in the rite before the night was over. I heard her soft cry of surprise as Leah set the urn on the ground between them. She seemed caught between flight and surrender as Leah kissed her on the lips and slowly began to remove her clothes, pausing after each article to murmur something to her, most likely words of support. Though it was too dark to see clearly, I am certain from her expression that the woman must have been blushing six shades of red but she was game enough, or believer enough, to stay where she was and let the rite continue. Just before moving on to the next chosen person, I saw

Leah lick her own finger then dip it into a tiny felt bag she wore around her neck. It came out coated with white powder which she placed on the woman's tongue. It must have been some sort of calming drug because it seemed to quiet her almost immediately.

(Calming drug! Well I had to set things down that way in the original journal, if only to protect myself should the little account ever fall into the wrong hands. It was heroin, of course, dear Aleister's drug of choice. He said it opened his mind to the spirits around him. He said that in its trance the spirits could talk to him, even dictate their messages. He said a great many things that would have been foolish coming from the mouth of a lesser person. I only know that though he used a great deal of it—mostly out of my presence since he knew I didn't approve—he never seemed to suffer any of the usual consequences, not even addiction. Perhaps this was due to some quirk in his makeup, or the rigid discipline described so well in Diary of a Drug Fiend. *Aleister might have said—had I ever asked—that it was only proof of his innate superiority to normal men; in short, his omnipotence. Sometimes I think that perhaps his "drug" was diluted to near impotency by some more innocuous powder, and his use more show than reality. I only know that while many of his supporters fell into the dark pit of addiction, losing family and fortunes to the murderous powder, Aleister throughout his life could always take it or leave it.*

(What a strange and remarkable man he was, Dierdre. And how odd that I only feel safe admitting such now, so close to the end of my life, so close to the time when God might object to this forgiving view of someone who considered himself His greatest adversary.)

Leah and the woman moved in front of two others. The four became eight. They danced round the fire, their self-consciousness gradually fading. Finally they served wine to the crowd around them. There was no passion in the rite. They might have been simply servants strangely unclothed. I suspect that Aleister had them all carefully in check and for good reason. When they passed an empty urn around for an offering to the gods, what the participants did not reveal in ardor they gave in funds. Even Noah contributed something, though he has hardly been one of Aleister's supporters of late. I cannot help but wonder if Aleister's powers caused the sudden loosening of everyone's wallets.

When the main goal of the night was safely stashed in the house, Leah went and stood in front of her lover, her priest. One of his arms cradled her breasts, one hand slipped between her thighs. With a single word, he changed the tone of the evening from controlled lust to uncontrolled passion.

I'd seen what followed before, but it never ceases to amaze me how quickly men and women with higher, nobler emotions can suddenly descend to the level of animals when plied with sufficient alcohol and mob fervor.

As was always the case with Aleister's rituals, there were more women than men in attendance. These set upon the naked males like voracious liliths. Only Aleister was allowed to pick his partners; only Leah, his scarlet woman, remained aloof. I have no idea if the pathetic men—though they hardly saw themselves as such—were up to the task of satisfying more than one or two of their partners, because I didn't stay in the yard to see. Instead I retreated to the house.

I wasn't surprised to discover Noah right behind me. He'd been drunk enough to stay for the beginning of the ritual, though I doubted that all of Aleister's powers would have been enough to force him to stay for the end.

I unlocked the cupboard where I kept my best Scotch. I poured us each a drink and we sat in the darkness of the sunroom. I faced the doors, glancing occasionally at the crowd, feeling less aroused than irritated as I wondered how much of my garden would have to be replanted in the spring. Through it all, I was aware of Noah watching me. The sounds from outside seemed muted, almost mystically so, the clinking of the ice in our glasses far louder, far more real, almost as revealing as speech would have been.

Outside things wound down, as physiology dictated they must. Everyone seemed to find their sanity quickly enough and followed with their clothes. There were none of the usual hangers-on except for the portly woman who was chosen first. She had dressed and was about to go when she began to sob uncontrollably. Leah put her arms around the woman but it did no good. Only a sharp word from Aleister quieted her but *it was still nearly an hour before she was composed enough to leave. Noah, dear that he is, drove her home.*

Aleister paid the December and January rent on the spot, then hoisted Leah over his shoulder. "The real rite begins soon," he declared and slapped her rump more playfully than hard. She screamed then laughed as he climbed the stairs with her as if he were scaling Everest and she nothing more than a half-loaded backpack.

Such a successful night for Aleister, but this morning when I found him in my sunroom, he seemed strangely subdued, unwilling to talk. He had a pile of papers on the floor in front of him, some already filled with symbols, others with notes. "The greatest work I will ever compose starts now," he said. "And you have helped me find the inspiration for it."

"Me?"

"The gods loved you. They listened. They gave you the gift we requested. They gave me one as well."

He pulled me down beside him. He kissed me, his tongue darting between my lips, pulling out as quickly; like a snake sensing the way into my soul. I wondered how I would react when he began unbuttoning my blouse, but he never did. Instead he let me go so quickly that I fell backwards, legs splayed. "Bring me some scotch and coffee," he ordered. "There's work to do."

Those were the last words he's spoken to me all day. When I put aside this journal for a bit and went into the kitchen, quietly, I stole a peek into the sunroom. He holds his pen tightly, like a dagger. He pays no attention to me.

Upstairs Hansi has begun to scream again. I wonder how Leah keeps from being driven insane by it.

December 28. Last night's silence in my apartment was irritating, if only because I was making every effort to maintain it and getting no notice, let alone thanks, for it. I finally went upstairs and knocked on Noah's door. He was off somewhere. I tried Leah's. She called for me to come in. I went through the apartment to her kitchen. The floor was filthy. There was a stack of dirty dishes in the sink, a bottle of Jameson whiskey open on the table, a saucer filled with it. Beside the saucer was a bottle of cream-colored liquid and a spoon. Hansi sat in his high chair, angrily beating a half-chewed cracker into soggy crumbs. Leah sat beside him. Her hair hung loose, tangled and unwashed. She probably hadn't done anything with it since the ritual last night, just as she hadn't bathed or even changed into clean clothes after she'd put her own back on.

"Have a drink," she mumbled and poured a spoonful of the liquid. I expected her to give it to Hansi, but instead she drank it, wrinkling her nose at its taste. I rinsed out a glass and sat across the table from her, watching as she tried to get Hansi to take a bit of milk. He batted the cup aside and lashed out at her like a little demon.

"What's wrong with him?" I asked.

"Teething." She dipped a finger in the brandy, slipped it between his clenched jaws and rubbed his gums with it.

"Teething. He's barely a year old."

"That's the worst time for teeth."

"Is it?" I stored the information for future reference. "What's in the bottle?"

"Something Aleister whipped up. It helps me sleep."

"Does it? I know something more effective." Without waiting for her reply, I poured a tablespoon of the brandy and slipped it into Hansi's mouth so quickly he never had a chance to push it away. His eyes became round, his mouth opened in surprise, as if his taste buds were in the back of his throat rather than on his tongue.

"You shouldn't have done that," Leah said. She tried to look angry but only managed to stifle a giggle.

"What did Aleister whip up?" I asked.

"Laudanum. A few grains of heroin. Valerian. I don't know the rest. It works, though."

"You shouldn't take that stuff."

"I know. I'm pregnant. Don't tell him, please. If you do, he'll make me stop."

She looked pathetic as she whined, pleaded. I didn't know what to do, so I took the bottle, found its cap next to the sink and put it in my pocket. "You tell him yourself or I will," I said. "Did you just find out?"

"I've known for two weeks but I won't tell him that."

"Are you sure? Have you seen a doctor?"

She shook her head, began to cry. "It feels just like last

*time, like I'm strung to my emotions and they're pulling me
here and there as if I'm some horrible overplayed puppet.''*

*I put my arms around her. I didn't know what else to do
except to suggest that she take a bath and fix her hair while
I watched Hansi.*

*I had to help her into the tub. Close up, I saw that she was
nothing more than skin over bones. I wondered where her
child would find its nourishment, and what would be left of
her when the pregnancy was over.*

*I left her in a tub half filled with water and went to check
on Hansi. The brandy had the effect I'd hoped. He'd fallen
asleep, his head resting on his arm, his dark hair flaked with
cracker crumbs. I carried him to his crib. His diaper needed
changing but there were some things I just didn't feel obli-
gated to handle.*

*I checked on Leah again. She'd dozed off. "I'm just getting
the shampoo for you," I called out as I passed her on the way
to the linen closet. I was pleased when she woke at the sound
of my voice.*

*With nothing left to accomplish, I left. The bottle was still
in my pocket, a comforting place for it. If Leah doesn't speak
to Aleister by tomorrow night, I'll do so.*

*Mother. Child. Lunatic messiah. Magick. Good Lord, what
have I gotten myself into? And where would I be if I hadn't?*

*(A poor and far more boring old lady, Dierdre. On this,
you can be sure.)*

*December 29. Leah never asked me for the bottle back. She
may have some more of it hidden away, but I doubt it. She
was far too nervous yesterday morning when she came down
to see me and ask me to be present when she told Aleister
about the child. She did so last night.*

*As she'd expected, he did not take the news well. He ex-
ploded then called her every name in his vocabulary. Some of
them scathed my ears; others, probably far worse, meant nothing to me. In fairness to him, I think he was more concerned
about Leah's health than upset about another child. She didn't
see things that way, reminding him that he was all too happy
to impregnate me.*

"And to take you in, and to raise that squawling little bastard as my own," he retorted.

"How dare you!" she said, her voice rising almost to the pitch of a scream. She lunged at him, her fingers clawing at his face. As he fought her off, they overturned an end table. In the next room, Hansi did what he was best suited for, he started to howl, his sounds adding another level to the mayhem.

I thought they could all use a dose of Aleister's soothing tonic but with their struggle going on between me and the door I had no choice but to move further back in their living room and watch things play out.

It was over as quickly as it began with Leah collapsed on the sofa and Aleister sitting beside her holding her hands and telling her that things would be all right. I went into the kitchen and brought back a towel moistened with cold water for him to lay across her forehead. He did, but not before blotting his own scratched face with it.

I fixed her some valerian tea, and put some in Hansi's bottle as well then left Aleister to take care of the situation. He joined me downstairs an hour later, carrying a small locked box.

"She and the boy are sleeping," he said. *"Hide this away somewhere for me. She doesn't need it. For the moment, neither do I."*

I didn't ask what it was, though I can guess. I did as he asked after he left. But then, I merely put it in a kitchen cupboard and sat with him. He looked older, sadder than I'd ever seen him.

"You said the child would be sickly," I reminded him, thinking that to anyone else it would hardly be the right thing to say.

"Not this child," he responded.

"You did something to it?"

"I don't have to; I just know."

January 4. Aleister was right. Last night Leah lost the baby. Throughout this seemingly long day, Angelina, Noah, Aleister and I took turns sitting with her. Sometimes she spoke to us, sometimes she swore. More often, she said nothing, just stared at the curtained window in her bedroom with glassy *eyes. She ate nothing until Aleister promised that after she was completely well, they'd try for another child, one conceived at a more auspicious time.*

He made it sound as if fate, not her addiction or his support of it, was to blame for her loss. It made her feel better. As for him, I doubt he felt any guilt in the first place though later he tenderly hand fed her, coaxing her to take every swallow of the soup I'd made.

At times like these, I am reminded of what he told me before we opened the door. In his own odd way he truly loves her.

January 12. After a week of frenzied writing, Aleister's inspiration ran dry. It may be Leah's condition. A pregnant Scarlet Woman is no less a vessel for his needs; but one getting over a deep depression can hardly muster the passion his work demands. And so Aleister has turned his attention to me. But though I may have let him use me before, I can't allow it now. It seems too much of a betrayal of my friendship with Leah, especially when she is still so weak, and fighting with what strength she has to overcome her addiction to the potions and powders he gave her.

She has become such a pitiful thing. Sometimes I don't know whether to cry with her or slap her until her defenses make her fight back. I think she needs a bit of both. As for Aleister, I think he is too harsh with her. He gives her nothing except the valerian and then only when she's so overwrought that she must sleep.

January 28. Aleister has turned into a hermit. He mediates in my sunroom and refuses to see anyone. He seems to have abandoned all attempts at seducing me, or anyone else for that matter, focusing instead on self-discipline as a means to inspiration. Since that virtue is so alien to his nature, it's requiring a great deal of effort, and I doubt that he's accomplishing anything with it. Still, he tries.

His aloof behavior is driving poor Leah insane. I fear for her life if she stays with him; and I fear even more if she goes, for she seems to have sacrificed every shred of decency and self-reliance when she decided to stay with him. And if she did leave, where would she go? Her family has all but disowned her. Her teaching position vanished when her pregnancy with Hansi began to show, and now there is no one in authority who hasn't read the newspapers' scandalous accounts of Aleister and his Scarlet Woman. With nothing else to do, she fawns over him when they're together. And when he comes into my sunroom to work, she camps outside my door like some stagestruck fan, waiting for me to exit so she can ask how Aleister is and if he has asked for her.

This afternoon while he was out replenishing whatever supplies he needs for his work, Leah came down to speak to me. We sat in my kitchen drinking coffee, saying nothing while Leah played nervously with her sugar spoon.

"He needs you," she blurted. "He tells me that he cannot do the work he must without you. I'm here to tell you that you should do what he asks. It's all right with me. I mean it's no different than when we hold a ritual, better even, since we're such good friends."

"Doesn't that make it worse?" I asked.

She looked on the verge of tears. I moved beside her and placed an arm over her shoulders. Had Aleister put her up to this? How could he be so utterly unconcerned about her feelings? "He said it can't be me. I don't understand. He won't explain." With that the old Leah reemerged from whatever shell he'd stuck her in, leaned against me and began to cry. "He says that his inspiration requires passion and until I find enough to go on living, I'll have none to spare for him."

Leah's lips twitched at the edges. I sensed her fear that he would leave her, a fear so strong it overrode everything else.

How Aleister must thirst for someone with spirit to defy him. How sad he must be to see the spirits of his chosen ones wither and die, drained by the power of his presence.

"He says that he needs you," she repeated. I can imagine him telling her this, speaking simply and without any display of passion or shame as if he wanted to hire me for some business position.

"No doubt he thinks he does," I said, and considered what we had done together, the incredible secret we share.

"I want it to be you. I want you to know that." She leaned forward and put her hand over mine. For a moment, it seemed that she might kiss me, beg me with her body. I imagined her *thin lips pressed against mine. The thought aroused nothing in me, not even pity.*

"Think about what I've told you," she said.

I didn't know how to answer, so I said nothing. This seemed to satisfy her. In a moment, she changed the subject, repeating some stupid gossip she'd heard about a neighbor. It seemed so trite somehow, so out of touch with our place in reality.

TWENTY

It was nearly five when Dierdre set the pages aside. Her head hurt from reading but she would have gone on if she hadn't made plans that evening. She felt impatient, uneasy. She could understand Grandmum's desire to know what had happened to these people, how their lives ended.

But that would be Grandmum's way of dealing with the matter, not hers. She'd already decided to read only up to the time she first entered the past. No need to know what happened afterwards when she was a part of things. She would find that future out as it unfolded, the way knowledge ought to come.

Sometime during the past few hours, Bill had come home. She could hear the muffled voices on his TV, his footsteps when he went to answer his phone. She waited a bit, then called him, to apologize directly for not being able to come to dinner.

"I understand. You probably have a lot to settle."

"Actually I have plans for dinner. And with so much to do, I should hardly be asking this, but does this building have cable?"

"It's included in the rent, even the premium channels. Doesn't yours work?"

"I don't even have an antenna."

"Do you have a line to the set?"

She put down the phone and checked. "I think Grandmum took it out."

"Or never had one in. I never saw a box on her TV."

"Do you have the cable company's phone number so I can call them?"

"You don't need it. There's cables for every apartment in the basement. All you need is a box to connect them to the set. I have a spare. Should I come down and give you a hand?"

She wanted to say no, to do nothing to encourage him. Yet, the thought of having the means to curl up with a drink and CNN or some mindless sitcom and put every strange event out of her mind for a few hours when the urge struck was too tempting. Besides, Bill was a neighbor and all she needed was a favor.

Soon, she was on hands and knees, wedged between the sofa and a living room wall, aiming a flashlight down a tiny drilled hole. "Can you see the light yet?" she called.

"Not just . . . wait a minute," he called from the basement. A metal connector came poking through. She grabbed and pulled out a few yards of cable, wedging it under a sofa leg while she went to unlock the door for him.

He had a box and a short set of cables in his hand. Within ten minutes he had the box hooked in and was sitting on the sofa arm admiring his work. "All you need is a VCR and you'll be set for anything. There's a good video store over on Seventh."

"I probably don't need one. I don't watch TV much. It's just that when I want it . . ."

"Believe me, I know. Stress reducer extraordinaire." He looked at the door, started toward it. "Well, I guess I'm done. You should call the cable company in the morning and tell them you're hooked in."

"Stay a little, have a drink. I have wine from the wake, and I think there's vodka and orange juice."

He followed her into the kitchen. "Are you going to stay here?"

"I guess so. I've inherited the building. You're mentioned in the will, by the way. Has the lawyer called you about it?"

"Yesterday. Angelina said she heard from him, too. Grandmum was a marvelous woman. A lot of people wouldn't have thought twice about their tenants."

"You were her friends. She was right to remember you."

"And I'm such a helpful sort of guy." He grinned.

She smiled in response, wondering why she'd been so reluctant to associate with him when an occasional dose of normalcy was just what she needed.

And he wasn't pushy the way she'd expected him to be. After one quick drink, he looked at the clock. "Early day tomorrow," he said. "And I have some calls to make before the last of the workaholics leave for home."

She started preparing for her evening out only an hour before she planned to leave. Though she'd intended to look casual, once she started putting on her make-up, she realized that the ending of their relationship should have a bit more drama, or at least some payback for how callously Frank had behaved in Calgary. She styled her hair, sweeping it back at the crown and turning the ends under in a fluffy bob. She added a bit more color to her cheeks, and chose a darker shade of lipstick, something to complement the black sheath that Frank loved. After one final appraisal in the full length mirror, she left to hail a taxi.

Bill was just coming in, carrying a bag of something that smelled like Indian take-out. He took a long appreciative look at her then whistled with friendly enthusiasm. "You said you were going out. I did't know it was a hot date."

"An old friend from Calgary, actually. I don't get a lot of chances to wear this dress."

"Find more," he suggested. "I guarantee you, you'll never have trouble hailing a cab in that."

Though Dierdre was a bit early, Frank had arrived before her. He sat at the black marble bar, staring at the patrons through the smoke-colored mirror behind it. He saw her coming when she was still a few yards away turned and whistled his approval. "You know I love that dress," he said. "Blondes always look so marvelous in mourning. Drink?"

She looked at the amber liquid in his glass. Frank was usually a vodka man. "Not your usual. What is it?"

"Manhattan. I figure when in New York . . ."

"You're no better than the Americans with their CC and Molson's at home."

"Another," Frank said to the bartender. "And . . . ?"

"Chardonnay," Dierdre said.

"Well, at least you haven't let the big city corrupt you."

"Not yet. It's trying, though."

They hadn't been a couple for more than three months, but here they were falling into the usual couples mode of conversation. It felt comfortable, normal; yet, everything had changed. Everything.

By the time they got her drinks, the maitre d' had their table ready, a secluded one in a quiet corner near the back. The room's walls and ceiling were smoke-glass mirrors, the carpet plush, the lighting dim. Every table had at least one candle, the larger ones in the center of the room trios of them. They reflected to infinity in the dark glass walls and ceiling, creating an illusion of spaciousness. It was the sort of place a boy might take his prom date in the hopes of seducing her, assuming the boy was very well off. She guessed the last because there were no prices on the menu.

"Menus like this make me nervous," she confessed.

"This is New York," he said as if he knew it so well.

Not her New York. "How's work?" she asked.

"Usual. Boring. I ran into your boss last night. He asked how things were. I didn't say anything about the funeral. I figured if you wanted to stay a week or two longer, I'd cover for you."

"How did you know that Grandmum had died?" She felt a twinge of conscience when she asked the last. She'd promised to call him so he could send flowers.

"After you left, I took to reading the *New York Times*. Hard to miss an obituary that size even if I hadn't been looking for it. When are you coming back?"

"I'm not."

"Smart girl! Get out of Cowtown while you can." He held up his glass, actually preparing to toast her decision. Didn't he realize that she was breaking it off for good?

Apparently not, because he continued. "I was hoping you'd decide to stay. There's no kind of life for you up there, or for me either. I was thinking how much more a good corporate attorney can make in a city like New York, that is, if you think we're ready.''

"Ready?"

"Well, if I relocate, I'll need a place to stay while I take a couple of law courses for passing the Bar and since yours is so large and we were planning to move in together—"

Incredible! He actually assumed she'd agree. So much for her notion of being irresistible; he thought her a pushover the way everyone else did. "Planning? You broke it off with me, remember?" she reminded him.

He played with the ice in his glass. "I was feeling damn insecure, Dee. I mean, I figured you were off to New York, that you wouldn't come back and I might as well just face the truth right away."

"You know I don't like crowds. Why did you think I would I want to stay here?''

"But you are . . . oh, I see. Well we could get a place somewhere close to the train line. With the kind of rents the Village charges, you could probably buy an estate out in the country and pay off the mortgage on the income from just your apartment.''

"I thought you didn't come to New York often. But you know the rental rates?''

He answered immediately, and smoothly, without a trace of guilt. "I admit that I looked at the *Times* classifieds. I was curious about where you were living."

Dierdre would have wagered that he'd done far more. At the very least, he knew the assessed value of the building. She was beginning to understand Suskind's blunt advice concerning prenuptial agreements and how wary she'd have to be even of men she thought she knew well.

She shifted the conversation to life in Calgary, information on shared friends. By the time their meals arrived he had steered it back to the subject of New York jobs and her suggestions on where they might live, along with another apology.

"I've never had the opportunity to give a person a second chance," she finally said, trying to sound upbeat, happy. She wanted to throw her glass of wine in his face. Instead she picked up her purse and headed for the restrooms. They were at the front of the restaurant between the coat room and the maitre d' station, out of sight of the dining room proper. No need for a scene, or even a parting harsh word.

She put on her coat. The maitre d' eyed her with a vague smile. "Your date just ordered our best champagne," he said.

"Did he? Well, he's welcome to it; on me." She paid the bill and went outside. At the corner, she hailed a cab.

Later, curled up on the sofa in the front room with a Fat Albert's Stuffed Turkey dripping cranberry sauce and mayonnaise on her dress, she watched two hours of sitcoms, more than enough mindless banter to clear away the stress of the last few hours. The phone rang a couple of times. She didn't answer it.

Nonetheless, she had odd dreams that night, and though she woke often she couldn't recall any of them.

It was nearly four-thirty when she heard Bill stomping around upstairs. Probably the normal start time for commuting to Boston, she thought, then rolled over and buried her head in the pillows.

The next morning—later than she'd planned—she settled into the kitchen with a cup of coffee and the morning paper. The national news was the same as always—talk of gun control and drug control and increased defense spending and crime as the United States played superpower while the country went to hell. At least it had been a peaceful day in her part of it. No local murders, not even a rape or shooting. Did that mean she could feel a little safer or that she should be particularly wary? No matter, she wasn't planning on being *here* tonight anyway.

With the past fast approaching, it seemed best to get on with the reading. She settled into the same place as the day before and continued.

January 28. The new year has come and gone and taken Leah with it. She's headed south to a warmer climate. The reason she gave is a need to see if Hansi's disposition would benefit from a change in the weather, though I am certain an escape from this harsh winter will be good for Leah as well. She's still overly thin, and prone to catching sniffles. Aleister thinks a couple of months with his brother, whom he describes as interminably dull, will restore them both to health.

The silence in the building is the best gift Aleister could have given me. And himself. He's working again, and we've settled into a sort of pleasant partnership. Non-sexual, at least for the moment. Though I think that with Leah gone I would be less reluctant, he has made no overtures, not even an occasional lewd remark. He has, however, been gone two full nights in the last week. I can well imagine what he's up to.

At least they finally have a cure for some of what he might catch, and midwives able to take care of what he might inadvertently give. I can't imagine that there aren't a half dozen nasty little Aleisters littering the route of his many travels. He swears it isn't so, however. I suppose someone like him would know.

Noah took me out for dinner last night, a sort of belated Christmas gift. Mine was hardly so pleasant. With my pregnancy just beginning to show, it seemed I ought to make him the first recipient of my lie. But when the time came to speak it, I found I couldn't do it. So, after swearing him to secrecy, I told him as much of the truth as I could—namely that I had been part of a sexual working with Aleister and the child was a result of it. I feel I owed him that though I cannot recall any reason why except what is hinted at in my journal and the deep affection I felt for him as soon as we met.

A missed opportunity, a cynic might say. But I often read that strange account, written while Aleister was preparing the sunroom, and feel like an amnesiac studying her own diary, struggling toward memory—uselessly it seems.

Noah revealed all the insight he has when he asked, "Is the memory I have of living in your apartment part of what your ritual changed?"

I nodded. "I can't explain anything more, but explanations make no difference anyway. What's done is done, and I wouldn't want things any different."

I knew this sounded callous, but I wanted to put any thoughts he had toward me well behind him. We finished the meal in silence. Only when I thought I was safely alone in my apartment, did I give in to the tears I'd been fighting. The first of them started me on a real crying jag. I hear such emotionalism is common in pregnancy, but I never expected that I'd succumb to it.

But I wasn't alone. Aleister had been working in my study. He waited until my outburst had run its course then brought me a cold rag from the bathroom so I could wash my face.

"I wish I could walk through the door and stay in the past," I said, struggling to get the words out between the sobs.

"If they didn't burn you as a witch, I think they'd make you wear a letter on your chest."

"An A for Aleister," I said, trying to smile.

"An A for your absolutely adorable ass, your ardor, your abundant aptitude, your angelic attitude."

I did smile then, and he kissed my nose. I smelled the incense hanging over his body like a cloak.

"I know exactly what you need," he said. *"Come."*

He took my hand and led me down the hall where he already had the candles lit at the four poles, the leopard skin laid across the floor. He'd been planning it all from the time he heard me come home.

(I knew where we were going as soon as he took my hand, Dierdre. I should have stopped him. I didn't. Not then, not for all the weeks that Leah was gone.

(Forgive me for my own impatience, child. My fingers aren't what they used to be. So I am not going to try to detail the countless times we performed our magick together during the next few weeks only to say that the result of that first night and all that came after, or so he swears, was the second half of a book you may read any time you wish since it's in the library, Magick in Theory and Practice.

(He had to go over the gnostic mass four times before he decided that we had it right enough for him to set down. Then, I think he finally settled because his body simply would allow nothing else.)

February 12. We have spent every night in each others arms, and part of every day as well. We fuck. He writes. That word—fuck—comes as hard to my pen as it would to my tongue, but the vulgarity describes what we have been doing better than any other I can think of. What we do certainly can't be called breeding, since I've already been bred. It can't be called making love, since love has nothing to do with it. Perhaps his notion of merging with his "Scarlet Woman" comes closest but I will not steal that title away from poor Leah.

Aleister received a letter from Leah yesterday. She is miserable. She wants to come home as soon as possible. She promises Aleister that she is a changed woman.

"Nothing like a huge dose of my brother's Christian intolerance to make her ready to accept anything I do as positively godlike," *Aleister confessed after he shared one of her letters with me. We were in bed at the time, his shaved head resting in the valley between my swelling stomach and my already-swollen breasts.*

"Are you going to let her come home?" *I asked.*

"Next month. By then the book will be done, she'll be properly contrite and hopefully Hansi will have his teeth. Besides, you'll be getting far too big for this sort of athletics and I need her if we are going to hold a ritual to consecrate the child.*

I would undoubtedly be in the center of it. I wondered what it would be like. I wondered if anyone would guess that though I may believe in his magick because I have no other choice, I have less faith in his gods.

(I also have not detailed the social results of the mess I was rapidly making of my life. Through all the gossip, only two men took a public stand in defense of my virtue. Noah, because of what little I was able to tell him, and Bob Dunglass, who through our year of working together had come to respect me long before he decided that he loved me.

(I'm not going to bother to transcribe the sections concerning my later and almost adolescent attraction to Bob Dunglass. Looking back on our relationship, I am reminded of the theory that girls grow up to marry men very much like their fathers. Of course, you know that after we married, I put all of the magick workings well behind me. And I will jump even farther ahead in my story to tell you that when the day came that Bob and I had our only child together, I rejoiced. And when I was well enough, I carried that child into the past with me and rejoiced even more.

(Do you understand what a marvelous thing I learned through that single act? How pleased I was to know that my daughter, Judith, your cousin Moira's grandmother, was no

less fated to be born than your own grandfather.

(And through this I knew that I would never have married Noah. He was fated for someone else. But enough skipping around. Back to the journal.)

Fated for someone else. Dierdre laughed aloud.

What followed were more pages of eroticism. If Dierdre had time, she might have read every word, absorbed every scene. Instead she skimmed until finally . . .

February 26. Leah arrived home this evening, looking better than I've seen her in years. Whatever trials she has undergone on the Crowley farm in Florida, dissipation wasn't among them. There was color in her cheeks I hadn't seen since she was girl, a bit of flesh on her bones. As for Hansi, he did have teeth and, as we hoped, was much better behaved.

"That's from having some decency slapped into him," Aleister declared. "That's something I heartily approve of, though I refuse to do it myself and Leah's never had the stomach for it."

I poured us each a drink. We toasted Christian virtue, pagan lack of it, and well-behaved children. Sometime during our festivities, Hansi fell asleep on the floor.

"Too much travel," Leah said and scooped him up. "Upstairs?" she asked Aleister, a vaguely erotic smile on her thin lips.

He nodded. He stayed with me a half hour longer, kissing me with what seemed like well-trained passion before he left.

I followed him into the hall and looked up the stairs. Leah stood on the landing outside their door. She'd shed all her clothes and let down her hair. It hung over her boyish breasts, making her look like Stoker's description of Dracula's wives.

And I wondered again, as I have before, what sort of an end will she come to when he finally leaves her?

The journal was quickly moving to the edge of Dierdre's time in it. She got up only long enough to pour herself another cup of coffee then continued on, reading as quickly as she was able, skimming when necessary, hoping to be finished by three. Finally, she came to the moment when past and present overlapped.

March 20. Yesterday for the first time in over fifteen years, I found Dierdre in my garden, or rather she found me. She was, judging from the startled expression on her face when she saw me, just returning from her first knowing stroll through this era.

It's been so long since we were chldren and played together, so long since we were friends. I wanted to laugh, to embrace her, but she shied away from me like a wild deer or one of the feral cats in the park.

And there was another reason I kept my distance as well. I know perfectly well why she came back.

I'm nearly twenty-three now. Did I really expect to live to a hundred or beyond?

I'm sick at the thought that she has come here to give me the day and the time and the cause. I'm sick at the thought that in seventy-two years I will cease to exist. And I'm most sick at the thought, and perhaps I'm wrong, that I will feel the need then to have her come and tell me all of it now just as I was told so much—too much!—about my mother and brothers, my father, even my son, when Dierdre and I were only children.

I suppose my attitude toward all of this will change in time when I grow old and conservative and less enamored of life's uncertainties.

What can I say to her when I see her again?

Aleister suggests that I start with Hello.

March 21. She's here again. We sat together and talked, briefly. As I expected, my death is imminent in her time. 1991. Few people live so long. I said that to her, tried to sound flippant, callous about it, though that's hardly the way I feel at all.

A stroke, she says. Painless, she says.

I don't want to know, and I suppose I will never forget the date. But I will write it down as I have recorded everything else, dutifully and without comment, in the little green note-book that I keep in the library desk. I try to think about what's recorded there as little as possible, and consult it only when necessary.

One thing bothers me—it has been so long since anyone visited from the future. Does that mean things are going well? I have no way of guessing.

After we spoke, briefly, she went off somewhere with Noah. He seems quite taken with her, but then he has a talent for finding himself in hopeless relationships.

(All of that seems no more than gibberish now. Of course things were going well, and so there was no reason for me to keep sending you or anyone back with odd notion that they ought to meddle in things. Besides, it's better not to meddle. As that stupid science fiction movie whose title I can't recall made so clear, you could inadvertently change something that would change you. Better to stay put and use the door like any other tool—only in an emergency.

(Is this my way of telling you to keep a steady head, to leave Noah to his era, to stop meddling in his life? I don't want to sound like some old biddy who thinks she knows so much, but I do, and when the romance of all of this wears off, I think you will agree with me.)

TWENTY-ONE

The rose silk dress, wispy, delicate and romantic, seemed so out of place over the black garter belt and seamed hosiery. But as Dierdre stood in front of the mirror pinning on the hat, she saw how well the gown suited her. Had Grandmum gone shopping with her in mind?

There was no way to ask her anymore.

Dressed, make-up applied in what she'd observed was in keeping with the era, she stepped through the door. Early, of course, but that was planned. Better he should find her waiting than see where she'd come from.

The sky was overcast, the weather warm and still, swollen with the promise of a storm. She sat on the bench, hands folded in her lap. The demure Victorian waiting for her beau.

He arrived a few minutes before five, coming out through Bridget's doors, looking a bit tired from a day at work. As he kissed her, her hat slipped off. He retrieved it, brushed the dirt off the crown. "I like you better without it," he said. "And the dress is beautiful, but so formal. I hadn't made any plans. Did you?"

"Not yet, but I know what I want to do. I want to pick your favorite formal dining spot in all of the city."

"Formal? Gage and Tollners in the Bronx, I suppose."

"We're going there tonight. I'm buying, and I won't have it any other way when I'm celebrating."

"What's the occasion?"

245

"I'm not going to back to Canada. I'm staying here in New York."

"Staying? Have you found employment here? If not, I can help you find something."

She wanted to laugh. To tell him everything. Perhaps in time she would, just as Grandmum must have somehow done with her Mr. Dunglass. "I don't need to think about that yet. I've inherited a bit of money from a distant relation. Quite a bit actually; enough to keep me well off even if I never work again."

"Well, I won't argue about the bill, then. But you have to give me time to change into something suitable, and I suppose we ought to call for reservations. Come up with me. I'll fix you a drink."

"I'll wait for you here instead."

She'd expected that Bridget might come out and join her, but if the woman was inside, she had no interest in talking at the moment. Instead, Aleister came and sat beside her.

He sat close enough to her that she could smell the incense Bridget had described in her journal, see in his eyes the full magnetism of the man. Without asking, he held her hands, kissed her cheek. "It isn't often that I see the results of my workings in the flesh, so to speak," he whispered in her ear.

She didn't know how to respond so she said nothing.

"I came to sit with you and ask you to tell me about your world."

"Packed with people. Filthy. Dangerous."

"Dangerous?"

"People are killed for the money in their pockets, sometimes just for the coats off their backs."

"And you think things are better today? I've seen people slit a throat for a scrap of food. There are whole sections of this town where no sane man will walk by day or night."

"In my time that extends to half a burough, and from what I read in the New York papers the police won't go there either."

"Sounds like an era in need of philosophy."

"Morality is a better word."

"We don't have time for that debate," he said. "What about magick?"

Dierdre frowned trying to think of some way to answer. "There's a lot of magicians, the sort that can make things appear or disappear or float in the air."

"That isn't magick, that's illusion." He looked disgusted with her ignorance.

"And there's a whole movement people call New Age. Believers burn incense and wear crystals for luck and protection. They listen to music to help them meditate."

"And that gets them prepared for? ..." he asked, leading her.

"To get in touch with their inner selves."

"Inner selves! That's all? That's it? What's the point?"

"There probably isn't any."

He squeezed her hands, painfully as if disciplining her for not knowing more, or through her to pain her world for not caring more. She hurried on, "There is a revival in Celtic music and research, and Tarot cards, and what people call parapsychology—divination or extra-sensory perception—mind reading, that is. There are New Age religions as well, but I only know a little about them."

"Then, damn it, say what you do know!" His grip tightened as if he could squeeze the answers out of her.

"Some of them worship the goddess. Others have a sort of Native American or Eastern slant. I heard of some that try to combine all the principle beliefs of the different religions into one." She recalled a seminar she'd once attended where she'd listened to a taped lecture by a woman dressed in white. "One of them believes that all truth comes from a few enlightened souls. These are the masters."

"Now that group is on to something. Continue."

"They believe in reincarnation. Souls return to earth knowing nothing of their past, but those of the masters who teach them somehow keep the knowledge of their previous lives."

"Yes!" He let go of her hands only to hug her. "You told me what I'd hoped to hear. Now, how am I remembered?"

He would ask that, and she had no answer except for the books in Grandmum's library, many of them with modern bindings. "Your books are still in print. I assume that they're read, and people still believe in what you taught."

That seemed to satisfy him. His lips curled up in a self-satisfied smile. She suspected that if he'd had hair he might be preening it now the way Frank did after she paid him a compliment.

She waited for another question but there was nothing. His interests had become so limited. She found him disappointing.

"I suppose I should go there," he said.

He spoke as if he, not God, made the decision on when he would be reborn. Or perhaps he was speaking of another door. Either way, she felt a need to discourage him. "There is one more important thing you ought to know. We have a venereal disease that kills those it infects. In spite of all the great advances in science, there is no cure. Those of us with any sense at all have become real puritans."

That seemed to put him off, enough that she doubted that she'd wake one morning to find him in her kitchen trying to cope with the JennAire range and Mr. Coffee.

"I want to ask you a question as well. I want to stay here with Noah. Can this be done?"

"Done? I never expected anyone to request this."

"You have too optimistic a view of the future," she replied.

"Apparently." He frowned. Long vertical lines formed in his forehead making him seem less contamplative than menacing. "The price on the magician would be too high. I won't do it, and I know of no one else who can," he finally told her.

"Can you explain?"

"Yes. But I won't." Though he still held her hand, he stopped looking at her. It made her feel as if he were royalty and she a servant already dismissed.

Noah joined them. He'd changed into a blue tweed suit with matching vest. It looked rumpled and oversized on him as if he were a little boy in his father's clothes. "Shall we be off?" he asked, holding out his arm.

"Through the gate, please," she said. "Goodbye, Mr. Crowley."

Noah said nothing. "I hate to see him anywhere near you, let alone holding your hand," he said once they were in the alley.

"It's rather hard to get it back once he takes it."

"Someone ought to slap his face."

"That's exactly what he wants. He'd find it arousing. So it's better to annoy him by being polite."

Noah looked at her, shocked for a moment, then broke into a grin. "You are so refreshing, and so right."

They drove north, then across an East River coated with a brilliant golden sheen in the hazy setting sun.

They dined in a Gay Nineties atmosphere, with flickering gaslights reflected in the dark-framed mirrors that covered the walls. Their waiter was dressed better than most men in Dierdre's time, looking almost military with the gold insignia on his sleeve proudly proclaiming his years of service to the establishment.

The food was marvelous from the turtle soup to the perfectly grilled steak to the spectacular cheesecake that ended the meal. By the time they finished it was after nine. The sun had long since gone down but the March heatwave and the charged stillness in the air had not diminished. This felt less like spring in New England than winter in the Mississippi Delta.

They walked a bit, far enough to work off a little of the meal. Noah drove her past the Customs House where he worked. Lights were still on in a few rooms inside. "We never quite shut down," he said. "Would you like to go inside?"

She shook her head, rested a hand over his.

They drove in silence to her house, his room.

No wine this time. No warnings, little discussion of any sort, really. Her dress lay in a heap on the floor the stockings and slip and corset and his suit above it. He was more sure of himself this time, but still not certain what to demand of her, even less certain that he should ask.

Any other naive lover would have made her impatient; with him she was merely greedy, wanting every part of him that he could give; giving every part of herself. She treated him to what she knew carefully; kissing his nipples, his stomach, the tip of his penis with deliberate playfulness, as if she were exploring his body rather than his inhibitions. Each time she'd feel him tense from an unfamiliar caress, she'd back off for a time, then return more insistently, pushing him into new territories, to new heights.

In the end it was her above him, his hands on her breasts, guiding her rise and fall. She cried out first this time, Noah a moment later.

The one who had boasted of a score of lovers before her had given her only a sudden intense pleasure, nothing more. The one who'd been too young, too inept, had made her feel older, wicked, nothing more. And Frank—so precise even in bed, the one who always made certain she was satisfied, had left her only satisfied.

This was something else entirely, something for which there was no simple, recognizable name.

Was this what Grandmum felt when she first lay with her Mr. Dunglass? Was this what Aleister felt when he first touched his Scarlet Woman? Yes, she could see how easily someone might confuse passion and magick, and even how the gods might be amused, aroused, appeased by such emotions, such earthly lust.

"Can you stay the night?" he asked.

"No one will miss me," she replied, and pressed her body along his side.

"Do you need anything?"

"I have what I need right here," she said and shut her eyes.

Bridget's warning returned, the concern muted to a whisper in her mind, *Not too long.*

Too long and you lose the messenger forever, Dierdre thought happily then contemplated poor quiet Mark in the heart of Manhattan or cousin Moira taking on the theater crowd. As Dierdre drifted off to sleep, she heard the clopping of hooves on the street below, the driver of the cart whistling softly.

The storm hit just before dawn, announcing its arrival with a heavy crash of thunder. Dierdre lay awake, listening to the noise, watching the strobes of lightning throw shadows on the wall, shadows that seemed to move with a life of their own, detached for the moment from the people who have lived there before and after Noah's time.

A strange night-thought, nothing more, but it stayed with her through the hour it took the storm to roll over the city and leave a gentle rain in its wake.

Dierdre rose, wrapped herself in a spare blanket, and walked to the bedroom window. Only the dim grey light growing on the horizon gave any indication of the coming dawn. The sky lowered, a cold steel grey. The city beneath it seemed still, serene, its sharp edges softened by the golden glow of the streetlights.

The screech of brakes and blare of a horn drew her attention to the street below. As she looked down University Place, she saw the slow moving carts and horses run through like ghosts by the harried nineties taxi drivers that seemed to be a part of modern New York even in early morning. She blinked and fought the image. For a moment it subsided, then grew stronger until past and present coalesced into an undulating hallucination of harsh mercury streetlights and flickering gas globes.

She stifled a scream and backed away from the window, toward the bed where Noah lay. He stirred, rolled over and reached for the place where she should be. When he did not touch her, he opened his eyes and sat up, running one hand through his hair. The color of it seemed faded. The hand itself looked thinner, his face faintly lined.

Had he grown older or was it just a trick of the morning light? Would he grow older still as she stood helplessly and watched? Would she see the old man he must have become whither and die, winked out like the era she would be forced to abandon whether or not she chose to remain on this side of those doors?

"What is it?" he asked.

"Noah, there's something I have to tell you. I think that when I do, you'll understand a great many things. Bridget and Aleister . . ." She could not look at him, could not watch him grow older and older. She stared beyond him, trying to speak words that refused to move from her mind to her lips. ". . . Aleister and Bridget . . ."

A sound so out of place in this silent era made her shiver. She whirled to look out the window and at a jet slicing through the pale morning sky. Stifling a scream, she pulled the coverlet tighter around her body and rushed for the door, not caring that she was leaving her clothes behind.

"Dierdre?" Noah called softly. After the confused words

she'd blurted, he must think she'd had a nightmare, or that she was caught in a nightmare still. "Dierdre, come back to bed. It's all right." To her his voice seemed hoarse with age.

She shook her head, her hand on the doorknob now. "Bridget and Aleister did . . . something . . ." she said, too frightened to speak the words. "No! Stay away from me. Let me talk. They . . . you know part of it, Grandmum, no Bridget told you. She and Aleister . . ." He was moving toward her, slowly as if to capture a wild, wounded bird. If he touched her, would his arms go through her? Would she condemn them both to madness? "Stop! Stay back!" she cried and bolted from the room, the apartment. Downstairs, she pounded on Bridget's door.

Crowley answered, wearing far less than Dierdre, his fleshy bulk filling the doorway. She pushed past him and ran down the hall, through the back doors and into the garden.

Noah followed close behind, the bathrobe he'd grabbed flaring out behind him. "Dierdre! Come back!" he cried.

She turned as she reached the yard and saw Aleister holding him back. "It's all right," she called to Noah. "I'll be in the garden at six tonight. If I'm able, I'll explain it all. If I can't come, tell Bridget and Aleister that you have a right to know."

She could say no more. Time twisted around her. She rushed to the old doors and through them.

Her stomach lurched. Her vision clouded. She fell to hands and knees, breathing shallowly. She swallowed down bile and waited for the sickness to pass. It didn't. Instead the room seemed to be shifting here as well, the beige wall of the past trying to impose itself on the dusty green one of the present, the worn oriental carpet becoming brighter beneath her bare hands. She could even feel the change in the pile as a vague vibration against her palms.

She heard a pounding and turned toward the sunroom door. Noah stood outside, his now-lined face and sparse grey hair dripping rainwater that merged with what she thought were tears, his aged features further distorted by the boundary between past and present. It was the face from the old nightmare that had haunted her for so many years, an expression less a leer than a shocked sorrow.

Her stomach heaved. She rushed to the kitchen sink, making

it just in time. After, exhausted and too frightened to move, she lay on the kitchen floor and stared at the ceiling. The modern fluorescent fixture shifted, reforming into an old three-bulb ceiling light she hadn't noticed when she'd been in the past.

She shut her eyes and heard Noah's voice, and Crowley's, their argument almost distinct enough to make out. She stayed where she was until the voices faded to a whisper. Still not trusting herself to stand, she crawled into Grandmum's room, and into her bed.

Someone was pressing the entry buzzer. She saw the multicolored reflection of police car lights on the hallway wall. Had she screamed when she fell through that door? Had she been gone longer than she thought, so long that someone had reported her missing? Were the police really there at all, or some new vision to add to all the rest? No matter, if they were really there, they'd have to break down her door if they wanted to talk to her in her present state. If she were fortunate they'd go away and leave her alone to try and find what was left of her sanity without benefit of an institution, a therapist or antipsychotic drugs.

She lay shivering under the covers with her knees pulled tight against her chest. It seemed that someone shared the bed with her, lying in her and around her like a ghostly presence. She stayed where she was, all energy drained by fear, until she gave way to exhaustion and slept.

When she woke it was well after noon. She felt alone again, all traces of the past gone from her memory until she saw the blanket on the floor beside the bed.

Hold on to something to bring back the memory—in this case, the nightmare. She began to cry, deep huge sobs, until exhausted and drained she could do nothing but lay staring at the ceiling contemplating her loss. She managed to drink a bit of orange juice before taking a shower. But even fed and washed and dressed, remnants of the terror remained.

Before she lost her nerve there was work to do. Dierdre pulled on a pair of sweat pants and tie-dyed T-shirt then took a pair of heavy wool blankets from the closet, a hammer and nails from a kitchen drawer.

She held the blanket in front of her and kept her eyes on

the carpet as she approached the old sunroom doors, refusing to look at the glass, let alone any sight beyond it. The closer she went to the door, the more ill she felt, the more disoriented. She considered sending Noah a note, tossing it through the door that afternoon, but even a glance at its handle made her knees feel weak. She fought back terror as she hooked one corner of the blanket then the other to the old curtain rod mountings. Then carefully, so as not to damage the carvings above the door, she tacked up the blankets covering the window. Later, she'd have someone put up a new set of heavy draperies.

And if she never pulled them open, she'd never risk seeing Noah again.

She recalled the promise she had made him as she fled. She couldn't keep it, couldn't meet him in the garden today or ever. Better she forget him as he would one day undoubtedly forget her, relegate him to the memory that would always remain, soft and insistent, in her mind.

Later, when she thought she was composed enough, she went to the closet intending to pack away what remained of the period clothing, and the sad memories they would bring. When she opened the door, she caught her breath and stepped quickly back. The dresses were arranged as they had been when she first saw them, with the rose silk gown hanging in its plastic cover along with the rest, the cape she'd purchased hanging with it, the hat wrapped in plastic on the shelf above it.

As if she had never been there. As if this time it had all been, truly, a dream.

PART THREE

Noah

"The oracle of the Gods is the Child-Voice of Love in thine own soul; Hear thou it."
—Aleister Crowley

PART THREE

Noah

TWENTY-TWO

The phone rang twice that day but Dierdre let the answering machine pick up. Late that afternoon, when she was feeling a bit more stable, she reviewed the messages.

Angelina had called both times, asking her to stop by as soon as she came home. Wanting company but not convinced it was wise to leave the apartment yet, Dierdre invited her over to share leftovers from the buffet.

By the time the woman arrived, Dierdre had fixed a small tray of cold cuts and cheeses and laid out plates and rolls, and a pot of tea—Lipton with slices of lemon.

Angelina's hair hung loose. She wore a blue and cream tie-dyed caftan and a pair of Birkenstock sandals. She hugged Dierdre then asked, "Sorry about showing up in my lounging clothes. Are you feeling all right?"

"Better," Dierdre said, knowing there was no way she could hide her red eyes or the emotions that had caused the tears.

"Good. Bridget and I always agreed that we never wanted anyone sniffling over us when we were gone." She poured the tea as if this was her buffet, then surprised Dierdre by taking most of the meat and piling it high on one of the rye rolls.

Dierdre watched her take her first bite, fascinated at how she'd misjudged the woman's diet. "What are you smiling at?

Did you expect me to be one of those pinched-faced greens eaters?'' Angelina asked.

''I assumed so. I thought you'd be convinced that animals have souls or something like that.''

''I am, but as Mr. Petra used to say, the same holds true for plants. And since I don't want to stop living, I eat what I like and try not to think about metaphysics while I chew.''

''You sounded worried on the phone. Was something wrong?''

''Very when the police are pounding on my door at five AM.''

So Dierdre had been right. She had screamed. ''Did they say why?'' she asked.

''A woman was run over by a truck early this morning. Apparently she had been in a high state of hysterics and running up the center of Fifth Avenue when it happened.''

''What does that have to do with us?''

''Nothing, except that witnesses say the same woman was seen running from this building a few minutes before her death. No one was sure which entrance she came out of so the police were trying to talk to everyone here hoping that someone could at least identify her.

''As soon as the cops left, I headed down to the block where the accident happened. There's a little cappuccino and sweets shop on the corner. I stopped in and listened to the customers. It seems that she hadn't looked like what most people would consider respectable. 'A junkie whore on some paranoid rush,' was the way one customer described her.''

''Can you think of anyone in the building—?''

''Hell no!'' Angelina interjected before she'd finished. ''Maybe she was turning tricks in the basement, or even keeping a place down there. I don't think anyone's been down there in years but an occasional furnace man or meter reader and them not recently. Who checks?''

''Bill was down there yesterday. He hooked the cable in for me.''

''Did he check every room? It's a pretty huge place.''

''You're right. I suppose I should go down.''

''Not alone you don't. She might have friends.''

"Maybe I should call the police back. Give them permission?"

"Then here." Angelina dug under the neckline of her dress and into what appeared to be her bra to pull out a rumpled business card. "They left me this number. Said he was on the normal day shift, whatever that means."

"Hopefully nine to five, or later." Dierdre dialed immediately, before she had time to think about putting it off. Enough had happened in one full turn of the earth. She didn't want to add any more questions to her already huge list.

Detective Malverne was just going off duty. At her insistence, he said he'd stop by on the way home. "You'll stay until he comes, won't you?" Dierdre asked.

"Until he goes, child. The last person anyone should trust in their house is a cop," Angelina replied.

They discussed the funeral over tea, then the charities Angelina believed that her friend had been supporting. Dierdre had just started heating another pot of water when the detective arrived.

Thomas Malverne was big enough at six foot and two hundred and something to inspire confidence, but there was a hesitancy to his speech, a quickness to his movements, as if he, like her, had experienced one too many shocks in the past few days and had not quite recovered. "You shouldn't of opened the door like that," he cautioned.

"You said your name before I buzzed you in," she replied.

"And the officers gave out my card to half the neighborhood. It could of been anybody out there."

"I'm sorry. I'm not from around here," Dierdre said, hoping he didn't see how ridiculous she thought this much caution to be. She started to ask about whether they'd identified the dead woman, but he cut her off.

"Can't talk about the case while it's under investigation," he said. "You got the keys for the basement?"

She got them from the desk drawer.

"Stay here," the officer ordered when Dierdre started to follow him.

"Here? I own this building. If there's something down there that I should know about, I would rather discover it in your company than on my own."

"All right, then stay behind me and be prepared to head back up if I tell you to."

The basement door was locked, the bolt showing no signs of an attempted break-in. The bare light bulbs were streaked with cobwebs but lit when Malverne hit the switch. From the looks of things no one had been down there in months, but Malverne aimed his flashlight across the stairs below them then asked, "Who else has a basement key?"

"Just the water man," Angelina called from the top of the stairs. "Bridget had the locks changed after the other meters were moved outside."

"Smart lady. Anyone else?"

"No," Dierdre replied. "Bill Coleman was down here yesterday, but he used my key. He helped me hook in my cable."

"Coleman. The one who hasn't called me. Remind him when you see him."

"He probably doesn't know about any of this yet. He leaves for work pretty early."

"Then he might of seen something." Malverne stepped off the bottom stair, Dierdre right behind him.

Four more bare bulbs, three to the right and one to the left, illuminated an open space at the base of the stairs and two long corridors running the length of the building with doorways on either side of them. The open space held a pair of old stationery tubs, a rusty toilet beside them, an assortment of wires and fuses, and a water meter.

Malverne started down the shorter corridor. "What is this? Tenant storage?" he asked, speaking loudly enough that Angelina could also hear.

"It used to be," Angelina called.

"Why don't you come down?" Dierdre called to her.

"Too many spiders. They crawl up my legs and I usually manage to kill them when I try to get rid of them. Bad luck."

"Neighborhood kook, is she?" Malverne whispered.

His voice must have carried. "Not the harmless kind either; you remember that, copper," Angelina yelled down.

A moment later, Dierdre heard her apartment door slam.

Malverne opened the nearest door. The natural light, filtered by a filthy basement window, revealed a large room with a number of wooden boxes. The nearest ones were open, showing stack of books inside. Dierdre suspected that the others held books as well.

The next room held more of the same, all of them raised off the floor on wooden crates. Malverne forced his way into the room on the end. It was empty except for a pile of rotting rags in the corner and another box of books, this one against the far wall. Above it was a window, cleaner that those in the other rooms, and barely closed. Malverne went over to it, pushed it shut with backs of his hands and fastened the turn-buckles. "You ought to put locks on all of these," he said.

"You don't think she was staying down here, do you?" Dierdre asked, looking for other signs that someone might have been sleeping here, living here. Shouldn't there be more than just the few rags Malverne had started picking through? Those were hardly enough to cushion the stone floor let alone provide warmth? He moved the box from beneath the window and pulled it open.

Dierdre held her breath, expecting used needles, perhaps a cache of drugs or money.

Spiders, and more books.

"People live where they can these days, but there's no sign of anyone staying here. Maybe on the other end. Come on."

The corridor was longer on the other side, apparently running the length of the building. The nearest rooms were empty. The next two were padlocked but time had ended all but the appearance of security. The hasps were rusted, the wood frames they were attached to soft with age. Malverne pressed against the first door and it swung open.

Boxes were stacked in one corner while furniture filled the rest of the room. Among the items was a large wood bedframe with carved figures in the headboard. Dierdre recognized it from Grandmum's description of it in her journal as one of the pieces from Crowley's apartment. Could these be his books? She saw what Malverne saw, places where the dust had been wiped away to examine an occasional title, but it didn't seem that anything had been taken.

"The really valuable stuff would never make it through the window," Malverne said.

Dierdre was less optimistic. She wondered if the "valuable stuff" was already gone and this only the leavings.

Malverne took one more sweep of the basement. Dierdre remained where she was, mentally cataloging the furniture. She was about to leave when she spied another familiar piece, one she'd actually seen before and might have overlooked now had the top not seemed less filthy than most of the others in the dingy space—a carved wooden box that held the letters Noah had written Bridget so many years ago.

Unless there were two similar boxes, this had been in the library yesterday. Now it was here. Another change, a small one, but not so small when it was added to the presence of the dress in her closet and the fact that Bridget MacCallum had died a day early. She took a piece of soggy tissue from her pocket and dusted the box off before picking it up.

"What you got?" Malverne demanded, speaking as if she were stealing clues from a murder scene.

"Letters sent to my great-grandmother. She died just a few days ago. I'd like to read them. Do I need your permission?"

She'd said it without any of the sarcasm she'd felt. He shrugged and looked around the room. "Go ahead. Nobody's been living here. But you oughta get bars for these windows or someone sure as hell will be."

"Thank you," she said and brushed by him, carrying the treasure up the stairs.

He followed her, locking the door and bringing the key into the apartment. Angelina sat on the sofa, eyes straight ahead, scowling obviously.

"I'm sorry," Malverne said to her.

Dierdre was astonished. She hadn't expected so much courtesy from a big-city policeman.

"You oughta be," Angelina retorted. "You know I did a few bits of work for the Big Apple Blues in my day. They didn't have a clue until they paid this kook to find them some."

"Police informer?" Malverne asked.

"Psychic consultant," Angelina responded. She looked at him, saw the change in his expression. "Yeah, one of *those*."

"Well, if you get the urge to pull out your ouija board and find something that might interest me, give me a call."

"A children's game. I'll need to touch something that belonged to the victim."

"Can't help you there, at least not at the moment. What cases did you work on?"

As she began describing them, Malverne moved closer to Dierdre. "You look a little worried about something," he said softly. "Why not open it while I'm here, just in case."

She did as he asked. The letters were there, as she'd expected. A stack of thin cream and pale green vellum envelopes that looked so delicate she thought they might crumble when she touched them; of ivory parchment yellowed to the color of old piano keys.

"Your name?" Malverne asked, pointing to the address. Until then, Dierdre hadn't noticed it.

"And my great aunt's," Dierdre lied. "These were her letters, sent here because she was always on the move. We have that in common."

". . . Then there was a handyman whose body was found up in Morningside. I managed to point them in the direction of the choir director over at . . ." Angelina continued.

"I gotta go," Malverne said to both of them. He reached into the box, doing what Dierdre had been afraid to do, lifting up the letters then looking under them. "No drugs . . . no spiders." He handed Dierdre another business card. This one had his home number on the back. "You be sure to get that window fixed. Call me if you discover anything we might have missed, and you . . ." He pointed to Angelina. "You let me know if you get any feelings about this case."

Dierdre followed him to the outer door. "Did it ever occur to you that she might have been hiding from someone in the outer foyer?" she asked.

"Yeah, it did. You know, you're not half bad at this. Call me if you think of anything else."

Dierdre went back to her apartment. "A strange man," she said to Angelina.

"Strange because he cares. He doesn't like it when bodies don't have names. And I don't like it when names have no bodies. Like your great aunt Dierdre."

Dierdre looked at her, torn between fear of confessing the truth, and fear of what would happen if she didn't. But now that Grandmum was gone, she needed someone to know what was going on. "That's because she's me!" she blurted.

"Impossible," Angelina replied then saw the fear in Dierdre's expression, the concern, the near hysteria. "Isn't it?"

"No. Bridget and Aleister . . ." Again, the words refused to move to her tongue. She felt as if that part of her were paralyzed. She might have tried writing them down if she wasn't convinced that her hand would fail her in the same way. "Wait!" she said and ran into the library, returning with the journal Grandmum had left here, opening it, making certain it began as she remembered.

Satisfied, she thrust it into Angelina's hands. "Read!" she ordered.

She waited, watching Angelina's face as she scanned the first two pages, watching her slip off her clogs and settle onto the sofa, intent only on the words.

Ten minutes later, convinced that Angelina was at least ready to believe, Dierdre turned her attention to the letters.

Most had only her name and a date on the envelope, as if he had hand-delivered them to Bridget. All were opened, though it was hard to tell if Bridget had done so or if age had destroyed the glue. They were arranged chronologically, as if whomever had put them away had expected her to find and read them. She opened the first and was pleased to see that Noah's handwriting, though small, was precise, as if he were taking pains to be certain that she would be able to read it easily. She'd have no trouble reading these. No, the real trouble would come in discovering how he felt when he left her.

She wanted to put off reading them, then realized procrastination would only bring its own torments. Better to get it over with, then mourn and move on.

TWENTY-THREE

March 30.

My Dearest. I heard your last words to me. I waited in the garden for you until hours after you said you'd meet me, then left feeling nothing but misery. Since then, days have passed and I've heard nothing. It seems as if you've fled my life forever but I will not give up hope of seeing you again.

I took your last words of advice and spoke to Aleister and Bridget, first separately then together. Neither of them gives me any answers. Aleister pleads complete ignorance, and beautifully enough that I almost believe him. Bridget says she does not know where you've gone, then tells me as if in the greatest confidence that you've always had a nervous disposition and that you will meet me in your own good time. She's lying about all of it; I would know that even if I did not know you so well. Bridget has always been a most transparent liar.

She did tell me one thing I believe, however. She said she would be certain these letters were forwarded to you as soon as she was able to do so. I hope this is soon. I hope you reply and let me know what it was that I did, or we did together, that made you run so abruptly from my arms.

I love you. Noah.

Dierdre took a deep breath and fought for calm. When she thought she could go on, she put the letter in its envelope and opened the next one. It was brief, a request that they meet on April 5 in the same little Hungarian restaurant. *I have to know what happened,* he concluded. *And I cannot imagine that you would leave me so confused.* He enclosed a phone number for his office and asked that she call.

The third letter was dated April 14.

My Dearest. In the last few days I have been thinking often of Bridget and Aleister and how they have evaded answering my questions. I believe that something they did—inadvertently, I hope—caused your hysteria. I wonder what you saw out there in the rain and what you saw when you looked at me sitting on the bed? Had they conjured some demon that leered at you through the window? One that stood between us?

Bridget laughed when I suggested this to her, but sobered immediately and repeated her promise to do whatever it takes to get these letters to you. I still have hope.

Last weekend I fled the city myself, traveling off to Boston to see my sister and her family. Louie said I have to tell you hello for him. Things are going well for all of them, but they informed me that my mother is not well. This damp weather is not good for her lungs and she has never really recovered from the bout of pneumonia earlier this year. I know that Barbara is taking care of her physically, but I am sure it is a joyless sort of caretaking. I think a happier and more interesting atmosphere will be better for Mother. I may have her move in with me for a time. My company will be livelier than Barbara's and Mother can see some of her old friends and make some new ones (I assure you that she would even be up to taking on Aleister who she has met on a few occasions). We'll also have an opportunity to consult with one of the better New York doctors.

Mother's not even sixty. It seems so sad that she should be in such pain.

Work continues to be tedious but rewarding. There's even hint of a promotion for me. Longer hours will come with it, I suppose, but I don't care all that much. At night I do little but sit in my apartment and set what seem like random words on paper. Yesterday, I jotted down a few lines of poetry concerning you. Lurid words, I confess, so much so that when I read them over I found myself blushing. Return soon, dearest, and help me understand all this delightful shame. Noah.

He'd get over her, Dierdre thought. In a way, he already was. Dierdre heard Angelina's soft cry of surprise, thought of her own first reaction to that journal, and opened another envelope.

There were three separate letters in it, written within a few days of one another and sent from White Plains.

April 18. Dearest. I have been here for the last two days helping Barbara take care of Mother. Her cough worsened before I was able to spirit her away from this drafty old house. The doctor here thinks the pneumonia has returned but can suggest no treatment other than to wait and see. We made up a bed for her in the kitchen and are keeping the room warm and a kettle of water always on the stove. The moisture makes it easier for her to breathe. One of Barbara's friends from church brought her a tea of willow bark and valerian that helps her sleep. We can only wait and hope for the best.

Dierdre looked out the window, the same window through which Bridget's mother had stared as she died. How difficult it must have been for her to limit her attention to just her family when so many were in need and she could so easily help them.

When I need to get away from this sad place, I take a walk. During the day, I take in my favorite scenes; at night I walk under the stars. Even now, under such sad

*circumstances, I revel in the peace of this place and wish
you were here to share it all with me. Noah.*

*April 25. Dearest. It's over. And after the last few days
of watching poor Mother struggle for every breath I am
thankful. Sylvia took her death as well as I did; Patricia
is far less forgiving. Though she does not say it, she acts
as if Mother had done something sinful and brought the
death onto herself. I reminded her that death awaits us
all, and even went so far as to add that it was only a
moment's passing from body and soul to soul alone and
then to God. She refuses to accept any of this. Mother
was damned. So am I and so is Sylvia.*

*I confess that the pity I felt toward her for her dreary
beliefs vanished. Only great effort kept me from proving
how thoroughly damned I must be by slapping her.*

*She tells me that things will be clearer after the serv-
ice. Sylvia and I would forbid her minister from speaking
but before she died Mother agreed to let her hold a short
service at the graveside following the wake, and I will
not go back on her final promise to my sister.*

*I pray that God has a sense of humor and Aleister
breaks with his practice and comes to the wake.*

All my love, Noah.

*April 30. Dearest. Not only did God answer my some-
what twisted prayers, but he topped them with a show I
could not have imagined. Mother would have loved it!*

*It began during what was probably only the middle
but what should have,in all decency, been the end of the
dreary graveside service Barbara's minister had arranged. It was clear that the preacher had never met
Mother, or if he had, never tried to know her. He cap-
tured none of her wit, her love of life, or her personality.
Instead he droned on about the pains of the afterlife
being far worse than anything we endure in this one,
citing Old Testament scriptures to make his point.*

*And if you think that I wanted to slap Barbara, you
can well imagine my thoughts toward her beloved spir-*

*itual adviser. These were getting nastier as each quarter
hour passed. Many of Mother's friends had left, and
those who remained were casting longing glances toward the road when I heard an automobile backfire on
the road outside the cemetery gates. Looking for any
excuse to get away from this congregation, I went down
to see who the late arrival would be.*

*It was Bridget and Aleister in the front, Bob Dunglass
and Angelina in the back. Bob and Bridget were dressed
in appropriate black. Aleister was wearing one of his
more flamboyant Egyptian robes and Angelina (bless
her!) was all in white, which she said was the appropriate color for sending a pure and beautiful soul directly to the throne of God.*

"You're late," I said.

*"Of course we are. We didn't come for the funeral,
we came to see you," Aleister said.*

*"Then you may have to wait awhile. It isn't over yet,"
I said.*

*Aleister looked up the hill at the black tent, the people
standing beneath it. "You mean the poor woman isn't
buried yet? What, are the damn Papists having a no-
vena?"*

*"She's been buried. Now Barbara's minister is speak-
ing as he has been doing since two."*

*Now once, after I'd had far more to drink than is ever
wise, I told Aleister about Barbara's late-life conversion.
He had drank far more than I but had obviously not
forgotten any of our conversation. "He's been speaking
nearly two hours? You allowed it?"*

*"Mother promised Barbara." I explained what she'd
said.*

*"Well, people on their deathbed are known for being
far too accommodating," he replied.*

*I couldn't help it. I started to laugh. It seemed that
all the sorrow of the last few days was dissipating in
that laughter. Every attempt to stop only made me laugh
all the harder. Tears of mirth and sorrow ran down my
face. Angelina held out her arms and I buried my face
in the folds of her soft knit sweater. One of Barbara's*

church friends came down to the gate to shush me. Aleister took her shoulders and spun her around. When she faced the gravesite, he sent her back up the hill with a most unchristian smack on the rump. She responded with a cry of surprise.

Aleister's actions had all the effect I'd hoped for. The woman joined the congregation so upset that the minister stopped the sermon and listened to her tell what had happened. He stormed down the hill. "What's going on?" he demanded.

Bob Dunglass took off his hat and stepped forward, one hand outstretched. "We've come to pay our respects."

"Well, you look respectable enough, and the lady, too, though she should hardly be out in her condition," he said nodding toward Bridget. "The other two should wait here, perhaps outside the cemetery gate until the service is over."

"You were invited to say a few words. I think you've said more than enough," I cut in.

"You mother's soul is at stake. You wouldn't want to jeopardize that, would you?"

The words seemed so shocking, so out of place, that I fell silent.

"His mother was responsible for her own soul. Your words won't change God's mercy," Bridget retorted.

"And how dare you think that the God of Abraham and Solomon, of John the Baptist and Jesus himself is so petty as to let the likes of you decide who is saved and who is damned," Aleister added.

The minister bristled. "I have studied the Bible all my life, sir. I think I know it well."

"Then let me tell you a little secret," Aleister said, moving closer to the man. "God gives you what you expect when you die. And so the good Mrs. Hathaway is with Him now. And you, my pickle-faced friend, will feel every bit of torment you think you deserve."

"Damn you, sir."

"Damn? I used to think so; I'm not so presumptuous now."

"Do you really think God cares about your opinion?"

"Do you think I care about His?"

"The Lord will have his way with you. You can be . . ."

The man's voice was rising to a feverish pitch. "Shut up, all of you!" I cried.

Barbara joined us. "Make them leave," she said.

"I've been tolerant of this man. I expect the same from you toward my friends," I replied.

"Then I'll go. I was planning on it anyway. I won't be at the house when you return to it, Noah." She got in the minister's buggy and he drove her away. The members of her congregation followed in theirs, all of them silent as if their minister had passed judgement on us all.

I walked up the hill. Sylvia met me halfway. "I'm sorry. I ruined everything," I said.

She shook her head. Her lips quivered but she was hiding a smile not tears. "I think Barbara is going to make a marvelous wife for the man. Exactly the sort of woman he deserves," she said, then turned to the others. "Please join us at the grave. I think it's time that Noah and I say a few genuine words about Mother."

I was not surprised that Mr. Dunglass and the women followed her but Aleister stayed behind. He thinks funerals nothing more than superstitious nonsense, and useless really once the soul is gone.

Angelina stayed at the gravesite after everyone else had gone, whispering as if Mother's soul were with her, taking comfort in her advice.

Later, when the five of us and my sister were alone at the house, Aleister gave a brief service not for the dead but for us, the living.

I allowed it as almost a way of cleansing the space of Barbara's influence, but I had not expected such a beautiful chant, or how at the end when he held aloft one of Mother's favorite crystal bells and rang it once, I felt at peace for the first time in days.

What is it about the man that makes him so brash and

annoying one moment, and so perfectly charming the next? I think that if I know him all my life, I will never be able to figure him out at all.

Dierdre glanced at Angelina and saw that the woman had almost finished the journal. Though there were only four more letters in the box, it seemed the right time for Dierdre to stop reading, and to wait for the questions Angelina would undoubtedly ask. But Angelina said nothing once she was done. Instead, she arranged the pages carefully and put them aside, then walked to the back of the house and into the sunroom.

Dierdre followed her, not surprised when Angelina unhooked the blanket and let it fall. Stepping back to the doorway, she looked through both sets of glass much as Dierdre had done that first time. "I could always feel that something wasn't right here, but I never would have guessed the reason," she said.

"No one could," Dierdre whispered. She glanced at the glass. Both showed a cloudy sky, the one on the left darker than the other. Even that discrepancy was too much, and she looked away, feeling vaguely ill. "Cover it again, please," she asked, backed into the kitchen and sat at the table.

Angelina joined her a few minutes later. "Is it really so frightning?" she asked.

"Now it is." Dierdre explained what had happened. "I wanted to stay there with him forever," she said. "Instead I discovered what happens if I stay too long."

"And so you left him, at a most inappropriate moment."

Dierdre hadn't explained all of it. "He told you?" she asked.

"Bridget did a few years later. By then it didn't mean much anymore."

"I wish there was some way I could tell him how sorry I am for everything. But I suppose that he died years ago."

Angelina nodded. "He was only thirty-three when it happened."

"Thirty-three! How?"

Angelina looked at her vaguely, the way she had when she tried to explain the events on the night of the fire. "He died . . . in the fire. He died when the steamer he was taking to

Italy exploded and sank . . . He died at the Abbey at Thelema following a fall. He'd gone seeking answers about something important.''

''About me,'' Dierdre whispered.

Angelina acted as if she hadn't heard. ''And he died . . .'' She stared at Dierdre; shocked, astonished. ''Everything shifts. Everything changes. None of it feels right anymore. That much I do sense, and always have.''

''Did Noah ever publish any more poems?''

''He had one book published in 1921, I believe. You'll have to read it.''

Dierdre started for the door. ''Grandmum must have a copy in the library,'' she said.

''No. She gave it to me months ago. I'm beginning to understand why.''

''Find it for me now, please. I have to know everything.''

As soon as Angelina had gone, Dierdre began reading the remaining letters. The first was written soon after his mother's funeral, describing the somber ceremony wedding of his sister and her minister. The next concerned her, and those she knew.

June 16th

My Dierdre. Aleister has left for Italy, taking Leah and little Hansi with him. Leah is expecting another child in a few months, and this time she seems more prepared to deal with the effects of her pregnancy. Aleister promises to take good care of her. I believe him, though I can't help but think better care would be to wait until after the child is born to take her a good way across the world to heaven knows where. He says this is his mission, however, and that he will soon found a great new religious order, one based on magick rather than superstitious nonsense.

I doubt that I am the only one who finds this idea strange.

A young couple has taken his apartment. I look at them, and their little girl and think about us, and what I had hoped would be our future.

And I admit that I feel like a fool.

*I do not know how many more letters I will write you.
I only wish you would reply, if only a line to tell me that
you are well and occasionally think of me. Your Noah.*

The last pair of letters were in an envelope addressed to
Bridget and mailed from somewhere else in the city. She
looked at the postmark and realized that some years had
passed.

December 8, 1923

Dearest Bridget,

*May I still call you dearest? You are, even now, my
dearest friend. Whatever your reasons for not telling me
where Dierdre vanished to no longer matter. Indeed,
now that years have passed, I sometimes think I know
where she wandered off to and understand all too well
your secrecy in the matter.*

*I was stronger when I was with her, more courageous.
I was ready to take chances with my life. I should be
able to remember how I felt then. That I cannot is my
failing, not yours, certainly not hers.*

*Tell her that and that what I intend to do is my de-
cision, and that I do not hold her in any blame, nor
should anyone.*

Noah

Guessing what was to follow, Dierdre's hands began to
shake. She set the pages down on the kitchen table in order
to read them.

*My Dierdre. These will be the last words I write be-
fore my life is over. I wish they could be beautiful words,
poetic ones, but that's hardly possible now.*

*I made you a promise and I broke it. I thought to
myself that Aleister was gone. There were no rituals being held in the courtyard. There were no unclothed ladies to scandalize the boys, no urns filled with glowing
coals to set the place on fire.*

Perhaps you know some of the story I am about to

relate, having read parts of it in the papers or heard of it from Bridget or one of your friends in the city the year that it happened. I won't provide the details, only the explanation.

At the time, 1920, Henry was nearly thirteen, old enough to wake his little brother and lead him to safety if they were in any danger. Even so, I felt some hesitation in taking them in after your warning and my promise, but I had no choice. Sylvia had fallen ill with scarlet fever and the boys had to leave the house immediately. With my brother-in-law's family living in Florida and his friends unwilling to risk their own families for the boys' sake, it was me or Barbara and her minister, and I would not subject them to Barbara, not even for a week or two. Worse, should their mother die, I would not have them in that man's presence, hearing his words of damnation when they would most need solace. So, at my brother-in-law's request and against everyone's advice, I took them in.

I confess that for the first few nights, I was vigilant. Then, after it seemed that nothing was going to happen, I went downstairs one evening, leaving my front door and Bridget's door open, so I could listen and run upstairs at the slightest strange sound.

I hadn't counted on the fire starting not in the apartment below but in my own kitchen. I hadn't counted on the boys being trapped in their bedroom, or on the fire setting off an explosion in the gas line that made it impossible for me to fight my way to their rooms to save them.

I tried, however, but my determination was no match for the flames. While I stood helplessly outside my own door, Bob Dunglass risked his life getting to the basement to turn off the gas lines. Bridget grabbed Bruce and baby Judith and ran to the side of the house, screaming at Henry to break open a window and jump. Henry managed to do the first, but belatedly, and as the glass broke, the fire inside flared outward. Both boys would have died instantly, she told me. I am thankful they were spared the added moments of pain and terror, but I feel nothing but guilt.

Once the gas that fed it was off, the fire spread more slowly. The couple next door who'd been trapped in their daughter's room were able to escape with their little girl. Firemen arrived with their hoses before much damage was done to Bridget's apartment. Only my rooms were destroyed, only my nephews died.

As for me, my burns have healed, enough that the pain they cause is mostly mental.

If only I had kept my promise to you. If only . . . ah, what's the point of endless speculation.

I write to tell you that you are blameless for all of this, and that I feel less than a fool for ignoring your warning. Aleister believes that we all keep coming back, that life and death are nothing more than turns on a wheel. May we be better blessed, apart or hopefully together, the next turn round. Noah.

Dierdre sat, staring at the letter, knowing why it had been written, and what those last words meant. All the grief had been wrung out of her hours before. What was left now was guilt for her foolishness, her stubborness.

Her stupid, ignorant pride.

She wanted to run to the sunroom door, throw it open and dash through it, into the past of shifting scenes, of aging faces, of Noah. She would blurt the truth to him and make him understand everything before running back to her world and the hours of insanity the trip would bring.

But first, knowledge. The sort she had not sought before she forgot that, as Grandmum had so tragically discovered, life and death belong to God and no one else.

So she waited until she heard Angelina's slow and steady footsteps coming down the hall.

Angelina set the books in front of her—a slim volume of poetry, beautifully bound in dark leather, and a second—a paperback titled *The Life and Times of the Great Beast.*

Dierdre opened the book of poems first. There were a pair of reviews taped inside the front cover; glowing remarks from the *New York Times* and a column by Edna St. Vincent Millay in the *Little Review*. Millay praised Noah's "simple eloquence and oddly innocent sensuality." Dierdre guessed what had inspired him even before she saw her name in the dedication.

To Dierdre . . . another place, another time, another turn.

Had he sent the book out as yet another message to her?

The door was uncovered, waiting. All she needed was the resolve. "How did he die?" she whispered.

Angelina picked up the paperback. As she turned to the index, a yellowed newspaper clipping fell out of it. Dierdre read the headline then passed it to Angelina to read aloud.

> *Local Poet drowns in Bay.*
>
> *Noah Hathaway, author of* Central Stories and Other Poems *and winner of the 1921 Crawford Endowment for the Arts, drowned yesterday off the 34th Street Pier. Mr. Hathaway was last seen early yesterday morning by the food vendor near the end of the pier.*
>
> *His body was pulled aboard a fishing trawler late yesterday afternoon after becoming tangled in the nets. Details of his death have not been released but it is believed that he committed suicide.*
>
> *Mr. Hathaway's growing success as a writer was marred by a series of tragedies beginning with the death of his nephews in the fire at MacCallum House on Washington Square three years ago and ending with the death of his sister, Sylvia Draper, earlier this year. According to one of Mr. Hathaway's neighbors, Angelina Laughran, he blamed himself for the boys' deaths.*

Angelina handed the paper to her. "Now it all comes back to me," she said. "I remember the reporters coming to my door. They're the ones who broke the news to me and took down the first words I spoke. I remember thinking how much Noah loved that river and the despair he must have felt when he jumped."

Dierdre looked down at the paper, wiped her eyes with the back of one hand to clear away the tears, and finished the account.

> *The funeral will be private. However, a special memorial service is also being planned at Healey's where*

Mr. Hathaway was a frequent participant in its Sunday evening readings.

Angelina picked up the paperback, turned to the index and found the last reference to Noah. Again, she read aloud,

Many of Crowley's closest associates fared even worse. On December 10, 1923 some years after having published his second, and many believe greater, book of poems, Noah Hathaway tied ropes around the cuffs of his pants, filled them with rocks and jumped off the end of a pier into New York Harbor. When informed of the young man's death, Crowley only remarked that he'd expected this news for some years.

"And so they blamed him," Dierdre said.

"So? They missed blaming him for half the misery he did cause, to those he loved more than anyone."

"Noah said that he waited for me for hours after I'd been expected. He should still be there." She forced herself to walk to the door, to get close enough to it to scan nearly all the yard. She could see the legs and shoes of a man sitting on the bench just outside the door, and guessed it was him. "I'm going through," she said.

"Dressed like that?"

"What better way to get him to listen? And . . ."

"Don't you understand? You can't do this."

"I have to. I caused Noah's death. It wouldn't have happened if it hadn't been for me. I have to set things right."

"And the boys? What will you do about them?"

"I've been thinking about this—logically, not just with my heart. The fire should have taken place at the turn of the century, just as most of our family still believes. Grandmum's father delayed it, but the event still had to occur. If my family hadn't caused the change, Noah's nephews would not have been the ones who died."

Dierdre grabbed the paperback and news article, and a copy of the *Times* from the pile in the kitchen. "If I can't tell Noah everything, maybe I can show him the truth. Don't leave until I come back. I'll need someone here."

Holding everything tightly against her chest, Dierdre walked toward the door. It seemed to take an hour to reach it, as if the air had somehow liquified and she was walking against a current that grew stronger with each step. She backed away and approached the door at a full run.

For a moment, it seemed as if she might break through. She saw Noah, saw Bridget sitting beside him. She opened her mouth to call his name but the air, the thick terrible current of it, filled her mouth and lungs. All she could make was a small, strangled sound.

Miraculously, Noah seemed to hear it. He looked in her direction, then stood and walked toward her, through her, into the sunroom. She felt him pass—the warmth of his body, the rough feel of his suit, even the gentle touch of his soul. Unable to breathe, to move, she felt the world close in around her. As her legs gave way, the current took her through the door, washing her unconscious into her own time.

When she opened her eyes, Angelina was sitting beside her, holding her tightly. The book and papers she'd been carrying were scattered across the floor.

Somewhere, just beyond her reach, Noah and Bridget were arguing about her. Dierdre could see them, could hear them as clearly as if they were in the same room with her, hear Aleister order them to stop, hear him drawn into the dispute.

She grabbed the newspaper and crawled toward the door, getting to within a few feet of it before the current pushed her back once more. She'd revealed the secret to someone and now the powers that had allowed it to open had exacted their revenge.

Tears came, unwelcome, to her eyes. She brushed them away, tried to think logically, to determine some alternate plan, finding nothing until Buddha entered the yard, tail held high. Someone had tied a black lace ribbon around its neck, an adornment the cat seemed most proud of. It pranced over to Bridget, curled happily round her legs. Aleister stopped arguing only long enough to hiss it away. The cat, ears back and wary now, moved toward the door, then paused again. Begging for another handout, Dierdre thought.

Still on her hands and knees, she searched among the scattered papers until she found Bridget's letter to her. Folding it into one long strip, she moved as close to the door as she could. "Buddha," she called softly. "Come on, Buddha."

The cat turned toward the door, ears pointed forward, listening. "Buddha," she repeated. "I've got a treat for you."

It must have understood the promise, because it began moving toward her. "That's it, Buddha," she continued. "Ignore the noisy people, come to me."

When the cat was a yard or so from the door, it stopped and crouched down, tail flicking anxiously. "Come on," Dierdre continued. The cat took another step forward, then lept back, all four feet off the ground at once. It whirled and ran for the wall, stopping for a quick look back before disappearing over the top of it.

Her last hope had abandoned her. Defeated, she pulled her knees tightly against her chest and leaned against Angelina, her rock in the shifting sea of time.

TWENTY-FOUR

It took the better part of the night for the effects of her attempted journey to wear off. Angelina stayed with her through it all, brewing her Valerian tea to calm her, holding her, promising aid when she despaired. "I'll help you set things right. It's not like I have no experience in these things."

"Not the same sort as Aleister, though. You said so yourself."

"We'll do what we can," Angelina countered. "But first you need your rest."

With Angelina's help, Dierdre managed to get an hour or two of sleep. In the morning, determination provided her main energy. While the coffee brewed, she was in the library, bringing up the files Grandmum had transcribed. There was only one short one beyond what she had read, written not as a journal entry, but as a letter to her. As she began it, she suspected that something else, far longer, was supposed to be there.

March 28, 1924

My Dierdre. The decision was difficult to make, but it was the only one open to me. I never told Noah the truth about where you had gone. I could not. My parents, my children, even your own life was in my hands. And of course I had promised, I would not interfere with the

*life of anyone outside my family; I'd seen the damage
that interfering within it had done.*

After you vanished into the future, Aleister spent some
time away from his own work, analyzing your disappearance. He determined that you have done something
forbidden, perhaps revealed too much to someone else,
and so shut the door on your travels into the past. He
believes this will affect you alone since nothing has
changed here. I tested his theory and yes I can go into
the past as before.

But your sudden disappearance affected Noah and
deeply. I gave him no real comfort. I was evasive with
him, even cruel, thinking it best to give him no hope.

Noah would claim he could sometimes hear you, but
not see you. I found this almost unimaginable since even
Angelina with her heightened sensitivity has never detected any oddity about the door. But then, Angelina has
never been in love with someone on the other side of it,
and love is a powerful force—greater even than the passion Aleister and I roused to create the portal.

I demanded that Aleister help me open the door for
you, if only for just one time. I reminded him that the
magick itself was responsible for Noah's despair, and
that we had a responsibility to help him. I thought that
perhaps you could come back, and find a way to let
Noah down gently so he could get on with his life.

I argued for days. He finally agreed because otherwise I would not let him alone.

"You provided half the magick for the first working.
You have an intellect nearly the equal of mine and you
are far more interested in solving this matter than I am.
Set to it, and bother me only when you have to," Aleister
told me and handed me a stack of books that reached
nearly to my chin.

For two weeks, I read and remembered, meditated
and charted, and plotted our assault on the will of the
gods, adding a bit of gut instinct for good measure. I
presented it all to Aleister. He read it carefully and decided that our combined passion would not be enough.
However, he has agreed to one final joining (as if his

*ego would possibly allow him to refuse!) On May 4,
beginning exactly at sunset, we tried. Sadly, we did not
succeed. We tried again in June on the night of the Solstice, still with no success. Aleister thinks it is because
something you did shut the door and you must be a part
of the ritual if we are going to reopen it.*

*Just before Aleister and Leah left for Europe, he made
a confession to me which I record for your sake. "You
and I made a life and opened the door," he said. "The
gods were pleased. Now, for whatever reason, they've
been angered. They'll want more than you are prepared
to give, Bridget. Give it up. For your family's sake, let
things stay as they are."*

*I took his advice for a time. I even took comfort in
Noah's mother's death, because handling the estate took
his mind off you for a time. But months passed and Noah
still spoke of you often. Then there was the fire and the
boys' deaths and he moved away. I saw him only once
afterwards, at his sister's funeral. When I heard the
news of his suicide, I sent Aleister a letter telling him of
it. He never wrote back, but that would be like him.
Death has never held any interest for him, and of course
he accepts no responsibility for any of it.*

*But I do. And I think that there are still ways to avert
this tragedy. I've taken all my notes and the information
Aleister handed me, and the exact times of various sections of our ritual and boxed everything up for you. I
hope you can understand the information. I pray you
can. Then perhaps we can work together to put in a
crack in the wall of years separating us, to rewrite this
sad history, and together save Noah's life. If this does
not work, do not despair. There is still another way, one
that will assure that he never meets you. I don't want to
do this. In my heart, I know it would be as terrible a
mistake as the one you made; worse, actually, since it
will be so deliberate. But if I must, I will.*

*And if all this fails, please forgive me as I have long
since forgiven you.*

Bridget.

May 4!

Dierdre still had nearly three weeks to research her side of
the ritual, and with both sides of the door working together,
it might open again. Then she would be sensible but sensitive.
She would tell Noah that their affair was too quick, too intense. She would tell him she was leaving for Canada and
promise to write. Perhaps she even would write, sending letters
via Bridget, and let them slowly lose their ardor, until he took
the hint and found someone else.

And the boys? Harder, but not impossible. She would remind Noah of his promise, tell Bridget everything and explain
her own theories on the matter. Together they could save three
lives.

Hopeful thoughts. Marvelous thoughts! But first she had to
find the box Bridget had mentioned.

She searched the library closet and found only business papers. She searched the desk, even the kitchen cupboards. She
called Angelina, but the old woman was no help. If the box
was still intact, it had to be with the others in the basement.

She had the flashlight in one hand, her keys in the other
and was locking her apartment door behind her when Bill
came down the stairs, still wearing his rumpled suit and carrying his briefcase. He had none of his affable slouch but instead
walked with shoulders back and spine stiff, a military sort of
bearing. "I'm glad I caught you. I was going to stop by your
place or Angelina's before I went back to work. Do you know
what this is all about?" He showed her Detective Malverne's
card.

"He's investigating an accident." Dierdre told him what
she knew about the woman and her death. "Witnesses say she
was seen leaving here."

"Here? That's impossible."

"Maybe she was trying the buzzers, hoping someone would
let her in," Dierdre suggested.

"No one tried mine." He sounded defensive, but then he
seemed to be so concerned about what she thought of him.

"Maybe she was hiding in the foyer, trying to escape from
someone on the street. That could explain why she ran. He
wants you to call him, though."

"Then I'll walk over to the station and ask for him. It's better that way."

"Better?"

"I come from a long line of anarchists. The family motto's always been 'never let authority into your dwelling. If you do, it will never leave.' " He started for the door. When she didn't follow, he turned back to ask, "Aren't you going somewhere?"

"I forgot something." She unlocked her apartment door, aware that Bill was standing at the outer door, watching her until she went inside. She waited until she heard him leaving the building before going downstairs.

The basement seemed darker without the comforting presence of an armed policeman; mustier too. A cobweb brushed against her arm as she made her way to the room at the near end. Thankfully, the window was still locked. Feeling a bit more at ease, she brushed the dust off the top of the nearest box and began digging through the contents, aiming the flashlight at the book spines so she could make out the titles. The first two boxes were all light reading, first edition hardcovers by Shirley Jackson and Frank Yerby and the like, covered with plastic and arranged in no particular order; the sort of books put away in the hope that they might one day be valuable. Mindful of how Grandmum had disguised her most important journal, Dierdre dug to the bottom of the stack, and opened any book that looked like it might have something else hidden inside it. Nothing, and nothing in the other boxes either except for other first editions.

The room where she'd seen Crowley's furniture looked more promising, too much so. Every box seemed to have at least one or two books that might be related to Crowley's work. There were also books by Helena Blatavasky and Montague Summers, something on rituals of the Golden Dawn, as well as volumes by Crowley himself. But the order of them, scattered through the boxes rather than arranged in one place, made her believe that she hadn't found what she was looking for. Had the box been taken, dragged off to be pawned for nowhere near its actual value?

She panned the flashlight around the floor. It was too damp to be dusty, but she noticed that the spot where the box of

Noah's letters had been sitting was still dark. She moved one of the cardboard boxes and saw the same type of spot beneath it. If something had been stolen, she should be able to tell.

As she searched, she paid particular attention to the dark corners and small spaces between the furniture. No dark spots, but beside the carved headboard was an outline in white crystal where something had been sitting, probably for a long time, before being moved. The item had been fairly large, two foot by three give or take a few inches. She crouched close to the mark and saw dark lines crisscrossing the inside of the rectangle.

There were paint cans stacked in the corner of the room. She moved one of these aside and saw a dark mark underneath it as well as the same sort of white ring around it where the metal exposed to air and damp had oxidized.

The box had been metal, possibly reinforced with wood. A trunk?

Her search went more quickly now. She moved from room to room, breaking down doors when she had to, panning the flashlight over the space, finding nothing that looked like the missing chest.

It was gone. She went to the end room and took another look at the window. It wasn't more than three feet across and no more than eighteen inches high. Maybe the trunk was thin enough to be taken away but she doubted it.

Which left someone with access to the basement keys. Someone like Bill, with obvious interest in the occult and the opportunity to take whatever he wished from Grandmum's huge collection.

She ran up the stairs and locked the door behind her, then paused in the foyer to hold her breath, to listen.

No droning of a TV upstairs, no footsteps, no sign that Bill had come back.

But he could, and anytime. Though she wanted to use her passkey and go rummaging through his books and papers now, she knew it would a mistake. Better to wait until he was off to work tomorrow, then make a slow, careful search, one which would leave everything exactly as it had been before she arrived. Besides, she had plenty of other things to read in the meantime.

But in the library, though there were many books about Crowley and by Crowley, biographies and critiques, essays and more, there was only one book she wanted to open—the little book of poems by Noah.

She picked it up, running her fingers over the soft leather binding, feeling something akin to the arousal of touching him the first time.

She read the dedication again, smiling as if they were together and he speaking it aloud. The first poems were on many topics, but as she read about what was certainly Grandmum's garden, artists on the Square, and other quick glances at New York life she was certain that they had all been written *to* her. Nowhere was this clearer than in the last poem in the section. Titled simply "Dusk," it was set on one of the New York piers, ending simply:

> . . . *The fog tiptoes in,*
> *curls round my feet, hungry and demanding.*
> *I tend to it, for a moment look away*
> *And you are gone.*
> *I stand alone in pressing lacy isolation.*
> *I call you.*
> *Reach out your hand.*

By the time she'd finished the first grouping of poems, Dierdre was crying, almost unconsciously and with less sorrow than joy that Noah would finally find beauty in the city. The second grouping seemed to be about her, as if he had dissected each part of her—her lips, her hands, her face—turning them into words, almost musical in their rhythm, their beauty. The third and last grouping was actually one long poem. Called "The Wheel," it paralleled the seasons of the year with the seasons of a man, ending not with death but with the promise of another spring, the promise the dedication had already explained.

To Dierdre . . . another place, another time, another turn.

For well over an hour, she was lost in his memory, her eyes closed, recalling, recalling, recalling. Aleister had believed in sex as a shortcut, meditation as the more arduous route. Well, he had his mantras and prayers and his scarlet women or what-

ever he called them, but she had the memory of Noah, her
inspiration, her love.

While she was reading, she heard the foyer door open and
close, steps on the stairs, Bill's TV. Curious about the police
case, she went upstairs and knocked on his door. As he opened
it, she smelled incense, saw a wide-screen TV in the corner,
an old recliner, and a bag of chips and can of beer on the
cluttered end table. He grinned when he saw her. "Well, hello.
And what brings you up to my door, finally?"

"I was wondering if the police found out anything more
about that woman," she told him.

"Malverne wasn't there so I talked to some other cop, a
sergeant, I think. Anyway, they did ID her. Just some
woman—kid actually since she was only twenty-one or so—
from the Bronx. I don't recall her name but it's sure to be in
the paper in the morning, buried somewhere near the back, I
suppose."

"Anything more about the building?"

"Nope. But the police were sure putting a lot of effort into
trying to figure out the connection."

"Malverne was hoping someone here could identify her.
Now that they have, I suppose they won't bother us anymore."

"Good. I can think of a hundred other cases that deserve a
lot more attention. Hell, everyone around here could." He
waved his arm toward the apartment. "It's nowhere near as
nice or as orderly as yours, but would you like to come in,
have a beer or something?"

She wanted to, perhaps have a quick look around while he
got it for her. But if she did, she'd never be able to resist the
temptation to make a study of every corner, every exposed
room. If he noticed, he might get suspicious and move anything of value well out of her reach.

Better to be patient, and wait for morning.

It was only midafternoon; tomorrow was such a long way
off. In the meantime, there was one important thing she ought
to do. She called Suskind at his office. "You said you have
someone there who does background checks. How long does
one of them take?" she asked the attorney.

"It depends on the individual. If he's lived in New York

most of his life, a day or two. If he moved around a lot, a week or more. Out of the country . . . well, you get the idea.''

"It's on one of my tenants, Bill Coleman.''

"The one mentioned in Bridget's will? You're in luck. This is going to take all of ten minutes, unless you want an update on him for the last five years since your great-grandmother ordered a report. She has it somewhere, probably attached to his lease. Check her desk. If you can't find it, call me back and I'll send you a copy of it.''

"That's not important. Is there someone who can skim it, and give me the most important information?''

"Judy's still here. I'll transfer the call.''

The report wasn't long. It took Judy all of five minutes to deliver a summary. "This was done five years ago, so adjust the dates. Bill Ellis Coleman, 48 now. Employed three months for Eastman Pharmaceuticals. Previous employers . . . well, it's quite a list, do you want them all?''

"No, but did he change jobs often?''

"Every six months or so. Moved around a lot, too, and apparently changed his name when he was nineteen. His parents were Charles Hirsig, a presbyterian minister from Dayton, Ohio, and Laura Coleman, a housewife from the same town. They divorced in 1961, following her husband's arrest for assault on Bill. The mother reclaimed her maiden name and her son changed his to hers as a show of support.''

"The father's name was Hirsig? Do you have the maternal grandparents' names?''

"Just the grandmother's, Leah Hirsig. We don't have the grandfather's name. I could check further for you but it might be hard to obtain.''

"It's not necessary.''

"Should I send you a copy of this?''

"No, what you gave me is fine. Just one more question. Do you have a date of birth for Charles Hirsig?''

"We do. 1925.''

Dierdre recalled the information in one of Crowley's biographies. Leah and Aleister had parted ways by then. Could they have reconciled long enough to have a son or was the father someone else? No small point, but more importantly what sort of life had that child experienced for the first few years?

Dierdre thanked the woman for her help and returned to Grandmum's library, pulling out a pair of biographies of Crowley, looking for the last references to Leah Hirsig.

There was no reference to another child, but a final entry for Leah provided some insight. She eventually settled back into the profession she'd had before she met "The Beast," that of a school teacher. Early editions of Crowley's biographies had respected her privacy by using a pesudonym, editing the text to include her real name only after she died.

What did Bill think of his lineage? Judging from his interests, a great deal.

Dierdre found plenty of other information to occupy her time, none as specific as what she sought, but certainly valuable. She studied the library section on the occult, pulling out two books by Crowley, his Confessions and a record of his magical practices. Both were arranged in diary fashion and covered the years he lived in New York.

In them, she found mention of a number of women used in his New York rituals, but none seemed to describe the young Bridget MacCallum. The rites themselves, all sexual in nature, were varied and mechanically noted. Yet there was a certain prudery in his language, a tendency to resort to Latin terms to describe certain obscene acts which made her wonder if he was really the libertine he made himself out to be.

One thing was certain, many of Crowley's rites from 1917 to 1919 centered around a desperate need for money. And there was something else—a sort of growing tension in the journal, as if he sensed that he was on the verge of a great magical discovery.

The Confessions were more helpful, filled with numerous references to Crowley's tiny apartment, his move to this building, some vague mention of rites conducted outdoors. His tone was that of one who had achieved some new and tremendous insight. Soon after he was in England, then in Greece. Apparently his quest for funds had been successful, since a man like Crowley would never travel second class. She suspected that he'd acquired some portion of the MacCallum fortune to sustain him.

Though it was still early, reading exhausted her. She was about to put the books away when she came across Crowley's brief, derisive comment about one of his students.

I told him that if he spent half the time he does in hounding me about my knowledge to seek out his own, he would be a mage of some power. He has the intellect necessary for greatness, but not the will, and without will there is nothing. All a seeker needs to assure success is patience and need. Unfortunately, he has neither.

She had both in plenty. The idea gave her hope.

TWENTY-FIVE

In the morning, Dierdre could hear Bill in his kitchen talking on the phone. It was after ten before he headed out. She
watched him through a crack in the front curtains. He wore a
suit, carried a briefcase and he headed in the direction of the
garage where he stored the company car.

A full day of travel, she hoped.

Just to be certain that he hadn't forgotten something, she
decided to read the newspaper first and give him some time
to get well out of the neighborhood. She paged through the
local news quickly, scanning the headlines. Nothing on the
girl, and nothing on the obituary page either.

Didn't a death deserve at least that much?

She found Malverne's business card and called him at the
station.

"I hear that you identified the woman you'd asked about
but I didn't see anything about her in the news. Is everything
settled?" she asked him.

"I suppose."

"Was she a . . ." Her voice trailed off.

"Hooker? Call girl is more like it. But not an addict and
not a regular in your neighborhood."

"And she died solely because of an accident?"

"It seems so. The lab work showed only trace amounts of
cocaine, more of some exotic prescription drug in her system,
a downer of some sort. She lived uptown in a pretty nice place,

so she wasn't a common streetwalker. But get some security bars on those windows or somebody will move in down there, OK?''

"Did Bill Coleman ever come to see you?"

"Yeah, I wasn't here so he talked to somebody else. He couldn't add anything to what you told me."

She thanked him and hung up.

Then, before she lost her nerve, she dug in the library desk drawer until she found the passkey for Bill's apartment.

She stood in front of the open drawer, holding it, wondering how to proceed, trying to form some plan to assure success, another to assure an excuse should Bill return while she was up there. He might even be waiting upstairs to see if she suspected him of knowing any part of Grandmum's secret. And if he did, and she discovered it then—.

Damn it! Her imagination was getting out of hand, and taking all her courage with it. She sat, one hand on the drawer pull, the other clutching the key, completely unsure what course to take.

She wished, with sudden painful longing, that Grandmum could be here to help her sort things out.

Ah, well, that was impossible, at least as far as Aleister understood things. She picked up the key, put it in her pocket, then went and sat in the front room. She didn't move from the chair for a quarter hour, then only to the phone. She called Bill and listened to the silence between the rings until the answering machine clicked in.

He's gone, she decided. She went upstairs and pounded on his door, keeping it up until she was sure there was no way he could claim not to have heard her.

Now that she'd created a situation that would be as embarrassing for him as for herself if they came face-to-face, she unlocked the door and went into the apartment.

Bill's living room was even more cluttered than her quick glance last night had revealed. The floor was littered with candy wrappers, aluminum cans and dirty dishtowels. And the only part of it not covered with a month-old layer of dust was the screen on the entertainment center and the leather recliner facing it. She was about to leave when she noted how neatly

the CD's were stacked beside the stereo, the alphabetically
listed movies in the glass-covered cabinet.

His nature was too neat for him to be so slovenly.

She headed down the hallway, past a bedroom—black
sheets and deep blue comforter, a kitchen—sparkling white
countertops above the original oak cabinets, and into a large
den with exits to both the kitchen and the hallway.

The last room held the most surprises. Here the clutter was
greater, but with an order to it all. Papers were stacked on an
oversized and well-polished mahogany desk. Books were arranged by category on the shelfs behind it. The wood floor
was clean and polished. A long narrow table took up most of
one wall. It was covered with a red cloth that reached nearly
to the floor. It had a pair of candles at either end, nothing else.
His altar, she thought.

In the center of the floor she saw a pentagram drawn with
different shades of paint, each tip of the star containing a different Egyptian symbol carved out of wood and held in place
by spikes attached just to the tip of each ray. Dierdre didn't
understand the full meaning of the carvings but three of them
were the same as the ones above the old french doors in her
apartment. Those same three symbols were also carved and
attached to the molding above the doorway leading into the
kitchen in the same fashion as they were above Grandmum's
sunroom doors.

Bill obviously knew a great deal about what Crowley had
done and was trying to duplicate the magick.

Had he found someone to act as his scarlet woman? If so,
did that nervous, lumpy man know enough to bring her to that
height of ecstasy that Crowley seemed to find so essential?
She shuddered at the thought of touching him, and moved
closer to the symbol, skirting its edges, looking for some sign
of what sort of magick Bill had worked here.

She found it in a few flakes of what seemed to be dried
blood in the center of the symbol on the floor, in more of it
coating the symbols above the door.

She felt sick, and a little dizzy. Not wanting to stay in the
apartment any longer than necessary, she quickly scanned his
shelves looking for books that might be Grandmum's diaries.
Nothing. Reluctantly, she pulled open the drawers of his desk.

The top ones were filled with handwritten files and sample packets of the pills his company distributed, making her wonder if the woman who had died had gotten some drug from him. The lower left-hand drawer held a small whip, a pair of sharp knives, a case of what looked like hatpins, and a bottle of alcohol to sterilize them. Crowley had used sex to provide a shortcut to power. Bill apparently used pain. She wondered if the pain had been self-inflicted or if he had found or purchased his victims. There were women who would let a man abuse them if he had the money to pay them well. And Bill had money; he'd hinted that he had a lot of it. Crowley's method, while far from pure, was hardly the abomination that Bill's was.

Had Bill succeeded? The only way to know would be to ask him, and she wanted to avoid that at all costs. Aware that he might walk through the door without warning, she moved in as orderly a fashion as she could through the desk drawers, through stacks of receipts and junk mail, and product literature from his work. She relied on her memory, well-trained from years of memorizing instructor's lectures, to help her keep everything arranged the way she'd found it.

In the bottom drawer, empty of anything else, she found a book wrapped in purple silk. Its red leather cover was inscribed with a gold pentagram, the pages in it filled with handwritten entries. Crowley had kept a magical diary; Bill had done the same.

She lifted book and cover from the drawer. Beneath it was a key, a simple design like the one she'd used at work to lock her files. It didn't fit the file drawer of his desk, which was unlocked and empty except for more work-related literature and samples, but the place where he had stored the key implied that it had special significance.

She studied the room, trying to see some hiding place she'd overlooked, settling finally on the altar table. She'd already lifted the cloth once, now she looked a bit more carefully and discovered a shelf a foot or so above the floor. She'd been looking for a trunk, but this could hardly be called one since it was less than two feet high. She pulled it out carefully, surprised at how light it was, and set it on the floor. As she expected, the key in her hand fit its newer padlock.

She opened it slowly, half expecting to hear an alarm or, worse, see some sort of nightmarish creature fly out at her. "Too many lurid movies," she mumbled to herself, then held her breath, suddenly uneasy. The feeling was strong enough that it seemed she had freed some invisible thing from the trunk, and that it was stalking her now, preparing to pounce, to protect these precious papers from any intrusion.

"These were supposed to belong to me," she said aloud, dispelling what had probably been nothing more than a phantasm conjured from her own imagination. She studied the trunk's contents—a trio of scrolls tied with black ribbon; a pair of books with strips of paper marking pages; yards of purple silk fabric; a short, fat, carved stick, more a phallic symbol than a wand; a trio of artist's brushes, and a dozen or so brass vials, their tops sealed with wax. Someone had also scattered desiccant pouches inside, probably to keep the contents dry. Nonetheless, the inside of the box smelled musty, as if it had been closed a long time.

She lifted the chest to the altar top so she could get a better grip on it. Though it was light enough to carry easily, the size made it awkward. She held it in both arms and headed for the front door when Bill's phone rang. She heard Bill's outgoing message, then his voice. "Dierdre," he said. "I kept the papers safe. I never even looked at them except to make sure they were what I believed them to be. I waited for you. Now stay where you are and wait for me."

"Not on your life," she mumbled, and pulled open his apartment door. Balancing the chest in both arms, she started down the stairs.

She was halfway down when Bill opened the foyer door. He walked to the base of the stairs and looked up at her, seeming to angle his entire body backward to do so. She wondered if he'd taken a fall, or thrown his back out. She hoped so. If she had to fight her way past him, she'd want him handicapped. She took another step down; he didn't move.

"You stole what was mine, now let me by," she ordered.

"I kept it safe for you," he countered.

"Let me by," she repeated.

"You're going to need my help, you know."

"The way you helped that girl, the one who died?" She'd

throw the chest at him if she had to, and bolt out the door.

"Be careful. Don't drop it," he said, as if he guessed what she was planning. "Stay where you are for a minute and let me explain." He spoke calmly, with his hands at his side but he still blocked her way, giving her no choice but to listen.

She expected some sort of hurried explanation, some excuse. Instead, he took off his suit coat and hung it over the newel post. His shirt and tie followed. His undershirt was stained in the front, as if he'd put it on dirty. He took that off as well and she saw a number of what looked like scratches across his shoulders. "Be prepared," he said. "It isn't as bad as it looks."

He turned his back toward her, revealing not scratches but welts, deep ones that crisscrossed his shoulders and, to a lesser extent, his ribs. Some had even broken the skin. Most of these were scabbed over, but there were two bandages as well, and one showed a bit of blood seeping through the gauze.

Dierdre had been warned, but she still felt faint as well as confused. "Who did that to you?" she asked.

"That girl did. I said I could explain. Will you let me."

She considered, and quickly because the chest she held grew heavier by the minute. "All right. But go outside. Wait for me there."

He pulled on the shirts and left his jacket and tie on the post. Dierdre saw him pause at the top of the steps then continue down, until he was out of sight.

She bolted for her apartment, placed the chest on her sofa then locked her apartment door and leaned against it. She needed a moment of calm to defuse and consider what to do. Calling the police seemed a logical next step but if she did, she'd likely lose Bill's help. And he was right, she needed it.

With Noah's life hanging in the balance, she decided to trust him, at least long enough to hear him out. She grabbed a sweater and went outside.

TWENTY-SIX

Bill was sitting on the bottom step, his back stiff and for good reason. A straight back kept the wounds from opening or the shirt from sticking to them. When he saw her, he stood and wiped the palms of his hands on his pants. The gesture seemed both old fashioned and juvenile, as if he were a little boy trying to make a good impression on a new teacher. She sat beside him. Though the day was sunny, the air held a chill and the marble steps, shaded by the stone walls on either side of the steps, felt icy against her body.

"I didn't know if you'd talk to me," he said. "I suppose I wouldn't blame you if you called the police."

"I considered it. Then I decided to listen to what you have to say first."

"Would you like the amended or full length version?"

"It's early," she replied.

"And it's freezing. Should we go inside?"

She shook her head. "Let's go over to the Square and find a place to sit. Then tell me all of it."

They found a spot sheltered from the spring wind and drenched in sun. It was warm there, and still early enough in the day to be pleasantly uncrowded. "All right," she said.

"First, do you know who I am?"

"I know you changed your name and that you're Leah Hirsig's grandson. Aleister's too?"

"I don't know. I think I am but it's more of a feeling than

anything else. By the time I first heard his name, Leah had
been dead for years. And Father never spoke of the man. It
was clear later that he hated Crowley with a passion he showed
for nothing else.''

"I read some of Crowley's biography. Your father must
have had a terrible life when he was young.''

"And spent the rest of it in a state far worse.

"Father believed in God with every atom in his mind, and
none in his heart. Not the fluffy sort of God good people like
Angelina pray to, but a God of judgement and retribution. He
went through divinity college and became a minister. Some
years later while he was assigned to a little Presbyterian congregation outside of Dayton, Ohio, he met and married my
mother. I was born a year later.

"Though he loved my mother, he was hardly a pleasant
man or the sort of father a boy hopes for. Though he never
raised a hand to me, I was terrified of him. He probably knew
it, Mother certainly did, but he did nothing to alleviate it. I
can't recall him ever hugging me, just as I can only recall
seeing him without his cleric's coat and collar twice in my
life.

"When I was about seven or so, Mother told me that Father
had lived his early years in desperate poverty as my grandmother moved through Europe taking one ill-paying job after
another, always terrified someone would learn of her past.
Eventually, her sister, my great-aunt Alma, wrote and invited
her to come to Ohio and settle. Mother told me this as a way
of explaining why he was so remote, so exacting, so obsessed
with order. Of course, I understood only a little of it, but I did
find myself suddenly fascinated by my grandmother.

"Until then, I'd thought of Leah as just a retired school-
teacher who had led a rather drab life. But after Mother spoke
to me, I saw her as a mystery that I had to solve.

"Leah would not answer my questions about her early life,
saying only that it was an existence she had put behind her
years before. I stopped asking about it, but I never stopped
wondering.

"She died when I was eleven. One of her younger sisters
had been living with her. When I was fourteen, that woman
died as well. I went to the house with Father to help him clear

it out so it could be sold. We were going through old letters when I came across one from a biographer asking for more information about Leah's relationship with Aleister Crowley.

"So I saw his name for the first time, and having learned it my curiosity about him could not be contained.

"I was no fool. I knew what would happen if I were caught with any information on the occult, let alone on someone my father would particularly despise. So I started my reading at the library, which had little to offer, then at the local bookstore. The sole employee was a whalelike sort of creature, and I would help him stock the bottom shelves. In exchange, he would let me take books into the back room and read them if I were careful to keep them looking new. After a time, I began doing more of his work in exchange for special orders. He gave these to me at cost, and I kept my library on a shelf in the back of the store. The more I read, the more I wanted to read. I don't know if we are related, but I felt a kinship with The Beast.

"In the meantime, the clerk's sloth did not go unnoticed. I was seventeen and just out of high school when the owner fired my accomplice and offered me the man's job. I hadn't been responsible for his departure and I needed the work. Dayton, Ohio, was not exactly a boomtown in the mid-fifties.

"The whale didn't see things my way. He phoned my father and told him what I'd been doing."

"He must have been furious," Dierdre said.

"Father didn't even wait for me to come home. He showed up at the shop, gliding serenely past me and the customers and into the back room. After seeing the truth of the matter for himself, he came to the cash register, smiled and said good morning to one of the customers who attended his church, even chatting with her until she left the store.

"As soon as we were alone, and with no word of warning, he turned on me. The first blow was so quick and unexpected that I fell. He kicked me a few times in the groin so hard I doubled up with pain. All the while he was screaming at me that I would never be like Aleister, that he would never allow it. Then he was on me, beating my head against the floor, as if he could beat the knowledge of that beast from my brain.

"He was my father. Much larger than I was, much stronger.

But even if I had the advantage of size, I could have never raised a hand to him. By the time I realized my life was in danger, I was too injured to fight back.

"He might have killed me if a couple hadn't come in and seen what was going on. The man pulled Father off me while the woman with him called the police. The police arrested Father and called an ambulance for me.

"They took Father to the station then released him with no charge. But the damage to his reputation had already been done. A sharp crime reporter with an interest in the occult noted the family name and the Right Reverend Charles Hirsig was unmasked as the son of the Scarlet Woman, or the Ape of Thoth, or the Whore of Babylon depending on which of Crowley's pet names for her looked most lurid to the editor that day. Needless to say, Father's congregation, taught by him to be unforgiving of far lesser transgressions, booted him out.

"I was in the hospital for two weeks. Father left town just days after I was released, on his way to a foreign mission assignment. Mother had already started divorce proceedings. Later she reclaimed her maiden name. I changed mine to match hers, not because I wanted to divorce myself from my grandmother, but because of my father and the scandal he'd caused.

"I stayed in Ohio with Mother until she died, then moved around a lot. But I never lost interest in Aleister. My research led me to Grandmum's building. Now I read whatever I can get my hands on. Unfortunately, my ability to practice the high arts has always been limited. My father's well-aimed kicks accomplished that. I suspect he would have been proud. According to my mother he never cared much for carnal pleasures anyway."

Bill wanted her to say something to him, Dierdre knew. A word of sympathy, of understanding, of forgiveness. She couldn't, not yet. "What about the girl?" she asked.

"Meditation is for monks with time on their hands, something we city dwellers have too little of. Aleister had the same problem; that was why he preferred sex magick to other methods. The last simple method is one that has been used by shamens for centuries—the dream state that comes with pain.

"I could hurt myself, of course, and I have." He paused to

roll up his sleeve and show her the scars left by burning cig-
arettes and lines from hot sticks of incense. "But I soon discovered that self-induced pain goes just so far.

"Then you came here. I was close enough to success with
my own door that I could feel you moving between present
and past. And I thought that the times when you were there
would be the most advantageous for my own success.

"I have a woman I occasionally use for my rituals, but she's
been out of town for weeks. The agency I called sent that
child over instead. She was all dressed in black leather from
her skimpy vest and bustier to her stiletto heels but she had
no idea of how to do things right. It was all some sort of sex
game to her. The minute she drew blood, she wanted to stop.
I persuaded her to go on but she was useless.

"It has to be serious, you see. It has to be real pain, but
she was too anxious to inflict it. If I hadn't been so certain
that that night would be my night of success, I would have
sent her home. Instead, I gave her a couple of tranquilizers."

"Wouldn't that make things worse?"

"They couldn't have gotten any worse. I thought if I could
calm her down a little, she'd follow my directions. Instead,
the pills had the opposite effect. Something snapped in her, I
don't know what, but in the space of two minutes I went from
being thoroughly bored with her abilities to praying for my
life. Needless to say, that situation made any attempt at magick
even more impossible.

"I screamed at her to stop. I begged her. She didn't seem
to hear me. I began to wonder who she thought I was. I managed to break one of the straps that held me and work the
other free, fending off blows all the while. I jerked the whip
from her hands and she ran to the front door and fled. I think
she expected me to follow, but I was hardly in any condition
to do so, even if I'd wanted to.

"You know the rest about her. But for me, the moment was
one of almost-success. I made my way back to the pentagram.
I sat in the center of it, my throbbing wounds throwing me
into a delerious state. And in it, just for a moment, I saw
Aleister and Leah in the room that used to be their room. He
seemed to see me as well, but as soon as he made a move to
acknowledge me, I was jerked back to my time."

Dierdre had no doubt that he was telling her the truth, but she still didn't understand. "Why do you want to go there?" she asked.

"Because he is the master. I want to learn whatever I can from him. And, I suppose, I want to know the truth about my father's father."

Dierdre considered this, silent for a long time.

"Face it, Dierdre, you need me, or at least that's what Grandmum's journal, or the most recent version of it, implies."

What could she say? She could use his knowledge, though as he freely admitted his ability to practice magick—at least in the manner Crowley preferred—was seriously hampered, a handicap she found more relieving than anything else. And since he'd discovered the truth about the door on his own, she wouldn't have to make matters worse by explaining any of it to him.

Most importantly, she believed his story. He seemed to doubt that, however, and went inside and got some literature on the drug he said he'd given the girl. Two of its uncommon side effects were increased agitation and violent behavior. An odd sort of tranquilizer. "Does your company sell much of this?" she asked him.

"Probably more than it ought to." He smiled nervously and looked away, as if afraid to ask what she intended to do. "I do feel guilty about what happened, but it was never my intent to cause her any harm," he added.

"Were you telling the truth when you said you never opened that box?"

"I exaggerated a little. I did open it, but only long enough to determine it was the one Grandmum had mentioned in her letter. As I expected, it had gotten far too musty. I put a drying agent in it, padlocked it and put it away in my own workroom."

"But why?"

"Why?" He looked at her incredulously. "The contents were never intended for me, but for you. There is no way I could ever work with something stolen from another. This isn't a matter of ethics, Dierdre. It can't be done. Do you believe me? Will you let me help you?"

She drew out the moment a lot longer than she needed to, saying finally, "We have a lot to accomplish. Are you going out of town in the next couple of weeks?"

"Boston on Friday, Hartford on Monday and Tuesday. But I can take off tomorrow if you want to get started then."

"Bill, if you're up to it, I want to get started now."

As they walked back to the building, she fell in behind him, watching his back. He'd made the beatings sound almost scientific, as if he felt no arousal from them. She found this impossible to believe, if only because there were so many different means to the same end—meditation and sex may have been Crowley's choices, but there were also drugs, and not just the illicit ones. Bill had access to things far more exotic. But he had chosen pain.

The thought sickened her, even more the strange fleeting fantasy of being the one holding the whip, of taking out her own years of frustration on some helpless person's back.

They decided to work in the sunroom, but before they began the studies, Dierdre pulled down the blanket covering the door. Stepping back, she looked out at the yard, cloudy there, perhaps rain later. It was Monday. Noah would be at work now. Later, she might see him sitting in the garden, waiting for her.

It would be terrible to see him just out of reach and know what would happen to him if she did not succeed. Yet, what better way to maintain her determination?

While she'd done this, Bill had gone upstairs to change. Now she sensed him standing behind her, watching her. She turned and faced him. "What do we do first?" she asked.

"We clear everything that's not needed out of this space, then we clean," he replied.

She wanted to ask him the reason, but before she could it came to her as if she had already known the answer and merely forgotten it. They were removing distractions and through labor claiming the space as their own.

Bill helped, though every time he had to lift something, he winced. His back must have hurt him terribly. Fortunately the wicker furniture wasn't heavy. They piled it in the corner of the kitchen along with the old Victorian floor lamps, until the only things left in the space were a narrow table along one wall, the brass ceiling fixture and the worn carpet on the floor.

Dierdre started to roll up the carpet. Bill tried to join her but she ordered him to stop. "You've done enough," she said. "In a minute you can help me drag it out."

She'd had no idea how filthy the floor actually was until she saw the sharp line marking the exposed and protected tiles, then something more, faint blue lines that ended where the exposed floor began. She stood and moved away from it. "Bill, come look at this," she called.

He put down the mop he'd been using to pull the cobwebs off the ceiling and came to stand beside her. "Not a pentagram," he decided after studying it awhile. "Far too elaborate."

"We may have the designs in the notes," Dierdre said.

"And now we know exactly where to place it. Things couldn't be starting out better."

She hoped so. She prayed so. They washed down the walls and remaining table with unscented soap, lemon oil and water, then started on the floor. With careful scrubbing, they managed to expose some of the faded lines. Others were completely gone, but if this was the symbol Crowley and Grandmum had used, they would have enough of the original to reconstruct it.

By the time they'd finished, it was nearly midnight. Bill carried the box into the room and handed it to Dierdre who placed it on the end of the table.

"Enough for one day," he told her. "This sort of work requires energy."

She nodded. She felt exhausted and not just from the cleaning. She could already feel the forces in the room, struggling with her, draining her will to continue. After Bill left, she sat crosslegged in what seemed the center of the symbol and stared at the old door, the light flickering beyond it.

She shut her eyes. She listened.

The voices were there, so faint they seemed like whispers in her mind.

When she opened them, she saw Noah standing alone in the garden. His back was to her. He stood there some time; waiting for her, she thought. She wanted to call to him, but his letters made her realize how cruel it would be if he heard her voice. So she sat, content to watch, until he took a step backwards then turned to go inside. His face had already grown distorted. Though she shut her eyes against the sight, it seemed that she could feel him moving through her, could almost feel his thoughts, his grief.

She imagined that Angelina must sense her ghosts this way.

TWENTY-SEVEN

Seventy-two years earlier, Aleister Crowley was having his own problems with trust. And his greatest act of magick was threatening to bring his pleasantly ordered life to an end.

He was aware that the main source of his power came from his unshakable confidence in it. Usually he attributed this confidence to his firm belief in reincarnation—for what after all constituted failure when one life flowed into another giving a soul one more chance to get things right? In his less philosophical moments, he viewed the confidence as nothing more than old fashioned British optimism inherited in abundance from his father.

The Crowley family could have led a comfortable middle-class life, but his father had chosen to give it all up and travel the countryside to preach the doctrine of a sect that made the Amish seem positive libertines by comparison. That the fire-and-brimstone message caused less conversions than derisive laughter did not diminish the man's zeal.

At least he hadn't been home very much, and occasionally he'd taken young Aleister with him on the travels, instilling in the boy a love of foreign places that stayed with him through his life. The man died when Aleister was eleven, of cancer of the tongue. Aleister thought it a fitting end for someone whose words had inflicted so much misery on his listeners.

If God existed, had He been unfair to His poor servant? Aleister wanted to say that he didn't care, but knew that his own actions proved that a lie. Soon after his father's death, he did turn his back on Heaven and start firmly down the path his father believed would lead to certain damnation.

Of course hell didn't exist. Instead there would be another body, another time. The only thing that would carry over into the next life was the psychic power achieved in this one.

Aleister was certain of this. By the time of his birth in 1875, Aleister had already led many lives, notable ones, powerful ones. He could recall details of the most significant of these, but even the more obscure sometimes brought flashes of memory. He'd experienced such a swift revelation when Leah came to see him—seen the two of them together in ancient Babylon. He'd acted on the vision and immediately claimed her for his own. She'd responded in kind, so quickly that he knew she shared the same feeling. Though he had moments when he doubted the wisdom of their union, it was a good one. They complemented each other. If Leah had one failing it was that she wasn't wealthy. In spite of this, her thin body and haunting eyes made a deep impression on those who came to hear him speak. She brought him luck.

And best of all, she seemed above petty jealousy, even where her friends were concerned. When he confessed to having an unexpected and intense attraction for her friend, Bridget, Leah merely looked thoughtful. Then, as he'd come to expect from her, she told him everything he needed to know about the woman.

"When we were younger, we were incredible," she said. "There wasn't anything that she and Angelina and I wouldn't try."

She described the lectures they'd attended. The times they'd paid mediums to tell their fortunes, how they'd scoured the dusty back rooms of bookstores for arcane diaries, or danced naked in front of an isolated bonfire like medieval witches. They'd been seeking the power to curse and bless, to fly, to see—if only for a moment—the elusive forest gods of their distant ancestors. Sometimes they had partial success—more than Aleister would have expected given their unfocused studies and the absence of any real teacher to direct them. Leah was a marvel, creative and supportive. Angelina's studies had given her real power, but contacting the dead did not interest him. Aleister was far more concerned about his effect on the living.

To that end, Bridget MacCallum was the one he focused on. Always attuned to its presence, he could feel his sort of power coursing through her. The fact that she seemed to despise him convinced him that they'd been adversaries in some past life. United with him in this one, she would be the companion he needed in order to accomplish his greatest work.

So he'd set out to win her support—first by moving himself into close proximity to her, later by giving her aid at a time when her need was even more desperate than his own.

And he had won—first her body for that incredible night of passion and magick, then her financial support, and finally the use of the possesions their passion had created. As his work continued and he set down page after page of instructions for his followers, he was constantly aware of her balancing the firm's ledgers, quietly working on correspondence in her library, or preparing a meal which she would leave within reach of his work desk, all without uttering a sound. A positively perfect arrangement, until that damned little fool had wandered in from the future and fallen in love with Noah.

Some of the damage the stupid creature had done was clear just minutes after she'd panicked and fled. Noah immediately turned on him, demanding to know what Aleister had done to her.

"Nothing. Why would I have any interest in her?"

"You have since she came here. I see you staring at her, talking to her, and I see the expression on her face when she's with you, as if she has no choice but to tolerate you. Is she one of your people? Have you forced her to stay away from me?"

"I assure you, Noah, that I don't give a damn about either one of you."

"She said you and Bridget have something to tell me."

Noah's voice had risen to nearly a shout, waking Leah. She opened the upstairs window and leaned out to see what was going on. Wisely, she kept out of it.

"She said she'll talk to you in the afternoon. It's late, Noah. Get some sleep, things will sort themselves out in time."

But of course they didn't. Somehow the stupid bitch had

managed to close the door—not completely for Aleister could
feel her lurking on the other side of it, could feel her fighting
to cross the threshold, could even feel her terror and despair
when she could not.

Pathetic, really, but not as much as Noah's reaction. He also
felt the girl's presence. He may have even glimpsed her for a
moment. Then she was lost to him, and seeing magick gone
wrong he naturally blamed the nearest mage.

Now, suddenly, the most important people in Aleister's life
were allied against him. Bridget wanted to know if there was
a way to tell Noah everything. Leah demanded to know what
"everything" meant. Meanwhile, Noah was camped out in the
garden waiting for his ladylove like some faithful puppy and
snapping at anyone who dared to call him a fool.

All of it most amusing, except for the constant distraction.
Aleister's greatest work ground to a sudden and disturbing
halt.

He solved the problem as speedily as he was able. He told
Leah as much of the truth as he dared then put her to work
editing the first half of his handwritten manuscript. He gave
Bridget the books and handwritten notes he'd made prior to
their ritual to open the door.

"What makes you think that *I* can do this?" she asked him.

"Because *I* know you can," he replied. She started to dis-
agree but he cut her off. "You are the one getting the benefit
from this. Don't you think you should be the one to do the
work?"

She saw his logic. "You will help me, though, won't you?"

"I will but you have to do something in return. Banish Noah
from your apartment and yard. Even his silence is annoying.
And spare me the questions except for two hours each evening.
I have my own work to do."

She did as he asked and a blessed though somewhat strained
silence fell over the house once more.

He had been working in her sunroom, but moved to the
library. He told Bridget it was to give her full use of the space
that had to be reconsecrated, but there was more to the truth
than that. He could feel a presence in the room, not a ghost
from the past but one from the future. Dierdre, perhaps, or

some descendent of hers, plotting the magick that would re-open the door.

He gauged their chance of success as just slightly greater than none, but at least their planning brought him peace. And as the days went by, he began to think Bridget might actually be able to succeed if only because her instincts were so keen.

There were many ways to prepare the mind for a ritual. Drugs were one, but she wisely refused to consider that during pregnancy. Sex was another, but in these later months not so easy. Fasting or any other forms of bodily denial were likewise impossible. This left meditation and emulation, and she used these together in the most incredible way.

The god she chose to commune with was Ptah, the bridger of time. Each morning at sunrise, she would spend an hour in meditation, her purpose to learn his purpose for her. The rest of the morning would be spent in doing his will. With no explanation other than this was what he asked, she sewed a robe of bright red-orange, the unbleached cotton dyed by her own hands. She fashioned a staff similar to that shown for Ptah in the Egyptian heiroglyphics, one made of walnut with a ram's head knob. She measured out a hexagonal shape rather than a pentagram on the sunroom floor and colored its lines with indigo ink she mixed herself by adding blessed water to the dye powder. Each new idea seemed less logical than the last, but she worked with such surity that he began to believe her inspiration sprang from some godly source.

Her afternoons were spent in study, first of his own notes then of his books and others. She made subtle changes in his rituals. When he asked the basis for these, she told him, "We must put our faith in the power of Ptah, we must trust it, not fear it."

A saccharine end for a god who had once demanded blood sacrifice, yet it seemed that the hint of a presence in the room had grown stronger. He stayed well away from it, lest he be caught up in her work and abandon his own.

And each night, just at sunset, Bridget sat crosslegged in the middle of the pattern she had drawn on the floor, and moved out of her body, seeking Dierdre, offering advice.

TWENTY-EIGHT

The morning after they had cleaned the sunroom, Dierdre and Bill examined the contents of the chest.

The information the scrolls contained was as detailed as Bridget could make it. They were to draw the symbol on the floor so that each line was exactly twelve feet long. It should be drawn with natural dyes, not paint. "Does she say what sort?" Dierdre asked.

"Better than that, she says she included it here."

Dierdre picked up one of the brass vials.

"No! Don't open any of them yet. Let's see what else is here first."

They went on, cataloging the contents of the chest from the notes enclosed with it, unrolling the scrolls on the desk. They were in English, for the most part written by Bridget, but there were sections in Latin and Greek, no doubt added by Aleister.

Angelina stopped by just as Dierdre and Bill were beginning to empty the items in the chest. She frowned when she saw Bill there, and all but dragged Dierdre into the hallway. "Why is he involved in this?" she demanded.

"Because I need someone who understands what to do."

"That's all? How many practitioners of Crowley's brand of magic do you suppose there are in a city this size? You can afford to pay the best of them for whatever you need."

"But I can't tell any of them what I'm doing. Look what happened when I managed to tell you."

Angelina's frown deepened. "I concede the point, but don't trust him with any more than you need to."

"Is there something you're not telling me?"

"No, but damn it I wish there were!" The old woman seemed as surprised as Dierdre by this outburst. "I'm sorry, maybe its just me and this infernal magick. I never could tolerate Aleister either, especially after he called what I do nothing more than astral necrophilia. Just promise me that you'll be careful."

Dierdre promised, but it was a lie. She didn't know much about what sort of ritual they would conduct but she suspected that trust would be at the heart of it.

As the days passed, Dierdre began to see the intensity Bill had hidden so well. She admired his devotion to his craft. He worked as tirelessly as she did, more even, because they would often stop working well after midnight. Then she could sleep in while he had to get up early to go to work.

The items Grandmum had stored for her contained sections of Crowley's published works as well as Grandmum's own notes. Crowley's magickal writings seemed deliberately obscure, and Dierdre wondered aloud how anyone could understand them without the help of a teacher.

"It's like math or physics," Bill explained. "Once someone explains the meaning behind the symbols it gets easy."

"So a student needs someone to explain?"

"Or they have to spend a lot of time in study."

"Did you ever work with a teacher?" she asked.

"Twice, but I didn't get that much out of it for what I had to pay. I prefer independent study, I suppose because it's how I started out."

As with her personal journal, Grandmum's notes on the ritual had faded in places, and a few of the pages were stained with mildew. Dierdre, with her limited reading ability, would have spent hours deciphering the letters. Bill, who knew Grandmum's handwriting as well as the basis for the ritual, had an easier time of it.

Though she didn't ask him to do so, Bill began to read Crowley's works aloud. Dierdre worked on absorbing them as she had her college lectures. The more she listened the more her talent for memorization returned. Soon she could recite back any complex incantation after hearing it just twice.

The trouble was, they all seemed wrong to her.

"We aren't opening the door; it's already open. I think that what we're doing is more like an apology for breaking a rule," she explained to Bill. "As for the symbol on the floor, it's almost right, but not complete. Wouldn't something else serve us better? This, for example." She sketched the elongated hexagonal-shaped pattern they'd discovered on the floor then added triangles at the narrower ends with the symbols of Ptah and Thoth in the center of them.

He considered this, then asked, "Where did you get this idea?"

"I don't know. It's just logical, I guess."

"Inspired is more like it." He opened a copy of one of Crowley's books and pointed to a mystical symbols. "You never saw this before?"

She ran her hand over the drawing, trying to recall. "I may have glanced at these, but that's all."

"Well, let me know if you get any other ideas like it. Where they come from may be as important as the ideas themselves."

A point she'd just begun to consider.

So each night, while the streets were quiet, and Bill went upstairs to sleep, she sat crosslegged in the center of the unfinished symbol on the floor, faced the door and intoned the odd Greek syllables of Crowley's invocation to Ptah.

For the next two weeks, Angelina stopped by to see Dierdre at least once a day, usually around midmorning. When she realized that only Bill's marked devotion to food kept the girl from forgetting to eat, she made a point of bringing fresh bagels and cream cheese from the bakery on the days he had to work. Then she'd sit with Dierdre, sharing the meal to make certain Dierdre ate it, asking how the work was going then waving off the details when Dierdre tried to explain them.

"That's all right," Dierdre admitted. "I'd be grasping at straws myself. But Bill says that he might have the knowledge, but I have the greater instinct. And I suppose, the greater fear."

"Fear, well I suppose it's natural that you would worry about Noah."

Dierdre played with her hands. "It's more than that. I keep thinking about another ritual in this place, and though we have to use incense and candles and the rest, the thought of any fire in this house worries me. But at least Bill takes my worries seriously. So we're taking every precaution I ask for. Let me show you what we've done so far."

She'd taken Angelina into the sunroom where they'd completed the symbol on the floor. Its center was a rectangle measuring some five by eight feet, with two triangles' apexes meeting, drawn off the two narrow sides forming a pair of stylized hourglass shapes at each end. There were symbols in each triangle. On one side were the earth symbols for success and change; on the other air symbols for truce and peace. At each corner of the main rectangle were thick fireproof tiles, all of them marked with the water symbol for love. The fire sign would be the incense itself.

"There is nothing in this room that would not have been used in nineteen nineteen," Dierdre explained. "We even went so far as to cut off the electricity to the room. Instead we'll use the oil lamps, as Grandmum and Aleister did. And of course there'll be incense."

"Aren't you afraid of fire?" Angelina asked.

Dierdre went to table already draped in yards of purple silk and brought Angelina one of the four incense burners they'd purchased. It was brass with a top that snapped into place and a tall wooden base. Angelina didn't understand. "I would think this would upset far too easily."

"Not when you do this." Dierdre unscrewed the top from the base, revealing a long wood screw. "Bill is going to drill out the center of the tiles. They and the burners are going to be attached directly to the floor. And though we can't have anything so modern as a fire extinquisher in the sunroom, there'll be one right outside along with a bucket of water.

"Things shouldn't get that far out of hand, not with you both here," Angelina said.

"We can't stop the ritual once it starts, so yes things could get dangerous before we're able to do anything about it. And I keep thinking of what Aleister said to Grandmum, about the price being too high. I know what Grandmum valued above all else. So do the gods they invoked. Bill thinks I'm being paranoid but I can't stop the worry. At least he's understanding. Someone with less knowledge would probably think me insane."

Angelina had expected Dierdre's patience for Bill to have worn off days before but Dierdre continued to praise him every time Angelina saw her. "You were right to let Bill help you," she admitted. "I would have done my best, of course, but all this science is beyond me; and probably would have been even when my mind was younger and sharper. No, don't try to describe any of the ritual to me, dear, just tell me how you feel about it all."

"I feel . . . No, I know that this is going to work."

"That's what I hoped you'd say. Now is there any news that doesn't have to do with Master Therion?"

"Well, Mother called twice. She wanted to come to visit next week, but I told her the weather was impossible this time of year and put her off until June. I wrote notes to some of the people who sent flowers, but there's still at least a dozen more to write and a stack of sympathy cards I haven't even opened." She pointed to the pile of mail on the end table. "And there are unpaid bills as well."

"If there's anything I can do to help, I certainly have the time."

"Do you? If I handle the bills and gave you the cards, could you write the thank yous for people you know well? We can both sign them. I know it's an imposition but you were as close as family, and you probably know the guests far better than I do."

The stack wasn't nearly as large as Dierdre had made it out to be, and they were mostly from people Angelina had at least met. She handled the last handful of thank you notes, then began opening envelopes, reading the occasional personal note aloud.

"Here's one from the nursing home," Angelina said. "It might be a bill. Do you want to open it?"

"Grandmum handled all the payments. This is probably just a card. You go ahead."

It was a card with a brief sympathy note and a postscript that Angelina read aloud,

*We keep a guest log for all our patients which we give
to the family after a resident dies. Sometimes relations
find it a helpful way to track down friends of the deceased. I'm sorry I didn't get it to you sooner but there
were only three people who visited Bridget regularly and
they were all at the funeral.*

Angelina handed the folded sheet to Dierdre, who glanced
at it, then took a longer, more intense look. "Is something
wrong?" Angelina asked.

"You're on it, of course. So is James Suskind. So is Bill,
four times with his last visit at 8:30 on the night before Grandmum's death."

"Did he say how she seemed then?"

She looked at Angelina, stunned. "He never said a word
about being there."

Angelina tried to hide her concern for Dierdre's sake. "I
wouldn't make too much of the fact. Bill has a secretive side,
all people like him do."

"Like him?"

"Believers. Magick makes its practitioners squirrely."
Though she was trying to brush off the matter, Dierdre still
looked concerned. "Why don't you ask him about it?" Angelina suggested.

Dierdre's voice fell nearly to a whisper as she replied, "I
don't know if I should. He's always so defensive."

The phone rang. When Dierdre went to answer it, Angelina
picked up the the visitor sheet and studied it, quickly folding
it up when she heard Dierdre's footsteps in the hall.

"That was Bill," she said. "He's stopping at The Hand of
Glory bookstore on the way home tonight and asked me to
meet him there. I have to go."

"Should I stay and finish the cards?"

"If you wouldn't mind." Dierdre dug in the desk drawer
and found Angelina a spare set of apartment keys. "Just lock
up when you go. I'd hate to have that policeman say 'I told
you so.' And don't say anything to Bill about the discussion
we just had, all right?"

"You're sure that's what you want to do?"

''Yes, especially now. We only have two more days to work together.''

But the doubt remained. That evening when she and Bill were studying one of the books she'd purchased earlier, Dierdre could feel it intensifying. It occurred to her that she had never asked Bill what price he would put on all this aid. Now that the time to do so had passed, she'd wait for him to bring it up.

She was prepared to be extremely generous.

TWENTY-NINE

Dierdre had dismissed Bill's actions much too quickly, then Angelina had even done the unthinkable. She'd not only made excuses for him, she'd also withheld information from that poor girl.

If she'd been honest with Dierdre, she would have said something about how Bridget had asked Bill to stay away from the nursing home. He'd even grumbled about it to Angelina. Curious, Angelina had called her old friend. Bridget had tried to laugh off her questions, making it sound as if Bill's solicitiousness had made her nervous.

Angelina had always suspected that it had been more than that.

It troubled Angelina to think that Bill might be controlling her but she couldn't avoid the truth. Controlled was exactly how she felt. She opened the visitor's sheet from Hudson Manor, studying it only a moment before realizing what it was that troubled her so when she'd first seen it.

The log was arranged with columns for name and date, time in and time out. Bill had scrawled in the date, his name and the time in. He had not signed out.

He might have been in a hurry, or the logs might have been put away when he left, but Angelina considered another, more chilling possibility. He'd been the last person to see Bridget alive. Could he have been there the morning of her death, not the evening before?

''Stupid old woman thoughts,'' she mumbled as she went about finishing up the notes. But the suspicion stayed with her, and when she was done she had no choice but to walk down the hall to the sunroom she hadn't been allowed to enter for days.

Yards of purple silk hung from the walls, gold tapestry covered the solitary table. There were cushions everywhere, candles and tiny glass oil lamps making the space look more like a shiek's tent than a New York brownstone.

Aleister would have loved what Dierdre had done to the space, Angelina thought as she walked forward to the little chest she'd only heard about and lightly touched its lock.

She almost expected to be burned, or shocked or even physically thrust back. Nothing happened at first, but gradually her curiosity grew stronger. She shut her eyes and in the silence of her mind glimpsed Bill scurrying from Bridget's room, quickly past the nurse's station, going to the corner before hailing a cab. But there was no hint in the vision of the time of his visit, or if this was even the last one he made.

''Stupid old woman thoughts,'' she said again as she retreated from the room and down the hall to the library to retrieve her bag and keys. Not certain what she intended to do just yet, she opened the desk drawer where Dierdre kept the building's keys and found the one for Bill's apartment.

She could always slip it back in the drawer later. Now she only prayed that she wouldn't have to use it.

Later that evening, Angelina had a long and stormy session with a difficult client. The man had exploded after her fairly innocuous reading. He'd even mumbled some silly curse as he left. She felt only amusement at his fury, an amusement that constrasted sharply with the anxiousness she felt far too often when Bill was at his most affable.

She was a good judge of people, she reminded herself. And she had never judged Bill well, yet she had defended him to Dierdre. She could argue that it was for Noah's sake, but she knew better.

She considered all the other little tricks he'd pulled over the last year, the most obvious being how he kept his distance whenever they were together, as if he feared what she would discover if she managed to get too close to him.

"Fight fire with fire," she mumbled as she sat in her dining room, paging through the few books she owned on Thelemic Magick. She finally found what she wanted, a simple but potent banishing ritual that required no special preparation save a few minutes of quiet meditation and controlled breathing.

After years of practice, she knew how to do this well enough. Only her pose had changed. After two rather embarrassing moments years ago, she had given up the lotus position for simple crossed legs. Later, sitting on the floor had to be abandoned as well. She could get down easily enough, but getting back on her feet . . . well, it was better to sit back in her Lazy Boy recliner than ask a client to help her up. Some things had to be expected when you were nearly ninety. Within a year, after she realized that those annoying little noises her clients had begun making were due to their belief that she was sleeping rather than meditating, she gave up all attempts at direct contact with the dead. She could hardly condemn her body for its weakness. She could only be thankful that she could still get anywhere she wanted to go on her own two feet and could pass easily for a woman in her seventies.

Bridget, whose face had shown every wrinkle from the time she turned fifty, used to say it was all the extra padding Angelina carried. It filled in the tiny lines and even the major crags on her face. The envious witch! Angelina knew better— it was the soul in the body that mattered. And while she believed that hers had aons of experience, it also had a youthful outlook and a willingness to attempt anything, at least once.

Thinking back on her life, it was a wonder she had survived this long.

Well, she had and she still had purpose to her clients and especially to Dierdre and poor Noah. She lit a stick of incense, unplugged the phone and stretched out in the recliner. A few minutes of deep breathing, a quick chant and she was ready. Standing, she faced east. She imagined her body filled with light and power. Then, using a walking stick she'd carved some years before, she drew a pentagram in the air and began the simple invocation to the gods.

Ten minutes later, ritual accomplished, she returned to her

chair, vibrated a mantra until she was back in the proper trance
state. Her soul, well accustomed to travel, left her and went
in search of Bridget MacCallum.

Angelina had no words to describe the afterlife. It existed
in a state outside of such normal physical terms as width or
height or time or distance. She understood that navigating this
alien landscape required power, not power caused by any special talent but rather one perfected by constant repetition. Anyone could do this, all it would take was the patience for years
of practice and a soul that was willing to respond.

Bridget had already shown herself willing. At the moment
of her death, she had stopped to tell Angelina goodbye. With
this thought in her mind, Angelina formed a picture of her
friend in the center of her consciousness. She waited.

They touched and in that moment, Angelina Laughran Petra
ceased to exist as a separate entity.

Two hours later, she returned to her body with a snap. She
stayed where she was, eyes closed, sorting the impressions she
had received into a cohesive whole. When she finally opened
her eyes, she was not surprised to find that her hands were
still shaking and her heart beating far faster than an old
woman's should have been.

The joining of friend with friend had been joyous, but Angelina had received one distinct impression. At the time of
Bridget's death, hardly unexpected and completely natural, she
had not been alone.

Angelina almost wished she hadn't made that contact. There
was no point to it. Bridget had died less than a day before she
was supposed to, and from what Angelina could determine,
her passing had been as peaceful as anyone could hope for. If
she told Dierdre any of what she suspected—a vague suspicion, she had to admit—the girl might break off her work with
Bill. At the least, she'd likely lose the trust that was so important in the work they were doing. If Angelina told the police—and assuming they believed her—Bill would be taken
in for questioning, perhaps held, and the ritual might never
take place.

Two days . . . that's all she'd have to wait before she told
her story to anyone, if she ever did. She decided to sleep on
the matter, and think about how to proceed in the morning.

She walked down the hallway to her bedroom, slowly and stiffly, feeling every one of her years. Her hands trembled over the buttons at the collar of her caftan, shook as they started the knee-highs she wore under it on the slow slide down her legs. She hurried the hosiery along with her feet, and let them stay on the floor where they fell. She'd pick them up in the morning when she was ready to put them on.

"How did we get so damned old, you and I?" she mumbled, speaking to Bridget as if they were still joined. "And why in the hell do I still hold on? You could have answered that, you old witch, gave me something useful in those hours we spent together."

Grumbling almost happily, she went into the bathroom, and started the tub. She made the water a little warmer than usual; she had to relax if she was going to get any sleep at all and there was no better place. When the water was high enough, she turned on the jets.

The bubble tub had been her idea, but Bridget had demanded that she equip it with security bars on both sides before she'd allow the addition. Now she wondered if there'd been a reason for the request. She never dreamed of drowning, though, so most likely Bridget was dictating with the voice of experience. "Older voice, remember that, you witch," she said, wondering if Bridget's soul was nearby, listening to her grumble.

She lowered herself into the swirling water, lay there for the half hour the timer allowed, then a bit longer, relishing the silence. Through it she could almost hear music coming from Dierdre's apartment, an occasional bit of chant.

They were practicing the ritual, committing it to memory.

Two days and it would all be over. She got out of the tub, put on her robe and went to fix a pot of tea. But in spite of the valerian and chamomile blend, in spite of the warm bath and relaxing massage, sleep came hard.

Angelina woke with a jolt in the center of the night. Sometimes a siren passing outside would have this effect, sometimes a bad dream. She could recall neither, nor anything else that might have jarred her awake. It was after four, hardly an appropriate time to be awake, particularly when a client was coming at nine.

She decided on another cup of tea, but as she put on her robe and scuffs she heard faint music coming from somewhere in the building, an occasional scrap of chant; Bill's voice, not Dierdre's.

He had to be taking tomorrow off from work, she thought, almost pleased that she wouldn't be able to use his key.

His voice should have been louder in her kitchen, after all it was the room immediately next to Dierdre's sunroom. But she couldn't hear it anymore. Had they just broken off? Curious, she returned to the bedroom, held her breath and listened. His voice again, clearer.

The room on the other side of the firewall had been Bridget's bedroom. They had no reason to work there. Could she be hearing Bill upstairs? She'd never been able to do so before but then she was rarely awake at this quiet hour.

A thought came to her, one more to add to the all the other troubling ones, why would he be meditating alone at this time of the morning?

Then another, more troubling yet: What did Bill, never known for displaying the slightest hint of altruism, hope to gain by helping his neighbor so conscientiously?

She might not call the police yet, she decided, but there was no reason why she couldn't do a little investigating on her own, if only to determine Bill's motive for being so helpful. Having Bill's key had only distracted her from her real talents. It was time to start using them.

THIRTY

Angelina waited until after her early client to pay a call on Dierdre and return her keys. She found the girl alone, reading over the ritual notes piled on the table in front of her. "I'd probably find it confusing even if I was a speed reader," she confessed, rubbing her forehead.

"You'll be fine. Isn't Bill around to go over things with you?"

"He's working today, finishing up some priority calls so we can have all of tomorrow to get the last items ready and make certain everything is committed to memory."

"Let's take a walk," Angelina suggested. "A little air will clear your head, make your thoughts a bit sharper."

"I'd love to, but I can't. The florist is coming later and I'll have to be here to let him in."

"Florist?"

"One of Bill's ideas. Purple and gold roses. Their natural scents are supposed to complement the rose and almond incense Bridget included for us. We're getting them early to give them a chance to open."

"An odd suggestion. Aleister was never one to take much stock in nature except as a force."

"Bill said it's an extra offering, and for luck." Dierdre managed a weak smile. "Of course, we'll need every bit of it."

"Now where's the confidence I saw in you yesterday?"

Angelina asked, trying to sound upbeat, encouraging.

"Exhausted. I don't think I slept at all last night, I was so nervous," Dierdre admitted.

"Take a nap," Angelina suggested.

"A nap? Why bother? The florist will only wake me up."

"I'll wait for you. I'll even watch for the delivery boy so I can catch him before he hits the buzzer." She sensed Dierdre about to argue, cut her off. "No, you're going to take my advice. It's more important that you work with Bill than by yourself. You won't get anything done with him tonight if you can't keep your eyes open."

She all but ordered the girl to sleep. Once Dierdre had gone, Angelina pulled a cookbook from her satchel and began to study recipes. She'd found just the one she wanted and was finishing up a note to Dierdre when the flowers arrived. She followed the delivery boy out and went home to assemble her spices.

Bill arrived at seven. By then, the foyer was filled with smell of hunter-style pot roast, spiced with cloves and thyme and basted with dark beer and brown sugar and a few more exotic ingredients from Angelina's cupboard.

Angelina let him into Dierdre's apartment. He stood in the doorway, holding pair of hot dogs and kraut he'd grabbed on the way home, the grease already leaking through the white paper wrapping. "What is that smell?" he asked.

"Dinner will be served as soon as I mash the potatoes," she replied. "I figured that since I don't know enough to help with the ritual, I'd do what I do best."

"Where's Dierdre?"

"Taking a shower. Poor girl was exhausted. I made her rest."

"Good for you, you got her to do something I never could. Here," he handed her the dogs. "Put these away for later while I go up to change."

She took them from him, resisting the urge to grip his hands, knowing it would look too suspicious. Once she'd begun receiving impressions in that manner, she began to realize how rarely human beings actually touched. Sometimes it took the greatest effort to get her clients to let her place even her fingers against their palms.

She'd set the table in the kitchen. As she expected, Bill sat across from her, so that most of the dishes were passed to him via Dierdre. For the most part, they ate in silence, as if any discussion of tomorrow night would ruin the ambiance of the meal. After they'd finished, Angelina asked a few questions, which started them talking, exactly as she'd hoped.

"You just go on with your work. I'll get the dessert," she said.

"Dessert, too?" Bill asked, happily astonished.

"Strawberry schaum torte," she replied. "The meringues are store-bought but the berries and cream are fresh."

As she passed behind Bill on the way to the refrigerator, she stopped, raised one hand to her face, laid another one hard on Bill's shoulder to keep from falling, her fingers on the flesh below his open collar. She felt him tense at her touch, but stayed where she was.

"Angelina, are you all right?" Dierdre asked.

For an instant Angelina ignored her, for another she didn't hear a word anyone spoke. Then, finally, in a strained voice, "Just a bit of dizziness. I don't usually eat such a meal, let alone expend the energy to cook one."

"Dessert can wait," Dierdre suggested.

"We'll be busy later," Bill reminded her, the picture of concern as he swung slowly around, took her arm and helped her back to her seat.

Dierdre assembled dessert while Angelina sat with eyes shut, breathing deeply, fighting for calm, or at least the look of it.

She'd learned nothing definite when she leaned against Bill, or at least nothing someone like Detective Malverne could act on. But she knew, with all the certainty her powers provided, that Bill's story to Dierdre had been little more than half the truth.

The other half was upstairs. And tonight, while the pair worked, she would have to go up and find it. She said nothing as she dug into her dessert, but the others didn't notice. They were already planning the night's work.

"You're sure you're all right?" Dierdre asked Angelina later, as she loaded the dishes into the dishwasher.

Angelina sat at the table, trying to look appropriately weak without causing any undue concern. "Just a dizzy spell. Most people my age have high blood pressure. Mine's just the opposite. A big meal pulls all the blood to my stomach and leaves me a little faint. I haven't cooked one like this in years," she replied.

"Well if you get another case of chef's fever, I'll be happy to help dispose of the quantities," Bill commented, waving a fork in her direction as he finished the second half of Dierdre's torte. As Angelina had hoped, his eyes were glazed over from happy gluttony. She could not recall ever having seen him this relaxed in her presence.

"Well, I guess I should leave the two of you to get some things done," Angelina said. She didn't have to pretend to stifle a yawn.

"You'll be all right?" Dierdre asked.

"After I take a shuffle around the Square. No, you don't have to come. If I fall over, someone will call an ambulance, especially in this neighborhood. Bodies on the sidewalk ruin the property values."

After she left them, Angelina sat on the stairs in Dierdre's foyer, fingering the keys to the foyer door and Bill's apartment, wondering if she should go upstairs now or wait until later.

She'd just decided to put it off for an hour or so when she heard music flowing from Dierdre's apartment; an atonal chant, soft and distant. The pair had apparently moved into the sunroom so they would hardly notice that she hadn't left the building.

"No time like the present," she said, mouthing the words. Perhaps it was fear of being caught, more likely of what she might find, but she suddenly felt even older than her years. Gripping the banister tightly for support, she began to push herself up the stairs.

She stopped to catch her breath when she reached the top and looked at the mismatched door that would have led to Noah's apartment, a door added to the space that remained after the fire. There was no usuable apartment beyond it, only a roughed-in attic used for storage.

She thought of Noah in these rooms, Aleister in the others just across the hall, how they would sometimes start talking and wind up sitting on the stairs they shared, often for hours when they had time to spare. Both of them had been so brilliant, but it seemed to her that only Noah had possessed a human soul. How sad Noah had seemed the few times she'd contacted him after his death, as if he were still mourning Dierdre's loss, still waiting for her somewhere far beyond the capricous waves of time.

"Angelina!" she whispered aloud, "What in the hell do you think you're doing up here?"

Where had the thought come from? Not her mind. Not her will. But what if she did go inside, find nothing then be discovered in the act. No matter what she said, she'd leave Dierdre with doubts. This could wait, couldn't it? After all, what was one more day?

The hand gripping the railing was shaking, as if the uncertainty were taking over her body. *Just get it over, with you stubborn old fool,* she thought, focused on the door to Bill's apartment, and walked decisively toward it. She didn't stop to think, if she had she might have thought too long. Instead she slid the key into the abandoned room's lock and opened it. As soon as she was inside, she shut the door behind her, then leaned against it, breathing deeply, willing herself calm.

When she was able, she moved through the rooms slowly, less concerned about missing something than about knocking over some of Bill's clutter, watching it fall, having him hear and know she'd invaded his domain.

She doubted that his response would be pleasant.

When she came to the room he'd reserved for his work, she paused at the threshold of it. Dierdre had told her how Bill had sensed her presence here, enough that Angelina would not enter unless there was a reason. She could feel none, except sadness, discouragement. There was a strange scent to the room as well, one lurking beneath the musk incense, a scent both familiar and unpleasant.

Shortcuts.

Where had the thought come from?

Dangerous hallucinations.

Aleister's words to describe bad magickal assumptions; spoken in Bridget's voice.

Angelina took a step into the room, then slipped off her

shoes and shuffled through it in a slow spiral toward its center, waiting for some hint that she should stop or some impression of what had happened here.

Nothing, until her feet touched the edge of the symbol on the floor. Then a feeling, that she'd reached some important place. Carefully, she got down on her knees and ran her hands over the painted lines.

She'd told the detective that she had to touch something that belonged to the victims to tell anything about them. She wasn't touching a possession now, but something more potent, the places where blood had fallen, staining the floor so that after each ritual he'd had to hide the evidence then mop up just in case his partner lost control and told. Now that she understood, the scent in the room made sense. A chlorine-based cleaner, then the musk incense to mask that smell.

She brushed her hands frantically over the floor, trying to feel for other places that would give more glimpses of what had happened here, what he had done, or ordered done to him. Nothing, but less certainty, until her hands brushed over a sticky spot on the floor. She jerked her hand back, thinking for a moment that she had touched something as potent as blood.

And she saw everything clearly, too clearly.

He'd always found his women easily, some in response to discreetly worded personals in those obscene specialty journals, others sent by phone services, paid to agree to whatever he demanded they do to him. Yes, Angelina decided, he'd told Dierdre that much of the truth.

Angelina lay on her side, her temple pressed against the sticky spot on the floor, the back of one hand on the place where she'd first felt some reponse from the forces inside her.

She ran her free hand across what floor she could reach, slowly, trying to find one more place willing to give up a clue. When she found it, she shut her eyes, and fell into a different setting in the recent past.

Oh, she'd been so good, this young woman, so expert with a whip, so willing to do more. And the more she did, the more Bill's mind moved down the wrong paths. He wasn't being tempted by some demon conjured from the underworld, but by his own masochistic tendencies, and the insanity of pain.

And in the midst of all that she inflicted, he saw what he thought had to be done.

No, the last wasn't completely right, but close enough.

"You're so good, no one has ever been so good. Now stop," Angelina whispered, repeating Bill's words.

"Is that really what you want?" The girl's body pressed against his back, her hands circled his waist, working on his belt, promising more than he wanted to consider.

"Let me go now. I need to get a goblet, a pair of them. We need to finish this."

She'd been paid to wound, not to dominate. She let him go, then did the rest that he asked, sitting crosslegged in the center of the symbol on his floor, preening at his complement. Angelina could sense that the girl had never been a part of anything like this before. She watched Bill fill the goblets with wine, then add a powder to each of them. She didn't question what it might be. The danger of the evening was too unfamiliar, the unfamiliarity too exciting. She drank, not noticing that he barely touched his own.

Her eyes shut, a silly girlish grin spread her painted lips, revealing a cracked front tooth, a small, almost-charming flaw. "Sleepy," she muttered, a little girl voice.

"It's all right, expected," he said then, ignoring her, he began to chant.

She lay on the floor, eyes closed, but he droned on, his voice and words acting with the drug, lulling her to sleep. When he sensed that she was ready, he stood over her, looking down, considering, wondering if he dared to move his workings to a different, more terrible level.

No, he had never done anything like this before, but the temptation had been too much.

He moved quickly before the first effects of the drug he'd given her had worn off, circling her wrists and ankles with the cuffs she'd used on him, rolling her onto her back, attaching her spreadeagled to the floor. He had no time to think of what to use to gag her so he settled on . . .

Angelina's hand pressed more tightly over the sticky spot on the floor, realizing finally what it was.

. . . duct tape. He assembled the rest of what he needed— a ritual knife he'd purchased for far more than he could afford because it was said to have belonged to Crowley himself, the black and purple candles, the incense burner. He lit the candles and placed them at the points on the pentagram,

Then he straddled her and undid the lacings on her black leather vest, pulling it open, touching her breasts, lightly, briefly. He sat there, back throbbing, eyes closed, meditating until he felt her stir beneath him.

She moaned, tried to move. When she could not, her eyes jerked open and she looked up at him. It took some time for her to understand what he had done, but when she did the last effects of the drug wore off in an adrenaline rush. He watched her eyes, how she tried to beg with them for her release.

He lowered the knife until its tip rested against the hollow of her neck then ran it slowly down her breastbone, pressing only when he reached her solar plexus, then only hard enough to break the skin.

She acted as if she had been stabbed, jerking on the bonds, thrashing her head from side to side until he gripped her forehead, holding tightly. Draining off her fear, adding it to his pain, mixing both together with the terrible rage he had suppressed for years, the rage at what his father had done to him.

The girl ceased to exist. The room as he knew it ceased to exist and he was lost in the overworld, seeking some anchor in a different time.

Had he succeeded then? Angelina didn't know, only that he'd tried for hours, having his best moments at the time that Dierdre had gone into the past and the door was partially opened in the space below his little room.

As for the girl beneath him, he wanted her terrified, held her that way until they were both exhausted. Then, inexplicably, he pulled an extra five hundred dollars from a drawer and let her go, pressing it into her hand. Stiff, still a bit woozy from the drug, exhausted by her emotions, and terrified, she had fled straight to the death he had not dared to give her.

The timing could not have been more perfect had the Fates arranged it. Dierdre fled back to this time, the girl died, and Bill had glimpsed his idol, and the room as it had been when Leah and Aleister lived here.

What had he deduced from this?

Dangerous hallucinations.

Another warning. This time Angelina knew exactly what it meant. With effort and the aid of a conveniently-placed chair, she pushed herself to her feet and started for the door. It was slow going. She felt as woozy as the girl must have been when she ran, as if she couldn't shake off the soul whose thoughts she had shared.

Her hands shook as she locked Bill's door behind her. She leaned against the wall for support as she made her way to the top of the stairs where she gripped the banister tightly before starting down. She made it nearly to the bottom when something struck her silently from behind. Her legs gave way completely and she fell forward. Her arms barely broke her fall and she cracked her head hard on the foyer's ceramic floor. She tried to move but her body felt as if some large and heavy weight were pressing down on it.

The tile seemed cool, almost pleasant against her bare arms and the side of her face, but strangely damp. She shut her eyes, intending to rest for just a moment before getting up.

It was nearly dawn and Dierdre and Bill were both exhausted, when he finally called it quits. "Get some sleep—a lot of it—tonight," he told her. We'll go over all of this one more time tomorrow afternoon." He took her hand and squeezed it. "No mistakes, that's the best we can aim for from here on."

This evening they'd finally discussed what Bill wanted from her in return for all this help. "Just your aid as my go-between with Crowley. Perhaps in time, I'll know enough to open a door of my own and go to him directly," he told her.

"We may have enough here," she reminded him.

He shook his head. "Only one can go, and it needs to be you."

So she'd promised to help in any way she could. This meant the door would stay open, that she'd risk seeing Noah again, but she'd find a way to deal with that.

They walked to the door where she hugged him goodnight, trying to get used to trusting him, to trusting herself. He turned to go when she looked past him and saw the heap at the bottom of the stairs on the other side of the foyer.

She cried out then followed Bill across the hall. He

crouched beside their neighbor, his hand on the side of her neck seeking a pulse. "Is she alive?" Dierdre asked.

"She is. Call an ambulance."

Dierdre rushed to do it, then came back and sat on the stairs. "She must have had a dizzy spell and tried to grab the newel post for support," Dierdre said. "I should have forced her to let me walk her home."

"She said not to," Bill reminded her. "And it's not like she doesn't tromp around the neighborhood at least an hour every day."

"You're right," she said, though she still felt guilty. She sat with her hand on Angelina's shoulder, listening to the growing wail of a siren, noting the lights flashing outside. She rushed to the front door to open it for them.

The paramedics were thorough, examing Angelina carefully before turning her over, laying her on a flat board, stabilizing her neck and putting a temporary splint on her arm. "It looks like a concussion and a broken arm. She's probably in shock," one of them said as they carried her out, leaving the driver with Bill and Dierdre.

"Where are you taking her?" Dierdre asked

"St. Vincent's is the closest and they're used to treating cases like this. Do you know if she had any insurance or any relations we should call?"

"I don't know of any family. As for insurance, Medicaid, I suppose. But don't worry about the payment, just take her to the best place. I'll make up any difference."

"I think St. Vincent's is best given her age," the man decided.

"Can I ride with you?" Dierdre asked.

Bill gripped her arm, leaned close. "You need to rest," he reminded her. "There's nothing you can do over there, anyway but lose some precious sleep."

"He's right, lady. Unless you're family you won't be able to stay with her anyway."

Dierdre jotted down her phone number and gave it to the man. "Have the emergency room call me as soon as they know something, please?"

"St. Vincent's? You better call them, lady. I'd wait until morning, though. The place can be a madhouse at night."

"Morning? All right." She leaned against Bill as she watched them go.

"Will you be able to sleep?" Bill asked.

"I'll do my best."

"I could give you something to help."

"I have some valerian tea from Angelina. I'll take that."

"If it isn't enough, call me. And don't get out of bed at six to phone the hospital either. I want you rested, understand?"

"Doesn't exhaustion induce a trance state?"

"No, just sloppy work." He kissed the top of her head, affectionately, and squeezed her hands. "Try not to worry, I'm sure she'll be fine. Now go to bed, little girl."

Yes, she'd done all that she could, she decided. She went into the bedroom and undressed. She'd forgotten all about Angelina's tea until she was in bed. But by then she knew she didn't need it. She said a quick prayer for Angelina's recovery, one deliberately vague about who she was praying to.

Less than a mile away, Angelina lay in a hospital bed. In spite of the painkillers they had given her, real rest was difficult, dreams and reality all jumbled together. Her body may have been out of commission for the moment, but her soul could still be active, so she watched and waited, calmly, convinced that she had been so rudely pushed out of the center of the terrible game by its most important, incorporeal, players.

THIRTY-ONE

Something strange was going on, Noah determined; something nasty and probably magickal. He'd sensed it even before his mother died, but in the days since the funeral, his certainty about this had increased.

He inferred that from the way Bridget had banished him from her apartment and garden—suddenly and with no explanation. He inferred it, too, from how abrupt she was with him whenever they met, answering his occasional questions about Dierdre with the same promise she'd given him before. Then she'd pointedly change the subject, and inquire about a mutual friend or his family. And the last few months, as much for the good of the firm as her own health, she'd slowly disengaged herself from the day-to-day workings of MacCallum Construction, finally laying complete responsibility on Bob Dunglass's able shoulders. So she shouldn't have been too busy to see Noah when he called or, if she was avoiding him, to see her old friends, but she was. Lately, Aleister had been the one to answer his knock on the door and send him away.

They were up to something, the two of them, and since he guessed that it concerned him, he was determined to discover what it was.

He moved his desk in front of the rear window in his bedroom. At night while he wrote, he would keep the window open so that he could listen to what was going on below. He never heard Aleister's voice, but he heard Bridget's often as she vibrated some ritual words. A long period of silence would follow, then another intoned prayer.

She was working, alone it seemed, and that was also odd. She had always shared that sort of work with him, letting him know about her successes and failures, which made him think this all somehow concerned him. So he eavesdropped as best he could. And in the long hours of silence, he wrote his poems, a related series that might as well be called *Dierdre*.

As the days passed, he began to feel a growing tension in that silence, familiar somehow. Since Bridget wouldn't discuss anything with him, he searched out Angelina, thinking that someone who had immersed herself so completely in spiritualism would be able to detect the presence of spirits.

"I thought what I felt might just be my imagination but if you sense it too, then it must be her or him. Should I ask her about it?"

"You could try. She won't talk to me. You might have better luck."

As he'd been leaving, Angelina had called Bridget to invite her over for a cup of tea. An hour passed before Angelina phoned him. "She says that she's meditating. She won't admit to anything else. She did tell me a bit about Aleister's work, though. His book is nearly complete and Leah will be starting the final edit of the manuscript sometime next week. If he's still writing then I can only assume that whatever she's doing is on her own."

Noah thought about what he'd seen from the garden on that night so many months ago. He had no reason to feel jealousy anymore, but he was still glad to know that the pair shared space but worked apart.

The weather grew warmer, enough that Bridget began leaving her sunroom doors open. Though his curiosity had abated somewhat, Noah could not help but hear her chants. Then, one night just as he was preparing to go out, he heard Aleister's voice as well.

He was certain that he'd never heard the words they were chanting, but they seemed familiar somehow. As they went on, the oppressive feeling in the building increased. Whatever Bridget had been planning was going to happen tonight. He changed his own plans, stayed in, and sat by the back window.

The air felt as charged as it did before a storm, the charge growing not over hours but over days.

Something was going to happen, something important, and he needed to be there to witness the outcome.

Dierdre didn't get out of bed to phone the hospital. Instead she used the cordless, then went back to sleep. She called twice more during the day, learning nothing except that Angelina was drifting in and out of consciousness and under observation. The nurses she spoke with assured her that this was perfectly normal and that for a woman of her advanced age, Angelina was doing remarkably well.

"Could I talk to her, for just a couple of minutes?" Dierdre asked.

"She's not awake enough to respond."

"If I phone the room, will someone hold the receiver to her ear? She might be able to hear my voice."

They'd done as she asked and she had spoken a few quick words that hardly said how much she hoped that Angelina would be home soon. She promised to visit the following day and tell her how everything had gone. "And if you're able to hear me, say a prayer for us and Noah."

A prayer. They'd need prayers tonight, she thought later that afternoon, as she went through the elaborate preparations for the ritual. She bathed in hot water scented by the herbs that Grandmum had boxed up for her so many years before, letting the air dry her skin before rubbing herself down with the oil, not just in the erogenous spots but everywhere. Upstairs Bill was doing the same.

She spent the remainder of the day sitting naked as a sign of innocence, crosslegged in the center of the indigo symbol, meditating in silence, paying as little heed as she could to the shafts of light moving into the room until it touched the base of the altar on the east side of the space.

She shut her eyes. She sent her mind to Bill's. She could feel when they touched, sense when he stood and slipped his robe, white for purity, over his body. She was with him when he lifted her robe, green and crimson for hope and contrition, and carried it down the stairs. She stood and faced the door, lifting her arms when he entered the room so that he could drop the soft folds of silk over her.

Together they lit the six oil lamps, set nearly to the walls to mark the points of an invisible hexagram—the symbol that linked heaven and earth. In their dim light and the long shafts of sun falling through the door, they spread rosemary and sweet grass over the floor around the indigo symbol and laid the petals that had fallen from the open roses in the center where they would stand. The brass pots of rose and musk incense were next—Bill had attached them to their tiles the night before. Now Dierdre lit them, intoning the polar guardians at each point.

They waited, feeling rather than seeing the moment.

Sunset.

"Raphael . . . Gabriel . . . Michael . . . Auriel."

They intoned the words again as they stood together, her back to his chest, their arms outstretched, her palms turned to press against his. As they expanded their auras to fill the room, Dierdre could almost feel hers merging with his, so attuned were they to each other.

Sexual magick had been out of the question. Dierdre didn't have Grandmum's enlightened attitude and even if Bill had thought himself capable, he possessed none of Crowley's power or charisma to overcome her reluctance. So they settled on a simpler ritual, one of meditation, supplication, petition, taking the heart of Aleister's ritual and substituting symbols and symbolic gestures.

They moved to the altar. Bill lifted his wand, carved of teak embellished with amethyst. She took her cup, also of teak. He poured into it the wine they would share and a drop of the the oil perfumed with myrrh and lotus that they had mixed together to annoint the symbols.

Moving back to their place before the alter, he drank from the cup then handed it to Dierdre so she could do the same, finishing it.

They faced each other, holding the wand against the cup, and together they began the chant Bridget had written down for them so many years before, a petitioner's prayer . . .

In the same room in another time, Bridget, draped in yards of red-orange silk, stood in the center of a similar design, one marked with Aleister's more optimistic symbols for dominion and success, peace and abundance. As he moved around Bridget lighting the incense at the corners and the oil lamps further out, his long indigo robe brushed against the sweet grass, releasing its scent. Through it all, she kept her eyes closed, head bowed in humility and recited the petitioner's prayer.

As she did, she could feel Dierdre in another time, intoning nearly the same words. Friend of her youth, someday youth to her antiquity. *Be with me soon,* she thought as she turned to face the man she had never loved but far too often had desired. His eyes glowed, some trick of the soft lamplight, as if he were the devil so many made him out to be . . .

The gods they'd invoked were moving through her, Dierdre decided. That must be why she felt so weak; why her heart pounded. Her mouth had become so dry that she could barely speak and she felt like the anchor in a maelstrom as the room spun around her. She kept her arms in front of her gripping the goblet, until she began to tremble. She gave enough warning that as her knees gave way, Bill was able to catch both her and the goblet. He laid her down gently in the center of the symbol. "This happens. Rest a moment," he whispered and laid a hand across her eyes. She shut them, and kept them shut as the room gained speed.

Half conscious, she heard Bill praying at the alter, saying her words as well as his own. She tried to speak them, but settled for thinking them instead, putting all the energy she still possessed into the prayer.

Even thought stopped before the end and she sank into darkness. Her last thought was of murky water and of Noah dying beneath it . . .

In the room above the sunroom, Noah sat at the open window, looking out at the twilight shadows in yard, listening to the chants, Aleister's voice as well as Bridget's.

He didn't need to hear their words to know that the forces that had been gathering in the building for weeks were about to explode. The air vibrated with them. He should be downstairs, a part of it, but this seemed more intuition than anything else until he heard Dierdre's name.

It seemed that he had been hearing her voice for days, calling his name so softly that the words registered only in his mind. Now he sensed that she was close at hand. If he thought that Bridget might actually answer, he would go downstairs and pound on her door. He decided to break his promise, instead, and play the Peeping Tom again. He grabbed his coat and went out the front door and round back to the alley and the gate.

He found it locked.

Did he dare break it? Risk an eviction for something as elusive as a feeling? He decided to go and get his car, to pull it up to the wall, stand on its top and pray he wouldn't be noticed. He'd just turned to leave when he heard Dierdre scream; in his mind, yes, but with such force that he knew it was real, and that she was indeed near . . .

Since the moment they had begun the ceremony, Aleister had felt an odd sort of déjà vu. He guessed that they had conducted this ritual before, here and now, but under markedly different circumstances. It didn't surprise him to think that they had failed once and would succeed now, for this was exactly the sort of altered fortune the door was intended to provide. And he wasn't surprised to feel another mage, another petitioner, familiar somehow, reciting words much like his in another time. As he and Bridget began their intonations, he could almost hear the echoes from the future, could almost see the pair sharing this space with them. It confused him, but only briefly. He went on, chanting his lines, listening to Bridget's response until he felt a sudden shift in the energy supporting the ritual. One of the pair in the future had made a terrible error He looked at Bridget and saw that she felt it, too. She frowned. He shook his head, and continued with hardly a break in his intonation. Bridget had done a remarkable job planning all of this. It would work. He and Bridget could do it alone. Oh, damn them all! *He* could do it alone if need be.

Then, so loud it could not have been in his mind only, he heard the bitch's scream and felt her terror . . .

THIRTY-TWO

Dierdre lay on her back, her body numb, her limbs leaden. Bill straddled her legs, facing the altar, chanting a new string of words.

She didn't know Greek or Latin, but more than once she heard her name. Then he raised his arms above his head, hands clasped together gripping something she couldn't see. This wasn't part of anything they'd planned. She tried to bend her legs, to stand, and realized finally that she was bound. Frantic, she looked at one of her arms, seeing the leather cuff, the long strap ending with a metal ring that attached it to the base of the incense burner. The other was also attached. She didn't have to see her ankles to know that they were fastened to a single post, her body forming a cross.

Bill stopped chanting and turned to face her, the lamplight reflected golden off the polished blade of his knife. It was wrong to upset a ritual, wrong to distract the mage, but she was too weak to remember that, too frightened to think. She screamed.

Bill crouched in front of her. "It won't do to break my concentration," he said, betraying no emotion but impatience. "But I suppose I have pause to explain if we're to go on."

"Go on?" she asked, trying to keep her voice steady, to find in this steadiness some source of calm, of strength.

"The bloody sacrifice, though more dangerous, is more ef-

ficacious; and for nearly all purposes human sacrifice is best,''
he said, reciting Crowley's words to her.

"Crowley was speaking symbolically. He said so himself,''
she replied quickly.

"He had to say that. Could he have dared to admit the truth?
And consider his own words to Grandmum. 'The price will
be too high.' This is the price, Dierdre. You're the one who
is going to pay it, and when you're dead, the door will open
for me.''

"We had an agreement. I said I would help you.''

"Help?'' he laughed without humor. "For years I've lived
off her help, practiced my skills through her handouts. I don't
resent that except that I would like just once to be the one in
a position to be generous.''

"But you are. Look how generous you've been to me.''

"With my skills, given in part by Bridget. Nothing else.''

"Bill, listen—''

"Shut up, or I'll fix it so you won't be able to distract me
the way I did to the other one.''

"You killed that woman?'' She thought of the serial killer
the police had been seeking. "And the others too?''

"Killed? You give my courage too much credit. No, I never
had a reason until now. Quickly, now. Any more questions?''

She thought of Noah, and how Bill's success could at least
save him. "If you succeed, will you promise to be generous?''
she asked.

"That depends,'' he said, his voice more gentle now that
she seemed resigned.

"Will you promise to tell Bridget about Noah and the boys.
She has to evict him, it's the only way I can be sure that he'll
survive.''

"You care that much about him after such a short time?''

"I won't have his suicide on my conscience when I die,''
she replied.

"Well, I suppose I can afford the favor,'' he said, a hint of
sarcasm in his voice.

"Swear.''

"Look, you—''

He took a step toward her. She tried not to show any fear.
"If you want me to do my part, you have to swear.''

"I can do it on my own if I must."

"Are you sure of that?" She arched her back, trying to loosen the strain on her arms and legs, and felt the bracket holding her right arm give ever so slightly.

She fell back flat before he noticed, watched him consider how to respond. "All right. I can afford this generosity. I swear on the memory of Aleister Crowley, and in the name of Isis and Osiris, the gods of death and rebirth, and on Ptah and Thoth and Ap-Uat the guardians of this door, that I will not let him die." He stopped, crossed his arms, a look of satisfaction on his face. "Enough?" he asked.

"Enough." She looked away, concerned that the triumph she felt would be noticed, dissected, seen for what it was.

"Then we continue. Say your part, as we rehearsed," he said. He lay the knife on her chest, the tip pointing toward the altar, then went and knelt above her, his knees just against her shoulders, his arms outspread touching her palms to palms, his breath warm against her cheek as he whispered the words, "And my Ap-uat, opener of the way, grant our petition," he intoned.

"And may Thoth, the measurer of time, grant it as well," she responded.

"And may Ptah, the bridger of ways and times, forgive us," they said together.

More words, these chanted in Greek followed. He stood and walked to the altar.

So many parts of the ritual had been redone that she had no idea how much longer she was expected to be a part of it. Desperate, she pulled hard on the loose strap, and felt it give way. The top of the burner came loose, clicking against the tile as it fell. Startled, Bill hesitated, turned.

She had only one chance. She jerked hard on the chain. Burner and tile came loose, glancing off his shoulder and hitting the altar. Sparks of incense scattered across the purple silk cloth. In the same motion, she grabbed the knife. Bill started toward her. "The altar!" she cried, looking past him to the fabric now covered with smoke.

Bill whirled and saw the flames explode across the altar. He rushed to it and grabbed one of the vases of roses, spilling the water on the worst of the blaze. The flames died for a moment, then came back stronger and with a pungent scent as if in the instant that fire touched water the water was consecrated into fuel.

Dierdre forced herself to look away from the death waiting for them both. She slashed at the strap holding her other arm, cutting herself as well as the thick leather. Reaching forward to slice the straps holding her feet she saw the flames roll down the altar cloth onto the floor, catching the dried sweet grass then the hem of Bill's robe. He beat at the fire with little effect, then ripped off the robe, stepping back into the symbol that seemed to offer the only protection from the hungry blaze while slapping out the few sparks that clung to his faded cotton shorts. "Get the fire extinguisher or we'll both die," she called to him.

He started for the kitchen door but the flames moved faster, fed by some force Dierdre could only feel, darting across the sweet grass to engulf the inside wall, cutting off that escape, cutting off even the new door, leaving only the old one open and ready. As the smoke thickened, the door became the only patch of light left in the smoke-darkened room, their only escape.

Dierdre sat up and slid forward until she could reach her feet. The motion caught Bill's attention and he turned and lunged towards her.

It had been years since she'd learned to throw a punch but the training hadn't left her. She hit him as hard as she was able, knocking him off balance. As he fell sideways, she stabbed at him with the knife. Though it barely connected, it was sharp enough to open a gash on his shoulder before he slapped it out of her hand. It bounced on the hardwood floor then went spinning to the edge of the flames now framing the door.

He looked at her, his face dark with rage, his hands in front of him, fingers curled and ready. With her legs still bound, there'd be no way she could fight him off if he got a grip on her neck.

Bill stepped toward her, then back, fighting his conscience and his inclinations. Killing with a ritual knife might be possible for him, but he was no murderer at the core. Now, though he knew his ritual demanded her death, he couldn't bring himself to touch her. With a growl of rage at his own weakness, he lunged toward the door and the weapon.

Working quickly, Dierdre felt her way around the strap holding her right leg until she reached the buckle. She managed to unfasten it when her robe caught fire. She beat at the flames with one hand while she felt for the buckle holding her right foot, quickly losing the battle with both.

She looked toward the door, not surprised to see that the room itself had vanished in a swirling haze of smoke and fire. The only clear path through it led to the door. It seemed as if the gods were announcing that the way had once more open to her, all she need do was free herself and run.

Bill was there as well, crouched in the cleaner air close the floor, trying to move toward the door, finding as she had so many days ago that the tides of time were still holding him back.

Dierdre's hands were blistered but she ignored the pain, tugging at the strap, trying to turn it so the buckle was more accessible. It had moved a few inches when she noticed Bill crawling toward her. His face was black with soot, his hair singed. "May Ap-Uat, the opener of the way, accept this sacrifice and grant our petition," he called and raised his knife, ready for the attack.

"No!" she cried, and with no time left to free herself did the only thing she could do, pushing the unburned fabric beneath the strap circling her leg. The flames devoured the leather and seared the side of her ankle. She jerked hard and felt the strap give a little just as Bill lunged.

She caught Bill's wrist, holding him back, thinking the words to one of the Christian prayers she often used in her meditation, "Dear Lord, ruler of all creation on earth and in the heavens, give me your strength." Perhaps God listened, because she managed to hold Bill away for a time before her blistered hands began to lose their grip. In that moment, she saw the flames spread to the door itself, circling the wooden frame, licking at the symbols Aleister had mounted above it. If those were destroyed, would the door shut forever? She thought so, thought she had failed. Then, as she was about to lay back and let Bill do whatever he wished, she saw a familiar face in the clear twilight just outside the door. "Noah!" She screamed his name, using all the force of the agony she could no longer ignore, hoping that through time and crackle of the fire and her own failing voice he could still hear her. "Noah, help me!"

THIRTY-THREE

As soon as he heard Dierdre's first terrified scream, Noah abandoned all thoughts of stealth. He ran to the gate and put the full weight of his body into breaking through it, slamming against it until the center of the gate rather than its metal latch gave way.

Noah forced his arm through the crack he'd made, and lifted the latch. Once inside he stayed near the wall for a moment, watching through the window as he had so many months ago. Staying in the shadows as best he could, he ran the perimeter of the yard to the sunroom door, praying that Dierdre would call him again before he reached it and give him some notion of where she might be.

As he neared it, he smelled smoke, acrid and unfamiliar. Dierdre screamed again, the sobs that followed suggesting pain. Not caring who saw him here, or what he witnessed, he ran to the door then skidded to a halt, astonished by what he saw inside.

Smoke, not just the scent of it now, but a thick cloud of it, poured out of the room, covering him. He coughed and his eyes watered, yet Bridget and Aleister stood inside as if nothing was wrong. Their voices remained clear and steady, making him wonder if the smoke was an hallucination, or magick, or if Dierdre had even called him at all.

The smoke thickened, stinging his eyes until he couldn't see them anymore. But he still heard Bridget and Aleister, chanting—his Greek to her Latin; his invocation, her response. They'd conjured this mirage, he decided, an illusion. His help would only be an intrusion and he ought to move away. But he couldn't, not until he knew that Dierdre's cry wasn't real and that she was safe. So he stopped just outside the open door and waited for the scene to shift itself into something he could comprehend.

Dierdre's scream, closer now, so close he ought to be able to see her, followed by his name, broken immediately by a fit of coughing. He took a deep breath and rushed inside.

Aleister vanished. Bridget disappeared. There was only smoke, smothering thick, and Dierdre's voice, screaming his name again as if she were right beside him.

She was here! He couldn't see her but she was here. He shut his eyes to clear the sudden tears then opened them to the full horror he'd only glimpsed a moment before. The room around him was on fire! He fought the instinct to turn and run. Instead, coughing, he tried to call Dierdre's name. Nothing came out but a hoarse whisper.

He heard her call him, and saw her on the floor with a man leaning over her pointing a knife at her chest. Noah didn't try to reason, or even to divert the man's attention. He had the element of surprise so he lunged sideways at the man, pushing him away from Dierdre and toward the flames surrounding them. "Dierdre," he called, crouching beside her and lifting her into his arms. "Dierdre, can you hear me?"

She didn't reply, only rested a blistered hand on his cheek, keeping it there as she shut her eyes.

Aleister couldn't see the smoke, but on some unconscious level, he could sense it. He couldn't hear Dierdre's cry for help, but the words she screamed were clear in his mind. When the ritual reached a moment where it would be appropriate to pause, he looked toward the open door, not surprised to see Noah standing just outside, his eyes squinted, his breathing shallow as if he looked into not the present but the future.

Noah took a step forward. Aleister watched in curiosity, in amazement, as Noah's body distorted then disappeared.

"The door is open," he whispered to Bridget. "And not in the way you ever expected." He gripped her hand and pulled her away from the altar and through the door on the far end of the house, the one that was just a door.

Smoke poured through the other doorway, billowing out into the yard. Aleister moved closer, feeling the temptation.

Dare he risk death to discover what lay on the other side of this working? It would be a quick run through a smoky room, through a familiar door, down a familiar hall then the safety of the street.

He'd risked his life in worse situations often enough, and he would have done it in a minute, if he had more certainty that he wouldn't be stuck there. No, he had books to write, a new form of ritual to nurture, seeds that needed to be planted before he could think of the future. Better to let the next incarnation take care of the future's needs.

But he was still curious, enough that he let go of Bridget's hand and moved toward the doorway, hoping to get some glimpse of what was going on inside.

Nothing but smoke and flames, the forms moving inside seeming more shadows than real. Until, unexpectedly, one of the shadows lurched toward the door. The man stopped just inside and looked directly at him. In spite of the man's blistered arm, and the raw patches on his shoulder and chest, his expression was one of joy. So this was the mage that had done the future working, and he recognized Aleister as brother, as teacher, as master.

Aleister could not have felt better than he did in the moment the man stepped through the door and took Aleister's outstretched arms.

Whatever Aleister had hoped to learn vanished in a moment as the man's expression shifted from joy to something worse than emptiness. Aleister had seen the expression before—in mountain climbers pushed past endurance who inexplicably gave up all struggle for survival, in men whose demons had been exorcized and had no life force of their own as replacement, in the zombies of the southern islands brought back to some half-life of slavery. The man's eyes lost their focus, their purpose, then fluttered and shut. The body, empty of soul, of life, lay heavy against Aleister's chest.

Recoiling, Aleister let the body fall onto the flagstones, and tried to hide the horror of what he'd felt, the realization that only the strength of his own body and the injuries to the other's kept him from being the one who died.

Later he'd sift through the details and the knowledge he'd acquired in an instant of touch. Later, he'd make sense of the event. For now it was better to move behind Bridget, to help her to her feet, to invent an answer to a question that had no answer, at least not yet. "It was the fire that killed him," he said.

Bridget moved away from him, toward the door. He didn't need to remind her to stop just outside. She stayed there a moment, then apparently satisfied by what she'd seen, she returned to Aleister's side.

"Do you suppose that we should roll the body back through the door?" she asked. "I mean, he belongs in the future, doesn't he?"

Aleister glanced toward the door, saw the smoke thin and die as the magick died. "Too late," he said. "I'll handle this. The notoriety should be more than a bit amusing."

"What about Noah?"

Aleister shook his head. For the first time in his life, he had no idea how to answer, and no inclination to lie.

THIRTY-FOUR

The fire had already begun to burn itself out as Noah lifted Dierdre off the floor, leaving only the outer door wreathed in flames, the heat making it dangerously impassable. He looked through it, out at the lawn where Dierdre's attacker lay motionless on the grass with Aleister crouched beside him. He saw Bridget walk to the door and stop just outside, staring directly at him. He nodded that they were both okay, then turned to the inside door, partly open, leading to a kitchen that was strangely altered. Clutching Dierdre, afraid of losing her again, he stepped through the kitchen door. Beyond it, he saw lights flashing through the front windows, throwing colors he'd never imagined onto the dark walls of the hallway.

A moment later, someone pounded on the front door. Dierdre stirred in his arms, coughed, and looked up at him. "It's all right," Noah said. He lay her on the sofa, covered her with his suit coat and went to open the door.

As it swung in, Noah stepped back, more surprised by the sight of the men outside than anything he'd witnessed so far. These were firemen, surely, but dressed like none he'd ever seen before. Two pushed past him, heading down the hall to where smoke still flowed from the sunroom. A third—a woman!—crouched beside Dierdre, covered her with a blanket then helped her outside where two other firemen were waiting with the truck, along with a pair of what looked like doctors. A crowd had gathered. They wore clothes of unfamiliar cuts, their colors vibrant in the glaring streetlights. Noah stayed close to Dierdre and tried his best to fit in. As they sat on the steps, the woman began giving Dierdre oxygen from some sort of portable tank while examining her injuries. A third vehicle pulled up, and a man dressed in a uniform and carrying a clipboard got out and introduced himself as the fire marshal before going inside.

The woman tending to Dierdre seemed less concerned about her blistered hands and legs than the cut on her wrist. "I think most of the burns are going to heal just fine on their own, but the one on your ankle may need a little attention. Just to play it safe, we're going to take you to the hospital to get checked over. You need a couple of stitches anyway." She wrapped the wrist tightly then added. "It looks like things are already under control in there. I'll go inside and find you something to wear home."

"Mine is the first room down the hall to the right," Dierdre said. As soon as she and Noah were alone, Dierdre looked at the firemen standing beside the truck and whispered quickly. "Let me give the answers, dearest. I'll explain everything when I get back."

"Explain?" He looked first at the fire engine, then the squad car behind it, the street, the crowd on the edge of the Square, and managed a weak grin. "Are you really sure you can?"

Dierdre started to answer but was interrupted by the two uniformed firefighters coming out, followed some minutes later by the woman and fire marshal. "We left a fan running to clear out the smoke," one of them told her before they left.

The marshal opened a book and leaned against the stair wall just below Dierdre. "You'll be happy to know that the only room with any real damage is your sunroom and even that seems minor. It appeares that the fire was out before we got here. Can you tell me how it started?"

Dierdre frowned, thought quickly, then gave the best answer she could invent. "I don't know exactly. I was burning some incense. I put it out and started getting ready for bed when I smelled the smoke. There's a fire extinguisher in the kitchen but it was jammed . . . Then the flames spread to the curtains blocking the way out. It all happened so fast."

"The extinguisher worked for us when we checked it. You

were probably just rattled and forgot how to use it. It happens.''

"Then my robe caught fire and . . . I ripped it off." She was thinking quickly now, taking deep breaths while her mind worked frantically to fill in the little details that always made lies seem truthful. "Thankfully Noah, Mr. Hathaway, is staying with me . . . He was just returning . . . from a dress rehearsal when the fire got out of control. If it hadn't been for him I'd probably be in your ambulance right now, on the way to the hospital if I were that lucky."

"You're going to be in a play?" The woman looked at Noah with happy interest. "I've been in a few myself. Which group."

"Provincetown Players," he said.

"I don't know them."

"They're very small," Dierdre said. "They're a local revival of sorts. I'm sure you'll hear about them soon."

"Well, I tell you. You're really lucky more damage wasn't done and that you're both all right," the marshal said.

"Could I see the room before I go?" Dierdre asked.

The request seemed odd to Noah, but not the others. They helped Dierdre up the stairs and down the hallway to the sunroom where an oversized fan was pulling what remained of the smoke into the backyard.

The fireman aimed a flashlight at the door frame, dripping with water and chemicals from their extinguishers. "The frame will need to be replaced but a good woodworker can make it look just like the other one." He motioned with his light to the opposite side of the room where the second set of old French doors were nearly untouched by the blaze. "Now you both be careful in this place, all right?"

"This place?" Dierdre asked. "Are you talking about the building?"

"It has a history of small fires like this one, and there's never a definite cause. Sort of like it's haunted or something," the woman whispered to her. "A stupid sort of superstition but in our line of work superstitions abound."

"Can I go to the hospital with Dierdre?" Noah asked.

"It would be better if you stayed here," Dierdre replied. "If the fire flares up again, you'll have to telephone 9-1-1 to get the trucks back.'' She kissed him on the cheek. ''9-1-1,'' she repeated. ''I'll be back as soon as they let me, dearest. I promise.''

He watched them leave, then ran his hands over the worst of the damage. The doorframe felt clammy to the touch, the charred places slick and wet. He looked over the fan and saw no sign of Bridget or Aleister, but the few minutes outside had begun to make him understand why.

He wandered through the apartment, noting the strange alterations, doing his best to touch nothing unfamiliar. Impatient for answers to what had occurred, he settled into the the most unchanged room, the library. He dug around on the papers on the desk until he found some typewritten pages that Bridget had written. He glanced at them and a few sentences in realized he had found what he'd been looking for. He sat at the desk and began to read.

St. Vincent's let Dierdre go a little after six. The emergency room physician wanted to admit her just as a precaution, something she refused to allow. So the hospital packed her a bag full of gauze and bandages, pills for pain and pills to fight infection and ointment to speed healing, and arranged an appointment with a burn specialist for the following afternoon.

Just before she left the hospital, Dierdre asked if she could see Angelina. ''The fire was right next door to her apartment. If she hears about it, she'll be worried. I want her to know that her apartment is all right,'' Dierdre explained.

''Visiting hours don't start until ten, but you can leave a note for her if you like,'' an Emergency Room nurse suggested, then looked at Dierdre's bandaged hands. ''Dictate it and I'll write it down,'' she suggested.

''Tell her that Noah Hathaway and I are both all right, and that her apartment wasn't damaged in the least. Tell her we'll both be waiting to welcome her home.''

Something about the way she spoke Noah's name, made the nurse look at her with interest. ''Smitten by him, aren't you?'' she asked.

''I'm going to marry that man,'' Dierdre replied, smiling for the first time since the ordeal had ended.

''Did you tell him yet?''

"Oh, he already asked me."

"And he saved your life. I can't think of a better way to start your years together."

And I saved his, Dierdre thought. She hoped it would be enough. On the taxi ride home, she prayed it would be—to Aleister's gods and to her own.

She found Noah asleep on the chaise, Grandmum's journal resting on his chest, a few books on the floor beside him.

She knelt beside him, wincing from the pain, thankful the worst of it was masked by the drugs she'd been given. "Noah," she whispered, and kissed his cheek, waking him.

He looked at her and smiled. "I tried to stay awake. I was afraid that if I slept I might wake and find it had all been a dream," he said, lifting the journal and rolling on his side so she could sit beside him.

"How much did you read?" she asked.

"Everything I could find, and my own poems, too. Funny to see things I'd thought were unfinished set down in print. The biography says that I simply disappeared one day, and that my landlady found the poems and arranged to have them published. It says that the mystery of my disappearance only added to my fame. But I think that my best work is going to be done posthumously."

"I'm so sorry, Noah. I wanted to stay in the past with you, but it wasn't possible."

"That was painfully obvious. Why did you run away that night?"

She told him everything she could of what she had seen and heard and felt. "Are you experiencing any of that?" she asked him when she'd finished.

"No, and I think I know the reason. Come in the sunroom with me," he said.

She didn't want to, not yet. But she followed. The damage was specific—the altar gone, the painted symbol on the floor nothing more than ash, the carvings above the door charred beyond recognition. Noah reached for her hand. When his fingers brushed a strip of gauze he grabbed her arm instead, gripping hard as he pulled open the sunroom door and led her through. The wall outside had no sign of a gate and the only sound was the ever-present traffic blaring on the streets around them.

Noah's arm circled her waist. "I think this is home now," he said and took her through the opposite set of doors, a near perfect match to the damaged set. She looked at the tiny squares, the dark oak frame and understood that the fire had been postponed some seventy years. Henry and Louis might even be alive somewhere. She wondered what they would think of a visit from their uncle Noah.

"There was an envelope addressed to us in the back of my book of poems," Noah told her once they were back in the library. "I thought I would wait and we could read it together."

"You read it to me," she suggested.

The envelope held a letter from Bridget and a trio of news clippings. The first delt with Noah's disappearance; the other two with the discovery of a mysteriously burned body in Bridget's yard. It was hardly a surprise that in the second article the reporter added some lurid speculations about where the body might have come from.

> . . . *After four days, the body remains nameless. An autopsy revealed a number of scars, apparently from operations of an unknown nature, and dental work well beyond that of current practices. Though there were signs of recent burns on the body, these were not severe enough to have killed the man and the cause of death is still unknown.*
>
> *Of greater interest was the single article of clothing the man was wearing—a pair of cotton undershorts apparently manufactured in this country by an unknown firm—which were printed and sewn in a fashion unlike any currently in use.*
>
> *It must be noted that the self-proclaimed master magician, Aleister Crowley, has been renting the apartment immediately above the yard where the body was discovered and that he was the individual reported finding it. It is speculated that the body materialized during one of Mr. Crowley's rituals, a point Mr. Crowley, in typical fashion, will neither affirm nor deny. Miss Bridget*

MacCallum, whose family owns the building, was not at home at the time the body was discovered. The only other tenant who might have seen something, Mr. Noah Hathaway, is on an extended vacation and could not be reached for comment.

Mr. Crowley has announced that he will soon be leaving for Europe where he intends to found an abbey based on the principles of reason over superstition, life over sacrifice as outlined in his recently completed work, Magick in Theory and Practice. *He will be holding one final gathering of his followers and the general public on Friday evening in the yard where the body was found.*

The morbidly curious are expected to attend.

"He must have reveled in it," Noah said.

"Read the letter, please," Dierdre said, moving closer to him, close enough to read the date over his shoulder, June 1923.

My best wishes to both of you, Bridget wrote.

It seems odd to wait so long to write you, and I have to remind myself that it will be years before you read this. Even so, patience has never been my best virtue.

The book of poems in which you found this letter would likely have been published anyway, but Noah's mysterious disappearance probably gave it extra recognition. The money from its sale has been placed in a special fund for the education of Noah's nephews. They are doing well, and I assure you that they will never set foot in this building again. I speak to their parents from time to time, and through them have been assured that there is no sign of any nightmares, or even troubling dreams. Our meddling would have caused their deaths, it was only right that we saved their lives.

I should add that I recently told Noah's sister (the sane one worth speaking to) where Noah went and why. She didn't believe me (who would!) but there is enough doubt in her mind that I think that the story will become a sort of family legend, one of those romantic tales parents tell their children on dull winter nights.

If you've read the clippings enclosed with this you know that the mage you'd been working with died, quickly and I think painlessly. Aleister, who is still shaken about the event four years after it took place, is not completely certain of the last. But from what Aleister was able to sense, he was not a person you would miss much anyway.

The paper notes that he died under mysterious circumstances. Truly he did, but Aleister says the reason is clear to him. I could not go back to a time in which I lived, nor can a soul return to an era in which it once lived.

Aleister says the loss of that life was hardly important and that it could hardly have been his most stellar incarnation.

Aleister tells me that he intends to meet you both again, and soon. Perhaps he's right about life and death and I will too.

Until then, my love to both of you, Bridget.

"Do you suppose Aleister meant those words as a promise or a threat?" Dierdre asked.

"More likely an imposition," Noah responded. "At least we have a few years to prepare for it." He lay an arm over her shoulder, drawing her closer.

Tears came to her eyes, surprising her. "This was hardly the ending I expected," she whispered. "I thought it would be me there with you. I have nothing to keep me in this time but a tenuous tie to my distant family. You had so much and I pulled you away from all of it."

"With the best of intentions. We'll be fine, I promise you."

She buried her head in the hollow of his neck.

As he kissed her she thought of Aleister's warning and of the horrible emptiness and terrifying dreams of Bridget's brother and father.

Nonsense, at least in this case. She had saved his soul. An auspicious beginning. As to the rest, they'd face it together, wherever they chose as home.

AFTERWORD

"Behold! I am yesterday, today and the brother of
tomorrow!"

—Aleister Crowley
Invocation to Thoth

Those readers who have a strong interest in Crowley and his
work will undoubtedly notice that I took some liberty with
Leah Hirsig's age, making her a few years younger than she
actually was when she met Crowley. However, the events of
their meeting are as described here.

Crowley did live in New York's Greenwich Village for a
number of years in a pair of apartments off Washington
Square, adding a most eccentric note to an already eccentric
era for that neighborhood.

For those interested in reading further on Crowley, there are
a number of excellent biographies, notably *The Great Beast*
by John Symonds and Crowley's own *Confessions* which he
describes with his usual humility as an "authhagiography"
(autobiography of a saint).

For those interested in Thelemic ritual, I suggest an excellent new release from Eschaton Books, *Future Ritual* by Philip
H. Farber.